Snowdrop's

Promise

By

Pearl A Gardner

Pearl A. Gardner

Print Edition

ISBN-13: 978-1500536145
ISBN-10: 1500536148

eBook Edition

ASIN: B00LWBD5US

Printed by CreateSpace, an Amazon.com Company
Available from Amazon.com and other online stores
Also available on Kindle and other devices

Pearl A. Gardner

Acknowledgements

I could not have written this story without help from my Granddad Ted, Grandma Ethel, my mother, Jean and mother-in-law, Alice. These four wonderful people are sadly gone from my life now, but they shared their war-time memories with me when I asked them to, years ago.

I'm so grateful to have known them, and they each played a part in not only shaping who I am today but in helping me find the courage to follow my dream and eventually bring their stories to life.

This account taps into their knowledge and experience of the war years. I have taken snippets of their histories, added lots of researched facts and shaped the whole into a work of fiction. I hope, 'A Snowdrop's Promise', is a novel they would be proud of.

Table of contents

Chapter One, June 1940

The clatter of falling crockery could be heard from halfway down the road and Agnes quickened her step. She was the clumsy one. She was always dropping things so she wondered who'd be in for a roasting this time. Making her way through the open door of Kingsway Café, she saw the dainty figure of Polly on her hands and knees cleaning up the mess of what looked like meat pie and mash from the linoleum.

"What you done, Poll?" Agnes hurried to take her coat off and tugged an apron from the hook behind the kitchen door. "And where's George?"

"He had to rush out. His mam took a turn for the worse." Polly wiped the back of her hand across her brow. "Can you get Mr Tolson another pie and mash while I finish clearing this mess?"

"You got the luck of the devil, lass. If George was to see what you wasted there… I mean, he's generous enough, but you know as well as I do that he can't stand waste!"

"Where's me dinner?" The old man at the corner table asked Agnes.

"I think you can see well enough, Mr Tolson. It's all over the floor!" Agnes tut-tutted as she tied the apron strings around her thickening waist. "Don't fret; I'll soon get you another plate." She hurried into the kitchen where Sally was busy plating up another dinner for the old man.

"What's up with George's mam?" she asked the cook.

"Not sure, but his sister came in earlier, all out of breath from running, so it must be serious."

"Poor George. I hope the old lass will be all right." Agnes took the laden plate and pushed through the swing doors, back into the café. "There you go, Mr Tolson. We gave you an extra bit of pie to make up for the wait."

"I'd a preferred a bit of a discount on the bill, lass." The old man looked hopeful.

"Not a chance, love. More than me job's worth." Agnes tucked a stray blonde lock further under her hairnet.

"Well, my job won't be worth much when George finds out about this." Polly rose to her feet clutching the cleaning cloth in one hand and a bucket in the other.

"No reason he should know, is there?" Agnes raised her eyebrows at her cousin. "I won't be telling him."

"You're a good friend, Agnes, but I might have to leave

here anyway before long." Polly dropped her eyes to the floor and put a hand to her stomach. "George won't let me stay once he finds out about this bastard little bundle," she whispered quietly.

"Polly!" Agnes was shocked. She looked closer at the rounded tummy on her cousin's slim frame and then at the girl's pink face. Polly's eyes were huge round pools of green and she hadn't bothered to tuck her hair inside the net they had to wear. It hung in loose dark curls over her shoulders. Agnes thought about telling her to tuck her hair away, but the younger girl's face was so full of misery that she didn't have the heart to tell her off. "What have you done, Poll?"

"I think that's going to be bloody obvious in a month or so, don't you?" Polly hurried behind the counter of the small café. "I've been a fool and I can't blame you if you say so, 'cause I know it meself."

Questions rose quickly to Agnes's mind, but she kept her lip buttoned. She knew Polly wouldn't want the customers to know the details of her private business. "What will you do, love?" she asked quietly, steering Polly farther behind the counter where they could talk with a little more privacy. "Does Charlie know?"

Polly shook her head. "How can I tell him?" she whispered, turning tear-filled eyes to Agnes. She blinked quickly and dashed the wetness from her cheek with the palm of her hand. "His wife just had their third only last month and on top of that he's been called up so he'll be off soon enough and might never come back!"

Agnes had a retort on the tip of her tongue, but she held it back. Polly didn't want to hear her opinion of Charlie Watson. Goodness knows she'd tried her best through the last year or so to persuade her cousin to end the illicit affair. She could see that no good would come of it. Charlie was a womaniser who only cared for himself. His poor wife now had three little ones under the age of four, and didn't seem to have a clue that her husband was a scoundrel. Heaven only knew how many more children he'd fathered around town, and now Polly had added herself to the long line of women this charmer had left with broken hearts and full bellies.

"Might be for the best, Poll." Agnes muttered. "I mean him going away, not... I mean, I didn't mean about him not coming back!"

"I know, Agnes. I know." Polly twisted her hands together.

"I should have listened to you. I should have resisted him, but he's so handsome, and the things he does to make a girl feel that she can't say no, well, I think you'd know, wouldn't you?" She smiled wryly at Agnes. "What with you having your little Harry and another on the way inside the first year of being wed, like."

"Yes, love, but I have the luxury of a wedding band on my finger to make it right in the eyes of them as point fingers. Not like you, eh?" Agnes flinched inside. She didn't like to point out her friend's flaws when she was just as guilty of sins of the flesh. She was lucky, though. She now had a husband, and that made all the difference, no matter that she didn't love him in the least, and didn't want the child she was now carrying. As long as things looked right on the outside, folks wouldn't point fingers and she could hold her head up when she walked the streets.

"Oh, Agnes! What am I going to do?" Polly shook her head.

"You'll be all right, love. Your mam and dad won't turf you out, I'm sure." Agnes lied and promised herself to go to confession the first chance she got. She knew Polly's dad, Bert, wouldn't stand the shame, and her mother, Hilda, would go along with her husband's wishes. Polly would be out on her ear as soon as they got wind of the package in her belly.

"I'm ready for some pudding." Mr Tolson called from his table. "What you got today?"

"I'll see to him." Polly hurried over to take the old man's order, leaving Agnes to serve a customer that just came in.

"What can I get you, Sam?" Agnes asked the tall young man.

"Pint pot of tea, please. I'm spitting feathers I'm that thirsty. This heat's a killer isn't it?" He didn't wait for Agnes to answer his comment on the warm weather, but went on, "And a meat pie dinner, love, when you're ready."

He took off his cap and Agnes couldn't help admiring his shock of bright-red hair. "Eeh, I'm always surprised by your hair, Sam. It'd look lovely on a lass."

"What's up, Agnes? Aren't lads supposed to have a lovely head of hair?"

"Sorry, Sam, I didn't mean it like that." Agnes was mortified and wanted the café floor to open up and suck her down to the basement. "I didn't mean to offend you."

"No offence taken, lass. I'm just glad of a bit of conversation with the girl of my dreams." He winked at her.

"Give over, Sam. I'm a married woman." Agnes blushed.

"Aye, well, if you weren't I'd be first in the queue."

"Don't be daft, Sam. I think our Polly would be more your sort, she is with most of the lads." Agnes tried to deflect the flattery.

Sam leant close and beckoned Agnes to lower her head to hear his whisper. "Now I'll risk giving offence, but not to you. Your Polly's nice enough, but she's getting a right name for herself with that Charlie Watson. You're a fine figure of a woman, and I wouldn't have to break me neck stooping to kiss you, would I?"

Agnes shot upright. "Sam Wood! You just watch your mouth and remember I'm married." Agnes tried to be stern, but couldn't help a small smile creeping through her tightly pursed lips.

"I've always had a soft spot for you, Agnes, but you never look the side I'm on." Sam put a hand to his brow and struck a theatrical pose. "I'm all of a dither when you walk by, but you don't even know I'm alive!"

"Oh, Sam! You are a one!" Agnes laughed along with his banter. "I'll get you that dinner."

"Hurry back, Agnes, so I can look upon your fine face again." Sam quipped as she hurried to the kitchen.

It felt good to be flattered, even if the chap didn't mean it. He was always the same when he came into the café, and she enjoyed the innocent banter with him. Sam was a nice man, and if things were different, maybe she would have considered walking out with him. But things were never going to be different. She was stuck with what she had for better or worse, God help her.

"By it's hot as hell in this kitchen today. Is it the same out front?" Sally, the cook, asked her when Agnes hurried into the kitchen.

"We've got the door open, but there's not a breath of wind to blow through to cool things down."

"My, you could cook eggs on them cheeks, what you been up to, lass? Is that colour from the heat or a guilty conscience?"

"Oh, I was just having a bit of a flirt with that Sam Woods out there, nothing a few Hail Mary's won't put right." Agnes lifted a pint mug down from a shelf and began to fill it from a large tea urn on the counter. "Another one of them pie dinners, please, Sally."

"Oh, you make me laugh you Roman Catholics. You can do and say what you like all day long and then a visit to the priest will clean the slate and you're free to start sinning from scratch the very next minute." Sally laughed and wiped the sweat from her face before she began to ladle gravy over the corned-beef pie, mashed potatoes and cabbage

"It's not like that at all!" Agnes protested. "I try to be good 'cause it's no fun having to bare your soul to Father Brennan every week."

"I doubt you'd have much to confess, Agnes." Sally smiled softly. "I bet you've never done anything worse than say an odd swear word."

Agnes blushed to the roots of her hair. Everyone thought she was a good Catholic girl. She never gave them reason not to think so, but she knew her heart was not pure. There were some things that even Father Brennan would never know about her. She was damned to spend all of eternity in flames because nothing on this earth would make her confess to her deepest, darkest sins. Her face drained of colour as the memory of her hidden past filled her mind. Trudie, her mother, knew a part of the secret and she took the knowledge to her grave, and was probably burning in hell right now because of it. Agnes's husband taunted her with the part of the truth that he knew, every chance he got, and if she'd realised what a bully he was, she would never have agreed to marry him.

"What have I said? Agnes? You look like you've seen a ghost!" Sally peered into Agnes's frightened, white face.

Agnes shuddered, shook her head to clear the awful memories, and took the tray with a plate of dinner and a pint mug of tea. "I'm all right. Just a bit tired with the bairn, you know? The first months are the worst; I was the same with our Harry. Best get this served." She hurried out of the kitchen and over to the red-haired man.

"Thanks, love, I'm ready for this." Sam picked up his knife and fork and began to eat the dinner quickly. "I've been working me socks off at the mill on Wilton Street, doing double shifts 'cause me brother joined up last month and they're short-handed, what with the big order an' all."

Sam spoke around his food and Agnes could hear her mother's words echoing in her head, 'Don't speak with your mouth full.' She ignored the remembered reprimand and continued to listen politely to the ginger-haired lad.

"I'm an engineer and I was going to join up as well, but Mr Binks, the big boss man asked me to stay at the mill a bit longer. He thinks highly of me, you know." Sam glanced up at Agnes and gave her a lopsided grin. "Not like some around here who don't even know I exist."

"Oh, Sam. You'd be the first one I'd look to walk out with if I weren't married with a bairn."

"That's music to my ears Agnes."

"Oh, go on with you, Sam."

"If you can get rid of the husband, I don't mind about the bairn. I like little ones."

"Even if they're not your own?"

"I don't mind. Really! My mam did a runner when I was little and I've only got me dad. I wish I'd had brothers and sisters. It gets lonely sometimes."

"I'm an only child too. So I know what you mean."

"Well, anytime you get lonely, you let me know."

"Don't hold your breath, Sam. I still have a husband, remember?"

"Oh, him! Well, I'll just have to dream then, won't I?" Sam frowned theatrically.

Agnes watched him shovel more dinner into his mouth and thought about getting back to work, but there was something about this man that made her want to stay and listen to him a bit longer.

"I'm joining up as soon as they get more men to take over in the mill. Being an engineer lets me off going to war, you know, but I can't stand by while everyone else goes off to fight, can I?"

"Will they let you join up?"

"The army needs engineers too, so I'm hoping they'll have me."

"The army needs anyone they can get by the sounds of things."

"Did you hear on the wireless about all them lads at Dunkirk? What a to-do! The Jerries had 'em pinned down good and proper, but all them fishermen and folks with boats went to get our lads. Them Germans have to be stopped or they'll be over here before we know it. Now Churchill's got settled in we'll give 'em a walloping, you'll see. Anyways, I'm determined to go over there to do my bit to stop Hitler if it's the last thing I do, and it might well be! The last thing I do, I mean. But I'm not afraid of copping it."

"Brave words, Sam. You take care over there." Agnes commented.

"If I didn't know better, I'd think you were starting to go soft on me, Agnes." Sam grinned up at her.

"I wouldn't want to see you killed, that's all."

"There's hundreds joining up now." Sam continued. "The mill has a big order for army blankets, so they're busy installing more looms. That's why I've been so busy, I'm in the gang that's fitting 'em, the looms, that is. They're looking for more lasses to work 'em, but it's mucky work, and most lasses aren't up to it cos it's hard, standing on your pins all day…" and so he continued his monologue, not appearing to need anything more from Agnes other than an ear for listening to him.

Agnes smiled to herself. "Well, I'll leave you to enjoy your dinner, Sam. I've customers waiting." She left him and went to serve a young couple who had just walked in.

The café usually got very busy at teatime when the factories and shops around town closed. She was rushed off her feet until closing time at eight, and they still hadn't had word from George, the owner, about how his mam was. She hadn't had time to talk to Polly about her pregnancy, but she knew she'd get more of that story on the way home when the two girls would walk along the cobbled streets and on together as far as the river, where they would cross the bridge and turn up Wharf Street to go to Polly's home.

Polly lived with her parents, Bert and Hilda, and two younger brothers in a back-to-back tenement at the top of Orchard Street. Agnes would collect her son from Hilda's care and take him home to an empty and cold house on Chapel Street. Bill had taken on the rent from her mother when they got married, but it was a struggle to make ends meet, especially now, with Bill away in the war. She managed because George, for all his bad-tempered appearance, had a heart of gold, and she was able to take most of her meals at work, or take home what didn't sell that day. She had a large portion of pie sitting in the bottom of her basket in the kitchen ready to take home. Harry would eat well tonight after she collected him from Hilda's house. They would never starve while she worked for George.

The last customer was paying Polly at the counter when George bustled through the doorway. Agnes looked up from cleaning tables and knew from the set of his shoulders that the news wouldn't be good. Poor George looked to have aged ten years in the last day. His face was grey and his shoulders stooped like those of an old man though he would only be in his late thirties as far as Agnes could tell.

"I'll just go through to see Sally before she leaves. Hang on a bit, will you both? I've summat to tell you," he said to them before making his way to the kitchen.

Polly shrugged as she saw the last customer to the door and locked it as soon as he had left. "What do you think he has to say to us?" Polly asked Agnes.

"We'll soon find out." Agnes inclined her head towards the kitchen door. "I can hear Sally crying so it won't be good, will it?" She rang out the cloth she'd been using on the tables and hung it to dry on the copper boiler at the back of the counter. "From the sound of it, I'd say that his mum passed away. She's been proper poorly for weeks, hasn't she?"

"What will that mean for us? Can George keep this place going without her support?" Polly glanced at the kitchen door. "It was hers by name, wasn't it?"

"Aye, but George has run it for years without any help from his mam." Agnes began to fear for her future. If George were to shut the café, she would really find it tough to keep the house on. "He can't close it. What would he do to earn a living?"

George came back to the counter with a grim look of determination on his face. "There's no easy way to say this, girls. My mam passed over early this afternoon."

"Oh, George, I'm sorry." Agnes offered at the same time as Polly.

"Girls, please! Save your sympathy. We all know she was a harridan. She ran this place tighter than a duck's arse, pardon my French, and when I took over when she got bad with her legs, she didn't like it a bit. Thing is..." George paused and scratched his head. "Well, I've come to realise that she was right about a lot of things, and one of them was borrowing. She never took loans, never asked the bank for a penny, and she managed to keep this place going on fresh air. I can't say I had the same luck. I've been running on empty for months, and the bank and the moneylender won't let me have any more, so I'll be closing up."

"When?" Agnes asked with a trembling voice.

"Now."

"You can't!" Polly gasped and clutched her tummy. "I need; no, WE need this job!"

"I'm sorry, girls. If there was any other way, you know I don't want to let you go." George shook his head. "I can't cope with the banks and the bailiffs and mam's funeral. I can't pay you for this week, but you can take owt you can carry from the kitchen, and come back for more tomorrow. I'll be around to let the bailiff fella in. I've been to see the moneylender. I didn't know what else to do. I knew I'd have the funeral to pay for and our Dorothy won't settle for less than the best for the old bitch."

"Oh, George." Polly was close to tears.

"So you see, I thought I could buy a bit more time, like, but, well, I can't! He's sending the bailiffs in and they're coming to take everything that isn't nailed down so they can sell it."

"I don't understand." Agnes blurted. "Just because your mam passed away, why do you have to sell up? What would you have done if she'd lived? I mean what if she didn't die, I don't understand? What difference will it make?"

"Well, I would have closed by the end of this month anyway, lass. Mam passing like this has just brought it forward a bit. The bank was at my heels already, and then the moneylender got wind of how much I owe to the bank, and now I have to find money to bury the old hag on top of paying the rent on this place. I have to find the weekly payment to the lender, and the bank. I still owe the butcher, the flour mill, the market traders and the fishmonger for last month's orders. They let me have tick, but I don't know how I'm going to clear all the debt. Truth is; there's nothing left. That cash till holds the only money I have to me name, and that's spoken for."

"What will you do, George?" Polly asked in a small voice.

"Think I'll run away to sea." He huffed. "The Merchant Navy might need a cook, and it would get me away from our Dorothy's condemnation. My sister hasn't taken it so well. She thought I'd have a thriving business to split between us as an inheritance. Not that she's ever done owt to help out. She saw her bit as looking after mam while I kept the business going. She's not too pleased that there's nothing to share out but debts."

"I'm sorry it's come to this, George!" Agnes went to get her coat and basket from the kitchen.

"Me an' all." Polly followed Agnes.

"Here girls, let me get you loaded up." George offered and

went with them into the kitchen. "Sally has been getting the bags ready for you. There's some dried stuff, peas and lentils, flour, sugar, tea and cocoa and some veggies and tinned stuff. If you can call back tomorrow, there'll be more when we finish clearing the shelves. Come before nine though, so the bailiffs don't see what we're up to."

Agnes took the large sack from Sally, and Polly took an identical one. They each hugged the small dumpy cook before turning to their boss.

"Thanks for this George, it will help a lot." Agnes swallowed the lump in her throat. "At least it should tide us over until we find something else."

"Aye, thanks, George." Polly nodded her head at the sad face of their boss.

"See you tomorrow then, bright and early, remember?" George bid them goodnight and locked the door behind them.

Polly was sobbing quietly before they left the back alley behind the café. "This bloody sack is too heavy! I'll never manage it all the way home."

"Give it here." Agnes took the sack from her daintily built cousin and placed some of the heavier items into her own sack before handing it back to her cousin. "There, do you think you'll manage that?"

"But you're carrying a bairn, same as me, can you manage?"

"What do you think, lass?" Agnes hefted her heavy sack over her shoulders and stood to her full height. She looked down at the top of her cousin's head. "I might be a big clumsy oaf, but I have me uses."

"Thanks, Agnes." Polly sniffed back her tears. "What are we going to do?"

"Well, you have to face up to your mam and dad and tell them about the bairn. I'm going to that mill on Wilton Street tomorrow and see if they'll take me on. Sam Wood was telling me they were looking to take on more lasses."

"You wouldn't!" Polly looked shocked. "That's hard work! You'd be on your feet all day, it's a sweaty business, and how will you manage with a big belly. They won't take you on if they know you're carrying a bairn. You can't, Agnes, you just can't!"

"Why not?" Agnes asked. "I've been on me feet in a sweaty business since I left school. Waitressing isn't so different, is it? There's no need to mention the bairn, I'm not showing yet. I'm not even four months gone. Besides, there's not much else around here that pays good wages. There're lots of men's jobs, but we can't be doing heavy work like the men do, not like some lasses are doing, because of our condition. When are you due, Polly?"

"Well, we'll be having our bairns within weeks of each other. This little bastard took hold about three months since. I've been hoping it was something else that stopped me monthlies, but when I started being a bit queasy in the mornings, well, that put the tin hat on it, didn't it?"

"Oh, Poll! Why didn't you tell me afore?"

"What could you have done about it? Like I said, I didn't want to think about it meself, I just hoped it would go away."

"Well, you know that it won't go away, don't you? I've told you before, Polly, that problems are best faced head on, but you never listen, do you?"

"I know, Agnes, but I'm that afraid of me dad. He's not a mild mannered man like me Uncle Seth was. He'll go bonkers. You know what my dad's like. I wish he were more like your dad was."

Agnes could well remember that her father was far from the gentle peacemaker his friends and fellow churchgoers thought him to be. She had first-hand knowledge of her father's temper. Seth would be alive today if he hadn't been so uncharacteristically hot-headed that night. "Well, tell your mam first. Hilda might talk to your dad and try to bring him around."

"Pigs will fly first. My dad's always in a bad mood these days. What with working all hours at the iron works and then doing the fire watches on a night. He's tired and snappy and he takes it out on us all."

"Well, you can't blame him, Poll. He's too old to join up and he wants to play a part in stopping this awful war. If the Jerries try to invade us, well, goodness knows what will happen." Agnes shook her head. "Our lives will never be the same again if Jerry wins this."

"What's the world coming to? All the young men are going to war. Now we've got women bus drivers, lasses working on the railways. They're even down the goods-yards, Charlie told me! They do a man's work for almost as much as a man earns too."

"I don't know what the world is coming to, Poll, but whatever I have to do to keep my bairn fed and a roof over his head, I'll do it. You should think about your own lot. How do you think your mam will take it?" Agnes asked, but thought she already had a good idea what the answer to her question would be.

"I think Mam will be more upset at me losing me job than bringing them another mouth to feed."

"Your wages went a long way to help put food on the table in your house, didn't it? But then your James and David bring a bit in with the work on the coal wagons at the pit, don't they?"

"Aye, but young lads don't earn much loading the wagons. They will in a year or so when they can go down the mine. I suppose dad can always get more shifts at the ironworks. He'd have to give up the volunteering at the fire watch, but, well, oh, I don't know, Agnes. I just don't know!" Polly stumbled and dropped her sack of food. She sat on a low wall and put her head in her hands and her shoulders shook as she began to sob loudly.

Agnes hunkered down beside her friend and put a comforting arm around the shuddering shoulders. "We'll find a way through this, Poll. You're not on your own, love. I'll help. If you need anything, I'll be here for you. You're not only my cousin, but we've been friends since we were in our prams, so I'm not about to leave you to cope with all this on your own."

Agnes wondered how much she could really do to help her friend, but they weren't just empty words. She meant every one of them. If Polly needed her, she would be there, no matter what. She owed Polly everything, but she hoped the girl would never know how much Agnes was in her debt.

Chapter Two, A friend in need

Agnes fed and changed Harry when she got home. The infant was hungry and tired and she knew he would soon want his bed. She popped him back in the pram and strapped him in with the reigns to keep him out of harm's way while she set about lighting a small fire in the cold hearth. The sun had been shining all day and it was hot in the little house, but she would have to start a fire if she wanted a warm dinner. The fire heated the small, black cast-iron oven that was built into the side of the fireplace. Harry had enjoyed his pie cold, but Agnes preferred bully-beef eaten hot. It didn't taste so bad if was warmed through. Harry watched her solemnly from his pram where he sat playing with a tin rattle.

"Won't be long now, Harry. I'll soon be done with this mucky work," she called to her son as she continued to work the leather bellows under the pile of kindling. The flames soon caught and she piled on small lumps of coal before sitting back on her haunches and wiping her brow on her apron. "There we are, all done. I'll wash my hands and we can have a play." She crossed the small room to the pot sink and dipped her hands in the cold water.

Agnes loved to play with her son. His smile and hearty chuckles had the power to lift her out of the deepest doldrums. After the day she'd had, learning of poor Polly's predicament, and losing their jobs on top of all that, she didn't know what she would do next. She wanted to take her mind away from the stress of her life, and playing with Harry was the perfect antidote to gloom and doom.

She'd told Polly that she was going to apply at the mill, but she didn't hold any hope of being taken on there, no matter what the red-headed lad had said about them being desperate to take on more lasses. She didn't know one end of a loom from the other. She had worked in her dad's bakery shop from leaving school, and then worked at the café with Polly. Both jobs were a far cry from millwork.

She went to lift Harry from the pram with her now clean hands and placed him on the rag-rug away from the heat of the blazing fire. "What you been doing all day, little man?" she asked, reaching to tickle his toes. "Has your Auntie Hilda been playing with you like I do?" She reached under his cotton romper and tickled his tummy and the eight-month-old baby let out a raucous squeal of merriment. "I know it's not ideal, son, but I have to work. I wish I could stay at home and look after you meself, but that's not going to happen while ever I need to earn enough to keep meself, so you'd better be happy with our Auntie Hilda."

Agnes continued to tickle and tease her son until he became tired of play. As his chuckles got quieter, she pulled him onto her lap and held him close. As his little body started to grow heavy in her lap, she began to sing to him. "*My bonnie lies over the ocean...*" She took Harry into her arms and rocked him close to her chest. "*My bonnie lies over the sea...*" The words of the song brought tears to her eyes, but she continued to sing, "*My bonnie lies over the ocean, oh, bring back my bonnie to me, to me.*" Agnes's voice broke on a sob, and young Harry added his wail to hers, picking up on his mother's distress. "Andrew will never come back here, Harry. Your daddy won't come back to us. Not ever! I'm sorry, son."

She soothed her baby and stroked his brow until he quieted and closed his eyes. She rocked him more, just to feel close to him a little longer. He was the image of his father, and her son reminded her so much of the man she loved with all her heart, but would never see again.

Agnes sighed and looked down at her baby. "I don't regret having you, my love." She kissed the top of his head before she laid him in the pram and covered him with a blanket. "You're the one good thing to come out of all the heartache and you make it bearable for me." When Harry was settled, she set about getting her own meal. She firmly pushed all thoughts of Andrew out of her head and began to focus on warming her dinner. She put the pie in the oven at the side of the fire to heat through. While it was warming, she filled the kettle and placed it on the hot plate on top of the small oven and began to get ready for bed. She shrugged her nightdress over her shoulders and a loud knocking startled her.

"Who's there?" she called to the door.

"It's me! Polly!" Her cousin's voice was high and shrill. "Let me in, Aggy. Please let me in."

Agnes hurried to open the door and ushered her friend into the over-warm room. Polly clutched a collection of cloth tied up with string, her face was wet, and her eyes were red and swollen from crying. Agnes's heart sank. Polly didn't have to tell her what had happened. It was clear as day that Hilda and Bert had kicked her out. It looked as if all her worldly goods were in the cloth bundle she held to her chest.

"I didn't know where else to go, Agnes. Can I stay with you? I'll pay me way. I'll get a job. I'll apply at the mill tomorra with you. I'll do anything."

Polly's eyes were dark and glossy as she pleaded, and Agnes thought she looked like an angel. Her dark shining hair hung down her back in rope like coils, framing her pale, dainty face. Even under a thick shapeless cardigan, Polly looked graceful and elegant. She was the very opposite of Agnes, and her elfin appearance always made the larger girl feel even taller and more cumbersome, but they had grown up together as cousins, became best friends, and were now closer than sisters.

"Please don't turn me away, Agnes. I can't believe me mam an' dad turned their backs on me." Polly let out a moan. "Oh, Agnes! They wouldn't listen. They don't understand. You'd think they'd never been in love."

"Well, we know that's not true." Agnes smiled gently at her cousin. "Auntie Hilda thinks the world of your dad and anyone will tell you the same. They dote on each other. At their age an' all! Folks at church are always commenting on how it is with your mam and dad."

"Maybe that's why they don't go anymore. Folks that go to Saint Paulinus are too nosey for their own good." Polly sniffed. "My dad says they're all hypocrites anyway. He didn't like the way Father Brennan preached about peace and love one week then spouted off about sending our young lads to fight in the war the next. And what a war that turned out to be!"

"You're talking about the last war, Polly. That was more than twenty years ago, and he still holds a grudge against Father Brennan." Agnes had often wondered why her Uncle Bert refused to go to church even though the family had been staunch Catholics. "Your dad went to France to do his bit didn't he?"

"Fought in the trenches just like your dad, but he won't talk about it. Nasty business he called it. Me mam says she nearly went mad with the worry of him being over there, and now my Charlie has to go and fight in this war. You'd think me mam an' dad would understand, wouldn't you?"

"Don't you think you're asking a bit too much, Poll? It's not like you can get married to your sweetheart and make everything all right, is it?"

"I haven't done owt that hasn't been done by many a lass around here. I was just unlucky is all."

"I'll not turn you away, Poll. How could you even think that I might?" Agnes took her cousin into her arms and let her sob on her shoulder. "We'll manage, love." Somehow, we'll have to, she thought.

Agnes shared her meal with Polly, and both girls settled on the rug in front of the fire.

"I can't believe it's so hot!" Agnes reached to close the damper on the fire to stop it burning so brightly. "It's only the beginning of June, so goodness knows what the rest of the year will be like. It'll be a no fun being pregnant through a blazing hot summer."

"Never mind the weather; it's the news in the papers that I worry about. All that business with the lads on that French beach being rescued by all them boats last month was terrible."

"Aye, Dunkirk wasn't it? They said thousands of our lads got killed there."

"They bombed Paris! Can you believe it? Belgium surrendered last month and now Norway has held their hands up to the Jerries. I'm that scared for Charlie. What if they send him somewhere like Dunkirk?"

"Italy has joined in now. Fancy them declaring war on us. I thought they'd have been on our side. I don't know where Bill is, but he'll be somewhere fighting this God-awful war. I hope he's making a good few of them Germans wish they'd never started it."

"At least we don't live in France or Norway or any of those other countries. We're safe in Britain." Polly sat forward and hugged her knees. "At least I hope we will be."

"Aye, they said, before Christmas, to expect the worst. They said we'd all be bombed, but so far they've only dropped a few on Scapa Flow in Scotland. Building all them air-raid shelters was a waste of time if you ask me."

"Well, the war's not over yet, Agnes. In fact, it looks like it's only getting started."

"Well, we've more things to worry about at home, haven't we, Poll? No use fretting about things we have no control over."

"Thanks, Agnes. You're right. I won't ever forget how kind you've been to me, taking me in like this." Polly leant back and snuggled against her cousin.

"As if I'd do anything other than take you in." Agnes patted her cousin's arm. "Are you going to tell me how you got yourself into this mess?"

"That won't take long." Polly shuddered. "I trusted him. I know I mean the world to him, and he said he'd be careful."

"Aye, well, words are fine before the event, but when they get carried away, they just can't stop themselves like they're supposed to."

"Charlie tried to use one of them rubber things, but he didn't like it, so we used the Catholic method. It's worked for ages so I couldn't believe it when I realised what had happened."

"You should have made sure he took more care. You knew he was married, Poll." Agnes chided softly.

"He doesn't love her. He told me she's like a dead fish in bed, and she has no affection for him."

"And you believed him? Even after he told you she was having their third bairn?"

"A man has needs, Agnes. I couldn't give him everything he needed 'cause it's not easy to get a time and a place to, to, well, you know what I mean."

"Oh, Poll. He really has you convinced, hasn't he?"

"If things were different, he'd have me afore her any day, I know it!" Polly defended her actions. "He loves me more than life, he told me so."

"And you were fool enough to believe his lies. Oh, Polly."

"He didn't lie, Agnes. I know he loves me."

"Then tell him about the baby!" Agnes raised herself onto her elbow and looked down at her cousin's stricken face, and saw her tears shimmering in the glow from the fire. She softened her voice. "If he loves you, he'll make the right choice, and stand by you, no matter what, especially if he doesn't love his wife. There is such a thing as divorce, you know." Agnes knew she was spouting fairytales. Anyone knew that Charlie Watson was only out for number one and would say anything to get into a girl's knickers. If he knew that Polly was having his child, she'd be discarded like so many other lasses before her, and Agnes thought that Polly was a fool if she thought otherwise.

"I can't do that, Agnes. Them three bairns have done nowt to deserve a broken home. I can't take their daddy away."

"Children can grow up without a father, Poll. My Harry's doing all right without Bill around."

"That's different, Agnes. Your Bill is off fighting a war, and God willing he'll be coming back to you like he did a few months back when he got sick leave. He's not gone for good, is he?"

"Charlie wouldn't be gone for good if he divorced Jane for you. He'd still be able to see his lads. Bill might be gone for good, Poll. Who knows with this war?"

"You don't seem too bothered about that. I couldn't stand it if Charlie were to get shot or blown up by the Jerries. Aren't you worried about Bill?"

"Of course I am. I wouldn't like it if Bill were to get hurt or worse. That bit of bother with his eardrum was bad enough to get him sent home for a few weeks. Daft thing got too close to the big guns when they were firing in that training camp. Now he'll always be deaf in one ear, but he survived and got better enough to go back and fight and he will again. But if he gets shot, then so be it. There's nowt I can do about it, is there?"

"How come you're so hard-hearted? I'd be beside meself just thinking about it, yet you sound so cold. You do love him, don't you?"

"Of course I love Bill. He's my husband." Agnes was finding it easier and easier to tell the same lie over and over. She didn't even feel the familiar twinge of guilt that sent her thoughts skittering towards the confession box. If the truth were known, she wouldn't care in the least if Bill didn't come home to her. She was better off with him far away, and if she thought she would never see him again, she would feel relieved. "Better get some sleep. We have a long day of job hunting tomorrow if the mill don't want us."

Agnes lifted the sleeping baby into her arms and the two girls made their way upstairs and got ready for bed. They settled down together in the double bed that had been Trudie and Seth's, but was now Bill and Agnes's.

"G'night, Aggy. Thanks again for taking me in." Polly mumbled before turning on her side. She was snoring softly in minutes.

Agnes found sleep didn't come so easily to her guilty conscience. She didn't love her husband, and never had. He was a distant relative, the son of a half-cousin of her Uncle Bert, who had lived a few streets away. He was persuaded to give an air of respectability to a wayward girl, and it seemed to

Agnes that he jumped at the chance. They'd grown up together, but had never been close. He'd been there in the background, attending the same schools, hanging around with the other children on the street, playing hide and seek, squat can and football in the back lanes. As teenagers, they'd all gone to the same church dances and charabanc trips to the seaside. Bill only ever had eyes for one lass, though, and it wasn't Agnes.

To be fair to Bill, he had done nothing worse than accept Trudie's bribe to marry her. His heart belonged to another, and he made no secret of that fact when he agreed to Trudie's plans. Agnes was lucky that the object of Bill's desire seemed to have no idea of his true feelings. Polly barely registered the fact that he existed. That made it easier for Agnes to accept her mother's arrangement, but she always felt Polly was missing out. Bill would have been much happier if it were Polly he'd been asked to marry, and Polly would have been better off too. If only her cousin wasn't so hell-bent on Charlie Watson, she might have noticed poor Bill Smithson. Agnes knew Bill had been waiting and hoping her cousin would grow tired of the affair and he was ready to jump in, if and when that happened. He was besotted with Polly, but Agnes hadn't realised how much he loved her friend until after she married him.

Bill made Agnes feel ugly and awkward at every chance he got. He was always comparing her to the pretty and dainty cousin, making Agnes feel even more cumbersome than she was. Bill didn't like the fact that she was taller than he was, and made her wear flat shoes when they went out together. He was on the short side for a man, and Polly would have been the perfect height for him, a fact that he referred to often.

Bill appeared to treat Agnes quite well under the circumstances. He paid for the upkeep of Harry, and he would pay for the one that he put inside her when he was home on sick leave when Harry was barely three-month-old. He refused to pay a penny for Agnes's keep, though. That was the deal he'd made with Trudie. The first child, and any children of their union would be his responsibility, but Agnes would never be his financial burden to carry. Her mother had made it plain that Agnes would always provide for herself. It was her punishment. As if losing the love of her life, only weeks after her father's death wasn't punishment enough. She would never forget that fateful night when her dad went into the river Calder. The memories were seared into her brain, and not a night passed when she didn't think of it.

That was the beginning of the whole sorry mess. Agnes shuddered and tried to push the dreadful memory of that awful night from her mind. If only her dad had been willing to listen. If only Andrew hadn't insisted on seeing him. If only, if only, if only...

Agnes allowed herself to think of the past when she was ready for sleep. She could not cope with the disturbing images during the daylight hours, but somehow the darkness helped to make the memories bearable. She had been the cause of her father's death, and she would never forgive herself, even if God might forgive her sin. She would never confess, so she would go to purgatory and be damned for all eternity. The times she had re-lived that night were countless. She ran through the events, trying to see if she could have done anything to alter what happened. Trying, in her head, to change what had been said and done to see if the outcome might have been different, but each time the episode she played in her mind ended when her father's lifeless body rolled from her arms and into the river, just as he had that night.

Chapter Three, The beginning

She recalled the first night they met in the springtime of 1938 at Ben Riley's dance hall opposite the town hall. Agnes was alone towards the end of the night as usual. At twenty-four-years old, she was used to being a wallflower. She often wondered whether it might have been different if Polly had still been with her. She knew that the lads looked at Polly first, and Agnes had to be content with her cousin's leftovers. Polly was the bonny one. Agnes knew she couldn't hold a candle to her younger cousin's elfin beauty. Agnes was too tall and she was heavily built, and the mirror told her she was nothing special to look at. Her dad was always telling her to straighten her shoulders and stand tall, but if she did, she was taller than most of the lads, and that put them off going anywhere near her.

Agnes was sitting by the wall in her usual spot. She was happy to watch the other dancers. She'd resigned herself long ago to life as a spinster, living with her mam and dad and looking after them when they got frail in years to come. Most lasses her age were married with bairns by now. She was the odd ball. The tall lass. The plainer cousin. She wasn't bitter. She knew she didn't have the same attraction that Polly did. She didn't begrudge the younger lass her beauty.

When the band started to play a slow dance she noticed a tall young man looking her way. She watched with amazement as the man left his seat and made his way over to her. When Andrew spoke, his Irish accent sounded strange in her ear, and it took her a moment to realise that he was asking her to dance. She nodded shyly and took his hand. When she stood, she was amazed to find that she had to look up into his eyes. He later told her it had taken him all evening to pluck up courage to ask her to dance.

She loved how he folded her gently into his arms and held her as if she'd been made of glass as they began the steps of a traditional waltz. His eyes looked down into hers, and she felt a tug in her insides that took her breath away. He was so good-looking with his dark flop of hair and twinkling eyes. He was smiling down at her, and her insides were trembling so much she had to lower her eyes from his face and concentrate on the dance steps so she wouldn't stand on his toes.

Within a few minutes, they were talking and laughing as if they'd known each other all their lives. Andrew kept glancing at her from the corner of his eye.

"I can hardly believe you are by my side, Agnes." He whispered as he led her back to the seating along the edge of the wall. "You're the best looking girl here, and you danced with me! It must be my lucky day."

Agnes felt flattered. "Go on with you." She lowered her head, hiding her blushes.

"Do you have to be home by a certain time?" Andrew asked. "Or does your daddy let you stay out a bit longer?"

"Me dad works nights, he has the bakery on Headfield Road so he's there baking most nights. He won't know whether I'm late or not." Agnes felt reckless. Her mam might have something to say if she was late, but she knew she could get around Trudie and she wouldn't tell her dad if Agnes asked her not to.

"Then will you come with me for a nightcap to the Scarborough hotel across the road?"

Agnes hesitated for a few seconds.

"I'll walk you home afterwards, I promise." Andrew's eyes twinkled down at her.

Agnes grinned at him and agreed to go the pub. Polly had gone off with her chap already, and although Agnes was upset that her cousin had left with Charlie Watson again, she couldn't do anything about it, so she may as well go with Andrew.

That was the beginning of a love affair that Agnes would forever regret, because the consequences of her love would cost her dearly. She didn't know then that Andrew didn't share her parent's faith. She hadn't realised it would be such a problem for her father. All she cared about was Andrew, and when she might see him again.

The following six months were filled with happiness for Agnes. Each day of those months was filled with Andrew. When she didn't see him, she was thinking about him, and he told her it was the same for him. He had recently begun to push for more than kisses and caresses in the dark, and she was finding it harder to refuse him.

"I can't get you out of my mind, Agnes," he told her as they walked hand-in-hand by the river on Sand's Lane, one cold November evening. "I can't concentrate at work and me boss has to chivvy me along to wake me from daydreams."

"So you dream about me in the daytime, do you, Andrew

O'Connor?" Agnes's insides fluttered. It felt so good to be walking and talking like this with her sweetheart.

"You fill my head, and my heart, Agnes. If I let myself think on it, I'd say I was in love with you."

Agnes stopped walking and turned to face Andrew. The lights from the gasworks at the other side of the river lit their faces as they stared into each others' eyes. "Say it again!" she demanded, smiling widely.

"I think I love you, Agnes Garrity." He leant down to kiss her gently on the lips.

"I'm glad, Andrew, because I think I feel the same way about you."

"Does that mean we're serious now?"

"Like a proper courting couple?" Agnes asked.

"Or a couple who intend to marry one day, perhaps?" Andrew stared down into her eyes.

"You want to marry me?" Agnes couldn't believe what she'd heard.

"I'm so sure of it; I'll make you a snowdrop's promise."

"What's a snowdrop's promise?" Agnes said, smiling up into his face.

"Well, it's something me mammy used to say to me and me brother's when we were pestering for something and wouldn't be quiet. She'd give us a snowdrop's promise and we'd know that we could have whatever it was we'd been blathering about, a little later."

Agnes looked puzzled. "I still don't understand. Why a snowdrop?"

"Well, the snowdrop is the first flower of spring. She shows herself while the snow is still on the ground and people are freezing and days are short with no sign of the warmth of springtime that waits just a month so away."

"So a snowdrop promises that the warmth of springtime will come? Is that it?"

"Just as surely as the sun rises each day, a snowdrop's promise can be relied on. A guarantee, you see. It's an assurance that what you are promising can't be broken, not by man and not by nature. So I'm making you a snowdrop's promise that I'll make you the happiest woman alive one day, Agnes Garrity."

"You really want to tie yourself to a big lummox like me?"

"Why do you always put yourself down, Agnes? You're tall and curvy, just like them pin-up girl pictures we have in the canteen down at the goods-yard. I bet you'd look just like one of them lasses if you put a swimsuit on."

"Oh, go on with you, I'm not like Ava Gardner and the likes!" Agnes couldn't help feeling elated at his words and her smile was radiant as she gazed up at him.

"Ava Gardner wouldn't be noticed if you were standing next to her. I bet you have a cracking pair of legs hiding under that shapeless skirt. I can't wait to see you in your underwear, Agnes Garrity."

"Andrew O'Connor!" She tried to sound stern, but couldn't keep the smile from her face.

"When you smile like that, you make my heart beat faster. You're so lovely, Agnes, and you don't even know it."

"I'm very glad you think so, Andrew." Agnes leant into his chest. "Even if I know that no one else thinks so. You make me feel pretty and graceful, and I love you for it."

"Do you love me enough to marry me and come with me to Ireland?" Andrew teased.

"I do!" Agnes giggled, and then sighed. "But with the way the world is, perhaps we'd better wait and see."

"Wait for what?" Andrew held her close and spoke to the top of her head. "For a war that might never happen?"

"Well, after all that rioting in Germany and the way they're treating the Jews..." Agnes shivered. "It's not right, and someone will want to do something about it before long. America has already brought their ambassador home from Germany."

"Aye, but politicians are always changing their minds, love. I wouldn't worry too much about a war. Chamberlain signed that peace treaty with Hitler and them others at the end of September, didn't he, so he won't want us to go to war after signing that."

"I still worry, Andrew. What if there is a war and you have to go and fight? Me mam and dad talk about it all the time. They still remember the last war. Me dad fought in France, and he's sure we'll have another war soon."

"Well, even if there is another war, my love, it won't stop us from getting married."

"But what if..."

Andrew silenced her question with a kiss and when he pulled away, he put a finger to her lips. "Shush, Agnes. If there is a war, we'd better get married as soon as we can so we can make the most of each other."

"Oh, Andrew, I don't know if me mam and dad would like that. I mean, they haven't even met you yet."

"We'll soon sort that out, love. Where would you like to get married?"

"Saint Paulinus is our church, so I suppose we'll have the service there."

"You mean the Catholic church on Temple Road?" Andrew looked puzzled. "You're Catholic?"

"Aye, Andrew, I'm a Catholic." Agnes said warily. "Is that a problem?"

"Not to me, Agnes. I don't mind who you pray to or how you do it. I was brought up Protestant that's all."

"On, no! That might be a problem to me dad."

"Let's not allow religion to get in our way. I left Ireland because the Catholics and Protestants couldn't get along. I thought it would be different over this side of the water."

"We do get along, Andrew. We don't have the same troubles as the Irish, and me dad drinks in the pub with men who go to the Thornbury Parish and the Methodist Chapels, so it might be all right."

"Let's not worry about it now, love. I'll win your dad around. Once he sees how much I care about you, he'll be begging me to marry you so I can make you the happiest girl in the world for the rest of your life, and if he doesn't we could always elope!"

"Oh, Andrew, you say the nicest things to me." Agnes hugged him closer and lifted her lips to kiss him.

"It's getting late." Andrew said as he pulled away after their kiss. "Will you be meeting your Polly to walk home tonight, or will I take you to the end of your street?" Andrew asked.

Agnes often met her cousin at the end of the evening so the two girls could walk home together. Polly usually spent her evening hiding away in some corner of a public house with Charlie, but the married man had to get home to his wife, and couldn't be seen openly walking out with his fancy woman. Their two boyfriends had never met, and Polly had only seen Andrew from a distance. Agnes didn't like to talk about Polly's affair, except to warn her constantly that she was playing with fire, and so Polly had made it clear that she wasn't interested in discussing the details of Agnes's love life. It was a strange arrangement, but because of Polly's illicit romance, that's how things had worked out.

"I said I'd meet her on the Long Causeway. You don't mind, do you?"

"Well, now that we're serious, perhaps I should be walking you home and meeting your parents before too long."

Agnes couldn't believe how her life changed so quickly. Christmas of 1938 was the turning point. Her father worked right up until Christmas Eve in the Bakery and expected Agnes to work more hours in the shop to cope with the holiday demand for bread and fancies. She was run off her feet, but somehow found the energy to spend precious time with Andrew at the end of the day. She was slipping into her coat on Christmas Eve, intending to meet Andrew at the dance hall when her father stopped her.

"Don't think you can stay out all night, young lass." Seth had warned. "Just because the shop is closed tomorrow, and you don't have to get up early, I don't want you out late. It's not right and folks are talking."

"Who's talking?" Agnes whirled to face her dad, surprised by what he'd said. "What are they saying?"

"They're saying as how you've taken up with a piece of Irish scum and I've been waiting for you to tell me yourself, but so far you've kept quiet, so I'm thinking you might have something to hide."

"I'm hiding nowt, Dad. I'd have brought him home for you to meet him afore now, but he works shifts at the goods-yard, and you work all night in the bakery, so it's never been a good time." Agnes blustered as she said the first thing that came into her head.

"Perhaps your young man could visit for his Christmas Day tea tomorrow?" Trudie suggested. "You won't be opening the shop on Boxing Day, will you, Seth? You can stay and have tea with Agnes's young man."

"I'll ask him, shall I, Dad?"

So it was arranged that Andrew would at last meet her parents and Agnes was excited and nervous at the same time.

Andrew was happy to be meeting her parents, and seemed pleased to be taking the next step in their relationship.

The afternoon proved to be a disaster. From being happier than she'd thought it was possible to be, she was thrown into a world of uncertainty. Her father had questioned Andrew about his background in Northern Ireland, and discovered he was Protestant.

"But I'm not a religious man, Mr Garrity." Andrew had insisted. "I don't have strong feelings either way. My country has been in turmoil for years because of religion that's why I came here. To escape the conflicts, you know?"

"But you were brought up to go to church, weren't you?" Trudie asked him, trying to soften the growing atmosphere between the two men.

"Aye, until I got old enough to think for myself, and saw what suffering the church caused in my country. I'm blaming neither side, mind." Andrew continued, "If I had my way, Catholics and Protestants would be put together and given a good shake to make them see sense. The world needs more tolerance that's how I see it."

"I'm all for tolerance, Mr O'Connor, but I'm telling you now, there'll be no mixed marriage in this family."

"But, Dad!" Agnes jumped to her feet.

"I've said me piece, and that's an end to it."

"I love your daughter, Mr Garrity, and I'd like to marry her. But I won't do it without your permission because that wouldn't be right. I was, no, we were hoping you might…"

"I've said all I'm saying on the subject. There's only trouble to be had from mixing the faiths in wedlock. I won't have it, and that's an end to it. You're to stop seeing him, Agnes. I won't have it. You've got away with being too much like your cousin for long enough, but it stops now. It ends tonight. Do you hear me?"

"But, Dad! You can't! Please!" Agnes pleaded. "I love him. I'm old enough to marry him without your permission, and I might just do that!"

"Agnes, I'll not go against your father's wishes. We should respect his point of view."

Agnes couldn't believe Andrew wasn't trying harder to convince her dad.

"But, Dad! Please!" She tried again.

Seth ignored her protests. "I think it's time you said goodnight to your Protestant friend." He picked up the previous day's newspaper and deliberately opened it on his lap, putting an end to further conversation.

Trudie nodded towards the door and Agnes took the hint. She and Andrew left without more argument. They walked to the end of the street together in silence, the heavy carpet of snow muffling their footsteps, the bright light from the moon illuminating the picturesque landscape.

"Don't worry, Agnes." Andrew took her into his arms and held her close. "This won't be the end of it, we'll wear him down, you'll see."

Agnes laid her head on Andrew's shoulder, feeling protected and safe in his arms. Her dad would change his mind. He'd have to, she thought.

However, Seth's stubborn adherence to Catholic values meant that Andrew would never be acceptable as husband material for his daughter. No amount of pleading from Agnes made any difference to her father's feelings on the matter, but she continued to defy Seth by seeing Andrew in secret. She told her parents that she was going out with Polly, and her cousin was happy to cover for her as it meant she also had an excuse and was free to see her lover.

"It's exciting, isn't it, Agnes?" Polly squealed as they made their way into town one January evening. They were each muffled against the cold sleet with woollen scarves around their heads and mittens on their hands. "Me mam said I was daft to want to go out in this weather to see a film."

"What are we supposed to be watching tonight?" Agnes asked. "We'd better get our story straight."

"Well, we're supposed to be going to the Pioneer Picture house, and they're showing a rerun of Alexander's Ragtime Band. We've both seen it before, so we'll know what to say if anyone asks us about it."

"My, you've done your homework." Agnes shook her head. "I don't know that I like all this sneaking around. I wish my dad would agree to me seeing Andrew properly."

"Well, my dad will never agree to Charlie, and I don't think Charlie's wife would be too keen either, so I'm happy to keep 'em all guessing what we're up to."

"Oh, Polly! I wish you wouldn't joke about it."

"What else can I do, Aggy? If I didn't make light of the whole situation, I'd go mad."

"Where will you meet him tonight? I mean where will you really be going?"

"We'll really be going to the pictures, but we're going to see that new Tarzan film. Not that we'll see much of it. Them back seats can get really cosy when the lights go down."

"Oh, Polly, you are a one!" Agnes couldn't help but smile. "I'm meeting Andrew in the Albion on Bradford Road."

"That's a long walk!"

"Aye, but it's far enough out of town so me dad's drinking

cronies won't venture there and we'll be safe from prying eyes."

The two girls walked as far as the Picture house together, and Agnes left Polly waiting on the steps as she set out towards her destination. She didn't like to meet in out of the way places away from prying eyes, but it was better than not seeing Andrew at all. They were getting closer, and she had allowed him to stroke her intimate places, and had felt thrilled by his touch. She knew it was wrong, but it felt so good, and Andrew always made her feel so special.

"You feel so good, Agnes." He told her often. "I can't wait to make love to you properly. We have to make your daddy see reason. I can't wait much longer. You're too tempting, my love."

Eventually, they were caught out. Someone from the church saw them and the gossips began to spread the news of their continuing romance. Her dad was angrier than she'd ever seen him, and banned her from leaving the house except to go to work in the shop. Andrew would wait for her, after his night shift at the goods-yard, so they could spend a few precious moments together in the mornings. When he did the day shifts, he'd call at the shop in the early evening before her father showed up, to walk her home, leaving her at the bridge over the river.

Then one evening Andrew suggested he speak to her dad again, saying that he would do anything he had to, if it meant he could marry her, and said it was daft to carry on as they were.

"We love each other, Agnes, and we need to be together." He squeezed her hand. "Surely your daddy will give in when he sees how much we mean to each other."

If only she hadn't agreed with Andrew that another meeting face to face would be the best way to go about persuading her dad to let them marry. Andrew had been insistent, though. He was sure he could convince Seth to change his mind.

"He'll have to listen to me, Agnes." Andrew held her hand tightly as they waited by the bridge, that cold February night. Seth had agreed to meet Andrew on his way into the bakery, and they were waiting for him. "He'll see how much I love you eventually, and he'll not want to see his lass unhappy, will he?"

"You don't know my dad." Agnes shook her head. "He'll not listen, Andrew. I told you..."

They quieted when they heard footsteps coming towards them. Her father appeared out of the darkness and stood a under the street lamp at the end of the bridge.

"Dad!" Agnes took a step closer to him. "You came."

"Well, lad." Her father said, ignoring Agnes. "I'm listening."

Andrew walked to her father, explaining his love for Agnes, telling of their future plans, talking of marriage, and then her dad exploded.

"Don't come anywhere nearer, lad. I'm warning you! My lass is not tying herself to a heathen such as you. You not being Catholic is bad enough, but I've been asking questions about you, and I've not liked the answers I've been getting."

"What do you mean, Dad?" Agnes began to shiver, but her shakes had nothing to do with the snowy weather.

"You ask him about his past in Ireland." Seth held a look of pure hatred on his face. "Ask him about the Irish lass he left with a belly full of his bastard before he scuttled over here to get away."

"That's not true, Mr Garrity." Andrew protested.

Agnes felt her chest tighten. "What's all this, Andrew?"

"You might well ask, lass." Seth pointed at Andrew. "That young man has a past you know nowt about, and you think I'll agree to you tying yourself to the likes of him for the rest of your life?" He took a step nearer to Andrew and squared up to him. "Over my dead body!"

"You've got it wrong, it wasn't like that." Andrew shook his head and turned to Agnes. "You have to believe me, Agnes. I never did anything with that lass. She accused me, but I knew it were someone else she'd been seeing. Everyone believed her, but I wasn't going to tie meself to someone I didn't care about. The bairn wasn't mine. I never went near her, I swear!"

"Then why did she say that?" Seth bellowed. "Why would she point the finger at you if she were seeing someone else, answer me that!"

"Because she was seeing a Catholic lad, and in the North of Ireland, if you're a Protestant, that's as good as making a pact with the devil himself. Her family would have lynched her if they'd known the truth."

Agnes felt the breath leave her body and she struggled to take another. Her dad was holding his tightly closed fists by his side, and Andrew turned his head to plead with her. "You have to understand me, Agnes. I took the blame to save her face, but I couldn't go the whole hog and marry her."

"Why didn't you tell me?" she whispered, shaking her head.

"There was nothing to tell. Some other mug married her and that was the end of it."

"That's not what I heard through my contacts at the church." Agnes's father's voice was harsh and he rushed at Andrew, jabbing his finger into the young man's chest as he spoke. "You were the one as got her in the family way, and coward that you are, you left her in a pile of trouble and high-tailed it over here to England to hide."

Andrew tried to step backwards to get away from Seth's prodding finger. "It wasn't like that. I told you!" He backed into the brick wall of the bridge. "If her dad knew she'd been with a Catholic lad, her life would have been as good as finished." Andrew sidestepped to get some distance between himself and Agnes's father. "I thought I'd got away from bigotry when I left my own country. I thought Britain would be more progressive, more open-minded! How wrong I was!"

"Dad, listen to him, will you!" Agnes pleaded. "It's the same thing with me and Andrew, only I thought you'd be more reasonable than the Irish Catholics. You're me dad, you're supposed to want what's best for me."

"What's best for you?" Seth bellowed. "You think this good for nothing Irish coward is best for you?" He lunged at Andrew and punched him hard on the temple. "I'll rot in hell before I let you marry a waster like this."

Agnes was shocked! Her dad was not a fighting man. He was usually the peacemaker in any troublesome situation. "Dad, stop it! What are you doing? Have you gone mad?"

She watched in horror as Seth punched Andrew again with more force, and when he went for him again, Andrew lifted his elbow to defend himself and caught Seth on the side of his head. The older man lost his footing and fell over the wall of the bridge.

Agnes heard the splash as her father's body hit the fast flowing water, but she didn't scream. She stood, frozen to the spot as Andrew took off his coat and jumped over the side of the bridge after her father. She was too shocked to move at first, but within a second or two she was running to the end of the bridge and down the steep banking to the water's edge.

She could see the splashes and ripples in the water and presumed Andrew and her dad were still fighting.

"Agnes!" Andrew's voice called over the water. "Agnes, your dad's unconscious. He'll need an ambulance," he gasped.

"Can you get him over here?" Agnes was lying on her stomach on the freezing bank with her arms held over the water. "Here, Andrew, push him to me." Agnes could see the splashes as Andrew slowly made his way to the bank with her dad's limp body under his arm.

As Andrew came close to the bank, Agnes took hold of her father's sodden coat and helped to haul him out of the water. Andrew pushed and she pulled with all her might until her father's head was in her lap with the rest of his body still dangling in the freezing river while Andrew caught his breath.

"Dad, oh, Dad!" Agnes patted his cold, wet face. "Wake up, Dad. Talk to me."

She saw her father's eyes flicker open, and then close again. He was like a dead weight. Seth had blood running from his nose and his ears and a nasty gash was oozing more dark liquid over one eye.

Andrew dragged himself from the water and went to pull Seth's legs onto the bank. "I think he must have hit his head on the way down. I'll go for help, Agnes. Try to keep him warm."

"Don't go, Andrew," Agnes pleaded. "What is this going to look like?"

"Who cares, Agnes? Your dad needs an ambulance."

"What have we done, Andrew?" She heard her father groan, and then he fell suddenly silent. Agnes leant down to put her cheek next to his mouth and realised that her father now felt heavier on her knee. She felt for a pulse at his throat. "Oh, my goodness. I think he's past help, Andrew. I can't feel his heartbeat."

Andrew knelt by her side and bent to listen to the older man's chest. He raised his head slowly. "Oh, good God in heaven, he's dead, Agnes."

"What will we do, Andrew?"

"I'll get help."

"No, wait!" Agnes's mind was whirling fast. Her dad had been intent on giving her young man a beating, but Andrew had fought back and her dad had fallen over the bridge. It was self-defence, but would anyone else see it like that? "How will it look, Andrew? You're younger and fitter than me dad. Who's going to believe you didn't mean to kill him?"

"I didn't! Agnes, that's not what happened. You saw what he was like!"

"Aye, I saw, but nobody else did, and nobody else would believe what I saw tonight. Everyone thinks my dad is a fine upstanding churchgoer, and I know he'd rather be a referee than a fighter. He's never raised his fists to anyone as far as I know."

"What are you saying, Agnes?" Andrew's voice was barely above a whisper.

"I'm saying that you might be taken before a magistrate for this." Agnes's heart was beating fast and she was trying to think ahead to see the way forward for them.

"But I didn't do anything."

"Then how did my dad end up dead!" Agnes hissed through chattering teeth. She shuddered, and then she began to sob. "Oh, Dad, Dad, what have we done?"

"Agnes, we haven't done anything wrong. We have nothing to hide. Let me go to get someone."

"I'm frightened, Andrew. They'll take you away. They will! They will!"

"I was only defending meself, Agnes. You saw how he went for me."

"Who's going to believe me dad thumped you?" Agnes asked through her tears. "You're twice his size, and everyone who knows my dad will tell you he doesn't condone fighting."

"Well, when you say it like that, I can see how you think it might look." Andrew stared down at the lifeless face in Agnes's lap. "But what else can we do, love?"

"It was an accident." Agnes took a deep breath. "No one can argue with an accident." She bent to kiss her father's cold cheek. "I'm sorry, dad. I hope you can forgive me 'cause I'll never forgive meself."

"Agnes, no!"

Andrew put out a hand to stop her, but Agnes rolled her father's head from her lap and let him slip into the dark water. The river carried his body downstream and out of sight in seconds.

"What will we do now, Agnes?" Andrew helped her to her feet and stood with his arms around her to try to stop her shakes.

"You have to go back to your digs and get packed. You can tell your landlady you had bad news from home and had to go back to Ireland."

"My, but you're a fast thinker. What about us? What will you do?"

"I'm not saying you really should go back to Ireland, but it wouldn't hurt to tell folks you've gone away."

"Where will I go?"

"I know a place." Agnes couldn't believe how her plan was coming together so quickly. "You only need to disappear for a few weeks. Once they find me dad and see it was an accident, you can come back."

"Why do I have to go away at all, then?"

Agnes reached up to touch his wet face. "Just in case they don't think it was an accident. I don't want you around for them to start pointing fingers your way. Me mam knew he was coming to meet us tonight. They might put two and two together. We can't risk it, Andrew."

Later that night, Agnes was in her bed but not asleep. Andrew was safely tucked up in an abandoned stable. She'd scrubbed her coat of all traces of blood and mud, thanking God that it was made of black wool and the stains wouldn't be noticeable. It was now hanging in front of the fire downstairs on the clotheshorse, where it would be dry by the morning. They often hung coats there when they'd got rained on, and the sleet was still falling outside. She'd tried to think of everything to keep them from being linked to her dad's unfortunate accident. It was an accident, she kept telling herself. "Oh, Dad, why did you have to lose your temper?"

She cried herself to sleep, but woke early, while it was still dark. She huddled under her blankets, shivering. The coldness was in her heart. She kept picturing her father's cold body in the river. "I'm sorry, Dad," she whispered. "But you left me no choice. I can't let Andrew be blamed for this. He didn't mean for you to fall and die."

Chapter Four, Hiding the truth

All Agnes had to do was wait. She knew the knock would come to the door, but she didn't know when that would be.

She repeatedly went over the events of the night in her head, trying to remember how things had escalated so quickly. She recalled her father's words and realised that Andrew had kept things from her. He'd explained, though. He'd told her father why he allowed that Irish lass to tell folks the bairn was his. He didn't want her to face the anger of her dad when he found out about the Catholic boy. Then Agnes realised that of all people, Andrew would have known that their own relationship wouldn't be easy. How could he take her to Ireland, she being Catholic and him being Protestant? It would never work, and Andrew had probably known that from the start. She gave him the benefit of the doubt, though, because she loved him. He wasn't to know that her dad would be as bad as the Irish father. English Catholics were more reasonable, or at least, Andrew said he thought they were or he would never have asked to speak with her dad.

She knew there was more to Andrew than he'd told her, but she believed him when he said he loved her and would do whatever it took to be with her. She didn't care about his past. It was his future she was interested in.

When the fateful knock on the door eventually came before she set out for the shop, Agnes managed to look shocked and upset when the policeman told her mam they'd found a body early that morning in the River Calder near Wakefield, and the papers in a jacket pocket suggested it might be Seth. When her mam broke down, Agnes ran to get her Auntie Hilda and Uncle Bert. Shortly after, Bert left to identify the body.

Events overtook Agnes quickly after that, and she felt she was living a nightmare. She grieved for her father and worried about her lover. The police were everywhere. They questioned her and Trudie about what happened that night. Trudie knew that her husband was going out to meet Agnes's chap, but Agnes had stuck to her story and said he'd never arrived at the meeting place, which she told the police had been in town. The police wanted to question Andrew, but couldn't find him. They questioned his landlady and got the story about bad news from Ireland calling him away suddenly.

Agnes knew the police were suspicious, but nothing could

be proved, and if Andrew were out of the way, no one would be able to discover what really happened. It was an accident, but she knew the police wouldn't think so. She knew the facts couldn't be proved either way, and didn't want to take the chance that it would go the wrong way for her sweetheart.

Andrew stayed in hiding, and Agnes helped to keep him safe. They were both afraid that if the truth came out, the authorities would presume the worst and Andrew would be locked away forever, or worse. When his picture appeared in the Thornbury Reporter with a story about her dad's suspicious accident, and a statement that the police wanted to talk with Andrew O'Connor, Agnes panicked. She waited until nightfall and sneaked out to the stables where Andrew was keeping his head down.

"They want to question you, Andrew." Agnes showed him the newspaper. "The police are looking for you and it won't take long for them to spot you if you ever show your face outside this building!"

"Hush, love, I'm safe here." Andrew took her into his arms. "No one knows about this place, right?"

Agnes nodded her head against his shoulder.

"Then I'll grow a beard before I come out, and no one will recognise me then."

"Oh, Andrew. It'll take more than a bit of hair to hide that face of yours." Agnes touched his cheek.

"What's it been like for you, my love? Are the police still asking you questions?"

"No, I think they've done with me for now. They're talking about an inquest, but they want to talk to you more than anything." Agnes buried her head in Andrew's shoulder. "I'm so scared, Andrew. What will we do?"

They talked long into the night and decided that they had to get him away from Yorkshire or away from England as soon as possible, but they would have to wait for things to quiet down before attempting to move him.

Agnes visited the disused stable buildings each day after dark, making sure she wasn't seen. She sneaked food from the house, and did without herself so her mother wouldn't notice the missing provisions.

Over the next few frightening weeks, as they made plans for Andrew to get away, their love became more intense, and when Andrew gently pushed for more than caresses, she acquiesced willingly, giving little thought to where it might lead.

"Agnes, I love you so much." Andrew told her as he held her in his arms. "I can't bear it that I have to go away. I might never see you again."

"Don't say that, Andrew. You made me a promise, remember? You told me the snowdrop's promise can be relied upon, so I know you'll come back to me."

"I will, Agnes. I'll come back for more of this loving." Andrew had swept her away with his intimate caresses, and she gave in to his pleading, believing that he would move heaven and earth to keep his promise to her.

She knew she was losing him, and she wanted to make the most of their precious last days and weeks together. She had no idea when she would see him again.

The last night she saw him would remain in her heart forever. She clung to him, crying and pleading for him not to go, but they knew he had to leave.

"Don't cry, Agnes. You're making it harder for me to leave you." Andrew held her to his chest.

"I'll never see you again. I know it!"

"Remember the snowdrop's promise, Agnes. We'll be together after all this has passed. We'll find a way."

"I hope so, Andrew, but we both know it's too dangerous. We can't risk you coming back. I can't see how this will ever turn out right for us."

"Like you can't feel the warmth of springtime when the snowdrop shows her face. We can't see what's round the corner. But you have to believe me when I tell you that I will make sure we can be together. Wait for me, Agnes. Like we wait for springtime when the snowdrop gives her promise. We will be together."

Under cover of darkness, the heavily bearded Andrew boarded a barge on the canal. Agnes stood on the canal banking as the bargeman threw the mooring rope onto the deck and jumped on board. She watched the narrow boat chug away in the moonlight as Andrew waved from the stern before disappearing below. He planned to make his way to Liverpool on the canals and then cross the water to Ireland. He told her he had relatives in Cork in the south, and they would ask no questions if he were to turn up, out of the blue, and ask for lodgings and a job. She hoped his plan would work. She wanted him to be safe more than anything.

Agnes spent the next few days listening out for news. She half expected Andrew to be caught and brought back, but after weeks had passed with no word of him, she knew he'd got away. She also knew that she might not hear from him for months. They had agreed that it would be too dangerous for him to contact her for the time being. Life seemed bleak. With her mother still grieving for her dad, and with Andrew gone, the house held a sad atmosphere. Agnes filled her days looking for work. Since leaving school she'd worked for her dad in the baker's shop, but she couldn't keep it going on her own, and her mam didn't know about the baking side of the business, so they'd had to put it on the market. They were hoping it would sell quickly at the greatly reduced price to give them something to live on. Trudie told her that her dad had a bit of money in savings, but that had been put by to pay for Agnes's wedding if she were ever to marry. The news of her dad's thoughtfulness was like salt in her wound. To think he had provided for the very event that he denied her was cutting. To realise that her hope of marriage to anyone was now lost as surely as her dad and Andrew were lost to her, was a bitter blow. Trudie wanted to keep hold of the savings, to ensure they would have something to fall back on in hard times. It soon became clear that Agnes would have to find another job.

Polly told her of the vacancy at the café where she worked and Agnes jumped at the chance. She was grateful that George employed her on little more than Polly's recommendation.

"If you're a cousin of Poll's that's good enough reference for me." George had nodded emphatically. "She's a good worker, so I'm betting you will be too. You can start on Monday morning."

It was as easy as that, and she soon got into the swing of things, taking orders and rushing about keeping the customers happy and supplied with food and drink in the busy little café on Kingsway Street. Polly had warned her that it would be tiring work, but Agnes wasn't afraid of that. She wanted nothing more than to feel exhausted at the end of the day. When she was worn out she slept before her mind had time to drift to thoughts of Andrew or her father, or the police investigation.

The case had been passed to the coroner's court, and was due to be heard within the next few months. Agnes was dreading the outcome. She and her mam would be called on to answer the same questions they'd already been asked over and over. Andrew was still a prime suspect because it was common knowledge that her father had taken against him. It was also well known by now that her father had arranged to meet Andrew the night before he was found in the river. No matter how many times she told the police that her dad never turned up for the meeting that night, the questions would then turn to Andrew, and she would be asked for the hundredth time where he'd gone and why he'd disappeared that same night.

Exhaustion helped keep the scarier thoughts from troubling her as she drifted off to sleep, but the nightmares still woke her in the early hours, and on those occasions she found it difficult to go back to sleep. Thankfully those dreams came less and less as the weeks went by, but she soon had something else to worry about. She hadn't had her monthly visitation since before Andrew left, and she was afraid that he'd left something of himself behind.

When she started to feel unwell in the mornings, Agnes knew she would have to tell her mother. There was nothing else for it. She hoped Trudie would be able to help her. Agnes had heard of special homes for girls in her predicament. She'd heard rumours that the church ran them, and for a small donation the unfortunate girl and the baby would be cared for until she could rejoin her community, with or without the bairn. She knew her mam wasn't without a bob or two now. The bakery had sold and although Trudie was upset that she didn't get what it was worth, she'd been happy to settle on the offer in return for a quick sale. She only hoped her mam wouldn't mind spending some of the money on helping her.

On a blustery April morning as they walked home from church services, Agnes decided it was time to tell her mam about her condition, and after a few false starts, she managed to reveal her fears.

"You think you're having a bairn, Agnes?" Trudie's jaw dropped and she stopped in her tracks. "Oh my goodness! On top of everything else, you saddle me with this!"

Agnes cringed as her mam looked up at her with her lip curled in distaste.

"Please don't be mad at me, Mam. I didn't mean for this to happen. I'm sorry, I am! You've no idea how sorry I am to put this at your door at this time. I know..."

"Sorry!" Trudie grabbed Agnes by the elbow and marched her the rest of the way home. "Sorry! Is that all you can say? I'll not talk in the street about this!" Trudie shook Agnes's arm. "You'll be a good deal sorrier when I've finished with you, young lady!"

Hours later, Agnes felt bemused. She'd thought her plan had been the one her mother would go for. She'd been thinking about it for days and it seemed the best solution. She wouldn't mind being sent away on the pretext of visiting relatives at the coast. The hard part was that Agnes would have to give the baby away at the end of it, and she didn't know how she could do that, but at least she could return home with no one the wiser afterwards. She already had a broken heart, and it couldn't hurt more than it did already. What would one more heartache mean, when added to the burden of guilt and sadness she already carried? She had prepared herself for the banishment and the ordeal of having her bairn adopted, but her mother had other ideas.

"I know his dad is your Uncle Bert's half-cousin, but that's not classed as a relative. The only link is through marriage, so there'll be no bar to the union."

"You can't mean it, Mam! Not Bill Smithson. He barely comes up to my ear! He's a stocky little upstart who's always thought he's better than the likes of us because he works at the bank. He won't agree to it. Why would he?" Agnes had protested.

"Because I'll make it worth his while!" Trudie narrowed her eyes. "I'll spend your dad's bakery money to keep you from bringing a scandal to my door. It will make a respectable dowry to tempt that lad."

"Mam! You can't! I won't! You can't make me marry Bill Smithson!"

"Well, you can't marry Andrew O'Connor, can you? That scoundrel hasn't had the decency to write you a note to let you know where he is. He'll be laughing at you, Agnes. Mark my words. He got what he wanted and now he's off to do it all again with another unsuspecting lass. I know his sort!"

"You've got it wrong, Mam. He loves me!" Agnes insisted.

"Love had nothing to do with the way he treated you, Agnes, but you're too infatuated to see it. Real love doesn't skulk in shadows. If he loved you, he'd have written by now. How long has it been?"

"He'll come back, Mam. I know he will."

"Not soon enough to give that bairn a name, Agnes."

"You can't make me marry someone else, Mam."

"I can and I will, Agnes Garrity. You got yourself into this mess, but I'll get you out of it in a way I see fit."

"No, Mam! Please! I said I could go to the nuns, Mam. I don't want to get married."

"You'll do as I say. Them homes for unmarried mothers aren't the kind of place I want a lass of mine to go to. They're full of young girls with loose morals who need a lot in the way of discipline to bring them back into line. The nuns know how to discipline wayward lasses, believe me. I've heard what them places are like. You're not like that, Agnes. I know you. You wouldn't stand it for more than a week."

"But Bill Smithson?" Agnes shook her head. "He's got a right soft spot for our Polly. He's holding out for her, so he'll never agree to have me. Why would he? Just look at me! I'm at least half a head taller than he is and no man wants to look up to his wife. I'm big and clumsy and Polly is so pretty..."

"Polly doesn't deserve a nice young man like Bill. Look at the way she's carrying-on with that married man!"

Agnes gasped.

"Don't think her shenanigans haven't been noticed. It's the talk of the town! I've had words with my sister Hilda about it, but she still lets her lass get away with it." Trudie touched the crucifix at her throat. "If they were a church-going family, she wouldn't be acting like a brazen hussy. Father Brennan would have something to say on it, you mark my words."

"Why don't they go to church, Mam? Bert and Hilda are Catholic aren't they?"

"They were brought up Catholic. It pains me to see how they've lapsed. But that's another reason why Bill's family would never let him marry a lass like Polly. So you see, this is the perfect way out for you both. He'll get over his fixation with her, and you'll have yourself a husband to give you some respectability."

"Won't it look odd that we just up and get married without any courtship? Isn't it too soon after me dad?"

"Let me worry about the details." Trudie went to get her coat from the back of the door. "I'll go and see the family now and put my proposition to Bill and Mary and Edwin. Bill's dad will go for it, I'm sure. You get started on the dinner. I'll expect it to be ready by the time I get back."

"But..." Agnes called as her mother closed the door behind her.

It was no good. Her mam had made her mind up. Agnes hoped Bill and his parents would laugh at her plan. She didn't want to be tied to a man who didn't love her. The only man she wanted was Andrew, but he was lost to her.

Agnes had no control over her fate, and all desire to fight her mother's plans had faded when she realised how helpless she was. She went along with the pretence of a whirlwind courtship with Bill because she didn't see any other way out. They met in the Crown Arms, went to the dances at the church hall and in town, and sat together in the pews at church service. Bill put on a good show for any prying eyes that might have been tempted to comment on the odd-looking couple. They held hands and he put his arm around her waist when they walked out in the busy town centre. He laughed loudly and made sure anyone within hearing distance would witness his words of endearment. He was different when they were alone, walking home in the darkened streets.

"You can let go of me hand, no one can see us now, thank goodness." Bill tugged his hand from her grasp. "An I've told you not to wear them sandals when you're out with me. I don't want you to make a fool of me, Agnes Garrity. It's bad enough to have folks thinking we're an odd match without you giving 'em cause to laugh at us by wearing them high heels. I know you do it on purpose to make me look daft. Well, I won't have it. Do you hear me?"

"I've never seen anyone laughing, Bill. I can't help being tall. I've always been big."

"Big! Pah! You make your Polly look like a child when she stands next to you. You wouldn't think you were from the same family. She's everything you're not and I got the short end of the stick, good and proper, didn't I?"

"You don't have to have any end of the stick, Bill Smithson. You could walk away now with no hard feelings on my part." Agnes tossed her head and hoped he would back out of the arrangement.

"And what would your Mam say about that if I did? The money is safely in my bank account now, and I'm not backing out so she can take it back."

Agnes shuddered. She knew it had taken more than the proceeds of the bakery sale to seal the deal. The pot of money in savings had been added to the dowry to make a tidy sum to convince Bill the marriage would be worth his while. Agnes had no idea how much it added up to, but she knew that Bill took every penny of it when Trudie offered it as her bride price.

Bill slowed his step as they neared her front door. "We get married next Saturday, just as your mam planned. That nasty business with your dad is all over now, so we can get on and do this without anyone raising an eyebrow and saying we don't have respect for the old sod."

The tiny wedding took place the following week, just ten days after the court inquiry into her father's death had finished. The coroner had recorded a verdict of accidental death as there was a lack of evidence to the contrary. The slippery cobbles on that night took the blame for her dad's fall. Even the scuffed up mud on the bank, and the bloodstains on the ground added evidence that her father had slipped on the cobbles, perhaps banged his head and fell down the banking into the river. It was an accident, plain and simple.

Even though Agnes knew that a verdict of accidental death meant that Andrew could return with no fear of prosecution, she had no way of contacting him. She didn't know where he was, and her pregnancy was beginning to show. She had no choice but to keep to the charade and marry Bill Smithson, and begin to live the lie that she knew she would hate through every minute of the rest of her life.

There were few guests at the wedding. Bill's father, Edwin, stood as his best man, Polly was Agnes's bridesmaid. They didn't wear the traditional bridal attire; there was no time or money for wedding dresses. Father Brennan joined them in holy wedlock, and Bill's mother, Mary; Trudie, Uncle Bert and Auntie Hilda were the only other guests to see the service performed.

She received congratulations from her mother and Auntie. Polly offered her hand to the couple, and Bill looked as if he might choke when he accepted congratulations from the girl he would have preferred to have standing by his side.

Her Uncle Bert came to give her a hug. "I hope you know what you're doing, lass." He whispered so only she could hear. "It's not what your dad would have wanted for you."

Agnes briefly worried about her uncle's words. Did he know about Trudie's deal with Bill? Did he know about Andrew? She didn't have long to think about what Bert knew or didn't know. The tiny wedding party went to the Crown Arms for a few sandwiches and a small cake. Their happiness was toasted with sherry and pints of ale, and before she knew it, Agnes was home in her bedroom with her husband.

Agnes had innocently thought she would be married in name only as there was no affection between her and Bill. She soon learned how wrong she was, when Bill insisted on his marital rights that first night as they'd settled into their marriage bed. Her mother had given them her room, and she'd moved into Agnes's single bed in the next room. Agnes didn't give it much thought. She didn't want to sleep in the same bed as her husband, but thought she'd need to do so to keep up appearances. She'd got ready for bed downstairs and when she slipped between the covers, she expected Bill to keep to his side of the bed and she to hers. When he rolled over towards her and his hands began to reach between her legs she pushed him off.

"No Bill, that's not part of the deal." Agnes had told him very firmly.

"That's not what was discussed with your mam and my dad." Bill placed his hand on her thigh. "Now be a good girl and let me in."

Agnes couldn't believe what was happening. Even though her belly was full of another man's child, it didn't put Bill off. He was determined, and threatened to cause a scene if she continued to object.

"But you don't even think I'm attractive! Why would you want to do that with me?" Agnes had pleaded with him.

"Because I can!" Bill said, with a look of arrogance settling around his features. "I'm surprised your mam didn't tell you your part of the deal afore now. You should know what to expect, after all, you're no shy virgin, as that lump proves!" He jabbed her in the stomach with a sharp finger.

"What do you mean? I don't know what you're talking about. What is my part of the deal?" Agnes tried to delay the inevitable. She realised what her part of the deal must be, and quivered to think of her mam discussing the finer details of the arrangement with Bill's father. She was more ashamed than she'd ever been, even taking into account her dad's accident and finding herself pregnant outside marriage. Allowing Bill to consummate the marriage was bad enough, but to know that her mother and his father had agreed that it would happen as part of the transaction was humiliating.

"A man has his needs, Agnes, and if you don't let me take my pleasure with your body, the deal is off. You and your mam can go find some other mug to take you on."

"You can't do that, we're married!"

"Aye, and we can get divorced just as quickly if we have a mind to, but I kept my part of the bargain. I married you, and the money stays mine no matter what, so it's up to you!"

Agnes's mind was racing. What could she do? She couldn't let him, but what would happen if she refused? It would all have been for nothing and she and her mam would be shamed.

She quietly turned to her husband. "You win, Bill Smithson, but I don't want you to kiss me."

"That's a blessing then, 'cause I've no inclination to kiss your ugly mug." Bill wasted no time in lifting her nightdress and moving between her legs. "It's a good job it's dark so I don't have to look at your big fat body, but a bit of flesh won't put me off. You all feel the same where it counts."

Agnes felt embarrassed and shamed at her husband's cruel words. She'd never felt pretty or even attractive. Andrew was the only man who'd ever made her feel that way. She filled her mind with her sweetheart's face, and imagined it was Andrew she was married to, but she couldn't imagine that her gentle Andrew was the one labouring above her so heartlessly.

Afterwards, when Bill was snoring beside her, Agnes was trying her best not to cry. She felt violated, angry and humiliated all at the same time. At the moment of Bill's completion, he had called out Polly's name and didn't seem to care who heard him. Is this what her life would be like from now on? Would she have to suffer the indignity of Bill's demands on a regular basis? How would she endure it? Agnes wiped her face on the bed sheet. She had no choice. Bill was her husband now, and whatever he wanted to do with her body she wouldn't be able to refuse him. It was his right.

Chapter Five, Living a lie

The job at the café was a lifeline for Agnes. She had no idea what Bill had done with her dowry, but not one penny of it ever came her way. She had to earn her own money. Bill had made it clear that he would not support her financially. That was part of the deal he had brokered with her mother.

When George took her on, he had no idea of her condition, but even though her pregnancy was evident within a few weeks of her marriage to Bill, he told her she could stay. She didn't know how she would have managed if he hadn't been so kind to her. She loved her work at the café.

Her mother had found a job too, and she worked a few hours a day at the local pub, earning a bit extra for her keep because Bill refused to pay for his mother-in-law too. Bill lived in the house and paid the rent and the bills to keep a roof over their heads. He gave Trudie a weekly allowance to pay for his food and for his clothes to be washed and ironed, but he was frugal with his wages and wouldn't pay for anything more than his own keep and a few items for the expected child. He was like a lodger, except for the fact that he shared Agnes's bed as her husband and expected all the privileges that went with that position.

Agnes's home life became increasingly unbearable. Bill and her mother frequently argued. Bill became more arrogant with each passing day, seeming to enjoy humiliating Agnes as often as he could. Agnes tried to ignore his insults, but Trudie was not so placid.

"You're starting to look like that barrage balloon that got loose and flew over Leeds a month or two back!" Bill laughed as he took a seat at the table, expecting to be served his meal.

"Why do you have to keep mentioning that she's getting so big, Bill?" Trudie started into him as soon as Bill made the comment on Agnes's enormous belly. "Why can't you keep a civil tongue in your head?"

"I'm only saying what any fool can see." Bill pointed at Agnes. "She's the size of a house, the ugly cow."

"That's not what you think when you're squealing like a pig of a night-time and calling out another lass's name so all and sundry can hear you!"

"Mam!" Agnes was mortified.

"I try to keep me peace, Agnes, but this one here would try the patience of a saint! I rue the day I made you that offer,

Bill Smithson. You're a bully and you're making my lass's life a misery!"

"I've never raised my hand to her! I'm no bully!" Bill got to his feet.

"There's more ways to hurt a lass than by striking her with the back of your hand." Trudie banged a pan of stew on the table. "It breaks my heart to hear the way you talk to her. My Seth would turn in his grave if he could see —."

"Well, he can't see." Bill interrupted her. "He's dead and gone, thank Christ. I couldn't do to live with that sanctimonious old man as well as an old crone and a battleship of a wife."

"I won't have blaspheming in my house!" Trudie stood her ground and faced Bill. "I'll put up with your insults if I have to, but I'll not have you taking the Lord's name in vain! Not under my own roof!"

"Your roof! Ha! I pay the rent on this place, so I'll say what I like, when I like. Your roof, indeed!"

"It's still my name on the rent book, Bill Smithson, and until you start treating us with a bit of civility, you'll be nothing more than a lodger as far as I'm concerned." Trudie squared up to the stocky man, wagging her finger in his face.

"We'll soon see how you change your tune when I stop paying the rent, then, eh?"

"Now, Mam!" Agnes tried to intervene. "Don't be causing arguments. Poor bill just got in from work and he must be tired and hungry. Let's have our tea in peace, can we?" She hated to take Bill's side, but it was the only way to stop the constant bickering in the small household.

"Just wait until I tell your father how you're behaving." Trudie wouldn't be calmed. "He'll not like what I have to say to him on Sunday in church. He'll not like to hear how you are behaving to the women in your life. He'll soon remind you of your responsibilities and sort you out good and proper, Bill Smithson!"

"You leave me dad out of this." Bill shoved Trudie away and began to pace the floor. "What goes on in this house is nowt to do with him. I'm a grown man and I don't have to answer to anyone, let alone me own old man."

"A grown man you say?" Trudie sneered. "Then it's time you started acting like a man!" Trudie wouldn't let it go. "A real man doesn't have to put his wife down every chance he gets to make himself feel he's bigger and better than she is. There's plenty of real men who treat their wives with respect, that's when they're not off fighting in this war. Now that's a real man for you!"

"What's that supposed to mean?" Bill yelled as his face grew redder and his eyes narrowed.

"You think that doing your bit for the local fire volunteers of an evening is enough to get you out of being conscripted?"

Agnes watched in horror as her mam started wagging her finger again. She was reminded of a dog baiting a bear, but knew that things had gone too far and her mother was beyond listening to reason.

"You make me sick! A fit healthy young man like you! Acting like the big I am at home and quaking in your boots every time the postman calls with a brown envelope. It'll come one day, you mark my words. All the other young men worth their salt have joined up voluntarily already, but not the likes of you! No!"

Agnes could see her husband was fit to burst a blood vessel. Her mam was going over-the-top and making Bill angrier by the second, but it would be Agnes who would be the one to suffer the consequences when Bill would surely reinforce his authority on her in the bedroom later.

"Now, Mam!" Agnes intervened yet again, as she often did these days. "Lower your voices, please! What will the neighbours think? It's time to stop name-calling and have our tea. Come on now, it's going cold."

"I'll have mine when I get back from the pub." Bill stormed to the door and put his jacket on. "I can't eat me dinner with that old witch staring at me. Her wizened mug is enough to give the Pope himself indigestion."

The two women flinched when the door banged shut, and Agnes turned to her mother. "Why do you have to goad him like that all the time?"

"Why don't you stand up to him? Why do you take his insults?"

"It's a small price to pay for being able to hold me head up in the streets."

Trudie's face crumpled and she brought a trembling hand up to her mouth. "I'm thinking it was a price too high, Agnes. When I think how hard your dad worked to build that business up, and now all the profits of his labours have gone to that insensitive, rude, obnoxious man! Well, I wish I'd never thought of making it a dowry for you. I'm sorry, lass. If I'd known what he was really like, I would never have made you wed him."

"Well, it's done now, Mam, and we have to make the best of things." Agnes pointed out. "But you picking arguments with him at every turn doesn't help. Can't you bring yourself to talk nicely to him, even if you don't agree with him; could you at least try to ignore him, like I do?"

"I wouldn't be doing my duty as your mam if I were to let him get away with half the things he says. I don't know how you put up with it."

"I put up with it because I have to, Mam. He's my husband for better or worse, and you of all people should be trying to support me after what we've done."

"We've done no more or less than was needed, Agnes. I know you got the raw end of the deal and I'm sorry. I wish there'd been another way."

"Maybe there is, Mam, if we bide our time." Agnes had been thinking of a way out of this mess since the day she'd said, 'I do.' "I could wait until the baby is born, then I could ask him for a divorce."

"What?" Trudie exclaimed. "Impossible! I won't hear of it! We'd be outcasts!"

"Well, that wouldn't be worse than what I am now, Mam. I feel I'm nothing more than a street walker where Bill is concerned. You don't have to lie beneath him of a night and pretend you're somewhere else until his needs are satisfied. You don't know what it's like for me to let him do that, especially when I know the only feeling he has for me is revulsion!"

Trudie's head dropped forward and her shoulders began to shake. "I'm sorry, Agnes. Honestly I am."

Agnes went to put an arm around her mother's shoulders. "Oh, Mam. We'll sort it out."

"We can't, love. You can't divorce him. You're Catholic. It wouldn't be allowed."

"Then I'll risk being excommunicated or whatever it is they do to divorced women. I can't live with him much longer, Mam."

"Don't do anything until the baby is born, Agnes." Trudie turned tear filled eyes to her daughter. "Promise me."

"Why, Mam? Why do I have to stick with him at all?"

"You can't get a divorce, Agnes, but Bill might not be around forever. There's a war on. He could be called up. He could be killed in action. It happened in the last war to thousands, and the newspapers think it will happen again with this war."

"Oh, Mam! You're clutching at straws."

"No, I'm not, Agnes. It could happen, and if it does, I'm working on a way to make sure the money comes back to us. Father Brennan has a solicitor friend and he's drawing up some papers for Bill to sign. Like a will, you know?"

"He'll never agree to it." Agnes shook her head.

"He will if the idea comes from Father Brennan."

Agnes froze. "Father Brennan? How much does he know about my sham of a marriage?"

"It's not like that, Agnes. Father Brennan still thinks you and Bill had a whirlwind romance, God help my soul."

"I feel bad about you not being able to confess, Mam. I know you worry about having the sin on your conscience."

"It's no sin to look after your own, Agnes. I feel God will understand."

"I hope you're right, Mam."

"Anyway, Father Brennan is advising all the young lads to make provision for their families before they go off to war, and he's arranged for a solicitor to come into the church to talk to them all and have the papers drawn up for them to sign in front of him."

"But Bill hasn't joined up. He isn't going anywhere!"

"Not yet, he isn't, but when all the lads are signing the papers at church, under the watchful eye of the priest, he'll be shamed into going along with it, you wait and see. When all the other lads are bragging about going off to fight, and your Bill is sitting pretty at the bank, it will be all he can do to hold his head up among 'em. He'll sign to make himself look good in front of all them brave lads, you see if he doesn't."

"And that will be something else he'll use to tease me and goad you with."

"He won't even mention it, Agnes, that's the beauty of this, don't you see?" Trudie smiled slyly. "He won't want us to know that the money could be ours again if anything should happen to him."

"No, I don't suppose he would."

"Then all we'd need is for God to be on our side and make sure Bill gets called up and sent to the front line."

"Oh, Mam! How can you talk like that? You're wishing him dead!"

"Don't you tell me you haven't wished the same thing more than once in the past few months? He's evil, is that man. He's wicked."

"He's been forced into something he doesn't like, Mam. You know it were his dad that saw the deal as a good opportunity for his son. Poor Bill would have preferred that it was our Polly that had got herself in the family way. He'd think he was in clover if that had happened."

"Aye, well that lass never did know when she was well off. Is she still gallivanting around with that married man?"

"Yes, Mam. She won't listen to me. She only has eyes for Charlie Watson, and never had any idea that Bill was sweet on her, so we can't blame her for this mess."

"Well, he's made it plain enough in this house where his true feelings lie. If I have to listen to another night of him yelling that lass's name out —."

"You'll say nowt more about it, Mam!" Agnes interrupted her. "What goes on in our bedroom is between me and Bill and nowt to do wi' you. Do I make myself clear? I've had enough of arguments."

Agnes didn't know how much longer she could keep the peace at home. War had been declared in September, but it had already been raging inside her home since May, when Father Brennan announced to the world that she and Bill were man and wife. The rows between her mother and husband were frequent, and hardly a day went by without strong words being exchanged. She preferred to stay late at the café to keep out of the way. Her mam did try to keep her tongue still after the talk they'd had after Bill stormed out that night, but there was still the odd skirmish, and the animosity between them was barely concealed.

Agnes worked right until the day Harry was born in late November of 1939. She was taken from the café in an ambulance after she collapsed behind the counter. There'd been no warning; no pains. She felt wetness between her legs then everything went black. She came to her senses in the ambulance, and that's when the first pain gripped her and she felt she was being sliced in two.

The wetness she felt before collapsing had been blood, but she didn't know that at the time. The placenta was torn, and the midwife at the hospital told Agnes that her baby was in danger of being stillborn. She was given drugs to make the labour progress more quickly, and Agnes struggled to stay conscious and pushed for all she was worth. This child would be the only link she would have to Andrew, and she was determined that it would survive. A doctor suggested Agnes should have a caesarean birth, but Agnes didn't want to be cut open. She pushed even harder, using the last ounce of strength she possessed. The birth was worse than anything she could have expected. Harry was a large baby, and she felt her flesh tear as he made his way out of her body. Agnes then had to endure the added pain of being stitched together afterwards.

The birth had appeared to be unexpectedly early and the fact that it was an emergency situation just made a complicated business so much easier to explain. Agnes knew Harry was actually born later than she'd thought he would be. After the traumatic experience of a hurried and painful birth, Agnes was thankful that the baby was healthy. A hospital stay couldn't be avoided after the ordeal she had endured, and she welcomed the respite from the constant arguments at home. She could relax in the maternity ward, where she could get to know her son during the peace and tranquillity of her recovery.

The day Hilda called to see her, with Polly close behind, looking pale and afraid; Agnes knew something bad had happened. Harry was in her arms, and she instinctively held him a little closer.

"I don't know how to tell you, lass." Hilda began.

Agnes clutched her son tightly to her chest, her mind filled with frightening images of policemen, her father's body, and Andrew in handcuffs.

"It's your mam, Agnes." Polly interrupted the imagined scenarios. "She fell down the stairs last night."

"Is she hurt?" Agnes knew by their faces that her mam was in a bad way. "Where is she? Did they bring her to the infirmary?"

"Brace yourself, lass." Hilda sat on the edge of the bed and touched Agnes gently on the shoulder.

"No! Not me mam!" Agnes shook her head. She could read the awful truth in her aunt's eyes.

"She died instantly, love. Broke her neck. She wouldn't have known a thing."

"How? Why? No! No!" Agnes struggled to take it in. What next? How much more could she take? "Not me mam!" Her sobs rang through the ward, bringing nurses to her side. They had obviously been warned of the news she'd just been told.

They offered sedatives that helped to soften the edges of her torment, and Agnes drifted into a grey world of fog.

Hilda stepped in to help out in the first days that Agnes was home after the birth. She came first thing in the morning and left late in the evening. She saw to the washing and getting the meals ready. She changed the baby when Agnes had fed him. Trudie's funeral came and went in a blur. Everything seemed unreal and distant to Agnes in her drug induced state.

Bill stayed long hours at the bank in the daytime and spent more time at the fire station, working late into the night. When their paths crossed he seemed lost for words, which was so unlike him. He didn't insult her, and he ignored the baby completely. She thought she might be able to get used to this new husband who seemed indifferent to her and the infant. If only her mother were here to see the change in him. Whatever the reason for his change of mood, she was grateful to be left in peace.

Agnes decided she didn't need the pills the doctor had prescribed to keep her senses dulled. She threw them in the river, preferring to feel the pain of her mother's loss so she could learn to deal with it. She often wept and Hilda told her it was the baby blues and it was normal, but Agnes knew her tears were for everything that had happened in the last year or so. She felt she could cry enough tears to fill the canal and still have more left. She cried for Andrew, for her father and for her mam. All the people she had loved were gone. She was left with a husband she didn't love and who didn't love her. How could she go on?

Agnes didn't know how she got through those dark days after her mam died. Christmas came and went with hardly a change in routine in Agnes's home. Hilda's love and care helped, but Harry was the shining light that carried her. The unbounded love she felt for her son was like a beacon of hope in her dreary, grief-stricken existence.

January brought the dreaded brown envelope for Bill. He had his call-up papers at long last, like thousands of other young men. The war was heating up. The Soviet Union had been expelled from the League of Nations before Christmas, and rationing had begun in Britain to preserve supplies in case the merchant ships were targeted. Agnes felt she was already living in the fallout of a war zone, and couldn't wait for Bill to go away for training. She missed her parents, but Bill had no compassion for her feelings.

"Silly old bugger deserved what she got!" Bill had said one evening when he'd finished his meal. "I couldn't have one dinner in peace while she was here to nag at me. Never shut up, did she?"

"My mother was only doing and saying what she thought was best for me." Agnes tried to defend her mam. "You were always goading her, you only had yourself to blame."

"What's that supposed to mean?" Bill jumped from his chair and began to wag a finger at Agnes. "I'll not be accused of any funny business. Your mam tripped and fell! I had nowt to do with it."

Agnes watched in amazement as Bill started to pace the floor. Beads of sweat stood on his brow, and he ranted as he paced. "She was always calling me names and putting me down. You're both the same. No respect!"

"Respect?" Agnes glared at her husband. "Respect can be earned, Bill, but you never did anything to earn it from me or me mam."

"I took you on, didn't I?" Bill yelled. "I was good enough to be the mug that married you and took on that brat!" He pointed his finger to the pram and crossed the floor to stand over the sleeping baby. "If I had my way, this bastard would be going the same way as his grandma."

"You leave Harry out of this." Agnes hurried to the pram and forced her body between her husband and the sleeping child. "He's an innocent in all of this, don't you dare harm a hair on his head." Agnes stood to her full height and looked down on Bill. "And if I ever find out that you had anything to do with my mam falling down them stairs, I'll swing for you, Bill Smithson. So help me God."

Bill backed away from her, grabbed his coat from the back of the door and shrugged it on. "Aye, well, that might be a fitting end for you too. Swinging on the end of a rope! Ha! That's if they can find one long enough!"

Agnes watched him leave and flinched as the door banged. The noise startled the baby and he began to scream his displeasure. She lifted him from the pram and took him to the fireside chair. Her legs were shaking and her heart was beating fast and hard in her chest. What had just happened? She felt that Bill was turning into a monster. She didn't recognise him anymore. His bullying and insults had become part of her daily existence, but this seemed worse. He had threatened her son. A defenceless baby. She meant what she'd said. She would defend her child from Bill at all costs.

Without Harry, her life would not have been worth living, and she might have ended up in the river like her father, by her own hand if it hadn't been for the infant in her arms. Harry kept her sane and gave her a reason to wake up in the morning. Her son was the only connection she had with the man who took her heart, and she loved them both with every fibre of her being.

Chapter Six, July 1940

The noise hit the girls each morning as they walked into the weaving shed. The mill was a cacophony of loud bangs, shouts and metallic clangs over the background rattle of working looms. They couldn't talk to each other as they had to concentrate on the looms in front of them. Rivers of wool threads wound down from above and their job was to stand in the mule gate and make sure the loom ran smoothly. From early morning when they filled up the weft until late into the afternoon, they watched, mended, changed the bobbins and cleaned, and didn't stop except to snatch a hasty meal at midday before continuing the endless slog of cleaning, yarn mending, and replacing the bobbins to keep the loom running.

By evening, they were dead on their feet and faced a long walk home.

"Hello girls." Sam joined them as they walked. "How are you settling in?"

"We're doing fine, Sam, thanks." Polly answered.

"I haven't been told off all day, so I must be getting it right." Agnes confided.

"I knew it wouldn't take long for a clever lass like you to pick things up, Agnes. That Doris is a slave driver though, isn't she?"

"Aye, Sam. She knows how to crack the whip and keep us on our toes." Agnes told him. "I heard the last of the new looms went in yesterday. Does that mean your job is finished?"

"That's right. I won't be around for much longer. I'm off to York for my army training next week."

"We'll be sorry to see you go, Sam." Agnes realised that she would miss the young man's flattery and banter.

"I knew you had a soft spot for me, Agnes." Sam grinned down at her.

"You're soft in the head, Sam Wood!" Polly elbowed Sam in his side as they walked. "Our Agnes wouldn't look at you when she's got a husband like Bill Smithson to take care of her."

"And I wouldn't dream of stepping on Bill Smithson's toes, but a lad can dream." Sam began to dance along the cobbles, holding his arms out as if he had an imaginary dancing partner.

"Oh, Sam! You make me laugh." Agnes smiled at the young man's antics.

"See you tomorra, girls." Sam danced away down the next street, leaving the girls to walk home together.

"I'll be glad to put me feet up for a bit when we get home, Agnes. I'll set the potatoes on to boil first while you get Harry from me mam's house."

"Thanks Polly. I thought we could have that tin of salmon with those few greens we got from Frank over in packing."

"Aye, he does well with that allotment, and he's always giving stuff to us lasses for a few coppers. Pity we can't dig for victory, we might be able to make a few bob, but all we got is cobbles out the back."

"What time would we have for digging gardens and growing vegetables?" Agnes smiled. "What with the millwork, keeping food in our bellies and clean clothes on our backs, and making do and mending when we get home so our clothes will last longer, there's not many more hours left in the day for owt else is there?"

"It wouldn't seem so bad if we got a decent dinner every day, but it's getting harder to make something appetising with what we can get hold of in the shops. Tinned salmon isn't much of a meal, but it'll have to do until payday and the new ration week starts."

"When do you get Bill's service pay?" Polly glanced sideways at Agnes. "I thought it was due about now."

"You know he doesn't send me all of it. We have an arrangement, Polly. Lots of married couples have arrangements where money is concerned."

"It's a downright disgrace if you ask me. I've been with you long enough to see that you're always short. A married man has responsibilities to his wife and children. I think Bill needs a good talking-to when he next gets home."

"Keep your thoughts to yourself, will you, Poll." Agnes snapped. "What me and Bill do with our money is our business and nobody else's."

"All right, keep your hair on." Polly trudged along beside Agnes. "I was only saying as how it don't seem right, you a mother and having to work alongside single lasses to keep bread on the table while me mam looks after your bairn."

"You'll be in the same position yourself in a few months, Poll. Have you thought who might look after your baby while you work?"

"I was going to ask me mam, but I don't think she will."

"It would be like rubbing salt in the wound, I'm surprised you even thought about asking her."

"It will be her grandchild, whatever the circumstances of how it came into the world. I didn't think she'd turn her back on a grandbairn, even if she doesn't want owt to do with me."

"She won't talk about it when your dad is around. When I pick Harry up, she avoids talking about you and the baby, 'cause Uncle Bert is usually having his tea when I get there. She'll ask how I am, and she even put her hand on my bump to feel the baby kick the other day, but she doesn't get chance to talk about you. I'm sorry, Poll. I have tried." Agnes reached for her friend and they clasped hands as they did when they were children, and swung their joined hands between them as they walked.

"I know, Agnes. I'm hoping she'll come around when me time comes. She'll be looking after your two, so one more wouldn't make much difference, and we'd be paying her, so she'd make a few bob from it."

"Don't hold your breath, Poll. You'll have to think of something else."

The two girls parted company after crossing the bridge spanning the river Calder. Polly went home and Agnes went to collect Harry from Hilda's care. As she walked, she mulled over the coming problems they would face. When their babies were born, both girls would have to return to work as soon as possible. The bairns were due within a few weeks of each other. The girls wouldn't be much help when the time came as they'd each be recovering from the births and looking after their own babies, and Agnes would have to care for Harry too. She couldn't pay Hilda to look after him while she was laid off with the baby and not earning anything. If Polly's baby were legitimate, life would be easier for them. Hilda would be eager to help with the children, but Bert wouldn't let her have anything to do with Polly. Agnes also worried how they would manage for money while they took the time off work to recover from the births.

Agnes was trying to save some of her wages to tide her over the month or so she wouldn't be able to work, but she knew that Polly wasn't doing the same. Polly lived for the moment, and if she had a few spare pennies, she'd spend them on anything that caught her fancy. To be fair, she was buying things for the baby, but the frilled bonnet and lacy shawl were luxuries to Agnes's eyes. A knitted hat and blanket would be more practical and a lot cheaper, but Polly wouldn't listen.

Polly was still seeing Charlie and Agnes couldn't persuade her to drop him. He didn't pass the army medical, so couldn't fight for Britain. Instead, he was still around and still carrying-on with Polly. She put her foot down about allowing him into her home, though. She drew the line at that. When Polly had brought him to the door a few weeks ago, expecting to be allowed to use the bedroom, Agnes had stood with arms folded over her rounded stomach and ordered him out.

She now regretted her hasty condemnation of the man who could ruin everything for her. She had no idea of his connection to her sweetheart until the other night. She knew they both worked at the goods-yard, but it was a big place, with hundreds of men employed there, and now some of them had been replaced by women. If only Charlie had passed the medical, and been able to join up and go away. With Charlie out of the picture, Polly might have been able to forget him and Hilda might have talked Bert around. With Charlie gone, Agnes's own life would be a lot less stressful.

She took a deep breath and stopped to lean on the wall at the bottom of Orchard Street. She couldn't forget the heated conversation they'd had. It played over and over in her head. Charlie knew things that she thought would stay hidden forever. She wished she'd known of his connection to her lover before she'd pushed him from her home.

"You might have Polly fooled, Charlie Watson, but you won't be fooling with her under this roof!"

Polly had pleaded, and Charlie had set his chin high while the two girls argued.

"He loves me, Agnes, have some sympathy for us, can't you?"

"I have sympathy for his wife. Poor Jane has to live with the disgrace of you two!" Agnes wouldn't be moved, and was glad to see that Charlie flinched when she mentioned his wife by name. "You're becoming the talk of the town, and I'm not sure I can put up with it at all, but I won't have it in my house!"

"I'm sorry you feel that way, Agnes Smithson. You come over all high and mighty like butter wouldn't melt in your mouth, but if truth be told, you're no saint."

Agnes had blanched at Charlie's words.

"What's that supposed to mean?" Polly had asked, glancing between them.

"She's not as pure as she likes to make out, that's all."
Charlie had sneered at Agnes. "You ask her about Andrew
O'Connor. Ask her what happened to him the night her dad fell
in the river."

"Andrew O'Connor? Isn't he that lad you were seeing
before Bill? The one the police were asking questions about?
What's he talking about, Agnes? What's all this about your
dad?"

Agnes had begun to tremble. It seemed that Charlie
Watson knew something about her secret, and she didn't want
to hear what else he knew. "Get out!" She'd screamed at him.
"Get out, now!" She'd balled her fists and began to thump at
Charlie's chest until he turned his back to take the blows as he
hurried through the door.

Charlie leapt down the stone steps to the cobbled road
and turned to the two girls standing in the doorway. "You ask
her, Poll." He pointed his finger at Agnes. "You ask her what
she did with Andrew O'Connor. You ask her where he is now.
She's no angel, Poll. I bet she knows more than she's letting
on."

"Shut up!" Agnes had yelled. "You know nothing!" She
desperately hoped her words were true.

"I knew Andrew. I worked with him down the railway
yards long enough. He had a lass he was keen on, never said
who she was, said her dad wouldn't stand for it, so it had to be
a secret. I don't understand all this Catholic malarkey; it's daft
if you ask me, that a girl can't court a man from outside her
religion."

Agnes listened to his words with mounting dread. She
began to fear that he knew more than he was saying and her
insides began to cramp.

Polly was looking from Charlie to Agnes, a puzzled
expression on her face. "What's going on? This Andrew chap
was your sweetheart, Agnes. I know he was, but what does he
have to do with your dad's accident?"

"The coroner said it were an accident. Andrew had nowt
to do with it." Agnes had stood firm, gripping the door to stop
her from falling to her knees as her legs were shaking so much.

"All I'm saying is that it was a bit fishy. A fine upstanding
Catholic man dies by falling in the river Calder on the same
night that Andrew O'Connor disappears. When I heard that this
fella that died was your dad, and you were Andrew's lass, well,
you have to wonder, don't you?"

Agnes had then felt the first glimmer of hope. Charlie didn't know anything. He was putting two and two together, and though he got the sum right, he didn't know for certain that what he came up with was the right answer to the puzzle in his head.

"You ever heard of coincidence, Charlie Watson? You have an overactive imagination that's what you have!" She spoke quietly, not wanting her neighbours to overhear. Curtains were already twitching along the street, drawn by the raised voices. "I'll thank you not to drag my dad's good name down to your level, God rest his soul."

"So you deny that Andrew O'Connor had owt to do with what happened that night?" Charlie cocked his head to the side. "The police seemed to think he might know something about it at the time."

Agnes blushed, she couldn't help it. She thought fast. "We were seeing each other for a time. It's no secret. Me dad was against it so we were going to break up anyway. When he got called away to Ireland that was the end of it. It's no big secret."

"Ha! Well, that don't explain how you reacted when I first mentioned him in your front room."

"I was upset with Polly and you for wanting to carry on your shenanigans under my roof! Can you blame me for not wanting a sin committed in my home?"

"I'm sorry, Agnes. I should have thought." Polly blushed and hung her head. "I never thought about your faith, love, and how it colours how you think about things. I won't ever ask again." Polly stepped onto the cobbles and reached for Charlie's hand. "Come on, Charlie, we'll go to the Crown Arms for a glass of stout."

Polly had led him away, but Charlie kept glancing over his shoulder at Agnes, making her feel guilty and afraid.

Polly hadn't mentioned it again apart from apologising when she got home later that night. Agnes hoped the heated conversation would soon be forgotten, but she feared that her secret might surface, and then her life would be ruined. She would never be able to hold her head up again. If only she had her mam to talk to. Her mam would have known what to do. She was the only person who would know how to help. She'd been good at keeping secrets. She was the one who helped to cover the truth of her pregnancy with layers of deceit. Her cunning had surprised Agnes, although she'd been against Trudie's plans at the time. She wished her mam could help her now. She didn't know how she was going to get out of this mess if Charlie Watson decided to dig deeper.

Agnes pushed from the wall with a deep sigh, and trudged up the hill to collect Harry. Hilda had him ready with his coat buttoned up and his balaclava on his little head.

"He's nice and warm with a clean nappy on, and he's had some mashed turnips and gravy with us for his tea, so he won't be hungry."

"Thanks Auntie Hilda. You didn't have to feed him, you know." Agnes didn't like to impose too much. She knew Hilda and Bert didn't have much to go around.

"He only eats enough to fill a sparrow. It's not putting me out, love."

"Say bye-bye to Auntie Hilda, Harry." Agnes lifted her son's arm to encourage him to wave. "We'll see you tomorrow."

"Just a minute, Agnes." Hilda put a hand on Agnes's arm. "Bert's late tonight, so I've got a minute to talk. I can't say owt about our Poll when he's around. You know what he's like."

Agnes waited. She knew Bert was the one behind kicking Polly out, but Hilda would never go against her husband's wishes, especially while he was around to hear her.

"Have you thought about what you'll both do when the bairns come?"

"We think about it all the time, Auntie Hilda, but we never get anywhere near sorting the problem." Agnes admitted.

"Well, there's this woman who lives down Headfield Road, near where your dad had the bakery. Anyway, she's thinking of starting a childcare thing. She says because of the war effort, lots of women want to work, but can't because of the bairns, so she's looking into hiring a room near the mill on Wilton Street, so it would be perfect for you two lasses."

"That sounds like a good idea." Agnes began to see how it could work. "How much would she charge, though?" She began to see some pitfalls. "Would she look after the bairns as well as we'd like?"

"That's just it, lass." Hilda sounded excited. "She's asked me to work with her. She knows I mind your little Harry, so I'll help with looking after the little ones, and the more bairns we get, the less we'll have to charge so we can make it so you can afford it. We only need to cover our costs and earn a little brass for ourselves for doing it."

"That sounds like a good idea, Auntie. I'll spread the word at work. I'm sure I could get a few lasses interested."

"That'll be grand. Tell our Polly I was asking after her, but tell her not to come here else her dad will have me skinned alive. If all turns out well, I can see her and the bairn at the nursery."

"She'll be over the moon, Auntie Hilda. Fingers crossed it all works out, eh?"

Chapter Seven, September 1940

The summer of 1940 passed slowly for the two girls. The war seemed closer to home with the factories and airfields all over Britain being targeted by German bombers. They'd even been audacious enough to come over in daylight and Agnes read stories in newspapers about eyewitness accounts of dogfights in the skies over Britain. So far, Thornbury had escaped the bombing, but the way things were going, it would only be a matter of time before the Jerries found the small mill town. They'd had a few warnings when the air-raid sirens had blasted through the quiet night, sending them scurrying for the relative safety of the cellar in the small hours.

Hitler had declared a blockade of the British Isles and merchant ships were attacked by German submarines. London had been bombed and Britain had retaliated by dropping bombs on Berlin. Many thousands of ordinary men, women and children had lost their lives on both sides, and it seemed to Agnes that this war was escalating into something much worse than the last one.

The long days of working in the heat of the factory was taking its toll on the pregnant girls. Each evening saw them trudging home with bowed heads and stooped shoulders. Agnes pushed Harry along, using the pram to help hold her upright. The early September evening was warm but close. Dark clouds were gathering in the eastern sky.

"There's a storm brewing by the look of them clouds." Polly pointed to the slow-moving dark mass.

"Well, we'd better get a move on before the rain starts." Agnes quickened her step. "I don't want to get a soaking on top of the day I've had. That supervisor, Doris Bates, wants to be strung up!"

"She was only saying as how you should be taking it easy, Agnes. She said the same to me."

"Taking it easy? She wants to have us out, that's what she wants. I know what she's about. If we take it easy and production drops, we'll be the ones for the chop, not her! Them twin lasses of hers left school in July and are both looking to be taken on in the mill because they can't get owt else and they're too young to join up."

"There are plenty of jobs, Agnes. We'll be all right, and some of the older lasses have gone off to work in the munitions

69

factories so there'll be their jobs to fill too. We don't have to worry about our jobs yet."

"I hope you're right, Polly."

"It's good to see me mam every day. I'm glad she came around." Polly tried to brighten their depressive mood by changing the topic of conversation. "I know me dad's a different story, but I think once this little one is here, he'll come around." She patted her rounded stomach. "I hope so anyway."

"He might, Poll." Agnes didn't want to get into this discussion again. Talking about the arrival of the babies was the last thing she wanted to talk about. She was dreading the arrival of Bill's child. She hated the fact that he had put it inside her with such cold-heartedness and lack of concern for her feelings. Whenever she remembered his painful squeezes and fumbled groping, and his sweating body heaving above her, she felt physically sick.

When Bill had come home for a week from his training camp, she'd worried that he wouldn't be able to go back to war. His eardrum burst when he got too close to the heavy artillery they were practicing with. He spent a couple of days in the hospital and was allowed home to recover. This time she didn't have her mother to help to protect her from his barbed tongue, and Agnes almost walked out.

"You're letting things slide around here, lass. What's a man to find to eat in an empty pantry?" He asked the first night he was home.

"There's rationing, Bill, and I can't afford more than I've got and what I've got is just enough for me and Harry. If I'd had more warning, or a bit of extra brass from you, I could have got some extra bacon for you. As it is, you'll have to make do with Spam."

"Bloody Spam!" Bill had turned his nose up at the meal she prepared for him. "Is that any kind of dinner to serve your man? You great lump of lard, you don't look like you're doing without a good square meal."

Agnes ignored the comment and carried on preparing the meagre dinner.

"So what do you eat when I'm not here? Who do you have around to fill your pantry for you?" Bill sneered suggestively. "You're obviously doing all right for yourself. Who's the mug? Who is he?"

"There's been nobody here but me and Harry. I work, Bill. That's how I pay me own way as well you know." Agnes didn't like the way the conversation was heading.

"Well, we all know you'd open your legs for a meal ticket, so it wouldn't be any different from what you do with me, would it?"

"We're married, that makes it different." Agnes cried. "How could you think that way about me?"

"Ha!" Bill guffawed loudly. "That's rich! That bastard package over there is proof enough that you're no vestal virgin, so don't act the innocent with me." Bill pointed to the baby asleep in the pram. "If you did it before, you can do it again. You can't blame me for being suspicious."

"Would you care?" Agnes challenged him. She'd had enough of his coarse and vulgar talk. "Would you? If I were to take up with another man, why would it matter to you? You don't care about me!"

"You got that right. I couldn't care less about you, but if you drag my name through mud you'll regret it, I'm telling you." Bill got to his feet and shoved her backwards until she had her back to the wall. "You try to make a fool of me by carrying on with anyone else while I'm away and I'll make sure you never want to do it again." He poked a hard finger into her chest with every word. "Do you understand me?"

He took his hand and stroked it down her cheek. When she didn't answer him, he took her chin between his thumb and fingers and squeezed, making her lips pucker.

Agnes pulled away. "Leave me alone! You're nothing but a bully."

"Bully, eh?" Bill came at her with his fist raised and Agnes cowered. "I'll show you what a real bully would do, shall I? Do you want me to give you a beating?"

"No, Bill. Please! I, please, don't." She begged as she sank to the floor.

"Well, that's as good a place as any to show you who is boss." He unbuckled his belt and dropped his trousers.

Agnes flinched, but didn't prevent him from having his way with her, and when he'd finished, she straightened her clothes and got to her feet. "Do you want that Spam now?"

"I'd rather have some proper food after that meagre feast I got between your legs. It's like doing it to a dead fish!" Bill fastened his belt.

"Spam is the only dinner I've got so you can take it or leave it!" Agnes hissed at him.

If she had anywhere to go, she would have walked out, but there was only Bert and Hilda, and they didn't have room for her and Harry.

She had to allow him his marital rights. She knew it was part of the deal, but he was so cold and cruel about taking what he considered was his privilege. He was supposed to put on a show of normality to their friends and neighbours, but he wasn't holding up his part of the bargain very well, and his indifference and brutality angered her.

She could take his nastiness on her own shoulders if that were the only place he showed lack of thought and respect, but when she watched how Bill was with her son, her anger and resentment grew deeper. Bill always paid his dues financially, where Harry was concerned, but he didn't acknowledge the child. From the day Harry was born, he might as well not have existed. Bill ignored her son, and every little act of her husband's unkindness towards her child drove another nail into Agnes's heart. She was glad he would be going away again soon to fight in the war. She'd be happier if he never came back, God forgive her for thinking such a thing.

She'd have to make sure she went to church on Sunday. Her sinful thoughts weighed heavily on her conscience, but in recent weeks she had been avoiding the church services that did nothing to help ease her burden of guilt. A few words of contrition to Father Brennan followed by any number of Hail Mary's could never take away the stain on her soul. It seemed meaningless to her now anyway. Religion had kept her from marrying her one true love, had caused the friction between her and her father, and ultimately led to his death.

Her religion now trapped her in a loveless marriage, and though her heart and soul cried out for a divorce, she knew she would never be allowed this while she continued with her faith. Agnes wondered whether she could bring herself to leave the church. Father Brennan and Saint Paulinus had been part of her since she'd been born and baptised into the church. She had refused to have Harry baptised, much to the chagrin of the elderly priest. Her son's father was a Protestant, so she wouldn't have him taken into the Catholic fold. She couldn't do that, and nobody would make her.

"The nursery is going well for mam and Enid, isn't it? How many bairns have they got now?"

"Err…" Agnes faltered. She'd been lost in thought, and struggled to find an answer. "I'm not sure, about twenty?"

"They'll be making a pretty packet out of this between 'em."

"They deserve it. They've been a life-saver for us lasses." Agnes was glad of the distraction of the chat with Polly about the mundane ordinariness of her life. Her private thoughts were too depressing. She made an effort to discuss their situation with her friend. "The bosses at the mill don't like it much. They say a woman with bairns shouldn't have to be working, but they can't deny that they need us."

"I can't believe they let us two and Elsie Ramsbottom stay on, even after they found out we was expecting."

"We're good workers, Poll. It would cost them dear to let us go now because they'd have to set on some young things like Doris's girls that would need to be trained from scratch."

"I hope they keep our jobs open when we have to take some time off when these little ones make an appearance." Polly touched her tummy as they neared the house. "When do you think you'll stop working?"

"I won't!" Agnes said firmly. "I'll work until I can't fit in the gate, or until me waters break, whichever happens soonest, no matter what folks like Doris Bates say."

"Will you be able to?" Polly looked shocked. "Will they let you?"

"Let them try to stop me." Agnes took out her latch-key and opened the door to their home. "Help me get the pram up the steps, Poll, will you?"

The two pregnant girls lifted the pram over the threshold, and then Polly set about lighting a fire to warm yesterday's leftover's for their meal while Agnes lifted Harry to the floor.

"My, look at him go!" Polly nodded at the crawling baby heading towards a small collection of toys on his hands and knees.

"He's a clever boy." Agnes smiled proudly at her son's achievement. "Your mam told me he was off, an' we've seen him shuffling on his bottom, but that's the first time I've seen him go like that."

"Eeh, you're missing out on seeing him grow up, Agnes. Why don't you take a few weeks off before the next one so you can spend some time with your Harry?"

"I can't afford to, Poll. I need the money."

"It's a disgrace the way your Bill keeps you short. Can't you complain to the army or something?"

"It's none of your business, Poll. Don't poke your nose in." Agnes spoke a little too sharply. "Sorry, love, but I've told you before, it's between me and Bill. Anyway," she added, "You're in the same boat. There's no man to pay your way. What will you do when the baby comes?"

"Charlie said he'll help. He earns a tidy bit down at the goods-yards, and they're always asking him to do overtime."

"But he has his own family! Anything he gives to you has to come from the pot he should be giving to his wife." Agnes tried not to sound too sanctimonious, but Polly exasperated her sometimes.

"Well, that's between me and Charlie isn't it?" Polly sniffed and held her head high. "So I think we'd better change the subject, don't you?"

Agnes sighed. "You have me there, Poll. Sorry." Agnes felt she'd been chastised and decided to do as Polly asked and changed the subject. "Did you hear the latest about London? Elsie was saying that it got bombed badly the other night. Her sister lives near the docks, and the next street to hers was flattened."

"Yes, they were all talking about it at dinner time. I heard Elsie saying her sister was thinking of moving back here for the duration. Can't say I blame her, can you?"

"Must be awful to live like that. We've been lucky so far. Hardly seen a German plane, and them we do see are just flying over."

"On they're way to Manchester and Liverpool by the sound of things. Thanks goodness there's not much around Thornbury to interest them." Polly shuddered.

"It's still no fun having to get out of bed in the middle of the night when the sirens go off. I've a good mind to stay where I am next time."

"What! And take a chance that they won't drop owt around here?" Polly looked shocked.

"Well, they haven't done so far, what makes you think they will in future?" Agnes went to the small pantry to get out a loaf of bread and some margarine. "I'll cut some bread to go with that bubble and squeak you're warming up."

"I don't know, Agnes. Charlie was saying that the Jerries would be very interested in what goes through the goods-yards along the railways, and we've got a good few of them yards not too far from here."

"Charlie says a lot of things to make himself sound important. I wouldn't put much store in what he has to say." Agnes hoped her words would sink in, but knew that Polly had Charlie on a pedestal and nothing she could say would knock him off it.

"You've always got it in for my Charlie! I wish you'd keep your thoughts to yourself, Agnes. If you can't say owt nice, you'd better say nowt at all, is what me mam used to tell me, and I'm telling you the same now." Polly clattered two plates on the table.

"So I can't speak me own mind in me own house now?" Agnes hated rows, but she couldn't let this one go. "I'm putting up with your shenanigans, giving you a roof over your head when no one else will, and all the while I'm trying to hold me own head up, despite what folks around here are saying about you and him, Poll. It's not easy for me."

"It's not easy for me either, Agnes." Polly shouted, but then lowered her voice and said quietly, "I'm sorry. I should look for a place of me own. I think I've outstayed me welcome, haven't I?"

"No, Polly. I'm sorry." Agnes went to give her cousin a hug. "I'm tired, and you're tired, and we're just getting snappy and grumpy with each other. I knew what I was taking on when I said you could stay, and I'm not going to turf you out now because of a few cross words."

"Oh, thanks, Agnes." Polly squeezed Agnes a little tighter before letting her go and turning to the bubbling concoction in the pan.

"But I wish you'd see sense with Charlie Watson." Agnes couldn't help trying to get the last word on the subject.

"That's enough, Agnes. Don't let's start again. Here's your tea." Polly put the hot pan on the scrubbed wooden table. "Come here, Harry, I'll feed you from my plate tonight, give your mam a rest, eh?"

"Thanks, Poll."

Agnes ate her food in silence, listening to Polly coaxing Harry to take a few mouthfuls. She wasn't happy with the way Polly and her lover were carrying on, but she had as good as condoned it by taking her cousin in. She was glad that Polly hadn't asked again for Charlie to visit with her in the house. She didn't want to spend any more time in the man's company than she needed to. He knew things that could blow her world apart much more effectively than any German Bomb.

Chapter Eight, November 1940

The postman knocked to give her the small letter. She recognised the writing and sat down to open it. Bill rarely wrote to her, and most of the time she didn't think about him or wonder what he was doing. He was a necessary thorn in her side and she put up with him, but that's as far as her feelings went towards her husband. The tiny envelope opened out to reveal the letter written on the reverse of the paper.

"*Dear Agnes, I know this will come as a surprise, but they are sending us home for a bit of a rest. I'm posting this from,* (The next few words were blacked out, courtesy of the censor), *so I'll be home in a week or so. Expect me about the middle of the month. All being well, I'll be around to see my own baby come into the world. Hope you are well. Best wishes, Bill.*"

The letter didn't say much, and held no words of affection, but she hadn't expected it would. Bill's news filled her with dread, though. He had no idea that Polly was living with her now, and she knew he wouldn't like it. Of all the young lasses she could have chosen to be best friends with, it had to be the one who Bill wouldn't want near him, especially since she was carrying another man's child.

Agnes had always known of Bill's feelings for Polly. He never made a secret of them. He had taunted her, telling her he imagined it was Polly under him when he was taking his marital rights with her. His words didn't have any power to hurt her. It might have been different had she loved him, but she didn't. She found his fumbling in the night distasteful, but he expected his wife to do her duty in that department. She had to consent or he would have left her, and the shame of that would have killed her mam just as surely as the fall down the stairs had done. So she endured his huffing and puffing and was grateful when the war took him away. Now he was returning, and Agnes didn't know what would happen when he arrived to find two pregnant women in his home.

"What you got there?" Polly asked as she brought Harry downstairs from his afternoon sleep.

"A letter from Bill. He's coming home for a while."

"When?" Polly asked as she placed the toddler on the floor.

"In a week or so." Agnes folded the letter and put it in her apron pocket. "Shall we go for a walk and get some fresh air?" She felt claustrophobic. The house was small and dark. Daylight barely filtered through the tiny windows, and she felt the walls were closing in on her.

Agnes recognised the familiar feelings of panic. Bill knew her secret and enjoyed hurting her with the finer points of her indiscretions at every opportunity. She hoped he would hold his tongue when Polly was around. Polly thought Harry was Bill's child, as did everyone else they knew. Agnes wanted it to stay that way.

They set out in the gloomy afternoon, and walked as far as the cricket field by the river, along Sands Lane, where little Harry could run around on his newly found wobbly legs. He was growing up so fast, a toddling boy already and his first birthday had been a week ago. The baby kicked and Agnes put a hand to her stomach. "Little Tyke!"

"Mine was at it last night. It's a good job it's Saturday with no overtime or I'd never have kept me eyes open at work today."

"Look at us! We must look like a pair of bookends with our matching bellies." Agnes managed a smile, the first in days. "I'll be glad when they get here and we can get around easier."

"Aye, it's no fun, bending over them looms to do the cleaning and stretching to fix the yarns is getting harder every day."

"Not much longer, two weeks for you and three for me." Agnes was counting the days.

"Is it as bad as they say, Agnes?" Polly asked nervously. "I mean, I know it'll hurt, but they say you forget all about it, so it can't be that bad, can it?"

Agnes remembered how bad it had been with Harry. She thought she would tear in two, but he had been a big baby, and she'd had a terrible labour, filled with panic at having to get the baby out quickly because her placenta was tearing. She hoped she wouldn't be so unlucky again. "I'm hoping for an easier time, and you should be fine, Polly. You're a strong lass and you know what to expect. I've told you often enough."

"I want a little girl, Agnes. I hope she'll look like Charlie. He has three lads, and I know if I have a girl she'll be special to him, you know what I mean?"

"It won't make any difference, Poll. He won't leave Jane, no matter whether you have a set of twin girls with angel wings and halos round their heads."

"I know." Polly sighed. "I can dream, though, can't I?"

"Yes, Polly. A girl can dream." Agnes didn't want to put a

damper on the afternoon by talking in depressing terms about what was in store for them.

Within a few weeks, they'd both have babies squalling at all hours of the day and night. The nursery had opened, in an old storage building by the mill and Harry was already attending. The young ones would be looked after there during the day while they continued to work. The nights would be a different matter altogether. Babies needed feeding at all hours, and they'd still have to get up when the alarm clock went off at the crack of dawn, even when they'd been up half the night. Polly didn't dwell on the realities of having a new baby. Polly was a dreamer. She still believed in fairytales and happy endings. Agnes knew there was no such thing as a happy ending. She often dreamed of a better future. She thought about how things could have been if her dad hadn't been so against Andrew. If only she'd been allowed to marry her sweetheart, the love of her life, her soul-mate. How different things would have been. Yes, a girl could dream, but she would always wake up to reality eventually.

"Let's get you out of that pram, young man. You can test your legs out for a bit." Polly lifted Harry from the pram and set him down on his feet.

"He can run around while we take the weight of our legs." Agnes spread the pram blanket on the grass and the two girls sank gratefully to the cold ground.

"Have you told Bill that I'm staying with you?" Polly broached the touchy subject.

"No, I haven't said."

"So he won't know that I'm pregnant either."

"No, he doesn't know."

"What will he say, Agnes? Will he let me stay?"

"He'll have to, where else will you go?"

"But will he be happy about it?"

"I don't know, Poll!" Agnes snapped. She had no idea how her husband would take it and was just as worried as Polly about his reaction to her lodger. "Sorry, I didn't mean to bite your head off."

"How long will he be home for?"

"I don't know. I don't think it will be for long. The way they're talking at work, this war is set to go on forever. I think Bill will have to get back pretty quickly."

"Well, that will make it easier for us, I mean if he's not going to be around for long. Oh, I don't mean! I mean, I know you must be desperate to see him, Agnes, and I know you won't want him to leave so soon, but, oh, there's me mouth running away with me again."

Agnes laughed. "It's all right, Poll. Don't worry about it. I know what you mean, and I think the same myself. With two babies and Harry in the house, I don't think he'll want to stay home for long once these two arrive."

"I see what you mean." Polly joined in the laughter. "The Siegfried line, or wherever it is they're fighting, will be a lot more inviting than a house full of screaming babies and steaming nappies."

"I don't know where he's been. He wrote where they were, but the censor blacked it out. I suppose he'll tell us when he gets here."

"I bet he's seen some terrible things, Aggy. The tales I hear from the other women at the mill. Mrs Johnson's son was killed at Dunkirk back in May. A mate of his came round to tell her how it was for them on that beach. She can't talk about it without crying. It must have been awful for the lads."

"We're lucky, aren't we? We hardly know there's a war on here. Except for the rationing and the odd air-raid siren, we're safe enough." Agnes pointed out.

"Don't laugh about the air-raids! We might not have had any bombs land around here, but we see and hear the planes go over and I hate it when we have to get into the cellar when the sirens go off."

"There's nothing of importance for them to bother with in these parts. The mills only make blankets and stuff. The iron and steel works is about the only thing they'd bomb if they had a mind to." Agnes said.

"Mr Fraser, the supervisor on the late shift, he said the railway junctions and marshalling yards will get it one day." Polly tipped her chin towards Thornbury goods-yards at the far end of Sand's Lane. "He said there're all sorts of important war stuff goes through them places, and he should know, his son worked over there untill he got his call-up papers." She pointed to the sidings sheds. "Mr Fraser said the Jerries will want to destroy our transport links so that means the railways will be a target, you mark my words. My Charlie's never said exactly what he gets through the yards, it's more than his job's worth to talk about it, but I know he's worried about being bombed too. I know he'd prefer to do the day shifts because there's less chance of bombers going over in daylight."

The girls looked to the railway line that ran on the viaduct at the end of the cricket field.

"The Honby marshalling yards are not too far away!" Agnes realised the major railway junction was only a mile or so from where they were sitting. "I've gone cold all over, just thinking about it!"

"They bombed Paris in June and look what happened there! France caved in without much of a fight."

"They've been bombing London for weeks over the summer and Coventry got it bad last week, but we won't give in. Even if they bomb every town in Britain, I can't see Churchill surrendering, can you?"

"Not while there's a British soldier still standing." Polly said. "They're still sending out call-up papers. Me mam must be worried about our James. He's almost eighteen, so if this war lasts much longer, he'll be sent for too."

"That's if he doesn't volunteer before then. He's a strong-headed lad, and I'm sure he'll want to go and do his bit."

"Me dad wouldn't let him. He'll mind what our dad says."

"I hope so, Polly. He's no more than a lad."

"None of 'em are. Charlie has been lucky in a way. He never knew he had a bad heart. Looks as strong as an ox, doesn't he? But he didn't pass the army medical, so it must be serious, 'cause anyone knows you'd have to be at death's door before the army refuse to take you on."

"He still works at the goods-yard, though, so he can't be that bad."

"It's something to do with a faulty valve. He's been excused heavy lifting. I think he does paperwork now. He'd know whether anything important went through the yards. He has to keep his mouth shut, though. He can't tell me anything, 'cause walls have ears and all that."

Agnes hoped Charlie could keep his mouth shut about other things too. She still worried about how much Polly's paramour knew about what happened the night her dad died.

They heard a droning noise and looked up at the darkening sky. Low clouds moved slowly above them and the air smelt of rain. Suddenly, a dark shape emerged from the cloud and sped over their heads. The small aircraft rose higher as it met the railway viaduct, and turned to follow the track towards the marshalling yards at Honby.

"That wasn't one of ours, was it?" Polly looked shocked.

"It was a German plane!"

"Did you see the black crosses on the wings?"

"Aye, it was a Jerry all right." Agnes shook her head. "It must have been one of them spotter planes. Do you think we should tell someone about it?"

"Who would we tell?"

"Your dad. Uncle Bert will know who to inform." Agnes was already getting to her feet. "I'll go see him now. He'll be back from the pub by now for his dinner, won't he?"

By the time Agnes got home, her back was aching. She felt she'd walked her legs off, but at least Bert knew what they'd seen and could report it to the correct authorities. He told her he thought the plane was scouting out the area for bombing raids, and she'd mentioned that she and Polly had been talking about Jerry attacking the marshalling yards only minutes before the plane flew over. Bert agreed that they could be a target, and hurried to get his boots and coat on to carry the message to his superior at the fire warden's station. They would, by now, be busy preparing for a raid, and positioning the new anti-aircraft guns in readiness.

"What did me dad say?" Polly asked as she got through the door.

"Let me get my coat off, Polly. It's freezing out there now, but it's nice and warm in here."

"Harry's had his supper and I put him to bed. I think all that running around in the fresh air has tired him out."

"Thanks, love. Your dad says we were right to report it. He thinks the railway junctions and yards could be in for it soon if that aircraft we saw was a spotter plane. That pilot would have seen that Thornbury and Honby could be targets for the bombers."

"Oh, no! What about my Charlie? He's on the night shift this week and he'll likely be working if they come. The bombers usually fly over at night, don't they? Oh, Charlie."

"Steady on, Poll. It might take a day or so for the Jerries to organise a raid and by the time they do, we'll be ready for them. Your dad says the home guard squad got new artillery guns for this type of thing and they'll be busy setting them up in a few hours. They'll be ready for Jerry and them bombers will be in for a big surprise when our lads shoot 'em from the sky before they get a chance to drop their bombs."

"Oh, Agnes, I hope you're right. Wouldn't hurt to tell Charlie, though. I'll go down there tomorrow before his shift ends and tell him."

"You'd have to get up at the crack of dawn if you want to get there before he leaves for home. It'll still be dark, and freezing out there. You might slip and fall, and in your condition, Poll you have to be more careful. You can't go! It's madness!"

"I'll be careful. I have to tell him, Agnes. You'd do the same in my shoes."

"You take care then. Mind your footing on them slippery cobbles."

"I will. Don't be such a worrier." Polly winked. "I'm off to my bed. Goodnight."

"Night Poll."

Polly was late into work the following morning. True to her word she had risen early and gone to warn her lover, but she had stayed longer than planned in the warm offices. Agnes knew all too well what her cousin had been getting up to. No matter how heavily pregnant she was, Polly wouldn't refuse Charlie anything, and her dishevelled appearance gave evidence that the lass had been up to no good.

Agnes could see the sly glances and raised eyebrows among the rest of the women as Polly hurried along the lane between the clattering looms and went to stand in her mule gate. Agnes couldn't help shaking her head and squeezing her lips together when Polly looked her way. It wouldn't do any good, though. Polly would never take advice, no matter who gave it, especially if it were about Charlie Watson.

At last, when they could take a break to eat the fish paste sandwiches that Agnes had packed she could ask Polly how Charlie had taken the news.

"Oh, you know, he said the bosses had already warned them of possible raids, and they have a shelter to go into when the sirens go off, so they'll be all right."

"So you didn't need to go this morning?"

"Well, he made it worth me while, so I don't mind." Polly smirked. "In fact, I might make a habit of early morning visits to the goods-yard offices. They're nice and warm and Charlie don't have much to do at the end of a shift."

"Polly!" Agnes tried to keep her voice low, "How could you?"

"Don't be such a prude, our Agnes. You won't let us have any private time at your place, and in this weather, there's not much fun to be had down at the cricket pavilion."

"The cricket pavilion?" Agnes looked puzzled.

"That's where we used to go for a bit of, well, you know what, when the nights were warmer and the cricketers had all gone home."

"Don't tell me anymore, I don't want to know!" Agnes said, firmly. "Come on, we'd better get back to work or Doris will have our guts for garters."

Chapter Nine, Birth and death

The sirens blasted through the night air and Agnes reluctantly threw the blankets back. She lifted Harry from his cot and made her way to the cellar. She now kept a mattress down there with spare blankets, but they were icy. She couldn't put her son on the cold bedding so she kept Harry in her arms and hurried back upstairs to get the warm blankets from her bed. She called Polly, but knew the girl could sleep through a bomb going off outside the window, so Agnes put her head around Polly's bedroom door, intending to go and shake her awake if she had to, but the bed was empty. Agnes sighed and pursed her lips. She could only guess where her friend had gone. The clock on the bedside table said four-thirty, but Agnes had no idea when Polly may have sneaked out.

She was halfway back down the cellar steps when the first boom shook the stairs beneath her feet. She grasped the banister and clung to her son as the second loud boom sounded seconds later, from farther away. She ran down the rest of the stairs and hunkered down with the toddler on the cold mattress in the darkness. Harry was crying loudly, and was not at all happy that his sleep had been disturbed. Agnes wrapped the warmer bedding around them, instinctively covering both their heads. As they cuddled in the cocoon, more bombs boomed in the distance, and Agnes felt the ground beneath her shudder. She was afraid for the rest of the town, but the bombs didn't seem to be falling near her house. She hugged her son and began to sing to him, and soon his lustful yells became quiet whimpers, until eventually he slept.

Agnes wasn't so fortunate. Sleep did not come to her. She was afraid of the noises she heard, and scared that people would be killed in the town. She stayed awake, listening to the rounds of artillery and distant booming of bombs being dropped. She couldn't believe it was happening. So far, they hadn't been affected much by the war. Not here in Thornbury. A lot of the men had gone to fight, and she knew that some had been killed or wounded, but the town itself had escaped the worst of the war until now. During the last hour or so, it sounded like the heavens had opened and hellfire was raining down. She hoped Polly was safe. She hoped her cousin had managed to make it to the shelters dotted around the town. She hoped she wasn't with Charlie down at the goods-yards, but she had an awful feeling that her friend was in danger. She couldn't wait for the raid to be over, but it seemed to go on and on.

Dawn was breaking when Agnes raised her head and shivered. She must have dropped off at some point. Harry was snuggled into her side and she glanced to the empty mattress and remembered that Polly had not been in her bed. "Oh, my goodness. Polly!"

Agnes pushed the blankets to one side, taking care to make sure her son was not disturbed. She ran upstairs to get dressed then readied the pram to put Harry into it. She didn't take the time to make breakfast, or even a pot of tea. She didn't stop to put a brush through her hair. Harry didn't like being picked from the warm bed and dumped into the cold pram, but Agnes ignored his complaints as she pushed him towards the river and up Orchard Street to Hilda and Bert's home. Smoke lingered in the air, and there was a smell of burning timber. The streets she walked through seemed unscathed, but people she came across told her they were all as scared as she was.

"It were a right pasting they gave us last night, lass!" An elderly man commented as he hurried by.

"Aye," Agnes called to his back.

"I heard they dropped one near the mill on Wilton Street." One of the girls who worked in the weaving sheds told her. "I'm on my way down there to see whether there's owt I can do to help."

"Have you seen owt of our Polly?" Agnes asked her.

"Sorry, Agnes. I've only seen me granddad this morning and he's been helping at the mobile canteen they set up for the fire-fighters."

"If you see her, will you tell her I'm looking for her?"

"Aye, I will. Hope you find her."

The town had lived through its worst night of the war, and the effect was evident in the white faces of the hurrying friends and neighbours. She had to get to her aunt and uncle's house. She had to let them know her fears. Bert would know what to do.

Hilda answered her insistent knocking within a few minutes. "Whatever is up, lass? You look dreadful. It's not our Polly, is it? She's not due for another two weeks. Oh, my! Where have they taken her? The infirmary is it?"

"Slow down, Auntie Hilda. I'm not sure where Polly is, or what's happened to her. I didn't know where else to go. Is Uncle Bert in?"

"He's just walked through the door, not ten minutes ago, love. He's been out all night fighting fires down at the goods-yard. You must have heard the racket. Kept us awake all night, them damned Jerries! It's a good job you and our Polly saw that spotter plane last week or we'd have suffered a lot worse. I don't think our lads got any of the buggers, but they made 'em turn tail and run before they could get rid of all their loads. We only caught a dozen or so bombs, and your Uncle Bert says them big planes carry as many as that each, and he said there were loads of them up in the sky circling around us."

"Auntie Hilda, stop!" Agnes interrupted. "Where did the bombs drop?"

"The marshalling yards in Honby took a few, and Thornbury goods-yard got one too, lass. Just as your Uncle Bert said they would."

Agnes sank to her knees in the hallway. Polly could have been at the goods-yard with Charlie. "Oh, no!"

"What's up, lass?"

"Polly, she was…" Agnes looked up at the older woman's puzzled face. "Oh, Auntie Hilda, I'm sorry. I tried to make her stop going, but you know what she's like. She wouldn't listen to me, and she's been sneaking out at all hours."

"You're not making sense, lass. Spit it out."

Bert appeared at the top of the stairs looking dishevelled. "What's all this racket? I've been up all night fighting fires and I need me sleep."

"You'd better come down, Uncle Bert." Agnes got to her feet and leant on the pram handle for support.

"You're scaring me now, Agnes." Hilda reached for her husband as he got to the bottom of the stairs. "She says our Polly… Well, she hasn't said, but she's going to tell us something, and it isn't going to be good news by the looks of her face."

"What's happened lass?" Bert asked quietly.

Agnes told them about Polly's early morning visits to the goods-yard to see Charlie when he did the night shift. "I think she might have been there with him when the siren went off. I hope they got into the shelters in time, but it happened so quick, didn't it? The planes were dropping bombs before the siren finished going off. I barely made it to my cellar steps in time."

"But you don't know for sure that she was there at the yards, do you?" Hilda insisted. "She might not have made it that far. She could be holed up in some air raid shelter on the way."

"They didn't give any of us much time to get to safety, did they Uncle Bert?" Agnes began shivering and lifted Harry from his pram. "And she still wasn't home this morning and the all-clear must have sounded hours ago."

"Come into the parlour, the fire will still be in, I banked it before I came to bed so it'd be nice and warm for Hilda, it should be warm in there." Bert led them through to the front room of the house. "Bring the kettle through, Hilda. We could all do with a pot of sweet tea."

"You'll have to make do with tea and condensed milk. I've no sugar left with the rationing. It doesn't go far, you know."

"That'll do, love." Bert pushed his wife through the door to the kitchen. "Now, tell me, whereabouts did Charlie Watson work, exactly."

"The goods-yard in Thornbury. That's all I know." Agnes said through chattering teeth. "I think he did paperwork, so maybe he works in the offices."

Bert's shoulders sagged and he flopped into an easy chair by the fireside. "Are you sure, lass?"

"No, I'm not sure. I'm guessing. And that's my best guess." She paced in front of the window and clutched Harry to her side, his legs hanging either side of her hip. "Where did the bombs fall, Uncle Bert? Will Polly be all right, do you think?"

"The offices took the worst of it." Bert put his head in his hands. "We didn't know anyone was in there, Agnes. We didn't know the office staff worked nights." Bert's shoulders began to heave long before the first sobs tore from his throat. "I was hosing the buildings down, trying to save what I could. I didn't know my lass, oh, Polly. Oh, no! I didn't know she was in there!"

"We don't know that she was, Uncle Bert. Not for sure!" Agnes's face was wet as she put Harry on the floor and went to cuddle her uncle.

"What is it?" Hilda bustled into the room with a tray of cups and a kettle. "Bert!" The tray fell from her hands and Hilda knelt by her husband's side and put an arm about his shaking shoulders. "Whatever have you said to him?" Hilda turned her worried face to Agnes. "Tell me what's happened to our Polly!"

Hours later, Agnes went home. Polly was missing and as far as they could tell, hadn't been seen anywhere since she went to bed last night. Hilda had scouted the neighbourhood, knocking on doors, and eventually Bert left to tell the fire wardens what Agnes feared. The office building down at the Thornbury goods-yard was a pile of smouldering rubble, but the fire-watch men had been working to remove it and search through the heap of debris, and now they were working with more determination since Bert went down there to tell them what he suspected. Agnes should have been getting ready to go to Mass, but even her guilty conscience could not prompt her to go. Her faith had never been strong, and in the last few months it had been tested to the limit. She didn't want to go and pray to a God that would take her best friend away so cruelly.

She fed and changed Harry and bundled him into his pram. She couldn't sit around waiting for news. She felt the need of company, so she turned the pram towards Orchard Street, intending to spend the time with her Auntie Hilda. As she got close to the river, she began to shiver. The day was bitterly cold, and seeing the bridge always brought back memories of the night her dad died. She pushed them away. Now was not the time to dwell on the past. The present was bad enough. She heard someone calling her name and looked up to see one of the older ladies from the church who had been a friend of her mam.

"Agnes, I'm glad I found you. I was hoping to see you at church, but when you didn't come to the early-morning Mass, and then you missed this one, well, I thought I'd better come to your house and tell you."

"Tell me what, Mrs Stoner?" Agnes was in a hurry to get to her Auntie Hilda's house, and didn't want to hear any reprimands about missing church service from this God-fearing woman.

"About your Polly. I don't have any time for your aunt and uncle, and they wouldn't thank me for turning up on their doorstep, no matter what the news. The way they turned their backs on Father Brennan, well! It's no wonder their lass turned out the way she has. I know she's no saint, that young Polly of theirs. My, she's the talk of the —."

"What about our Polly?" Agnes gripped the pram handle tightly, bracing herself for bad news.

"Oh, yes, well. She took a tumble last night. Don't know what she was doing out so late and the weather as it was. Like an ice rink on our street, it was..."

"Where is she now?" Agnes interrupted impatiently.

"At the infirmary, I think. My Stan found her on the street on his way in from the pub. He'd only gone out for the one pint, you know? A pint helps him sleep, but then everyone knows that. Mind you, none of us got much sleep last night, did we? Them Germans are getting a bit too close for my liking. They say the goods-yards got it last night, and the mill nearly took one too. It fell it the river and caused a right old mess. There's mud all over the mill yard —."

"Mrs Stoner! Please!" Agnes was getting impatient. "What about our Polly?"

"Oh, yes. Well, my Stan found her on the cobbles outside our house, like I said. I don't know how long she'd been there, but she was frozen through, poor lamb. She'd hurt her leg, twisted her ankle, I think. Anyway, I got her some blankets and kept her warm. I know she's a wilful little scoundrel, but there's such a thing as Christian charity, isn't there? I couldn't leave her to freeze, could I?"

"Very good of you, Mrs Stoner, I'm sure you'll get your rewards in heaven for that little act of kindness." Agnes was now eager to get to her aunt's house and wanted to cut the conversation short.

"Oh, and she was having contractions by the time we got to her, and the baby was almost born outside my house. Thankfully the ambulance made it in time but I think it must have been born on the way. She was well into the pushing stage when they lifted her into it."

"Oh, my goodness!" Agnes was overjoyed and worried all at the same time. Polly was alive and would have the baby by now too. "Thank you Mrs Stoner, Thank you, thank you, thank you!" Agnes took hold of the woman and danced her around in the street before giving her a hug. "I have to go tell my auntie." Agnes began to push the pram up Orchard Street. "Thanks again, Mrs Stoner, see you at church next week."

Agnes hurried as fast as she could and was out of breath when she began banging on the door of her Auntie Hilda's house. She didn't wait for her knock to be answered. She flung the door wide and shouted, "She's alive! Our Polly is alive!"

When Bert returned from the goods-yard, he was grim faced. Nothing had been found so far, but it had been a two-story building and the bomb had levelled it. The men were searching through heaps of rubble and it was no easy task. His face lit when Agnes told him Polly was not under the debris.

"She's in the infirmary, Bert. She's all right!" Hilda had hugged her husband. "Our lass is alive and by the sound of it, we have a grandbairn too."

"That's grand news." Bert ran a hand through his sparse hair. "I'm dead on me feet, but I know I won't rest until I've seen her with me own eyes."

"Let's have some dinner first, it won't be visiting time until this afternoon." Hilda suggested.

"I'll have me dinner and then call at the goods-yard again to see if there's any news, and then I'll meet you at the infirmary."

Agnes went with Hilda to the infirmary and they found Polly on the maternity ward. She was not badly hurt by the fall on the icy cobbles. A bruised knee and twisted ankle were the worst of the injuries. The fall had shocked her body into an early labour, and the baby was now in special care as a precaution. Little Alice was born in the ambulance on the way to the hospital, and had screamed her displeasure from the first second she was out in the cold air.

"I'm so glad you came, Mam. You don't know how happy I am to see you." Polly sat up in the iron bed and grinned at her visitors. "Wait until you see her. She's so tiny, and such a sweet little thing. I'm not a bit worried about her. She has a fine pair of lungs, that's what the ambulance lady said. It felt strange to have a woman ambulance driver, but she was ever so good. She knew exactly what to do, and I had our little Alice with no bother at all."

Bert came into the ward and made his way to the bed, twisting his cap in his hands, his head bowed low, and took a seat next to his wife. "Hello, Polly."

"Dad!" Polly smiled. "I'm so happy to see you."

"I can't wait to see your baby." Hilda smiled but avoided Polly's eyes. "Are you all right, love? Are you sure you're not hurt?"

"Only my knee and my ankle. I'll soon mend." Polly beamed at them all. "Has anyone told Charlie yet?"

Bert jumped to his feet and looked as if he wanted to run away. Hilda touched his arm and he sat back down.

"No, Polly. No one has seen him." Agnes put her fingers out to touch Polly's hand. "We think. We thought that…" She couldn't finish.

"They searched the rubble, Polly." Bert's eyes filled with tears. "They found a body, love. We think Charlie Watson was in the buildings that got bombed down at the yards last night." Bert blurted the words quickly as if to get the bad news over with, but he didn't stop to see the devastation they caused. He turned and left without another word, leaving the women to gasp, open-mouthed at his back.

"No!" Polly whispered and shook her head. "He's wrong. Charlie isn't dead."

"Shush, love. Don't get upset." Hilda squeezed her daughter's hand.

"Don't get upset!" Polly shouted. "Why would I get upset? You're telling me the only man I could ever love has gone and died, and then you tell me not to get upset!" She let out a shriek and then clamped a hand over her mouth. She shook her head vigorously and moaned. Her white face turned questioning eyes to Agnes. "It's not true, Agnes. Tell me it's not true."

"I wish I could Poll." Agnes watched as her cousin seemed to shrink before her eyes.

"No, it can't be." Polly started crying quietly. "Not my Charlie. Please not my Charlie."

Chapter Ten, Confession

Polly insisted on attending the funeral a week later, even though Agnes had tried to advise her against going. When she returned home, Polly was ashen faced. The family had turned her away and she only got to see Charlie's coffin from the church wall. She didn't get to say goodbye as she wanted to, but Agnes had warned her she wouldn't get near.

"You can go later in the week, Polly, when everyone else is at work, or about their business." Agnes had tried to comfort her cousin. "You can visit his grave and say your private farewell."

"Why did they have to be so mean?" Polly cried. "I'd as much right to be there as the rest of them!"

Agnes bit her tongue. She knew that Polly had no rights at all, but it would do no good to point that out to her friend. She was in no mind to listen to reason.

"I can't believe he's gone, Agnes. I can't imagine that I'll never see him again. He never got to see his little girl. She'll grow up without a daddy. He would have come to me. I know he would. I just know it."

Agnes let her ramble on, knowing that Polly needed to let off steam. "I'll make us a pot of tea, love. You look frozen through."

The late November fog had clung throughout the day, and the freezing mist seemed to penetrate the clothes they wore. Agnes tried to keep the fire banked high to ward off the cold in the house, but when she left the hearth to fill the kettle, the cold air was waiting to snatch the warmth away from her hands and feet and face. "Sit by the fire, Polly. You're shivering, and little Alice will need a feed soon. Get warm, love, before she wakes."

"I don't think I'll ever feel warm again, Agnes. I was given the cold shoulder good and proper, I can tell you!"

Agnes snapped. "What did you expect, Poll! I warned you! I told you not to go, but would you listen?"

"He loved me, Agnes, and I loved him, that gives me the right —."

"That gives you nothing, Poll. They see you as a brazen hussy who's not worthy to lick the boots of Jane Watson. She was his wife, Polly. You were his mistress. There's a big difference and you're fooling yourself if you think otherwise." Agnes watched her friend's face crumple and went to put an arm around her shoulders. "I'm sorry, love. You should forget you ever knew him and get on with your life. I know the truth hurts, but the sooner you face it, the better you'll feel. It's the only way, love."

"I'll never feel better. I'll always feel just as I do now. I miss him so much!" Polly's sobs grew louder, and Agnes rocked her to try to give some comfort.

Alice's cries rang out from the open bottom drawer of the dresser that was her crib. "She wants her feed, Polly. Shall I get her for you?" Agnes got to her feet and was already reaching for the baby. "I'll change her for you while you get yourself ready." Agnes offered, and began to strip the infant.

Little Harry got up from the rag-rug where he'd been quietly playing and came to see what his mother was doing. "Baba," he said in his baby voice.

"Clever boy, Harry." Agnes smiled at her son. "Did you hear that, Poll? Harry said his first proper word."

Agnes finished cleaning and dressing the screaming baby and handed her to Polly, who waited for her baby with a bared breast. Alice began to feed immediately, and the silence was bliss.

"We'll have to get used to double that noise soon." Agnes stroked her large tummy. "We'll soon have two babies, Harry, and then you'll know about it."

Both women heard the door catch rattle and turned to see Bill, in army uniform, step into the room.

"Bill, you're here!" Agnes stated the obvious.

"Looks like it." He glanced from Agnes to Polly sitting by the hearth. "What we got here?" His face was impassive, but Agnes grew nervous.

"Hello, Bill." Polly managed a brief smile before turning her attention back to her daughter.

"Polly is staying with us for a little while." Agnes said and quickly added, "I hope that's all right with you, Bill. You see, the baby's dad was killed last week and was buried earlier today, so she's had a tough time." Agnes hoped Polly would go along with her edited version of events. Bill didn't need to know the details of Polly's irresponsibility.

"What about Bert and Hilda? Can't they look after her?" Bill spoke as if Polly wasn't there. It seemed he was doing his best to ignore her presence.

"Me mam and dad have enough to cope with." Polly answered him. "Dad works all day and is doing the fire watching most nights, so he needs his sleep and wouldn't get any with a baby in the house." Polly gave Agnes a knowing sideways look. "You don't mind, do you, Bill? It'll only be for a few months until she's sleeping through."

Agnes watched her husband as he began to slowly take off his army-issue coat, then bent to remove his boots. Lying came naturally to her, but she felt uneasy that Polly was hiding the truth too. "How long will you be home for?" she asked.

"About a week. We go for some special training at the beginning of December. They're sending us…," he hesitated. "Well, I'll be going away again soon."

"That's all right then." Agnes said without thinking. "I mean, I didn't mean it's all right that you're going, I just thought, that, well…"

"I won't be around long enough to mind what happens in my own house when I'm not here!" Bill shook his head. "You do have a way with words, Agnes." He grinned, but Agnes knew it wasn't a sincere show of approval. "Come here and give me a kiss, sweetheart." He held his arms open, gesturing for Agnes to go to him.

Agnes faltered, but knew that Polly would think it odd if she didn't do as he asked. She stepped into his arms and he squeezed her too tightly. "Careful, you'll hurt the baby." Agnes tried to squirm from his hold, but his mouth came down on hers and almost smothered her as he kissed her deeply. She tried not to shy away from the intimate embrace.

"I missed you, Agnes. Did you miss me, my love?" He asked as he let her go, his face a picture of sarcasm.

"Err, of course, I missed you, Bill." Agnes answered automatically, hoping the side-play between them was going over Polly's head. Her cousin seemed engrossed in the baby. "Little Harry missed his daddy too." She thought she'd better include her son to back up the illusion of wedded bliss they were acting out for Polly's benefit.

"I bet he does." Bill's eyes rested on the toddler. "He's getting a big lad now. He's the image of his daddy, don't you think so, Polly?"

Agnes cringed inside at Bill's words, knowing they were a snipe at her.

"I think he favours his mammy." Polly said as she lifted the baby from her breast and put her over her shoulder to pat her back. She quickly covered her breast when she noticed Bill was staring at her with an odd expression on his face.

Agnes didn't miss the exchange and began to tremble inside. What had she done? Having Polly in her home, knowing how her husband felt about her, was madness. She saw it now. How could she ever have thought it would be all right? Polly still seemed oblivious of Bill's feeling towards her. She was so wrapped up in her own misery that she would never have noticed anything amiss between Agnes and her husband, but she hadn't thought about Bill's response to living with the girl of his dreams under his own roof.

"I didn't hear that you'd married, Polly. Who was the lucky lad?"

"No one you know, Bill." Agnes answered for her. The less he knew the better. She hoped gossip wouldn't reach his ears in the short time he'd be around.

"His name was Charlie." Polly said quietly. "He loved me, but he's gone now and I have to get used to that."

"Please tell me it wasn't that waster you've been seeing! Not that Charlie Watson you were carrying-on with!"

"What if it was!" Polly's eyes filled with tears. "What's it got to do with you?"

"Another bastard under my roof!" Bill shook his head. "What's up with the bloody world? It's gone mad!"

"Bill, mind your language, please." Agnes hoped Polly was too upset to notice what Bill had said.

"What are folks around here saying about this little setup?" Bill waved his arm around, pointing at the two young women.

"It's not a setup, Bill. I had nowhere to go and Polly kindly took me in." Polly was wiping her face and sniffing. "I'll look for somewhere else if it's a problem for you," she said quietly.

"I'll get the tea." Agnes bustled about setting cups out on the scrubbed table and brewing the tea. Her hands were shaking, but she had to do something. She had to try to divert the atmosphere of tension that was growing in the room. She didn't think Polly had noticed anything untoward between her and Bill so far, but it would only be a matter of time before the girl realised all was not as it seemed in the Smithson home.

"So Charlie Watson is dead, is he?" Bill asked. "Well, there's no need for you to be alone, Polly." Bill seemed to have a sudden change of heart and seated himself opposite Polly at the other side of the hearth. "I suppose it won't matter much to me whether you go or stay. I'll be off again soon so I can't object if I'm not around, can I?" Bill leant to pat Polly's knee. "It might be nice to have a pretty young face around for a change. A good-looking girl like you won't be alone for long."

"Bill! She's just come back from Charlie's funeral, don't be so unfeeling!" Agnes could see the look of longing on her husband's face, but hoped Polly didn't recognise it for what it was.

"I'm only saying what's staring me in the face. You're a bonny lass, Polly. I'd have you any day!"

"Bill!" It was Polly's turn to reprimand him this time, though she had a small smile playing around the corners of her mouth. "How dare you say such a thing? With your wife here too! What's poor Agnes to think?"

"Don't worry yourself, Poll. I know Bill is trying to be friendly to you, though he has an odd way of doing so."

"What's odd about admitting what's obvious? Your cousin is a lovely lass, and I'll keep on telling her so, because it's true."

"Eh, Bill. You are a one!" Polly smiled softly at her friend's husband, and it was clear to Agnes that his flattery had found its mark.

Agnes watched the small interchange with mounting dread. What had she started by taking Polly into her home? She served the tea and tried to keep her hands from shaking. Her insides were doing somersaults and it wasn't the baby moving. Her sham of a marriage would not last long if Bill and Polly were to get close. Without the cover of a church blessed marriage, her life would be exposed as a sham too.

"Here's your tea." She thrust the hot cup at her husband.

"That's not much to quench a man's thirst. I think I'll go to the Crown Arms and have a pint or two. You don't mind, do you, Agnes, my love?" His smile reminded Agnes of sly fox stalking a rabbit. "I won't be too late, so mind and keep the bed warm for me."

Agnes shuddered and couldn't bring herself to answer him. The thought of being intimate with him was repulsive to her. She'd hoped he would be sensitive of her advanced pregnancy and leave her alone, but his comments suggested that it would not be so. She tried to smile, but her lips trembled as she watched him put his coat and boots back on.

"I'll see you later, Polly." Bill aimed his last remark at the young girl feeding her baby. "I bet you'd make it worth my while to come home to, lass. Any lad would be glad of the sight of your figure after a long stint away from female company."

"Give over, Bill!" Polly chuckled. "I've just had a bairn, so I'm not in great shape under these clothes."

"You'll soon get your figure back, lass." Bill glanced at his wife's large tummy. "I don't hold out much hope for Agnes, though. She's the size of a house!"

Agnes almost jumped from her chair, but forced herself to stay calm. To be talked of by her husband like that, was hurtful, and shocking. She couldn't look at Polly for fear she would open her mouth and spill the bitter bile that rose in her throat.

"Cheeky!" Polly glanced at Bill from under her lowered lashes. "Agnes will have a lovely figure again soon, you wait and see." Polly glanced at Agnes and raised her eyebrows. "She's always had nice curves. Not like me. I'm too skinny ordinarily. Wait until you see me when I've lost the baby fat. You won't be so fast to compliment me then."

Agnes knew her cousin was trying to help smooth over an awkward situation, but in her eyes, she was making it worse. Poor Polly had no idea how Bill felt, and she was adding coal to the flames.

"I know what you look like, Polly. I've seen you around, remember? You were always one to make a boy feel like a man." He turned to Agnes. "Not like some. On second thoughts, don't wait up, Agnes. I've gone off the idea."

Agnes felt she couldn't breathe. She watched Bill leave and jumped when he slammed the door behind him. Harry started crying at the loud bang, and baby Alice began to fret at her mother's breast.

"Come here, son." Agnes held her arms out and Harry ran to her. "There, there. It's all right."

"What was all that about?" Polly asked as she held the baby over her shoulder to burp her. "He didn't seem too happy to be home. He never even spoke to little Harry!"

"I think he might have had it rough wherever he's been. Perhaps that's what it is that's making him tetchy and cruel." Agnes lied. Finding excuses for her husband's behaviour came effortlessly to her. She couldn't let Polly guess the truth.

Agnes woke to the sound of her husband stumbling around the bedroom. She lay still, not wanting him to know that she was awake. She listened to him cursing as he stubbed his toe on the cot and groaned inwardly as she heard her son whimper at the disturbance.

"Don't you start, you little bastard!" Bill hissed. "If it

weren't for you, I'd be sharing the bed in the next room instead of getting between the sheets with the ice queen." Bill thumped the cot, but not hard enough to wake the toddler. "Damn that bitch that made me do it," he mumbled, "I never wanted to. Dangling that money in front of me like that. She, she… well, she got what she deserved, hic! Taught her a lesson, didn't I?" Bill started giggling softly.

Agnes froze. He was drunk, and still staggering around getting undressed, but he was talking to himself, and his words were sending chills through her. What had he done? He was talking about her mam. She hardly dare take another breath in case she missed his muttered words.

"Stupid old crone thought she'd got the better of me, didn't she? Making me sign them papers with the priest to make sure the money went back to her whore of a daughter if owt happened to me, hic!" Bill burped loudly, tossed his trousers in a heap and sat on the bed. "Well, a lot of good it did her. I'm not going anywhere, anyway, but them papers are burned now. She didn't like it when I told her that, did she?" He giggled softly again and the bed shook. "And she ain't gonna tell no one I signed owt since I made sure she couldn't open her fat gob again."

Agnes flinched as he climbed into bed beside her. She couldn't help it. She had heard every word of his confession, if that's what it was. She lay very still as Bill settled down for sleep, still muttering under his breath. She tried to keep her breathing slow and steady so he wouldn't realise she was awake, but her heart was hammering painfully in her chest. She tried to remember what he'd said, to make sure she had heard what she thought she had heard. He as good as admitted killing her mother. Was he responsible for the fall down the stairs? Did he push her? What about the signing of papers? Did Trudie really go through with her plan and have the priest make him do that? Is that why he did away with her mother?

Bill's snoring told her he had quickly fallen into a drunken slumber and she knew from past experience that he probably wouldn't wake for hours. She carefully left the bed and crept downstairs where she sat by the banked fire, but no matter how close she got to the glowing embers, she couldn't get warm. She was chilled to the bone, and couldn't stop her shivers.

She was married to a murderer. She was trapped and she realised that she would have to find a way out. She couldn't lie with him again. She couldn't live with him, knowing what he had done. How could she go on? What would she do? She sat by the fire all through the night, and when little Harry began to make his morning noises, she still hadn't thought of a plan.

She went quickly up the stairs to get her son, hoping Bill wouldn't wake at the commotion he was making. Harry wanted his breakfast, and didn't care who heard his demanding squeals.

"Shush, Harry. Come on, son." She picked him from the cot and glanced at the sleeping form, snuggled under the blankets. Bill was still fast asleep. Agnes hurried from the bedroom.

She went through the motions of feeding her son and getting him ready for the day that he would spend at the nursery. She packed him some food, clean nappies, a change of clothes and his favourite toy car into a small cloth sack, while he played on the rug. She packed her own dinner of beef paste sandwiches and a flask of tea into her bag. She put her gas mask over her shoulder, put Harry's mask into the pram and was ready to set out to go to work, but her legs didn't feel strong enough to carry her.

She wished she could be more like her mam. Her mother would have known what to do. Trudie had wasted no time making sure Agnes's sin was covered over and hidden. Her mother was to blame for the awful predicament she found herself in now. Perhaps Trudie hadn't been as wise as Agnes always thought her to be. She certainly hadn't thought ahead to the consequences of her plan.

Polly came down the stairs with Alice in her arms. "I thought I heard you moving about. You're not going in to work today, are you?"

"Why wouldn't I?" Agnes tied her scarf around her head.

"Your Bill only got home yesterday! They won't expect you in work. He's only got a week before he goes back."

"Look, Polly." Agnes didn't know where to begin. "I know you think Bill and I are…, well…" She couldn't go on. Polly's puzzled, innocent looking face was more than she could bear.

"Go on!" Polly insisted. "You and Bill are what?"

"Nothing, Polly. I'm just tired. I have to get to work. I don't want to be late." She put Harry in the pram, loaded the bags at his feet with his gas mask and pushed it to the door. "Be careful, Polly." She tried to think of some words that would explain the whole sorry mess, but nothing came to her. "Just take care, will you."

"Don't worry, Agnes. I won't break. I'll get over it eventually. Most women do, don't they? I'll be all right."

Agnes knew that Polly thought she'd been referring to her situation with Charlie's death, and with the way she was treated by his family at the funeral, but she couldn't tell her any different.

She left the house in the cold, dark, pre-dawn frost and set out to town. She couldn't tell Polly that she would be spending the day with a murderer. She was convinced that Bill was a killer and she knew that he wanted nothing more than to have Polly by his side. Goodness knows what lengths he would go to, to make that happen.

Chapter Eleven, Madness

Harry came running towards her on his stubby toddler legs and though she was bone weary, she lifted him high and spun him as he liked her to. "Hello, little man. Have you had a nice day with Auntie Hilda and your friends?"

"He's been good as gold, Agnes." Hilda bustled over, a baby in her arms. "They're not all as easy as your Harry. I've had me work cut out today. I think we might have to take on another lass to help, or stop taking in more babies."

"That's good news for the nursery. You and Enid must be making a mint with this little lot!" Agnes looked around at all the infants and toddlers playing on the floor or in wooden playpens. "You must have twenty bairns in here."

"Thirty when they're all here at once, but some lasses work in shifts, so we don't have 'em all at the same time, thank goodness. We wouldn't be able to cope!"

"You will still have room for your Alice and this one, won't you?" Agnes asked, uncertainly, touching her large tummy.

"Don't you fret yourself. We'll find room for our own kin. I can't believe you're still working, lass. You've only got a week or so to go, haven't you?"

"Aye, but Harry was, err," she almost said late, but everyone thought he was early, so his birth date would tie-in with her marriage to Bill.

"Oh, aye, I remember. He was early, wasn't he?" Hilda said, absently. "Well, it'll come when it's ready, they usually do."

"Yes, I suppose so." Agnes busied herself getting Harry into the pram and tucking the blankets around him. She'd nearly slipped up, and Hilda was too close to the truth to make any more slip-ups. She knew her mother would not have mentioned anything to her sister. The shame would have been too much for Trudie to bear. Hilda knew nothing, and it had to stay that way.

"When is Polly thinking of going back to work? She'll not want to lie around the house with your Bill home, will she? She wouldn't want to be under his feet. Best thing for her is to get back to work. She needs to take her mind off that Jack the lad she just buried and get on with her life."

"I don't know what Polly's plans are, Auntie. I'll ask her. She's still feeding Alice herself, but I think she'll put her on the bottle in a day or two, she's more than a week old, after all."

Agnes didn't mention her husband. She'd been thinking about him all day but hearing his name made the small hairs on the back of her neck stand on end.

"Afore I forget, did you hear about George, your old boss at the café?"

"What about him?" Agnes was mildly interested.

"He's scarpered, that's what! Enid saw his sister down the market. I think they went to school together. Dorothy, isn't it? His sister's name?"

"Aye, she's called Dorothy." Agnes was half listening to Hilda. Her mind was racing ahead to when she would get home. She didn't want to face Bill again after what she'd heard last night, but she couldn't escape it.

"...so anyway, he left in May, just after he shut up shop and she thinks he joined the merchant Navy to get away from the debt collectors, and they've been after her for the brass he owes ever since. I told Enid, they can't get blood from a stone, so she'll be all right. Anyway, he got wounded and he's back now. It's a right bit of gossip, though. Kept us going all day, that did. Well, what do you think on it? Who'd a thought it of George, eh?"

"I hope he's all right. The Germans started attacking the merchant ships in June, didn't they?" Agnes frowned at her auntie.

"He'll come up smelling of roses that one, you mark my words. Got the luck of the devil hasn't he?" Hilda didn't really need an answer. She was happy to rattle on, telling the gossip and relishing the details.

"I'd best be off, Auntie Hilda."

"Sorry, lass. I'm keeping you from your tea, and you'll want to get back to your Bill. How long's he home for?"

"Just a week I think." Agnes couldn't help thinking it would be seven days too long.

"Well, you make the most of him. What them lads have to put up with, don't bear thinking about. You make sure you spoil him and send him back with some happy memories."

Agnes shuddered. "See you later, Auntie Hilda."

"Aye, lass. See ya tomorra."

Agnes bounced the pram down the two steps outside the nursery building and began to push it towards the bridge over the river. Although it was cold, she didn't want to hurry. Her steps were slow as she made her way home. She was in no rush to see her husband again. When Harry began moaning and fretting, she realised that he would be hungry and she couldn't dally any longer. Resignedly, she began to walk faster and soon reached the corner of Chapel Street. As she neared her front door, she could hear laughter and music. She hesitated a few seconds before opening the door and pulling the pram inside behind her.

"You're back, then!" Bill's loud and jovial voice sliced through her nerves. "Thought you'd got lost! Polly said you should have been home half an hour ago."

"I got talking to Auntie Hilda. You know how she goes on." Agnes said the first thing that came into her head.

"Aye, me mam could talk the hind leg off a donkey if it stood still long enough." Polly shook with laughter, and Agnes was appalled to see that her cousin's cheeks were red. "We made a bit of corned-beef hash for tea." Polly laid plates on the table, and then brought a large pan from the range. "Your Bill is a right laugh, Agnes. We've had a grand day, and he's helped with peeling the spuds when Alice wanted a feed."

"Where did that come from?" Agnes pointed at the shiny new wireless that stood on her mantelpiece. "We don't have money for luxuries like that, Polly."

"I bought it on me way back from seeing me mam and dad this morning." Bill rose from the chair where he'd been sitting with the baby. "Thought this place could do with a bit of music to cheer it up, it were like a morgue in here."

Agnes slowly took off her coat then lifted Harry from the pram and set him on his feet. The toddler stood close to Agnes's skirts, hiding from the loud man in the room who was like a stranger to him.

"Well, Polly has just lost the father of her child!" Agnes pointed out firmly. "You can't expect things to be jolly."

"All your Polly needed was a tot or two of rum and some good company. Ain't that right, Poll?"

Polly had the grace to blush as Agnes took a sharp intake of breath. "Your Charlie isn't cold in his grave and you're behaving like, well, like..."

"I can't hide away forever, Agnes. You said so yourself. You can't have it both ways. Either I forget him and move on or I spend the rest of me life living like a widow in mourning. I'm not a widow, as you so clearly pointed out yesterday, so I don't need to wear black and I'm free to do whatever I want."

"And if she wants to have some fun, where's the harm in that?" Bill raised his eyebrows at Agnes and didn't try to hide the sly implication in his words. "The wireless is a gift to you both. Think of it as an early Christmas present seeing as how I won't be here to celebrate the festive season with my lovely wife and family."

Agnes cringed inside, and hoped Polly couldn't hear the sarcastic undertone in his voice.

"See how generous I am with my hard-earned cash!" Bill waved his hand theatrically at the gleaming machine.

"There's better things you could spend that money on." Agnes deliberately made it clear to Bill that she knew what money he had spent on the wireless.

"Don't look a gift horse in the mouth, Agnes." Polly said as she spooned hash onto the plates.

"Be careful to mind what your cousin tells you, Agnes. Gift horses can have a nasty nip if you don't treat 'em right." Bill said as he took his seat at the table, giving Agnes a spiteful glare over Polly's bowed head.

Agnes swallowed nervously. Before last night, she might have retaliated and stood up for herself and her opinions, but now she knew what her husband was capable of, she felt it wiser to stay quiet and back down.

She sat quietly, with Harry on her lap, feeding him from her plate and snatching the odd mouthful for herself. "Your mam asked when you'd be going back to work. There's a place for Alice in the nursery." Agnes tried to start a normal conversation in an attempt to lighten the tension.

"She's not weaned onto the bottle yet." Polly said around a spoonful of hash.

"Well, you'll need to start paying your way here again, soon. I can't carry us both, Polly. What with Bill's baby due any day." She emphasised that the baby she carried was Bill's child, hoping to gain favour from her husband.

"Agnes. Have some sympathy for your cousin." Bill patted Polly's hand that rested on the table. "She can't go back to work so soon after losing the baby's dad, and like she said, Alice isn't weaned off the tit yet."

Agnes blushed. To hear a man talk of breastfeeding, and in such a coarse way, was offensive to her, but she couldn't rise to him. She didn't dare.

"If it's a question of money, I'll pay Polly's share of the bills until she can face going back to work."

Both women looked shocked, and Polly's mouth fell open. "You can't do that, Bill! It wouldn't look right!"

"That's madness! How would that look to folks? What would your mam and dad say?" Agnes added her voice to Polly's.

"To hell with things looking right for everyone else. I've had a belly full of making things look right. I can do what I want with *my* money."

Agnes knew that he'd stressed the word, 'my' for her benefit and she closed her eyes and turned her head away from his sickening smile. "So be it." Agnes said quietly. "Have you had enough, son?" she asked Harry, as her son turned away from the next spoonful of dinner. "Let's get you ready for your bed then."

Agnes left the table and went to set the kettle to boil for some warm water to wash her son. She busied herself getting Harry cleaned and changed and listened to the lively chatter between Bill and her cousin over the steady drone of the wireless. This can't be happening, she told herself. What could she do? She couldn't tell Polly to leave him alone, she'd think Agnes had gone mad to suggest that Bill was making a play for her. Polly would see Bill as nothing more than a kind benefactor, and that would suit Bill's purposes down to the ground. She could do nothing to prevent the mess that was coming. She knew Polly, and she knew Bill. Polly was easily led, easily fooled, and would believe black was white if it meant she was getting the best of the situation. Bill was a determined opportunist and Agnes knew he would make the most of his present circumstances. She couldn't wait to get away from them and when Harry was ready for bed, she took him to the bottom of the stairs. "I'm turning in, it's been a long day."

"Keep them blankets warm tonight, love." Bill sneered at her. "I missed out on the home comforts last night, but I'll not make the same mistake again."

Agnes cringed, but realised there was nothing she could do to prevent his unwanted attention. She couldn't make a fuss with Polly in the house to hear her protests. If she did, it would be the topic of conversation with the gossip mongers for weeks if anyone got to know that her marriage was a mockery.

Agnes didn't dare fall asleep. She was beyond being tired. She was exhausted. She'd had no sleep the previous night and had been on her feet all day at the mill. She was dreading her husband joining her, but she could still hear the music from the wireless, and the quiet voices of Bert and Polly were lifting and falling, interspersed with laughter. Polly didn't take long to put

Charlie Watson firmly in her past. She probably didn't realise that Bill was flirting with her. Polly was so naïve, for all her wantonness.

Agnes shuddered. She was cold as ice. When the cramps began, she thought it was because she'd been shivering so hard. When she felt the wetness gush from between her legs, she knew it was the baby. She lifted from the bed and pulled off the soiled sheets, wrapping them into a ball to wash later. She got out the spare sheet and made the bed again before getting dressed.

When she got to the bottom of the stairs, clutching her belly, two flushed faces turned towards her. Bill was sitting on the rag-rug, leaning his back against Polly's legs. They both held a glass of dark spirits in their hands.

Polly jumped up quickly, and Agnes was sure she saw a flash of guilt cross her friend's face. "Is it the bairn, Agnes?" Polly asked, a little too brightly. "Shall I send Bill for the midwife?"

"I'm supposed to go to the infirmary. They said it could be bum first, it hadn't turned last time I was checked."

"Should we send for an ambulance?" Bill asked, getting slowly to his feet.

"Get the midwife first, Polly." Agnes bent double as more ferocious pains gripped her. "Mrs Wilks will know what to do, and if, ooooooh, just a minute…" Agnes began to pant while the pain ripped through her insides.

"I'm on my way." Polly grabbed her coat and was putting her arms into the sleeves when Bill stopped her.

"You can't go and leave me with her like this." Bill took hold of Polly's arm. "What will I do if the bairn wants to come out before you get back?"

"It'll be hours yet, Bill. Don't panic. I'll be back soon." Polly dashed out of the door.

"How far away does the midwife live?" Bill asked, scratching his head.

"Not far. Don't worry, Bill. I'm not about to give birth just yet. You'll have time to get down to the Crown Arms where you can stay until it's all over with." Agnes straightened her back as the pain subsided and she sank into the fireside chair. "Just wait until Polly gets back, will you? You've nowt to fret about." She didn't like to ask him to hang around, but knew she couldn't handle the bairns if they woke.

"Aye, well, if you say so."

"I do say so, Bill." Agnes felt the strong pull of the next contraction and doubled over in the chair, groaning loudly.

Bill began to pace the floor, running his hand through his hair. "Bloody hell, Agnes! How much longer?"

Agnes waited for the pain to pass and leant back to look up at her husband. "Are you impatient to see your little one?" She asked with a note of steely irony in her voice. "Will you be any kinder to this one than you are to my Harry?"

"What's that supposed to mean?"

"You've never looked at him since you got back. He's supposed to be your son, Bill. What are people going to think if you don't even talk to him? You could at least pretend, for the sake of the boy if nothing else. You made a promise to my mother, but I suppose that means nothing to you since she's not around to remind you."

"I promised to support your bastard. I never said I'd treat him as me own. I'll pay for his keep, but that's as far as it goes. He's not mine and I won't pretend he is."

"That's not fair, Bill. He's a child. He's not responsible for this mess we're in."

"No, Agnes. That guilt rests fair and square on your shoulders, so you've only yourself to blame if you think your bastard got the short end of the deal."

"I'll admit my sin. I know I did wrong, but I don't have murder on my conscience." She blurted before she could stop herself.

"So how come your dad ended up dead? I know he didn't fall in the river as the police told your mam. He was pushed and I've got a good idea who did the shoving!"

"You're mad! You don't have a clue about what happened that night, so don't pretend you do. But while we're talking about pushing and shoving, I think you know more than a thing or two about that method of doing away with someone."

"What's that supposed to mean?" Bill stopped his pacing and stared down at her with narrowed eyes.

Agnes shrank back into the chair. "You need to be more careful what you say when you've had a few too many." She gripped the chair arms as another pain tore through her stomach. She let out a loud moan and lifted her knees

"We're here, Agnes!" Polly burst into the room with Mrs Wilks at her heels.

"Get your coat on, young man. We don't need you around

for this bit." The midwife hurried to take off her coat then rushed to Agnes's side. "How long between 'em, love?"

"About two or three minutes, I think." Agnes gasped.

"Are you still here?" Mrs Wilks aimed her remark at Bill.

"We haven't finished this conversation." He threatened, menacingly as he pulled on his jacket. "Not by a long chalk!"

Polly watched him leave and turned to Agnes. "What did he mean? He looked fit to spit nails into you. What's going on?"

Agnes let out a moan and drew her legs up to her chest again. "Oh, I think it's coming," she groaned.

"No time for chatting, lass. Get that kettle boiling and fetch me some clean sheeting. This bairn is in a right hurry to get born."

Two hours later, Agnes held a robust baby boy in her arms. The lusty cries announced his arrival to the household, waking Alice and Harry from their sleep. The toddler now sat by his mother's side peering up at his baby brother with large eyes. Polly sat at the other side of the bed, cradling baby Alice in her arms.

"It's over, at last." Polly smiled at Agnes. "After all these months of waiting, we have our babies and they're both little belters."

"I'm glad it was easier this time." Agnes admitted. "I was scared it was going to be the same as Harry. If this one had come bottom first, as they thought he would, I think I would have died. I couldn't have gone through another bad delivery."

"Well, thank goodness you didn't have to. What you going to call him?"

"I don't know. I suppose Bill will want a say in that." Agnes shrugged. She didn't care what the child would be named. She wasn't surprised that she didn't feel the rush of emotion for the baby that she had felt when Harry was born. Harry was the son of the man she loved. This baby belonged to Bill. She had disliked Bill before, but in the last day or so she had realised what a monster he was, and now she hated him. She didn't want anything more to do with him. She had decided that she would ask him for a divorce and release him from his obligation. Never mind that she would be ostracised. She could live with that. She couldn't bear to live with Bill now she knew he was responsible for killing her mother. He could take his child with him. She didn't want it. She could never love the child of a monster. She could feel pity for it, but she could never love it as she loved Harry. She reached for her older child and pulled him close to her.

"Don't you fret, Harry. Your mammy still loves you."

"He's too young to get jealous, Agnes." Polly said. "I wouldn't worry about that."

They turned when they heard the door downstairs bang shut.

"That'll be your Bill. I'll make meself scarce." Polly got up to leave.

"No, Poll. Don't go." Agnes grabbed her cousin's hand. "Not yet. Please!"

"Don't be daft, Agnes. Bill will want to spend time with his new bairn and you. I'll be in the way. I'll just be though there." She pointed to the next bedroom. "I'll take Harry with me, just for tonight, so you can get some rest."

"No, I want Harry to stay with me." Agnes cuddled her older son closer.

"All right, love. You know best." Polly called down the stairs, "Your new son is up here, Bill. Mrs Wilks knew where to find you, didn't she?" She turned back to Agnes. "I bet he's three sheets to the wind," she whispered.

Bill pounded up the stairs two at a time and fell through the bedroom door. "Where is he? Where's me boy?"

"Take him!" Agnes held the infant out to her husband. "He's all yours."

Bill stood still, staring at the tiny bundle in Agnes's arms. "He's so small."

"Course he is, you daft thing." Polly pushed him to the bed. "Go on. Pick him up. He won't break. You held my Alice and she survived!"

Bill stepped forward and took the baby into his arms. Agnes watched his face transform. If she didn't know better, she would say that Bill was showing a softer side to his nature, but she knew that a softer side didn't exist in monsters. He was hard and mean to his core.

"We'll call him Thomas, after me granddad. He'll like that, will me dad." Bill gazed down at his son as if he couldn't lift his eyes away. "Is that all right with you, Agnes?"

Agnes couldn't believe she had been asked for her opinion. "Call him what you want, it's all the same to me."

"Thomas it is then." Bill sat on the edge of the bed, cradling the infant close to his chest.

Polly left the room with a smile aimed at Agnes and closed the door behind her.

"Bill." Agnes waited until he turned to look at her. "I've been thinking, and I want a divorce."

"What?" Bill's face screwed into a dark frown. "We can't get divorced. Divorces cost money. Lots of money. Father Brennan would never allow it. Besides, we have this little one now to take care of."

"We have two little ones to take care of, but that doesn't make a difference to how I feel. I don't love you and you don't love me. We were daft to agree to this in the first place. We should call it quits now before anyone else gets hurt because of our lies."

"I won't let you divorce me, Agnes. You can't. You have no reason and the lawyers will want to know why you'd want to leave me. You won't be able to tell them the truth without it all coming out and you're the last one to want to have those old coals raked over. You've got too much to lose. We both have. We can't get divorced."

"You've got money. Lots of it. My mother's money would pay for a divorce and you'd still have lots left. I know you haven't spent any of it. Well, at least I haven't seen any evidence that you've spent it, except the wireless downstairs."

"What about the church? Catholics don't get divorced. It's just not done! We'd be shunned. I'd be a laughing stock!"

"I don't care what the church or anyone else thinks. This is our business, no one else's."

"What about the bairns? I thought you wanted a respectable home for your bastard! I've kept me word on that score. He wants for nowt. You'll not keep me from seeing this little one. He's mine, and I'll not have you take him away from me."

"You can have him." Agnes said quietly.

"What did you say?" Bill looked aghast.

"I said you can have him. I don't want him. Take him. Take him wherever you want. I don't care. I don't! I don't care!" Agnes began to sob and couldn't stop. She didn't know where the sound was coming from, but it felt as though her chest was being torn open. She clutched at Harry, who began to cry, and then the new baby started to yell too.

"Polly, get in here!" Bill shouted. "She's gone mad!"

Agnes could hear the doctor's deep voice downstairs. He had given her a sleeping tablet, and told her she'd be good as new in the morning, and if she wasn't they were to send for Mrs Wilks. She could hear him talking with Bill and Polly, but couldn't hear what they were saying. Her world had gone foggy, and she couldn't think straight.

She remembered asking Bill for a divorce, and telling him she didn't want his baby, but after that, things went hazy. Harry! Where was Harry? She needed to hold her son, but he wasn't there. She didn't have the strength to call out. She mumbled his name, and felt herself falling into a deep dark hole.

Agnes spent the next few hours in a deep, drug-induced sleep. Eventually, when her brain began to function again, her mind was filled with nightmares. Her father's face loomed over her, his features contorted with anger and pain. She tried to talk to him, but the sound of the words got stuck in her throat. Her father's face was replaced by that of her mother. Trudie was singing softly, *"My bonnie lies over the ocean..."*

"Mam!" Agnes called in her mind, but the words were silent and went unheard.

Andrew appeared, silhouetted by bright light at the far end of a long dark tunnel. He was running, but she couldn't tell if he were running away or towards her. "Andrew!" She tried to run down the tunnel, but her legs felt as if they were moving through deep water. She was drowning. She was in the river Calder struggling to stay afloat. Her dad's body was floating next to her and she screamed.

"I'm here, Agnes." Polly's voice broke into her dream and she felt the weight of her friend sitting on the bed beside her. "Wake up, love. You're having a bad dream."

"Polly?" Agnes opened her eyes to a gloomy room. "Harry! Where's Harry?"

"He's downstairs playing. Bill's keeping an eye on him and the two babes, you don't have to worry. Are you thirsty? The doctor said you would be when you woke up. Here's a nice pot of tea I just made. I heard you stirring and thought you'd be ready for this."

"Thanks, Poll." Agnes sat up and took the cup. Her head still felt foggy, but she began to remember little snapshots of the previous day. "I had the baby. A boy?"

"Yes, Thomas is downstairs. I fed him for you. I've plenty of milk for the two of 'em until you're strong enough to feed him yourself."

"Oh." Agnes nodded, not daring herself to speak.

"Bill said you got a bit upset, and started saying some silly things."

"Did I?" Agnes could remember what she'd said.

"I told him you didn't mean it, and you'd be saying it because of the pain of the birth and what have you. You didn't mean it, did you?"

"I don't suppose I did if you say so." Agnes took a sip of the hot tea.

"That's a girl. Drink that down, you'll soon feel better. Shall I get the baby for you?"

"No!" Agnes said, sharply. "I mean," she tried again in a calmer tone, "I'm not ready, I'm still half asleep with that tablet the doctor gave me."

"Do you want me to give you a few minutes to come around?"

"Yes, please, Polly. I'll be right as rain when I've had this." She lifted the teacup and tried to smile at her friend.

"All right, love. Shout me when you're ready, we're just downstairs."

"Thanks, Poll." Agnes watched her close the door quietly and tried to stem the tears that welled into her eyes. How was she going to cope? What would she do now? The previous day's events came back clearly now, and she began to wish she'd never woken. She wanted a divorce, but Bill had made it clear that he wouldn't agree to it, and without his consent, or a good enough reason, she couldn't take it to the courts. She had good reason, but there was no way on God's Earth that she could tell anyone without also telling them her part in the sad, sorry story.

She had given birth to the baby, but she didn't know how she could be a mother to Bill's child. She would have to pretend to love it. Their secret had to stay hidden. The only way was for her to keep up the charade of the loveless marriage and play the part of the doting wife and mother to both her children. If only Bill would leave her alone, she might be able to pull it off. If he didn't insist on having his marital rights, it would be bearable, but the thought of him taking his pleasure with her, brought goose bumps to her skin.

Maybe she could talk to him about it. Perhaps if she

agreed that he could take his pleasure elsewhere as long as he was discreet. Polly had been carrying-on with a married man. It wasn't so unusual. Perhaps Bill would find someone to accommodate him. Then she realised that Polly was the only other woman he would want, and she couldn't do that to her cousin. Polly didn't deserve to be shackled to a murderer any more than Agnes did. What about baby Alice, Harry, and now Thomas? Her dad had died because of her love for Andrew. Andrew was living in exile because of their love. Her mam had been killed by her husband. Agnes was trapped. She would have to continue the charade, no matter how she felt about it. Too many lives had been wrecked already, and more could be ruined if she didn't.

She finished the tea and took a deep breath. "I can do this," she told herself before she called out for Polly to bring the children to her.

Chapter Twelve, Chance encounter

Bill was getting ready to report to his unit who were temporarily based in a town a few miles away. He would be leaving first thing in the morning. She knew he would be confined to barracks until they shipped him out to goodness knows where, and she was relieved. At last she could have some peace. During the last few days she had convinced herself that she could cope with him being around, knowing that it wouldn't be for long. The doctor had told Bill to go gently with Agnes, and not to expect anything on the physical side of things, because of her delicate condition. She knew the doctor had been referring to her mental health, but was happy to go along with the doctor's diagnosis if it meant that Bill would leave her alone in the bedroom.

Agnes spoke to Bill only when she had to and hoped Polly wouldn't guess at the growing distance between her and her husband. Thomas was an easy baby so far, thank goodness. Even his birth had been straightforward compared with Harry's. Thomas was much smaller, and she had suffered no damage when he slipped from her body after three or four pushes. She couldn't take to him, though. The love wasn't there. She felt nothing when she looked at her new baby, and the times she felt obliged to hold him, she couldn't wait to put him down or pass him to someone else.

She didn't feel the need to soothe him when he cried, or make him more comfortable when he messed, and she didn't want to feed him. Fortunately, Bill and Polly were eager to step in when the baby needed anything. Polly was happy to offer a breast to the baby when Agnes made excuses that her milk hadn't come in yet. Bill's son took to the bottle straight away too, and Agnes was happy that she wouldn't have to endure the close contact of breastfeeding with, what she considered, was the child of a monster. She didn't mention that she had taken Epsom salts to ensure her body would not produce the milk her baby needed. Thomas was content with a bottle and Agnes had been surprised when Bill offered to feed his son.

"That's it my son." Bill cooed as the baby latched onto the bottle teat. "Drink it down, there's a lad."

"You're a natural, Bill!" Polly commented as she put her own baby to her breast at the other side of the hearth.

"I think I'll take Harry for some fresh air." Agnes couldn't stand to watch the scene of domestic harmony when she felt so tense inside.

"It's blowing a gale out there." Polly said. "Are you mad?"

"I must be." Agnes snapped. "That's what you think anyway, so you won't be disappointed when I prove you right, will you?"

"Don't be daft, Agnes. You know I didn't mean it that way." Polly frowned. "We know it's the baby blues making you a bit down, don't we, Bill?"

Agnes looked at her husband for a response, but he made a big fuss about getting the baby to burp. "Come on, Thomas." Bill patted the tiny infant's back gently. "You'll have room for more if you get them nasty bubbles out of your tummy."

"Put him over your shoulder, Bill. That always works with my Alice."

Agnes closed her eyes and turned to Harry, who was standing by the door with his thumb firmly inserted into his mouth. "Let me get your coat, Harry." Agnes wanted to leave the cloying atmosphere of her house. She got Harry dressed for the blustery conditions and tied a woollen scarf around her head. "I'm taking the pram. You won't need it, will you?"

Polly shook her head. "No, you take it. The babies can sleep in the bottom drawer together. There's room for both babies if we top and tail 'em."

"See if you can get us a nice bit of something for our tea, lass." Bill pulled out some bank notes from his trouser pocket and held them out to Agnes.

"That's enough money to feed us for a month." Agnes's mouth fell open at the unexpected generosity.

"Well, I'm off tomorrow so I want a nice send-off. See if you can get some best frying steak from that butcher on the market. And another bottle of rum wouldn't go amiss."

"But that will cost a fortune, Bill!" Polly chuckled and her eyes sparkled in the firelight. "But I suppose you're worth it."

"Some might think so!" Agnes couldn't help sniping as she took the proffered money.

"Are you sure you're up to walking all the way to the market?" Polly asked. "It's only five days since Thomas arrived, and the doctor said he was worried about you."

"I'm not made of glass, Poll, but if I don't get out of here soon I really will go mad." Agnes opened the door and pushed the pram out into the gusting wind. She slammed the door behind her, cutting off the good-natured banter that continued between her husband and her friend. She didn't want to listen to them playing happy families together.

In another world, she might have been happy for them. If Polly had realised Bill's feelings for her much sooner, her cousin would probably be married to him by now, and the babies they crooned over would be ones they'd made together. Agnes couldn't stay cross with Polly for long. The girl was responding to Bill's kindness in the only way she knew how. Her cousin had always been a flirt and popular with the lads because she didn't know any other way to be. It was unfortunate that Polly had picked Charlie out from the crowd of admirers that flocked around her. She didn't know he was married, but by the time she discovered he was, it was too late. She was in love with him and wouldn't give him up. Poor Bill hadn't stood a chance since the day Charlie Watson made his move. Now Charlie was gone, and Bill was wasting no time in trying to fill the hole in Polly's heart.

Agnes shook herself as she walked along, pushing the pram to the market at the other side of Thornbury. How could she think of Bill in sympathetic terms? He'd as good as admitted that he'd killed her mam. The conversation they'd been having before the midwife turned up and kicked him out had not been resumed. It seemed Bill was happy to let things lie and hadn't mentioned it since that night. Agnes had been afraid to bring it up again. She hadn't felt strong enough, emotionally or physically, to deal with the implications of his confession. She didn't know whether she would ever be strong enough.

Rain started spattering down on them, and Agnes stopped to button the rain canopy to the hood on the pram to protect Harry from the downpour.

"My, this weather is wilder than the storms I saw on the Atlantic."

The familiar voice boomed from behind her and she whirled quickly. "George! What are you doing here?" Agnes was surprised to see her old employer grinning at her through the rain.

"Do you have time for a cuppa, Agnes? We can get out of the rain for a bit over there." George pointed to the market café.

"I'd love a cuppa, George." Agnes didn't hesitate. This man had been kindness itself to her in the past and she was curious to know whether the gossip mongers had been right about him.

With the pram safely parked at the top of the cellar steps of the café, Agnes settled by the steamy window with Harry on her lap and watched George ordering the tea. He looked thinner, and she noticed he walked with a slight limp.

"Where have you been hiding, George?" she asked as he placed two mugs on the table and a small glass of milk.

"I got the bairn some milk, is that all right?"

"Perfect, George." Agnes helped her son to take a drink from the glass. "Thank you for this. I was ready for a sit down and a rest."

"You been working hard? I heard you got set on at the mill."

"I've had a few days off. I have a new baby at home now, he's five days old. Polly has a baby too, a little girl."

"Congratulations to you both, but what you doing out so soon? From what I know about havin' bairns, it takes a couple of weeks at least afore a lass can get back on her feet."

"Them's old-fashioned ideas, George. There's a war on now, remember." Agnes quipped, making light of her situation. "Talking of which, I heard some things about you too."

"Oh, aye?" George lifted his eyebrows. "What you heard?"

"That you ran off to sea just as you said you would."

"You heard right, then." George took a sip of his tea and winked at her over the rim of his mug. "Wanted to be like that pirate that gets all the girls. Bluebeard, is it?"

"Oh, George!" Agnes laughed. "Go on, then. Tell me all about it. Where did you get to and what did you see?"

"Well, I didn't get to see many lasses, but I saw a lot of sea. I worked me arse off, pardon my French, and then got sunk by a submarine and left for dead in the water."

"Oh, no! George, how awful!" Agnes was shocked by the blunt statement that didn't begin to explain the horror of what she imagined his experience would have been like. "What happened?"

"We got torpedoed. The ship went down quick like, and the lads scrambled for any bit of floating stuff they could grab hold of. I was in a bad way. If it weren't for me mate, I might have been done for, good and proper."

"Were you wounded, George?" Agnes asked.

"Me leg caught a lump of shrapnel and me head took a bashing, but I'm all right now."

Agnes shook her head. "This war is awful, isn't it, George? The news gets worse every day."

"Aye, well, I can't do owt else to stop 'em, now I'm disabled and out of the service. I hope our lads can give 'em hell because they deserve it! Every last one of 'em."

"How did you survive? What happened after the ship sank?"

"I wasn't alone, lass. There were about a hundred of us that played dead. None of the lads wanted to be taken prisoner. Well, I didn't play dead. I was knocked out, like. But when the other boys saw that the little rowing boat full of German sailors left me alone when they thought I was dead, they all pretended to be dead as well, see."

"So the Germans didn't check any of you?"

"I don't think they could be bothered. They only surfaced to check what kind of stuff we'd been carrying so they could tell their captain. We'd have been extra mouths to feed so I think they were glad they didn't have to take any of us on board. I wouldn't have liked to go on one of them things anyway. It would be like being inside a tin can." George shook his shoulders and blew a raspberry, and Harry laughed at the older man.

"Oh, George, you make it sound so ordinary, but I bet it was very frightening for you all."

"Well, to tell the truth, I didn't know owt about it until I woke up in another ship. We got picked up by one of our own that was following us. Now I'm back here with nowt to do but twiddle me thumbs."

"Are you staying at your Dorothy's house?"

George blew through his pursed lips, making Harry giggle. "That woman! She's enough to send a man barmy. I tell you, if we were to send her to Germany, old Hitler would surrender in less than a day!"

Agnes smiled. "Oh, George, she can't be that bad."

"No, she isn't." George shook his head slowly. "She took me in and gave me a home, and she didn't have to. I know I left her in a right old pickle."

"What are you going to do now? Do you know?"

"Well, I've been thinking of making me way to Ireland."

Agnes's heart missed a beat. Andrew had gone to Ireland.

"I've done me bit in this war, and I'm no good to work on

the ships anymore. I've no ties apart from our Dorothy and she makes it plain that she'd be better off with me out from under her feet. So I reckon I'd be as well going somewhere where the war can't touch me anymore. The south is neutral, so if I can find a way to get over there, that's where I'm headed."

"I hear Cork is a lovely place." Agnes tried to sound casual, but her insides felt wobbly.

"All of the south is meant to be like a picture postcard. The grass there is green as emeralds. That's why they call it the Emerald Isle. I'd like to see as much of it as I can. Travel around like, work here and there to pay me way as I go."

"Do you think you might visit Cork on your travels?"

"I might. What's in Cork to make you mention it twice? Do you have some family there?"

"Not exactly, George." Agnes briefly wondered whether she could trust George, but decided it wouldn't be worth the risk to tell him more than he needed to know. "I know someone who went there. That's all. He might still be there, but I'll never be sure."

"He?" George winked. "Old flame is it?"

"Something like that." Agnes smiled with trembling lips. "He meant a lot to me once."

"Before your Bill, eh?"

"Yes." Agnes felt bad to be keeping the details to herself, but no good purpose could be served by telling George the whole sordid tale.

"Tell me his name and if I bump into him, I'll tell him you were asking after him shall I?"

"Oh, George, would you?" She couldn't help the grin that split across her face.

"By the look of that smile, I'd say you'd be glad of a word from him, too. Shall I give him your address?"

"No George, no need for that." Agnes knew that Andrew would know where to find her. "Just tell him," she faltered, wondering what she would say to him if ever she got the chance, and then it came to her, "Tell him it's safe for the snowdrop to honour her promise."

"That's a strange message, but I'm sure I'll remember it, should I come across him. What's his name again?"

"Andrew O'Connor."

"That name rings a bell. Wasn't he the lad the police wanted to question about your dad's accident? His name was in all the papers that's why I remember it."

Agnes went white as the blood drained from her face. She felt faint and took some deep breaths.

"Eeh, lass. Don't take on so. I'm not going to say owt. What's your business is your business."

"George, we had nothing to hide. We did nothing wrong! I swear it!" Agnes whispered.

"I believe, you, Agnes. I know you, and I know you're a good girl. Whatever happened that night your dad died, I know it wouldn't have had owt to do with you."

"Thanks, George." Agnes sighed with relief. "It was an accident, as the coroner said it was, it was complicated, and..."

"Look, lass. You don't have to explain to me. I'm no saint meself, but I do know that sometimes things happen that you can't help. Some things can't be explained easily, and I'm guessing that's what happened with your dad, am I right?"

"In a way." Agnes didn't want to say anymore on the subject.

"Then we'll leave it at that." George patted her hand. "Where you off to now?"

"The butcher. Bill wants some steak for his tea."

"Steak, eh? That'll cost you. Don't he know there's a war on?"

"Aye, he does. He goes off to fight next week. He's leaving tomorra."

"Then you get him the biggest piece of prime rump you can get, lass. He'll need his strength if he's off to fight them buggers. Pardon my French!"

Agnes took her leave of George outside the café and went to do her shopping. She walked with her head high, despite the bitter wind that whipped her scarf about her head. George was going to Ireland and might bump into Andrew. Even though she knew the likelihood of the two men meeting was slim, she couldn't help but hope it might happen. If Andrew was still in Cork, and if George could give him her message, there might be a chance that she could see him again. Even though she was still married to Bill, she hoped Andrew would understand the situation. Agnes felt Bill was just a minor irritation now, and one she could get rid of by divorce one day. Surely it was only a matter of time. The day suddenly seemed brighter, and she walked home with a lighter feeling in her heart than she'd had in months. Knowing that Bill was leaving the next day was like having the cherry on top of her happiness cake.

The wireless was blaring loudly from her house as she

neared the door. She pulled the pram up the step and through into the music-filled room and called over her shoulder, "Will you turn that racket down, I could hear it halfway down the street! The noise will hurt the babies' ears!"

Agnes banged the door closed and began to take her coat off.

"Sorry, Agnes!" Polly jumped up to turn the dial on the wireless.

"Leave it, Polly!" Bill pushed the girl away from the mantelpiece. "You know I can't hear it if you turn it down."

Agnes could tell her husband had been drinking, so decided not to make a scene. "I got us that steak you asked for. A nice bit of rump."

"That sounds grand, Agnes." Polly went to help unload the packages from the pram. "And a big bottle of rum, too." She picked up the bottle and waved it at Bill.

"Just in time, we polished off the last bottle this afternoon, didn't we, Polly?" Bill made a grab for Polly's waist and swung her around in a clumsy attempt at striking a dance pose with her. "We've been having a bit of a drink and dance to celebrate me last day at home, though poor Poll is hindered by her sore ankle."

"So I see." Agnes bit her lips together so she wouldn't be tempted to say anything else. She didn't want to argue with her husband or Polly. Not on his last night at home. Even she couldn't be so cruel. What did it matter whether they were having fun together? It's not as if she cared if he were attracted to another woman. She felt nothing for him, and Polly deserved more than she'd had so far in her love life. She wished they wouldn't act so free with each other while she was there to witness their flirtation. She felt humiliated, but it was obvious Polly hadn't realised what was going on, though Agnes could see from the hateful look on Bill's face that he knew exactly what he was doing.

"I got some pig's knuckles and dried peas too. I thought I'd do us a pea soup to last us for the next few days. I hope you don't mind that I spent more of your money on food for us, Bill." She made a point of mentioning that it was his money, but she wasn't ashamed of spending it. She wouldn't be able to work for a week or so, and money would be short for the girls when Bill left.

"That sounds grand, Agnes." Polly took the parcel of peas and limped to the sink. "I'm sure Bill won't mind providing for his growing family. I'll put these to soak, will I?"

"Put these in too, Polly. Pig's knuckles can be tough if they're not soaked first." Agnes bustled about emptying the pram of the various packets of provisions she had bought. "I got some bacon for your breakfast, Bill." She hoped to sweeten his temper with the offering. "I used the last of our ration as I thought you'd like a good bit of English breakfast inside you before we send you off to war."

"That's grand, Agnes. I'm sure your Bill will appreciate that you thought of him."

"It's nice to be thought of by me own wife." Bill smirked and opened the bottle of spirits. "Anyone would think she'd gone soft in the head the way she's fussing around me and buying me treats with me own money!"

"I can take it back to the butcher if you don't want it, Bill Smithson!" Agnes rose to his bait and immediately regretted her words. She spoke in a softer tone to try to smooth over the spat. "Why can't you just be nice for once?" she asked, her eyes pleading for some understanding. "Can't we have one pleasant evening together without bickering before you leave us?"

"Glad to oblige, my love." Bill leered at Agnes. "Anything you say, Agnes. I'm all yours for the taking, and by the sounds of things, you'll be all mine tonight, doctor's orders or no doctor's orders!"

Agnes froze in the middle of taking Harry from the pram. She held her son close and used his small body to hide her face from Polly and Bill. What had she said?

"Shall we have a tot of rum with our tea to keep the cold out?" Polly tried to hide her embarrassment at the intimate talk. "I'll get some clean glasses from the pantry cupboard."

The wireless was still blaring music from the mantelpiece, and Bill crossed the room to take Agnes into his arms when Glen Miller's, 'In the mood,' began to play. He lifted Harry from her grasp and placed the boy on the floor. "Run away and play, lad, I want to get your mam while she's in the mood for fun."

Agnes had no choice but to allow him to whirl her around the room. His rum-perfumed breath fanned her throat and his hands were everywhere. She tried to hold him off and keep him at a distance, but he was stronger than she was and held her even tighter as she struggled.

"Please, Bill! Not in front of the lad." Agnes tried to push his groping hand away from her bottom.

"He's too young to know what I'm doing." Bill grabbed a handful of her soft flesh and squeezed.

"Ouch! Bill, stop it!" Agnes tried to pull away.

"Get yourselves upstairs if you want to be doing them sort of capers." Polly giggled as she came back into the room and set the glasses on the table. "We don't want to watch your shenanigans, do we, Harry?"

Agnes looked at her son, standing by the pram with his thumb in his mouth. He was looking at her with eyes full of tears. "That's enough, Bill!" She found the strength to push Bill away and went to comfort the child. "It's all right, Harry. We were just playing."

"Spoilsport!" Bill started to pour three glasses of rum.

"Not for me, thank you." Agnes inclined her head to the drinks. "You know I don't like strong spirits."

"You're a right wet blanket; do you know that, Agnes?" Bill picked up the third glass and drank it down. "But it won't go to waste. Me and Polly can have a drink and get a bit merry. We don't need you to join us." Bill sneered at Agnes behind Polly's back. "Your Polly knows how to have fun, don't you, girl?" Bill took hold of Polly's shoulders and spun her into his arms. "You'll have a dance with me, won't you, Poll?"

"Err, Bill, I was about to get our dinner started." Polly turned a worried face to Agnes. "And, and, err, me ankle isn't up to waltzing yet."

"You two enjoy a dance together." Agnes took Harry with her to the pot sink in the corner of the room and sat him on the wooden drainer. "Harry can help me get the vegetables ready." She turned her back on the two revellers. She didn't want to see what liberties Polly would allow her husband to take while they danced. She knew that something had started between them, even if Polly wasn't admitting it to herself yet. Agnes was glad that Bill would be leaving the next day. She couldn't bear the humiliation much longer.

Later that night, Agnes pretended she was asleep when Bill eventually came to bed. He and Polly had stayed up until the small hours, and although the music from the wireless masked their voices, their drunken laughter filtered through the ceiling to Agnes's ears and made her feel angry and afraid. If only Polly had realised years ago how Bill felt for her, none of them would be in this awkward position now. If only Bill could have married Polly, Agnes would have been free to go to the home for unmarried mothers as she'd planned, but then she would not have Harry to love. She couldn't wish things had turned out differently because if they had, she wouldn't have her son.

Bill fell into the bed and put a heavy arm over her side, groping clumsily at her flesh. Agnes moaned sleepily and shrugged him off.

"Oh, no you don't, Agnes Smithson." Bill roughly pulled her onto her back. "You as good as promised me earlier, and you wouldn't see a man go without on his last night, would you?"

"Bill, it's only five days since I had your bairn." Agnes reminded him. "It's not seemly. I'm still sore."

"You're not too sore to go gallivanting around the market all afternoon. If you can walk to the other side of Thornbury and back, you can open your legs for me."

He yanked the hem of her nightdress and Agnes heard it rip. "Bill, please!"

"That's more like it. I like to hear you beg for it." His mouth slobbered over her throat.

Agnes opened to him because she didn't want to make a scene with Polly in the house. "Please don't shout Polly's name at the end?" she asked him. "Spare me that, at least."

Agnes held her breath while Bill laboured over her, and was grateful that it was over in a few minutes. Bill grunted, but didn't shout anything incriminating, and she could breathe easier when he finally dropped into a deep sleep.

Chapter Thirteen, Christmas wishes

Agnes started back at the mill two weeks before the Christmas holidays. Polly looked after the babies at home, and Harry went to the nursery to be looked after by Hilda and Enid. It was a temporary arrangement until Polly felt she could return to work. Agnes was losing patience with her cousin. Alice had been an easy birth, and Polly wasn't limping now, though she used her ankle pain as an excuse. She said she couldn't stand on it for long without it starting to hurt. Polly also pointed out that she'd be saving them money by looking after the babies as they wouldn't have to pay the nursery fees.

Agnes thought that Bill's contribution to Polly's rent was also a deciding feature in the girl's decision to stay at home. He had kept his word and was paying for her cousin's share of the housekeeping too. Although Agnes was happy to accept the money, she was far from happy about the circumstances. It didn't look right in her eyes, and she knew that it wouldn't seem right to anyone else who might hear about the arrangement.

Polly was still supposed to be mourning Charlie, but she hardly mentioned his name. Instead, it was Bill this, and Bill that. She seemed to want to sing his praises every chance she got. Poly's praise of her husband was grating on Agnes's nerves, but she daren't say anything to the girl. Polly thought the sun shone from Bill's backside, and Agnes couldn't tell her otherwise without telling her everything else, and she couldn't do that. She would have to put up with things, and hope Polly would grow tired of hero worship and move on to someone else.

Hilda and Bert had invited the girls for Christmas dinner, and they arrived in a flurry of flapping coats and pram blankets. The wind was howling through the streets as they pushed the laden pram along the cobbles. Polly carried Alice close to her chest and Harry shared his transport with baby Thomas. Harry sat under the hood, and the baby lay at his feet. Agnes had bags dangling from the handle filled with gifts and contributions to the meal. Both girls carried gasmasks and handbags over their shoulders and walked with their heads bowed into the wind.

"I hope Auntie Hilda will like the mittens I knitted for her."

"Oh, Agnes. Them knitting-needles haven't been still since you got them off that second-hand market stall."

"Well, you've got to admit that I saved a fortune. This, 'make do and mend' that all the magazines are telling us to do, is a good idea, you know. I got two woollen jerseys and the needles, and the whole lot cost next to nothing. I got a bagful of wool once I unpicked them and unravelled the yarn."

"I can't wait to see what you knitted for me from that blue yarn. It's such a pretty colour."

"Well, you won't have to wait long."

Hilda welcomed them and soon had everyone seated in the parlour. It was a tight squeeze, but Polly's brothers, James and David sat on the floor with Harry to give the girls room on the small sofa. The pram was pushed behind the sofa where both babies slept peacefully, despite the loud chatter.

"Here's a nice cup of tea to warm you through. By, it's cold as the North Pole out there."

"Thanks, Mam." Polly took a cup from the tray.

"I think me and the lads are having something a bit stronger. I got some bottles of ale for us." Bert got up to go into the kitchen.

"You're not giving the lads ale, Bert! They're not old enough!"

"Come on, Mam! I'm eighteen next month. A bottle of ale isn't going to hurt. It's Christmas!" James protested.

"Well, David is only sixteen, and if he can't have one, neither can you! It's only fair." Hilda turned a stern face to Bert.

"Eeh, lass," Bert said gently. "Our James is signing up next month on his birthday, and we wanted to make this Christmas special didn't we?" He reached to pat his wife's hand. "We can relax the rules for one day, can't we?"

"Well, I think he's too young for that an' all. It don't seem two minutes since he was like that little one there." She pointed at Harry. "But he's off to fight a war. I can't believe it."

"Can we have a drink or not, Mam?" David was eager for permission.

"Oh, well, if your dad thinks it's all right. But just the one, mind you!"

Bert jumped up to get the beer.

"So you're going to be a soldier, James?" Agnes asked the young man.

"No, I want to join the Royal Air Force. I want the chance to shoot some of them bombers down before they can drop their bombs on me family."

"Don't build your hopes up too much, James." Polly told him. "Not everyone can fly. Some have to stay on the ground and fix the planes and what not."

"Well, I won't mind what I do. As long as I can help stop this bombing. Look what they did to Coventry! Manchester and Liverpool got it bad this week. Innocent folks are dying. They're not bothered where the bombs drop, houses, hospitals, schools!"

"We're doing the same to them." Agnes said quietly. "It's not all one-sided."

"Well, they started it first!" David said.

"Let's not spoil our appetites with war talk." Bert handed the boys a bottle of ale each.

Hilda got to her feet and went to turn on the wireless. "How about a sing-song until the chicken's cooked? They'll be playing carols and such today, I expect."

"You got chicken?" Agnes's eyes flew wide. "I haven't tasted chicken in months."

"One of Bert's mates at the fire watch keeps chickens, and he's been rearing some for the pot. We swapped some turnips and leeks and a couple of winter cabbages for a little bantam. It won't go far with all of us, but I've done lots of stuffing and made some Yorkshire puddings, so we've got a feast to come."

"It sounds grand Auntie Hilda. I can't wait."

"We brought some bottled plumbs we got from Frank at the mill. He works in the packing shed and has an allotment. His wife bottles all the fruit, and she makes jam and chutney and suchlike. It's a right little goldmine he's got going on the side." Polly told them.

"Aye, some folks seem to be making the most of this war." Hilda laughed. "Can't blame 'em, can we?"

"I've got some presents in that bag. Shall I give 'em out now before we have our sing-song?" Agnes reached for the bag hanging from the pram handle.

"Eeh, you shouldn't have, Agnes!" Hilda leant to get a better look at the bag. "The government wanted us all to buy bonds to help with the war effort instead of spending brass on presents."

"Well, who's got spare cash for war bonds round here?" James said.

"I didn't spend a lot, and they're all homemade, so don't expect much." Agnes began to hand out her newspaper wrapped parcels.

"We got Harry something as well." Bert disappeared again and brought a brightly coloured little wooden boat from the kitchen. "We did a swap shop at the ironworks. All the lads brought things in that they didn't want anymore, and anyone who put something in, could take something else out. It needed a lick of paint, and I wish I could have got him a new one, but I think it'll do."

"Oh, thanks, Bert. That's lovely." Agnes watched her uncle give the boat to Harry and her son smiled widely.

"We didn't get owt for the babies; they're too young to know owt about it anyway." Hilda turned on the wireless and the sound of orchestral music filled the room. "Well, that's a long way from jingle bells!" She burst into laughter.

Christmas day passed happily. It seemed there'd been an unspoken agreement between the warring nations to keep the peace over the festive season, but when Boxing Day was over, the bombing began again in earnest. Sirens sounded all over the country and Agnes and Polly took to sleeping in the cellar with the children so they wouldn't be disturbed at night. It wasn't ideal, but it was better than getting up and moving everything down two flights of stairs in the blackout.

By the middle of January, they took to sleeping in their beds again. The raids had reduced around Thornbury, but they knew that various parts of the country were still getting bombed. James had enlisted and was doing his initial training near Warrington. Polly worried about her brother, and knew her mam was not happy about her eldest son going to war.

Agnes and Polly were feeding their babies. They were seated either side of the hearth and the fire sent a warm glow over the domestic scene. Harry was already tucked in bed and the girls were enjoying some peace and quiet before they went to bed too.

"Me mam is that worried, but our James wouldn't be put off. He was determined to join up. You heard him at Christmas, didn't you?"

"He's a brave young man." Agnes smiled at her friend then shook her head. "So many are getting killed. When will it end, Polly? I wish we could see an ending to the blasted war soon."

"Well, it can't end soon enough for me mam. She listens to the wireless every night, hoping to hear that we're winning such and such a battle, or someplace has surrendered to us. I don't understand it all meself, and I don't think Mam does either, but me dad explains everything to her. He's clever is me dad."

"Uncle Bert is one in a million. Look how he's come around to little Alice after all he said about not wanting anything to do with you or the bairn before she was born."

"Aye, well. It would have been a different story if Charlie hadn't been blown up." Polly's face crumpled. "I'd rather have Charlie back than see me dad happy over our bairn."

"Now, Polly! Don't get upset." Agnes pulled the bottle from Thomas's mouth and the baby complained. She picked him and put him over her shoulder and began to pat his back. "Charlie is gone, but you have to move on. I thought you were feeling better about the whole business."

"I loved Charlie, Agnes! I can't close the door on my feelings just because he's not here anymore. I wish he were still alive with all me heart. I really do!"

"I didn't mean that you should forget him, Poll." Agnes said, softly. "But you have your mam and dad on your side now, so that has to help, doesn't it?"

"It helps with Alice, but they can't replace what's in here." Polly touched her chest.

"Someone will, one day, you'll see." Agnes thought she knew who that someone might be.

"Charlie was the only one for me, Agnes. I can't see me falling for anyone else like I fell for him. I don't think I could take up with another chap, I still feel so sad."

"I don't know, Polly. Look at how you enjoyed flirting with my Bill." Agnes couldn't help it. Polly had seemed a different girl when Bill was home. She'd been happy and laughed a lot, and Charlie wasn't cold in his grave then.

"What are you saying, Agnes?" Polly's eyes were wide. "I never flirted with your Bill. He was kind to me. He lifted me spirits when I was feeling low. He's a good man, Agnes, but I'd never flirt with him. It wouldn't be fair to you. I'd never do that. What kind of girl do you think I am?" Little Alice began to fret at the empty bottle teat. "Now look what you made me do. She'll have a belly full of wind now."

"I'm sorry, Poll. I didn't mean it like that." Agnes said to keep the peace. "I just meant that, well, it's time that you had some fun, it's allowed, you know."

"You've said it before, I know. I'm not a widow, so I'm free to start to live again." Polly was patting little Alice's back. "I don't feel ready."

"Do you feel ready to come back to the mill and earn your keep?" Agnes thought she might as well throw that comment into the conversation. "You can't expect my Bill to pay for you indefinitely."

"I don't expect owt! He offered, Agnes. You heard him."

"You didn't have to accept, though. What will folks think if they find out?"

"Who's going to tell them?"

"Oh, I'm going to bed." Agnes rose from the chair. "We've been over this a hundred times and you still don't seem to understand, Polly."

"Understand what?"

"That it's humiliating for me to watch how you can live in clover because of my husband's money, while I have to go out to work to keep clothes on my back and food in my belly."

"Well, as you've told me often enough, whatever arrangements you and Bill have over money is your business."

Agnes hurried to the bottom of the stairs. "Well, he hasn't got a bottomless pot," she said over her shoulder, "So you'd better think about what you'll do when he's spent it all."

She didn't wait to hear Polly's reply. She hurried upstairs and put Thomas in his cot. She covered him to make sure he was warm enough, but didn't stoop to kiss him. She climbed into the big bed beside Harry and touched his little face gently. "She'll never understand, Harry. Our Polly is so innocent. She genuinely thinks Bill was simply being nice to her. If she only knew the truth."

Agnes snuggled under the blankets, but her thoughts wouldn't settle. If she still went to church, she would be praying for answers, but she hadn't gone to a service since Bill came home on leave. She couldn't confess to wishing her husband was dead. She tried not to think uncharitable thoughts. Bill didn't deserve to die by enemy fire. He deserved to hang after being judged and found guilty of killing her mother, but she knew that would never happen.

She couldn't worship a God that would allow a war like this one to continue, let alone do nothing about the troubles in her own small life. To Agnes's way of thinking, God had let her down badly. If it weren't for the constrictions of her religion, she would be married to Andrew by now, and little Harry would know the love of a good father instead of the indifference of a monster. Her second child would have been conceived with love, and she would have adored him just as much as she did

Harry. As it was, she could barely look at Thomas without feeling anger at his father for treating her so badly. It wasn't the baby's fault, but she found it difficult to feel anything for the tiny infant.

She had thought she would be able to cope with her life, especially with Bill away, but now she had another worry niggling in her brain, and try as she might, this wouldn't go away. She hadn't had her monthly visitation since the baby came. Up to now, she'd thought it might be usual for a woman to miss a couple of months before regular periods returned. She'd asked a few mothers, at the mill, but they didn't tell her what she wanted to hear. Doris told her that she went six months after the twins were born before her monthlies were regular again. Another lass joked that she didn't get chance to find out because she was pregnant again within a month.

Agnes couldn't pretend to herself any longer when her breasts began to feel tender a few days ago, and then this morning she'd felt unwell. She couldn't deny it any longer. She was having another of Bill's babies, and the thought if it growing inside her made her annoyed and embarrassed. She was infuriated at the way Bill had taken her, only day's after Thomas was born, and she was ashamed that she had let him. Even though she told herself that she'd had no choice, she wished with all her heart that she could have found the courage to refuse him, and the strength to stand up for herself. She knew she would never let him touch her again, no matter what the consequences. She would rather live with the shame of everyone knowing about Harry not being Bill's child, than live under the same roof as her husband and suffer the indignity of his mauling her whenever he wanted to.

She couldn't find it in her heart to love baby Thomas. He was her son, but because Bill was his father, she saw her baby as tainted. She couldn't look at the infant without seeing a picture of his father looming over her and the image filled her heart with hate, leaving no room to love the child. She looked after him and took care of his needs, but she couldn't bring herself to love the offspring of her loveless marriage. Now she would be saddled with another. How would she cope? How could she bear it? She needed to find a way out of this mess, and her thoughts were instantly filled with Andrew. If only he would come for her. If only George could find him and deliver her message. She knew he would come if he knew it was safe.

Then Agnes realised that Andrew would be in for a shock

if he did come looking for her. She was carrying another man's child, had two sons already, and was still married to Bill. So much had changed since Andrew left on that barge a couple of years ago. The world had gone to war and Agnes's life had changed beyond anything she could have imagined. How could Andrew save her from the reality of how things were now? Would he want to? She couldn't blame him if he turned on his heel and ran right back to Ireland. She was no longer the Agnes he'd fallen in love with. She wasn't the young, carefree girl he'd compared with the film star pin-up pictures with firm bodies and pretty smiling faces. She had borne two children and her body carried the signs of motherhood. She already had another on the way. She was fooling herself to think Andrew would still find her attractive. Few men had seen beauty in her before Andrew came along, but even less would give her a second look these days.

She might never know how Andrew would feel. She thought it would be unlikely that George could find him. Ireland is a big place. Despite what she knew to be the facts of the situation, she couldn't help holding out the smallest hope that Andrew would turn up on her doorstep one day. Even though she knew the outcome couldn't be the happy ending she had in her mind, it didn't stop her from wishing for him to come to her and dreaming that he would.

Chapter Fourteen, Love grows

Hilda was elated. "Did you hear the news last night on the wireless?" She took Harry from Agnes's arms and set him on the floor by a pile of wooden blocks. "He loves to build towers with these," she told Agnes. "Just watch him."

Agnes smiled as her son's chubby hands grabbed at the blocks and began to stack them one on top of the other. "He's so clever."

"Now, back to the news. Did you hear we took Tobruk?" Hilda walked Agnes to the door of the nursery. "Sounds like we had help from the Aussie lads, but they were saying on the wireless as how this might be a turning point. We've got them on the run at last!"

"Well, that's good news." Agnes felt Hilda's excitement. "Let's hope it helps to bring this war to an end."

"Well, your uncle said there's still a long way to go. Was your Bill out there in the desert? He might have helped to win that battle. You should be right proud of that husband of yours."

Agnes couldn't help feeling that she hoped Bill had been among the casualties, but immediately felt bad for wishing him harm. That would be an easy way out for her, and she'd imagined getting that fateful telegram so often that she felt sure she could fake the expected response though she knew her heart would be rejoicing at the news.

"What about James, any news of where he's going next?" Agnes threw the spotlight off herself by mentioning the subject closest to her auntie's heart.

"He's off to Canada! Can you believe it? He did his initial flight training in Devon and he got his wings. We're that proud of him, our Agnes."

"He's done well, hasn't he?" Agnes was happy for her cousin, but she knew that pilots in the RAF usually had short careers and was scared for him. Hilda didn't seem worried about the long-term prospects for her son, though.

"More than half the lads in his group didn't qualify, you know. The ones that failed have to go into ground staff occupations. They said our James has a flair for flying, and he's changed his mind about fighter planes and they want him to train on the bigger ones. He goes to Ontario in a few weeks, imagine that."

"Who'd have thought it of our James?" Agnes was pleased the young man was doing what he wanted to do.

"He's a good lad. He writes every week you know."

"That's nice that he thinks of you, Auntie Hilda. I'm sure he knows how much you worry about him."

"What about your Bill? Have you heard from him lately?"

"No, Auntie Hilda, but you know how it is. The post isn't as reliable from overseas. Your James has only been in Devon so letters can easily get through. It might be different when he gets to Canada."

"Aye maybe you're right. Watch your footing out there, them steps are slippery. I've dosed 'em wi' salt, but this freezing rain will wash it off in no time." Hilda opened the door to see Agnes out.

"Thanks, Auntie. I'll see you at teatime."

Agnes slid and shuffled her way towards the mill entrance on the frozen street. The path was treacherous, but she made it without mishap. She wasn't expecting to enjoy the day's work. She'd been put in charge of training Doris's twins who'd been set on the previous week. They were proving to be chatterboxes and didn't concentrate on the job nearly as much as they should have. She couldn't complain to her supervisor about them because Doris was their mother and she wouldn't hear a word said against her girls.

She walked into the weaving shed and ignored the wall of noise that assailed her ears. She'd got used to the clanging and the rattling of the looms. She made her way to the mule gate where the twins were threading the weft and began the long day of chivvying the two girls along.

Agnes was glad when the whistle blew to let the women know it was dinner time. She pulled out an iron stool and took out her sandwich and flask of tea. The twins sat on the floor either side of her and took out their paper packets that Doris had packed for them early that morning.

"What you got today, Agnes?" Rebecca asked. "We've got fatty bread."

"Mine's not much better, it's potted beef, but I think there's more fat and gravy than beef in it, it's that watery to spread it."

"Our mam goes to that butcher up Wood Street. His sausages are really good. He doesn't make 'em taste like sawdust as some do." Jessica said around a mouthful of sandwich.

Agnes struggled to tell one girl from the other, but remembered to look at their smooth foreheads, Jessica had a mole above her left eye, and it was the only distinguishing feature to tell the identical twins apart. "Thanks, Jessica. I'll remember that. I like a nice bit of sausage and mash."

"What's Poll going to have ready for your tea tonight?" Jessica asked Agnes.

Food was the chief topic of conversation for the girls. It seemed that the rationing concentrated their minds on the scarce commodities. Film stars and music were the next favourite topics, after gossiping about what was showing at the pictures or who they might be going to see the films with. Agnes humoured them as much as she could, but their conversation was a million miles away from the thoughts that occupied her head these days. What she wouldn't give to be as young as they were again. If she could go back in time, and know what she knew now, her life would be so different.

"We're having pancakes made with dried egg, me mam says." One girl said.

"Yuck! I hope she makes plenty of gravy to smother the taste. I hate powdered egg." The other twin said.

"Do you help her make the tea?" Agnes was half interested, and joined the conversation to be polite.

"Only if we have to," said Rebecca. "Mam prefers to do it herself, because —."

"She says we get in the way." Jessica finished her sister's sentence.

"Do you help your Polly make your tea?" Rebecca grinned knowingly at her sister and Jessica smirked.

"No, she usually has it done by the time I get home." Agnes didn't miss the exchange between the two girls, and wondered what the secretive looks were about.

"Will she be coming back to work soon?" Jessica asked, "After all, her little bastard is almost two months old now."

"That's enough! I won't hear you use words like that in my company!" Agnes was outraged.

"What's up, Agnes? Our Jess was only saying what everyone else is thinking."

"It's shameful the way she walks the streets with her head held high as if she never did anything wrong, when Jane Watson can't bring herself to go out for the shame of it." Jessica looked up at Agnes. "She won't be made welcome back here you know."

"What do you mean?" Agnes asked.

"The lasses will send her to Coventry. They'll not talk to her after the way she turned up at the funeral like she did." Jessica said.

"The cheek of it!" Rebecca added.

"Well, it's plain that you two have your minds made up about my cousin, but let me put a few things straight." Agnes didn't like gossip, and wouldn't stand for these young things to get away with talking about something they clearly knew nothing about. "The only reason Polly fell for Charlie Watson was because he was a charmer and she didn't know he was married. He was the one who did wrong, not Polly! By the time she knew about his wife, she was in love with him." Agnes knew she should stop, but the girls had goaded her. "You can't help who you fall in love with, and you two would do well to remember that before pointing your fingers and wagging your tongues." Agnes poured the last of her tea from the flask. The drink was barely warm, but it was wet and would help to calm her nerves.

"I'm not feeling all that hungry, Jess, do you want the rest of my sandwich?" Rebecca asked her sister.

"You're not coming down with that flu are you?" Jessica felt her sister's forehead. "You do feel warm."

"Me mam said she thought she had a fever this morning, but said she'd work it off. I don't feel hot, I feel cold." Rebecca got to her feet. "I think I'll get back to work. That will warm me up."

"I think we should all get back to work." Agnes packed her dinner bag and got to her feet. "Dinner time is over, come on girls."

When Agnes collected Harry at the end of the day, Enid came to greet her. "Eeh, lass. We've had a right day today."

"With my Harry?" Agnes thought she meant something had happened with her son.

"No, lass. He's good as gold. It was your Auntie Hilda. She went out to get some milk and slipped on the steps. She's only gone and broke her leg."

"Oh, no! Where is she now?"

"Well, the ambulance took her off to the infirmary, but she might be home by now."

"How have you managed here on your own?"

"It hasn't been easy. I wish we'd set a lass on as we said

we were going to. I'll have to find someone quick, now. Hilda won't be fit to come back for a good few weeks."

"I'd best get back and see if Polly knows." Agnes tucked Harry into the pram and set off at a brisk pace, holding onto the pram so she didn't lose her footing on the slippery paths.

Agnes made it home in one piece and hurried into the house. Polly was standing by the fire, stirring something on the hot-plate.

"Your mam had an accident, Polly."

"What!" Polly turned from the oven, the spoon dripping gravy on the rag-rug. She quickly put it back into the bubbling pan. "What happened, is she all right?"

"Enid said she broke her leg. They took her to the infirmary, but Enid said she might be back home by now."

"Will me dad know?"

"I don't know, Poll. Enid has been on her own all afternoon with all them bairns so she won't have had time to send word. Maybe the infirmary got a message to him?"

"I'll nip round to see. You don't mind, do you? Thomas and Alice have had a feed and should be asleep for an hour or so."

"You go, Polly. I'll see to the little ones." Agnes handed Polly her coat. "I'll keep your tea warm."

Agnes watched Polly rush out. "Mind your footing!" she called after her before she closed the door on the cold.

She took Harry from the pram and checked the two wooden dresser drawers that lay end to end on the floor down one wall of the kitchen. The babies slept soundly, tucked into the nest of blankets, one in each drawer. Agnes sighed as she looked down at the sleeping faces. Alice was so pretty. Her dark lashes fanned her cheeks and her little button nose stood above her pink rosebud lips. She was the typical magazine image of the perfect baby. When Agnes looked at her younger son, she saw Bill's face looking back at her. The infant was blowing little spit bubbles in his sleep, and his lips were glistening. His shock of dark-brown hair curled on his wrinkled forehead, and he looked to be frowning.

"Baba, Mama." Harry wriggled to get down from her arms.

"Yes, Harry. That's your brother." Agnes set Harry down by Thomas's makeshift cradle.

Harry reached a tiny hand to the baby and gently stroked his brother's cheek with chubby his fingers. "Ahhh, baba."

Agnes smiled at her older son. "You love your brother, don't you son?" She copied Harry's show of affection and touched her youngest son tenderly on his wrinkled brow. "It's not his fault that his daddy is a monster. I wonder what you're frowning about, young man?" Agnes felt something stir inside her. "I don't suppose I've given you much to smile about, have I?" She touched the baby's chin and his lips twitched. His cheeks dimpled and he smiled in his sleep. Agnes felt an upsurge of emotion that almost choked her. Her feelings for his father were nothing to do with this little innocent baby. She had foolishly allowed them to cloud her maternal instincts. This baby was part of her too, and she saw that now. Harry had made her see that he was just a baby. A tiny infant who needed to be loved. "I'll try to do better by you, Thomas. I will, you'll see."

Agnes slowly got to her feet and set about getting Harry, his supper. She kept one eye on the toddler who was fascinated by the babies in the drawers. He touched them gently and toddled to get the small rag doll that Polly had made for her daughter to put in with Alice, and then brought his little boat to Thomas's bed. "Careful, Harry. Thomas is a little young for that, yet." Agnes took the boat from Harry and gently laid it at the bottom of the drawer. "I'm sure he'll be glad that his brother is so generous with his toys." She scooped Harry into her arms. "Let's get you fed, little tyke."

Agnes fed and changed the babies after Harry was in bed, and put them upstairs for the night. They rarely woke in the night now, except when they were disturbed by the air-raid sirens, which didn't happen too often, thank goodness.

She'd taken more time with Thomas tonight. Both babies had been in good moods and were smiling and cooing as she bathed them in turn, in front of the fire. Alice had always made Agnes feel protective of her. She was small and dainty, like a porcelain doll. Until now, Agnes's heart had been hardened towards her youngest son, but something had changed. Harry had shown her that Thomas was just a baby in need of love. If her eldest child could give love so freely to his little brother, Agnes felt she could do no less. When Thomas began to smile in his sleep, his little, dimpled cheeks had won her over.

She felt she'd turned a corner with Thomas, and was determined that her life would improve from now on. She had a new life growing inside her, and although it would be difficult, she could learn to love this one too. She refused to dwell on Bill coming home. It might never happen, and if it did, well, she'd deal with that when the time came. She would ask for a divorce and she would make sure she got it. She'd make a new life for herself and the children without him. She'd faced pointing fingers in the past, and she could face them again. Gossip never hurt anyone. She'd already given up on the church so it would be no hardship if the church gave up on her.

Polly arrived in the middle of Agnes making her resolve. The cold air rushed in behind her and she slammed the door shut against the howling wind. "My goodness, it's freezing out there, and set to snow again before the night is out, I'll bet."

"Is your mam home, then?"

"Aye, she is, but she won't be any use to man nor beast for a good few weeks. I stopped to make them all some chips and sausages, I had my tea with them, so we can save the meal I would have had here for tomorra if that's all right, Agnes. If you don't mind having the neck of lamb again, I can do a few more potatoes to make it go further between the two of us, and maybe some dumplings."

"That'll be fine, Poll. How is Auntie Hilda?"

"She's on tablets for the pain, so she doesn't seem too bad. Her leg is strapped from the ankle to her thigh and she can't bend it. Dad brought James's bed downstairs for her, she can't make the stairs."

"Let's hope there are no air-raids then, she won't be able to make it to the cellar, will she?"

"My dad will carry her if he has to. You know what he's like. He won't see her in danger. You should have seen how he fussed around her tonight. He made sure she was comfy and could manage to shift herself over the bucket if she needed to do, well, you know what."

"By, it's grand to see how much your mam and dad mean to each other. They might come over all brusque and matter of fact in front of folks, but when something like this happens they show their true colours don't they?"

"Aye, Agnes. Me dad were beside himself when I got there. Couldn't do enough for her, but she was hungry and he can't cook to save his life!" Polly laughed.

"Good job you went round there then."

"I'll have to go round a lot more, too. She won't be able to get up and walk for a few weeks." Polly cleared her throat. "I might have to move back home, Agnes."

"Well, if you have to, you have to, Polly. We'll manage."

"Mam asked if I'd take her place at the nursery too. Enid can't manage by herself, and they were thinking of taking someone on before this happened, so it might be a permanent thing. You don't mind, do you?"

"Why would I mind?" Agnes remembered the earlier conversation she'd had with the twins about Polly and realised this could be the perfect solution for her cousin. There would be no reason to upset the girl by telling her of the unwelcome gossip if she weren't going to return to the mill. "It would be lovely to know you'd be looking after the little ones, only now you'll be getting paid to do it."

"You'll have to tell Bill I don't need his charity anymore, when next you write to him." Polly looked shamefaced. "Especially as I'll be earning and moving back to me mam and dad's house."

"I'll send him a note, but it might take some time to get through. I'm not sure where he is and I haven't heard from him since Christmas when he sent that card."

"You must be worried about him, Agnes. You've been looking a bit peaky. I bet you're not sleeping well, are you?"

"No, I'm not, but it's nowt to do with worrying over Bill." Agnes let out a long sigh. "You might as well know, Poll. I think I'm having another bairn."

"What! So soon!" Polly gasped then grinned. "My but you two didn't hang about! Your Thomas was only a few days old when Bill left!"

"I didn't think it were possible to get pregnant again so quick."

"I think you and Bill are just like my mam and dad. All tetchy and argumentative in front of folks, but behind closed doors, it must be a different story." Polly was smirking as she looked at Agnes.

"It's a very different story, Polly." Agnes shook her head. "Though you wouldn't want to know what's it's really like." Agnes thought it would be so easy to open up to her cousin. If she could confess the truth about her sham marriage and Bill's cruelty, it might make it easier to bear, but she didn't want to burden the girl with her troubles, and she couldn't take the risk that she'd keep it to herself.

Chapter Fifteen, Supporting a friend

Polly started work at the nursery the next day, and Agnes felt she'd left her little ones in good hands when she walked into the mill entrance. She didn't relish another day of listening to the juvenile chatter of her two charges, but at least their thoughtless comments couldn't hurt Polly now she had another job. Agnes had Polly's note in her hand to give to the supervisor.

"Where's Doris?" Agnes asked the man in charge of the looms.

"She's got the flu. I think we're going to be short-handed for a time, her two lasses have it as well."

"I've got a note from our Polly. She's left. Who do I give it to?"

"Better take it straight up to the office, lass, and get back down here quick-smart. Like I said, we can't afford to waste time with the workforce going down with this flu bug."

"Doris and the girls seemed all right yesterday."

"So did half the other lasses that haven't turned in this morning. Watch yourself, Agnes, You look a bit peaky."

"I'm all right, Mr Driver. I'd better get on." Agnes made her way up the iron staircase to the offices on the upper floor of the shed. She knew that the flu was going around, but to have so many go down with it so quickly was a bit scary. She felt well so far, and hoped she stayed that way. She didn't want to get ill and pass it to the children and Polly.

Agnes knocked on the door and entered when a voice called her inside. "I have a note from me cousin, she's not coming back." Agnes handed the letter to the girl behind the desk. "She was off after having her baby, but she has another job now."

"Thanks, I'll let them know to add another vacancy to the list." The girl took the note and dabbed at her eyes with a crumpled handkerchief.

"Are you feeling all right?" Agnes took a step backwards. "There's flu going about, you're not poorly are you?"

"Oh, no, it's not the flu. I'm perfectly fine, thank you. I just got some upsetting news. I had to go and tell Mr Binks, and I could see the boss was upset. He thought a lot of Sam Woods."

Agnes put a hand to her mouth to smother her gasp of fright.

"Poor Sam was shipped home this week. He got wounded

and they say he's in a bad way, by all accounts. I liked him, you know. He was a good sort."

"Well, if they shipped him home, he still *is* a good sort." Agnes was relieved to hear that Sam was alive, and tried to cheer the girl up as she was obviously upset. "It's not as if he's dead, is it?"

"No, but I think he lost a leg or an arm or something. Mr Binks was upset when I went to tell him the news. Sam's dad phoned earlier, but he didn't like using the telephone, and it was all a bit rushed, so I didn't quite understand the details."

"Oh, poor Sam!"

"His dad was asking whether there was anything Sam could do here at the mill. He wants to give his son something to aim for, a job, like, you know? I told Mr Binks and he said he'd see what he could do. Sounds as if poor Sam is very down in the dumps."

"He would be if he lost an arm or a leg as you said. Were you sweet on him? Is that why you're so sad?" Agnes dared to ask.

"Goodness, no!" The girl quickly wiped her face. "He was a laugh, that's all. We were all fond of him in the offices."

"Well, you still *can* be fond of him, can't you? He's not dead and gone, and maybe he can come back and make himself useful once he's recovered."

"It wouldn't be the same though, would it, with him being maimed." The girl shuddered. "I don't think I could look at him, in the same way, if he had something missing."

"Well, that's no way to think!" Agnes was shocked by the girl's callous attitude. "What about poor Sam?" Agnes could feel her anger rising, and decided it was time to get back down to the weaving shed. "Does his dad still live down near the goods-yard?"

"Coronation Road, I think, but I don't know the number without looking it up in the files."

"That's all right. I'll find it." Agnes left the snivelling girl and hurried down to her mule gate. She was determined to visit poor Sam as soon as she could. He'd done his duty and got maimed doing it, but that didn't mean he was any less of a man, and she wanted to let him know that. If people were treating him like that insensitive office girl, it was no wonder he was feeling so low.

"Get a move on, Agnes. We've got to finish this order by Friday with or without Doris and the others." Mr Driver shouted over the clanging racket of looms starting.

"You can count on me, Mr Driver." Agnes began to set up the weft in earnest.

By home time, she was exhausted. She hadn't stopped for a minute, and only had a short break at dinner time to eat her sandwich and drink her flask of tea. The other girls looked just as tired as they hurried out of the shed at the end of the working day.

"Thanks girls." Mr Driver called to them. "You did us proud today."

"Little good it'll do us. You won't be paying us anymore, will you?" One lass called back.

"You'll get your rewards in heaven, lass." Mr Driver shouted.

"Aye, well some of us might get there sooner than others with this flu bug going around." The girl shouted back.

"They say they're dropping like flies all over town and taking to their beds. I hope I don't get it." Another girl said to her companion.

"Nobody's died though, have they?" Her friend asked.

"Not yet." Someone answered.

Agnes shuddered. They had enough to worry about without adding a flu epidemic to the list. She hurried to the nursery and hoped the children would be all right when she got there.

"Hello, Agnes." Polly called from the other side of the crowded room.

Mothers from the mill were collecting toddlers and babies, packing little bags and putting on their coats and woollen hats. Agnes made her way through the busy throng and joined Polly at the window. Their two babies were snuggled side by side in the pram and Harry was holding the handle looking up at his mother with a small smile.

"Are you ready to go, Harry?" Agnes asked her son.

Little Harry nodded solemnly.

"I have to stay a while longer, Agnes. Some mothers work the late shift and aren't done until after eight. Can you see to these and get 'em ready for bed without me?"

"Course I can, love. I'll save you some of that neck of lamb, keep it warm for you, eh?"

"Thanks Agnes. I don't know what me dad will do tonight, though."

"He can go to the chippy for one night, can't he?"

"Yes, I suppose so."

"I'll get a big pan of hash done tonight. I'll get the little ones in bed and start on it then. I'll do enough for all of us and you can take it round before work in the morning so they just have to warm it through tomorra night."

"Oh, Agnes, you're so kind. Me mam will be so grateful."

"Don't work too hard, Poll. I'll see you later."

Agnes picked Harry up and perched him on the bottom of the pram. "Come on, son. Let's take these little ones home, shall we?"

Polly moved back to her parent's house on the Saturday, using the pram to cart her few possessions and baby Alice through the streets. She'd promised to come back on the Sunday afternoon to mind Harry and Thomas while Agnes went to visit Sam Wood. Agnes missed her cousin on the Saturday evening. The house had seemed too quiet without Polly's lively chatter. She'd put the wireless on for company and listened to the news broadcast. The newsreader sounded bright and jolly as he told the British public that the troops were doing well and had captured Derna, a town one hundred miles from Tobruk.

As Agnes drifted off to sleep that night, she wondered whether Bill had been one of the fighting men that captured the desert town. She knew he was somewhere in the desert from his brief letters commenting on the heat, and his complaints about the dust getting into everything from the water canteens to his socks. She couldn't find it in her heart to wish that he was safe, but she no longer wished him dead. Too many people were dying in this war or getting terribly hurt.

She had mixed feelings about seeing poor Sam Woods that afternoon, but she felt she should go. He was a good man, and he didn't deserve what had happened to him.

She left Polly in charge of the children and set out to Coronation Road. She asked a neighbour which house the Woods lived at, and then went to knock on the brown wooden door. Her heart was thumping rapidly in her chest as Sam's father, Peter, showed her into the warm parlour. She had no idea what to expect, and was apprehensive about seeing Sam's injuries. She need not have worried, and at her first sight of him, she felt relief wash through her.

Sam was seated at the table by the window, concentrating on the construction of a model boat.

"I hope you don't mind me coming to see you, Sam." She began. "But the girl in the office told me you were back, and—."

"Agnes!" Sam started to lift from the chair, and then sat down again quickly. "You don't mind if I don't get up, do you?"

"Of course not!" Agnes glanced nervously at Sam's dad. "You, err, you stay where you are. That looks impressive." She went to sit opposite him at the table and nodded at the pieces of the model scattered around.

"Will I make us a brew?" Sam's dad asked from the doorway.

"Aye, dad, if you like. It looks like Agnes has made herself comfortable." Sam's voice sounded a little tense.

"Oh, sorry." Agnes jumped to her feet. "I don't mean to intrude. I just, err, I thought, I wanted to see if you were all right."

"Came for a look at the war wound, did you?" Sam swivelled in the chair and stuck out his left leg. "Take a good look then! Everybody else that's been has had a good gawp."

Agnes took a fleeting look at the stump of his leg enclosed in bandages. She could see he had lost a foot. The bandaged limb ended just below his knee.

"Seen enough? Can I put it away now?" Sam was uncharacteristically caustic, and turned his head abruptly to look out of the window as he manoeuvred his damaged leg out of sight.

"I'm so sorry, Sam. That's an awful thing to have happened to you." Agnes was shaken, but she'd come to try to cheer him up, and she thought she knew how to handle a man in a bad mood. She'd had enough practice with Bill over the last few years. She hadn't realised how down and bitter Sam would be. She didn't know where to start to help him feel better.

"Aye, well, now you've seen it, you can go and tell your friends about the poor cripple." Sam continued putting his model together and didn't look at Agnes.

"I wouldn't do that, Sam." Agnes hated to see him like this. "You're not a cripple in my eyes. You're still the same Sam I remember before you went away."

"You're wrong, Agnes. I'm a long way from that lad. Losing a foot does that to you."

Agnes was relieved to hear that Sam had lost the bitter tone she'd heard in his voice. He just sounded sad now.

"Do you mind if I ask you, how did it happen?"

Sam glanced up at her and she saw suspicion in his eyes. "Why do you want to know?"

"I thought it might help you if you talked about it."

"Most folks want to know the gory details so they can gossip about it and glorify the story over a pint down at the pub. I don't want to be the poor, pitied soldier that folks point at and whisper about."

"I'd never do that, Sam. You should know that."

Sam raised his head and gave her a small smile. "I know, Agnes. You're a good lass. I know you mean well, but I'm not a charity case either. You might be earning some good deed awards from Father Brennan for visiting me, but you've done your Christian duty now, so I'll let you off the hook and you can go back and tell them you cheered me up good and proper."

"It's not like that, Sam. I came because I wanted to see you. I'm done with the church. Father Brennan is a stranger to me now. Religion has caused me nothing but heartache so I decided I can do without it."

"My, now it's my turn to be nosey." Sam raised his eyebrows. "What happened to turn a good Catholic girl against God?"

"It's a long story, Sam, and I'm sure it's not nearly as interesting as the one you have to tell."

Sam's father came in carrying a large brown teapot. "I'll get the cups then I'll leave you to it. Do you need owt else, lad, before I get off?"

"No dad. I'll be fine with Agnes."

"Well, I'll only be gone a couple of hours." He left the room and quickly returned with cups and a jug of milk. "There's no sugar left, you'll have to do without."

"Thanks, Mr Wood." Agnes reached for the teapot and poured the tea. "Where you off to, anywhere nice?"

"Just to the Scarborough pub for a pint with me mates. I haven't been for a week or two, what with our Sam needing me. He's a bit better now, though, aren't you, son?"

"I can manage for a few hours, Dad. I keep telling him I'm not a baby, but he won't listen."

"Well, I'm listening now. I'll get off. You'll be able to see yourself out, lass, won't you?"

"Yes, Mr Wood. Though I hope I'll still be here when you get back."

"Planning a long conversation then, are we?" Sam tilted his head to one side and raised his eyebrows at her again.

"That depends on what we have to say to each other, doesn't it?" Agnes copied his expression and they burst out laughing.

"I can see I'm leaving him in good hands. See you later." Mr Woods closed the door softly behind him.

"It's good to see you smiling, Sam. You looked so tense when I first came in."

"I've not had much to smile about, Agnes."

"I can see that, you just showed me."

"Sorry about that. It's just that I feel like a freak show, you know? It makes me so mad when folks call around to gawp at me."

"Do visitors really do that?"

"Most of the neighbours came round for a look when I was still laid up, and I ended up throwing a crutch at Mrs Pickles."

"Poor woman. What did she do to upset you?"

"I think she said something about getting a wheelchair and taking up a musical instrument. She mentioned the corner of the market where buskers sit to beg a few coppers —."

"Oh, my goodness!" Agnes interrupted. "I would have thrown both crutches at her. The cheek of it!"

"Well, she meant well, I suppose. I don't have many options to earn a living now, do I?"

"Why not?" Agnes asked. "You've still got both your arms, and your head still works, I presume."

"Aye, but arms and a brain won't get me far if I can't walk to work, or stand to do a job."

"You must have been told about them false legs you can get. Wouldn't you want to try one of them?"

"There's a waiting list for 'em. I've got me name down, but it might be months before I get one."

"Well then. That's not too long to wait, and while you're waiting you could start to look around and see what you might want to do." Agnes remembered her conversation with the girl in the office. "What about returning to the mill? I'm sure they could find a use for you there."

"As I said afore, Agnes. I'm not a charity case. I'll not take kindly to being given peanuts for pottering about looking busy."

"I'm sure the bosses wouldn't think of setting you on if you couldn't pull your weight and earn a wage for doing so."

"Well, I can't do that without both me feet." Sam picked up a piece of his model. "This is all I'm good for now, Agnes. Fiddling about with toy boats."

"That's a fine-looking boat, Sam Woods." Agnes smiled at him. "But you'll progress to bigger things before too much longer. You've got time on your side. You'll get stronger and fitter and by the time you get that new foot, you'll be good as new."

"Is that a promise?" Sam looked sceptical.

"It's a snowdrop's promise, Sam. It's guaranteed."

Agnes stayed with Sam until his dad returned from the pub, and Mr Woods came back to the sound of laughter.

"My, it's a long time since I heard that sound in me house." Mr Woods said as he came into the parlour.

"Thanks for coming, Agnes. You've been a tonic, lass." Sam's eyes sparkled when he smiled at her.

"Same time next week, lass?" Mr Woods asked her.

"If that's all right with Sam."

"If you're sure you want to spend your Sunday afternoon with a wounded soldier."

"Well, I'll have to see if Polly will mind the bairns again." Agnes realised it might not be so easy to make it a regular event.

"You could bring 'em with you next time." Sam suggested.

"You wouldn't want to be pestered by a toddler and a young baby."

"I don't see why not." Sam lifted his face to Agnes. "If it means I can see you again."

Agnes felt a little flutter in her chest. She could see that Sam was reading much more into her visit than she had intended, but she couldn't back out now. He seemed so much more cheerful than he'd been when she arrived. "See you next week then."

Agnes hurried home through the cold streets. She knew Polly would want to get home to make tea for her family, and she had stayed much longer with Sam than she had planned.

Harry ran to her when she came through the door, and

she scooped him into her arms to cuddle him close. "Did you miss me, young man?"

"I've tried to keep him occupied, but he kept looking at the door and sucking his thumb." Polly was feeding one of the babies. "I haven't had the energy to do anything, but feed and change these two little ones. I'm feeling a bit off it myself. I hope it's not this flu bug that's starting."

"You do look a bit flushed, Polly."

"I'll be all right. Your Thomas had his bottle half an hour ago. I'll finish feeding Alice then I'll get off."

"Sorry I was so long, Poll. Sam was really down when I got there."

"How bad is it for him?"

"He lost a foot. The bottom half of his leg is all in bandages, and he's feeling sorry for himself, you know?"

"You spent all afternoon talking to someone who was miserable? That must have been depressing for you."

"No, I think I cheered him up. At least I hope I managed to show him a silver lining to his dark cloud. I enjoyed talking with him, and I'm going again next week."

"Careful, Agnes! You're a married woman, folks will talk!" Polly warned.

"Let them talk!" Agnes felt more cheerful than she had for months. "A few wagging tongues can't hurt me."

"They might hurt Bill if he should hear that you're visiting a single man."

"Who's going to tell him? Bill is miles away."

"Just be careful, that's all I'm saying." Polly cautioned.

"I'm only visiting a war invalid. It's not like I'm walking out with him or anything."

"Well, you couldn't do that if he has a foot missing, could you?" Polly put her hand to her mouth. "Oh, dear. That didn't come out right, did it?"

"Don't worry about it, Polly. I know what you meant." Agnes started giggling. "You do have a way with words sometimes."

"I'd better get back to get the tea on. If I don't get home soon, I can see me mam dragging herself off the sofa to start without me. You know what she's like."

"Thanks for looking after them this afternoon, Polly" Agnes saw her cousin to the door.

"Yes, see ya tomorra at the nursery, Agnes."

Chapter Sixteen, Illness and death

Agnes was ready for stepping out of the door on Monday morning when a loud knocking interrupted her putting the little ones into the pram. David stood on her doorstep with baby Alice in his arms, wrapped in a thick blanket to keep her warm.

"Come in, David." Agnes opened the door wider to let the young lad in. "What's the matter?"

"It's our Polly. I think she's got the flu. She's hot and sweaty and talking in riddles. Me mam sent me to get the doctor, but she said can you take Alice to the nursery with your two, 'cause we can't look after her today."

"I'm not sure Enid will be able to cope without Polly either, but I'll take her. Tell your mam not to worry. I'll keep Alice here with me until Polly gets better. Has she had her breakfast?"

"Aye, me mam gave her some porridge, and me dad gave her a bottle before he went to work."

"Your dad?"

"Aye, well, we're all pulling our weight. I packed Alice's bag for the day. Well, I packed it when me mam told me where everything was."

"That's good then." Agnes took the baby and the small bag and put them in the pram with her own children. "You'd better hurry to the doctor. Sounds as though your Polly needs him."

"She's blathering on about all sorts. Mumbling like, you know?"

"That'll be the fever. If the doctor can't see her straight away, you get some cold water and sponge her down. Especially around her head and neck. You have to cool her down."

"Oh, I don't know if I could do that."

"David, listen to me!" Agnes knew she was asking a lot of a young lad. "Your mam would be doing it if she could. You have to bring her temperature down. It's important! That's what's causing her to talk rubbish, She'll be hallucinating."

"I'll try, Agnes." David said as he left.

Agnes made her way to the nursery with a heavily loaded pram and hoped Enid wouldn't turn her away. She needed to work or there would be no food on the table next week.

"Our Polly has gone down with the flu now." Agnes told Enid as she bounced the pram up the steps and into the warm nursery room. "Will you be able to manage?"

"I got me sister, Vera, to come in today. She could see we were struggling, even with your Polly helping us."

Agnes nodded to the unfamiliar older woman and turned to Hilda's friend. "Are you sure you can cope, Enid?"

"I can't turn the lasses away, can I? You need to work, but if this flu gets any worse, we'll have to shut up shop, and then what will all you young mothers do with the bairns?"

"Well, let's hope everyone gets better soon." Agnes helped to unload her packages of baby gasmasks, bags of nappies and bottles and food. Then she lifted Harry to the floor and left the two babies in the pram.

"You get off, love. We'll see to them." Enid nodded to the infants in the pram. "See you at five-thirty."

Agnes left the nursery and hastened to work. She had a busy day ahead of her. The mill had some big orders to fill, and the girls were rushed off their feet with half the workforce down with the flu.

As she began setting up the loom, her fingers worked mechanically. She could do the job with her eyes closed, and her mind began to drift to the children. It wasn't ideal to put them in the nursery every day. She only got to see them for an hour or so at each end of the day. Agnes felt she hardly knew her children anymore. Harry seemed such a sombre little chap, but he still loved her to tickle him and make him giggle. She couldn't remember the last time she had played with Harry like that. She was always too tired or too busy with Thomas. She was constantly weary these days, what with working long hours and a new baby growing inside her, sapping her strength. She would have to try to spend more time with her bairns or they would grow up to be strangers to her, and she didn't want that for them or for her. This life was not fair on them. If only Bill would agree to give her more money, she could drop her hours and go part time. She'd have to write to him about the baby she expected, and to tell him of Polly's change of circumstances. Perhaps he would agree that she needed extra money, especially with another of his offspring on the way. She decided she would have nothing to lose by asking.

Halfway through the morning the mill whistle sounded to stop the looms. All the girls looked up from their mule gates and realised pretty quickly that it was the air-raid siren they could hear over the noise of the slowing machinery. It would be the first time they had actually had to use the mill shelter in the basement of the large building. They'd done practices for daylight raids, but this was no practice. The girls hurried to form an orderly line, and Agnes saw the fear on the faces of her work colleagues, and knew her face held the same panicked look. A daylight raid! The Germans were getting bolder.

"What about the bairns in the nursery?" One of the women asked.

"Enid will get them to safety." Agnes said, with more confidence than she felt. How would the two elderly ladies manage to get all those little ones into the Anderson shelter behind the nursery building? She wanted to run outside to help get the youngsters to safety, but she knew the bosses wouldn't let anyone leave. The wardens would be enforcing the rules to anyone seen outside during an air-raid. She followed the others into the bowels of the building where she hoped they would be safe.

Within a few minutes of getting settled on the benches lining the walls, the workforce heard the first explosions as bombs detonated close by. A woman screamed and a few more started crying.

Mr Binks, the mill owner, stood and began to sing, "*Pack up your troubles in your old kit bag...*"

More voices joined in as the song continued, and together the workers tried to drown the noise of the dropping bombs and the drone of the aircraft overhead.

As the voices swelled, Agnes watched Mr Binks talking with her boss, Mr Driver, and thought she'd try to ask them about Sam Wood. She knew that Mr Binks liked the young man, and hoped he would be willing to help him. She pushed her way through the singing crowd and tugged gently at Mr Driver's sleeve to get his attention.

"What is it, Agnes?" Mr Driver asked.

"I was hoping I could have a word with Mr Binks."

"What about, lass?" Mr Binks looked at her expectantly.

"It's about Sam Wood, Mr Binks. I went to see him and he's quite depressed because he thinks he won't be able to work again, but I told him that's nonsense, because he's only lost a foot and he can get one of them false ones and he'll be good as new, won't he?" Agnes knew she was babbling, but she was nervous at speaking to the mill owner.

"All right, lass. I hear you." Mr Binks smiled at her. "You tell him to come and see me when he gets up and about. He's a good worker, and cheerful soul, I'll be glad to help him out."

"Oh, thank you, Mr Binks, but he wouldn't want your charity, sir. It would have to be a proper job." Agnes dared to insist.

"I only have proper jobs, lass!" Mr Binks laughed loudly, but his laughter was cut-off by the ear-shattering blast of an explosion close by.

A few women screamed and all eyes turned to the stairs at the entrance to the basement. It looked as if most of the workers were thinking of making a run for it. Agnes felt trapped, but knew she was in the safest place. She hoped the children were safe too.

"They'll be after the goods-yards again because they didn't get them last time they tried." Mr Binks told Mr Driver.

"I heard they were targeting factories as well, so the ironworks might be getting a pasting too." Mr Driver looked anxious.

"Well, I wouldn't be too sure about that." Mr Binks said, and added, "I heard they miss more targets than they hit. It's the civilians in towns and the houses roundabout that get it. It's criminal what they're doing to this country."

"I thought we were having a sing-song!" A voice called out then started to sing, "*Roll out the barrel...*"

Nervous voices joined in around the basement, but the sound of weeping overshadowed the bravado. Agnes tried to sing along, but her heart wasn't in it. She was too worried about her children. The last bomb was so close and the nursery was right next door.

An hour later they heard the all-clear siren, and the workers jumped to their feet and made a dash for the door. They clearly all had the same idea and wanted to go and see what damage had been done outside. Mr Binks shouted above the general hubbub, "Order, ladies and gentlemen! A bit of order, please! Now form a line and we'll all get out of here a lot quicker. Remember the practices!"

Eventually, two lines were formed and the workers filed upstairs to the weaving shed.

"Right, ladies, back to work." Mr Binks called to them all. "Let's get them looms moving, we're losing business because of this bloody war!"

Agnes couldn't think about work, and knew the other

mothers would be as worried as she was. She timidly approached the mill owner. "Please, sir. Can we check on our bairns first? They're next door, and we'll work twice as hard when we get back, once we know they're safe."

"We won't take long, sir." Another woman added her assurance.

"Go on, then." Mr Binks shook his head and smiled at Agnes. "We won't get any work out of you until you're sure your little ones are all right, will we?"

"Oh, thank you, sir." Agnes nearly dropped a curtsey, she was so grateful, but stopped herself, and turned to the door instead. She was closely followed by more of the mothers who had bairns in the nursery.

"Can I check on me dad, sir? He's bad with his legs and I know he wouldn't have made it to the shelter." Another woman asked.

"Go on then." The mill owner flapped his hand at the door.

"My bairns are with me mam on Coronation Road. Can I go check on them, sir?"

"Look! Wait a minute all of you." Mr Binks's loud voice halted the hurrying women. "We've lost enough time with them bloody German bombers, another hour won't make much difference. You can all go check on your loved ones. You've got an hour, but then I want you back in the shed and raring to go, all right?"

A big cheer rang through the shed as the workers hurried to the exit.

Agnes turned to the mill owner. "Thank you, sir. You know we'll all work twice as hard when we get back."

"Go on, Agnes. Away with you and check on your family."

The mill entrance saw a mass exodus as women and men ran in all directions. A dozen or so ran to the nursery next door with Agnes, and they were all relieved to see the building still standing and the children all safe and playing happily.

Agnes picked Harry up and cuddled him close. "Did you manage to get them all to the shelter, Enid?" she asked.

"Aye, we did." Enid told her as she rocked a pram with a baby in it to soothe its crying. "It was a right struggle, but we got 'em all inside before the bombs started dropping. I couldn't believe it when I realised it were really happening! A daylight raid! I ask you? Them Germans are getting far too daring for my liking."

"We were all scared in the mill basement. It sounded as if the bombs were dropping right outside."

"Does anyone know what the damage is, yet?" Vera asked.

"Not yet." One of the mothers answered. "We just came out from the mill shelter."

A young girl came running into the nursery calling for her child. "Where is he? Where's my Ronald?"

"Over here, love. He's right as rain." Enid pointed to a toddler playing with a train on a track.

"Oh, I'm that glad!" The lass sat by her son's side. "Two bombs dropped over the other side of the bridge. It sounds as though some houses got blown up. One lad I saw was saying that two houses were flattened at the top of Orchard Street."

"Oh, no!" Agnes sprang to her feet. "Which side?"

"I don't know, but the wardens are all over the place and they're stopping people going up there.

"Polly!" Agnes felt her knees go weak.

"What about Hilda? She can't walk. She wouldn't have been able to get to the cellar and Bert would have been at work." Enid looked anxious.

"I'd better get up there." Agnes ran to the door.

"Let me know what you find, lass." Enid called to her as she raced away.

Agnes ran all the way to the bridge, and had to slow because of a stitch in her side. She could see smoke curling into the grey sky from the direction of Polly's street.

"Oh, no. Please no. Not Polly." Agnes clutched her side and began to hurry forward. As she neared the bottom of Orchard Street, she could see the debris strewn over the cobbles. Fire trucks and police wagons were parked haphazardly among piles of rubble. Firemen, policemen and wardens were everywhere. An ambulance pulled into the top of the street as Agnes was stopped by an air-raid warden.

"You can't go up there, lass. It's too dangerous."

"My auntie and cousin might be under that rubble. Do you know which house got flattened? I can't tell from here."

"Not sure yet, love. Stay here out of the way for now, eh?"

Agnes tried to get her bearings. The familiar street was gone and had been replaced by smouldering heaps of bricks and broken furniture. A narrow wall stood two storeys high between wide open spaces where houses used to be. Ragged orange curtains fluttered at an open, broken window, and Agnes could see the contents of a wrecked wardrobe flapping in the breeze. A bed was teetering on smashed floorboards high above an exposed parlour. The devastation rendered her speechless. She stared in shock at the horrific scene.

"Agnes!" Bert's voice shook her to her senses. "I just heard. It's not our house is it?" Bert's arm came about Agnes's shoulders and he squeezed her reassuringly. "It won't be my Hilda."

"I think it is, Uncle Bert." Agnes put an arm around her uncle's waist as he sagged heavily against her. "I recognise your bedroom curtains. No one else had bright-orange window hangings, did they?"

"Our Hilda liked to have bright colours around her." Bert said, absently. "Our David will have made sure the women were safe in the cellar. They'll be all right, Agnes. You'll see."

"But there's nothing left, Uncle Bert. How can they be all right!" Agnes's voice shook.

"Stay here, Agnes. I can see my Cousin Edwin over there." Bert left her standing at the bottom end of the street. "Edwin!" Bert shouted. "What can I do? That's my house over there. Have you got anyone out yet?"

"Come over here, Bert." Edwin beckoned Bert over.

Agnes watched Bert's cousin, her father-in-law, talking and could see Edwin didn't look as if he were giving Bert good news. She held her breath and watched her uncle start to pick his way over the rubble that used to be his house.

There were several men in various uniforms working to clear a space in the rubble, and a voice called out, but Agnes couldn't hear what was said. She watched as the men worked more frantically to clear the broken bricks and masonry.

"Get a stretcher, we got someone here!" A voice called and Agnes watched her uncle drop to his knees. Bill's father went to Bert's side and put a hand on his cousin's shoulder.

She couldn't hold back any longer and hurried to join Bert and her father-in-law. "Who they found, Uncle Bert?" Agnes called, ignoring the shouted warnings from the uniformed men, telling her to get back.

"They think it's our Polly, but she's covered in muck and buried under some heavy lumps of wall."

"Careful there, Agnes." Her father-in-law, Edwin, warned her. "Don't get too close. The rest could come down any minute."

"Is she alive, Uncle Bert?"

"She's been talking to the fireman that found her. He's down there with her now." Edwin answered her.

"Are they getting her out?" Agnes tried to peer into the dusty gloom of the hole in the ground.

"I don't know." Bert slowly got to his feet and carefully approached the edge of the cavern that the working men had exposed. "Agnes! Oh, lass, come here." He reached a hand to her.

Agnes clasped his hand and followed him, watching where she put her feet. The ground was covered in broken glass, bricks and shattered wood. It was treacherous underfoot. As she reached his side, she peered into a dusty and smoky hole that she knew had been a cellar. A pile of rubble filled one side by the cellar steps. The stairs were miraculously clear of debris, and Agnes's gaze followed them down to the deep mound of rubble at the bottom on the cellar floor. She could see the exposed shadowy form of the top half of a body, with debris covering the lower half from the chest down. "Is that Polly?" Agnes froze. She couldn't breathe.

"Polly!" Bert called.

The fireman leant down to the injured girl as if to listen to her. Agnes watched him nodding then he turned to beckon them to come down. "Be careful!" he cautioned. "Make your way round to the steps, that's the safest way down."

Agnes followed her uncle, treading carefully, but quickly, in their haste to get to Polly. When they reached the dusty body, the fireman made way for them. He shook his head at Bert and said very quietly, "She's not got long."

Agnes wept as she knelt by Polly's side. The young girl was covered in dust, and the lower half of her body from her chest down was under the massive heap of rubble.

"Don't cry, Agnes. I'm all right. I can't feel anything." Polly whispered.

"Where's your mam?" Bert asked, his voice barely a murmur.

"We helped each other get down here. I pushed her and she pulled me. We thought we'd be safe." Polly coughed and they waited for her to get her breath back. "Oh, Dad. I'm sorry." Polly gasped and was struggling for breath. "She's under here somewhere with me."

"Oh, no, lass. Not my Hilda. Not your mam."

"She was near the back. Close to the cellar steps, Dad. She copped the lot when it came down." Polly took another ragged breath. "It would have been quick. I never heard her scream."

A tear escaped Polly's eye and Agnes watched it clearing a path down her cousin's dusty face. It didn't seem real.

"Our David?" Bert asked.

"He went out to get something in for tea." Polly tried to smile. "He wasn't here."

"He might be safe then." Bert sighed and touched his daughter's dirty face.

"Agnes?" Polly's eye flickered to Agnes.

"I'm here, Poll." Agnes crouched by her friend.

"Will you look after Alice for me?" Polly's breathing was getting shallower. "Me dad can't look after a bairn. David's too young." She was struggling to speak.

"Don't you worry about Alice. She'll be like me own, Polly." Agnes promised through her tears.

"Thanks, Agnes. Knew I could count on you."

"Save your strength, lass. We'll soon have you out of here." Bert's face was wet with tears.

"I'm done for, Dad." Polly coughed again and they heard the rattle in her chest as she struggled for air. "I can't feel me body. It feels like I'm floating. I'm not scared."

"Hush, Poll. Your dad's right. They'll have you to the infirmary in no time. We'll get you fixed up."

"I can see Charlie." Polly's face broke into a radiant smile. "What you doing here, Charlie?"

"What's she saying?" Bert glanced at Agnes and they exchanged a puzzled look.

Polly's eyes closed and she stopped breathing, but it took a few seconds before her dad and cousin realised she had gone.

Chapter Seventeen, Funerals and friendships

Saint Paulinus church was packed for Polly and Hilda's funeral. People who had pointed fingers at Polly and shunned her for the affair she had with Charlie Watson, now sniffed hypocritically into handkerchiefs. Church folk who gossiped about Hilda's lapse of faith now embraced Bert back into the fold to say farewell to his wife and child. Black was the predominant colour of clothing among the congregation, but uniforms of all services were also represented. A few men wore army khaki, one or two had navy blue, and a few, like James, wore the grey-blue uniform of the Royal Air Force. He had managed to get two days compassionate leave before being transferred to Canada for further training. Air-raid wardens, firemen and ambulance personnel were also present, sitting among friends and relatives. All were there to show respect for the dead, and support for the living.

Agnes had left the children with Enid's sister, Vera, who kindly offered to mind them. She told Agnes that she'd been to more than enough funerals in her time, and she thought Hilda and Polly could go to their maker without needing her to give them a personal send off. "I said a prayer for them at the vigil last night." Vera said as Agnes left her at the house.

Father Brennan conducted the double service. Agnes listened to the words of the Requiem Mass. She stood for the hymns, and knelt to pray, but her lips remained closed and her heart felt a million miles away from the reality of the Mass. Her thoughts would not have been welcomed by the priest if he could read her mind. What use was a God to her if He allowed these awful things to happen? Polly was young with all her life ahead of her. Why kill Polly? Hilda had a heart of gold, and a loving family. What had she ever done to deserve such a brutal ending? What did God gain by taking their lives?

When the funeral service came to an end, Agnes followed the congregation as they filed outside to the graveyard over the road. She held her Uncle Bert's arm, and James held him at the other side. The poor man could barely walk.

David tagged along behind them with Bert's half-cousin, Edwin and his wife, Mary. The young lad had been mercifully spared the same fate as his sister and mother because he'd been out shopping for their tea. He'd taken refuge in an Anderson shelter in town, but the firemen had told Agnes that even an Anderson shelter would not have been enough to save anyone if it were to suffer a direct hit. Bert's house was blown apart by a bomb that fell on the roof, descended through the floors, and exploded in the parlour. That's why there had been so much damage. The neighbouring properties were smashed beyond repair and would have to be demolished.

The small northern town had suffered many deaths and injuries. The infirmary had been inundated that day, and the churches all over town were holding funeral services through the following week.

Standing in the graveyard with her Uncle Bert, her parents-in-law and her cousins, Agnes looked down into the double grave that would be her Auntie Hilda and Cousin Polly's final resting place. She couldn't believe that she would never see either of them again in this life. She dashed her tears away. She'd shed too many already, and her eyes were sore from crying. She glanced away from the men who were lowering the coffins into the gaping hole in the ground, and noticed the snowdrops waving their pretty heads all over the graveyard. She remembered Andrew's promise to marry her, but even the snowdrop's promise was not enough to lighten her spirits on this terrible day. She lifted her eyes away from the flowers and a bright mop of ginger hair caught her attention.

She was drawn to Sam's concerned face. He was dressed in his army uniform, supported by his crutches. He was standing back from the central group of mourners with his father. He nodded to Agnes, a sympathetic smile on his face.

She tried to smile an acknowledgement to him, but her lips trembled.

Father Brennan began the final committal, and Bert began to sob. It took all of Agnes and James's concentration to hold him upright until the priest had finished.

When it was over and the gravediggers moved to begin filling in the earth, Bert had to be pulled away. "Come on, Uncle Bert. We have to go." Agnes gently tugged on his arm.

"I can't leave them. Not in there!" Bert cried.

"Dad, they're not in them coffins." James tried to reason with his father. "They've gone to a better place, Dad."

James put his arm around his father and led him to the churchyard gate where Father Brennan was shaking hands with everyone as they left.

Bert seemed to stand taller as he approached the priest, and he held out his hand to Father Brennan.

"It was good to see you here today, Bert, though I'd

rather it had been another reason to bring you back to church. I'm so sorry for your loss." The priest's Irish brogue brought memories flooding back to Agnes of another voice with an Irish lilt, but she quickly brushed all thoughts of Andrew from her mind, today was not the time, and this was not the place to be thinking of her lover.

"Don't be a stranger, son," the priest was continuing, "We're here to help you through this difficult time."

"I know you mean well, Father, and I'm glad you took the service for my girls, but I won't change my mind. I didn't agree with the way the church encouraged young lads to go off to die in the last war, and I'm not saying we shouldn't have gone. You know how I feel on that score. There was no choice in my mind. We had to fight, for just the same reasons as the young lads are fighting now. Evil has to be stopped." Bert straightened his shoulders and glared at the priest. "But the church should stay out of politics!"

"I'm sorry you feel that way, Bert." The priest bowed his head slightly. "You know, the God I serve is a forgiving Lord. He'll welcome you back into his arms anytime you feel you can make your peace with him."

"I've no argument with God, Father. I'll say my prayers and live my life in the best way I know, but hell will freeze over before I set foot in your church again for anything but weddings and funerals." Bert marched away on stiff legs and James hurried after him.

"I'm sorry, Father Brennan." David looked apprehensive. "He's upset; he doesn't know what he's saying."

"You're a good boy, David. Look after your father, now."

"Come, son." Edwin led the young lad from the churchyard. "Let's go help James with your dad."

Agnes followed her mother-in-law and politely touched her fingers to the priest's proffered hand, but hurried through the gate before he could draw her into a conversation.

"I know you're upset, Agnes." Mary said as she fell into step beside her. "But there was no reason to be rude to Father Brennan."

"I wasn't rude. I just didn't have anything to say to him."

"I would have thought you'd have plenty to say as you haven't been near the church in months." Her mother-in-law sniffed. "Does our Bill know you're not attending Mass?"

"I've no doubt you'll have told him." Agnes didn't want to get into a fight with Mary. "I barely hear from him these days."

"He'll be too busy to be writing letters, I expect."

"Yes, I suppose so." Agnes answered absently.

"That's why me and Edwin wanted to talk to you, Agnes. I know today probably isn't the right time, but we never see you, so I told Edwin I'd have a word."

"You know where I live, Mary." Agnes stopped and turned to face her mother-in-law. "You could call around any time to see your grandchildren."

"My grandchild is what I want to talk to you about."

Agnes sighed heavily. Mary and Edwin had made it clear that they would never think of Harry as theirs and it annoyed her enormously.

"There's no need to get all huffy with me, Agnes Smithson. You know what I'm about to say, and it has to be said. Our Bill would have sorted this himself if he were home, but —."

"If this is about getting Thomas baptised, you can forget it. It's not going to happen." Agnes told her. "If Bill wants to arrange something when he gets home, then that will be his decision, not yours."

"Well!" Mary puffed out her chest. "I'm only thinking of my grandson. It's not right that he isn't baptised already. Father Brennan said, only last week —."

"I don't care what Father Brennan or anyone else says! I'm with me Uncle Bert. Hell will be a cold place before I set foot in that church again."

"Well, I never!" Mary stepped away from Agnes. "If we'd known what you were really like, we would never have agreed to our Bill marrying you. We thought you were a good Catholic girl."

"Well, me getting pregnant should have given you a clue that I wasn't!" Agnes couldn't help rubbing it in.

"I don't have to listen to this!" Mary started to walk away. "I wish we'd never said yes to your mother's proposal."

"Well, that makes two of us. We can agree on something there!" Agnes called and watched her marching away.

She didn't feel like going to the wake, but knew it would be expected of her. She sat on a low wall and waited until she felt a little calmer before getting to her feet to follow the rest of the mourners. As she rounded a bend in the road, she saw the familiar red hair of her friend. He was leaning against a wall with his crutches under his arms.

"I thought you'd already be down in the Crown Arms." Agnes said as she reached him.

"Me dad's on his way down there. I told him not to wait for me. I take ages to get anywhere on these things." He waved a crutch in the air.

"I'm glad you're here." Agnes smiled up at him. "I don't think I want to walk into the wake on me own. I know everyone is talking about how I don't go to church anymore, and they already condemn Bert and the boys for not going. It's like we've changed into devils in their eyes."

"I wouldn't go that far, Agnes. They gave 'em a good send-off, didn't they?" Sam said quietly. "I'm surprised so many turned out after the way most of the town condemned your Polly as a harlot."

"I think most of 'em were there for Hilda." Agnes watched the procession of dark-suited men and women walking down the hill, making their way into town. "And, of course, for me Uncle Bert. They still have lots of friends, even though they gave up on the church."

"It's a tragedy, what happened to Hilda and Polly, and folks come together at times like these, don't they?"

Agnes took a deep breath and let it out in a long sigh. "It's a tragedy all right. Me Uncle Bert is like a lost soul. They've all moved in with me for the time being. I don't think Bert knows what to do next. I don't know how he'll cope without Hilda."

"Life goes on, Agnes. It has to."

Sam tucked his crutch under his arm and touched her shoulder.

Agnes looked up into his eyes. "I sometimes wonder whether it's worth the effort of carrying on when things like this happen."

"It's always worth the effort, Agnes. You never know what lies around the next corner."

"Judging by the way my life has gone in the last few years, I can only see more of the same waiting round the next bend for me. It's not much to look forward to."

"Then think of your bairns, Agnes. Harry and Thomas need you and now little Alice too. I heard about your promise to Polly. You can't let her down. Those three little ones will keep you going, I'm sure."

"There'll be four of them soon, Sam. I'm having another one." Agnes touched her stomach.

"So soon! How? I mean, I know how." Sam blushed.

"Sorry, Agnes. That didn't come out right at all. I meant... well, I don't know what I meant. I was shocked that's all."

"It's all right, Sam. It was a shock to me, when I found out. Bill was only home a week, and Thomas was born the second day he was home, so it's a mystery to me too." Agnes shook her head. "I had an easy time of it with Thomas, so I suppose everything got back to normal pretty quickly. Sorry, Sam. I shouldn't be talking women's talk with you like this." Agnes swallowed and looked away. "But I'm still getting used to the idea. The doctor said it happened like that sometimes. All it takes is once."

"I don't mind how you talk to me, Agnes. We're friends. You've been a good friend and I'll be there for you whenever you need me. I've always had a soft spot for you, lass. You know that, don't you?"

"I do, Sam." Agnes didn't know what else to say. She couldn't look at him. She didn't want to encourage Sam's feelings for her. She didn't think it would be right or fair.

"Your Bill will have been pleased with the news, wouldn't he?" Sam asked.

"He doesn't know yet. I was going to write to him before our Polly got killed, and now I'll have to write to tell him about that too. He'll be devastated."

"Were they cousins too? Were they close?"

"Oh, aye." Agnes huffed. "You could say they were close." She decided she'd better change the subject, she didn't want to tell Sam about the complicated relationship she had with her husband. She wouldn't know where to start. "I spoke to Mr Binks, the mill owner, during that raid. We were cooped up together in the basement, and I told him you were hoping to get one of them false legs fitted."

"Why would you tell him anything about me?" Sam's voice held an edge of suspicion.

"Because he was interested in you."

"I didn't think he'd remember who I am."

"Well, he did!" Agnes grinned up at him, happy to be talking on a safe subject. "He thinks a lot about you an all!"

"Does he?"

"Aye, and he said for you to go and see him when you're back on your feet, as it were."

"Why would I do that?"

"So he can give you a job you big daft lad!" Agnes smiled and punched him gently on the shoulder.

"I won't be a charity case!"

"Mr Binks doesn't believe in giving charity, you should know that. He said you were a good worker before and he said he remembered you as a cheerful soul. Go see him, Sam."

"Maybe I will and maybe I won't."

"You'd better, Sam Wood. He's waiting to hear from you. Don't you let me down, now."

"I'll think about it. Can I walk you down to the wake?"

"Yes, we'd better get going before people start talking about us." Agnes started to walk slowly into town, allowing for Sam to hobble along beside her.

"You don't have to worry, Agnes. No one will think you're up to no good with a cripple like me."

"Don't ever call yourself that in front of me, Sam Wood!" Agnes tried to keep her voice light. "You're more of a man with one leg than most around here who have a full set of limbs."

"Do you really think so, Agnes?" Sam hopped along on his crutches beside her.

"Well, you wouldn't win a race against any of them that's for sure!" Agnes smiled and glanced mischievously at the ginger-haired lad. "But you've got guts, and you've got gumption, so I think you'll do all right."

"It's nice that you think so, Agnes. It makes me feel better to know you don't think of me as less of a man because of this." He waved his stump in the air before taking the next careful hop with his crutches.

Agnes felt the first warning signs that Sam might be thinking of her as more than a friend. She quickly dismissed the feeling and thought she was imagining the look of longing in his eyes. She couldn't think of anything to say to him and they walked along, side by side, in silence until they were almost in the centre of town.

"What you going to do when the new baby arrives?" Sam spluttered out of the blue. It was obvious he'd been thinking about her. "You'll have no room in that pram of yours for another little one. Will you get a hand-cart to get them all around?"

Sam was smiling, and she was glad to see he was trying to make light of the awkwardness that had grown between them in the last few minutes.

"Oh, Sam!" Agnes laughed. "I've no idea what I'm going to do, but I'm sure I'll think of something."

"You should stop working, Agnes. It's not right that a

mother of three little ones, soon to be four little ones, should be working as you do."

"I've no choice, Sam. I have to put food on the table."

"What about Bill's army pay? That husband of yours shouldn't be leaving you short. The men I knew sent every penny home to their wives. There's nowt to spend it on anyway over there."

Agnes fell silent again. She couldn't explain to Sam, and she didn't want to hurt his feeling by telling him to mind his own business.

"I'm sorry, Agnes." Sam stopped as they reached the steps of the Crown Arms. I overstepped the mark, didn't I? I am sorry. It's none of my business."

Agnes smiled sadly, she couldn't help it. Sam was so nice. He was so likeable.

"Where is he? Do you know?" Sam asked her.

"I'm not sure. In his letter he wrote about the heat and the dust, so I think he's somewhere in the desert. He's in the Seventh Armoured division now if that means anything to you. I think he was involved in that battle for Tobruk."

"He'll be a desert rat, then. That's what the lads are calling them. Vicious fighters they are. They're getting a reputation for being brave and standing their ground."

"Well, that first bit sounds like Bill." Agnes shuddered, and thought her husband would fit in well with a bunch of ferocious and daring soldiers. He'd already killed before he left Britain's shores. She didn't think he'd fit the description of being brave. Bill was a coward, and the only way he knew how to stand his ground was by being a bully.

"I'll bet you're proud of him."

Agnes couldn't bring herself to look into Sam's eyes. Proud wasn't a word she would have used when thinking of her husband.

"Shall we go in? It's getting cold out here." Agnes climbed the few steps into the pub and watched Sam valiantly hop up them with the aid of his crutches. "I don't want to go in there." She confessed to Sam. "When they've had a few, the knives will come out, and everything will descend into arguments and back stabbing. It's always the same at wakes."

"Well, if you'd rather not go in, Agnes." Sam hesitated. "We could go back to the house if you'd prefer."

Agnes saw that same look of longing in Sam's eyes again, and was almost tempted to go and spend some time alone with this lovely man, but common sense told her to go to the wake. "I'd better show my face or I'll never hear the end of it. Missing me own auntie and cousin's wake! Whatever will folks say?" She tried to smile and make light of the circumstances, but her heart was being drawn to Sam. She didn't know where these new feelings would lead her, so she chose to ignore them for now and push them aside. She didn't need the complication of a new love in her life when the old one was still burning so brightly in her heart.

Chapter Eighteen, Revelations

The cold winter gave way to spring, just as the snowdrops at Polly and Hilda's funeral had promised. Agnes had seen lots of changes during the last few months. Her house had become more crowded, but she didn't mind that her uncle and cousin moved in to live with her. Where else were they to go? Bert and David moved into Polly's room, and Agnes had the three children in with her. Harry shared her bed, and the two babies slept end to end in the cot.

Bert had asked her to give up working at the mill. He told her that he would pay her an allowance for himself and David, and little Alice. Agnes accepted his offer, but said she preferred to keep on working, if only part time, because she liked to spend time being useful, and making army blankets for the fighting men might not sound much, but it gave her a purpose. It also meant that she could continue to see Sam. He lifted her spirits and made her laugh. She didn't want to give up contact with her friend, and she knew it would be frowned upon if she were to see him too often outside the working environment. He asked her frequently to go for a drink with him, or to see a film at the picture house, but she refused every time. She liked him a lot, and if she were honest, she liked him more than she should, but she couldn't encourage him. It wouldn't be fair to Sam.

Agnes had a letter from Bill in answer to her note about Polly's death and the expected baby. She had waited a long time, expecting a reply to her letter, and the tatty envelope arrived at the end of June. She was relieved to read that he had agreed to increase her allowance to help pay for Alice and the new baby. He explained that he'd always been fond of Polly and Alice, and he would be happy to accept Polly's child into his growing family. Polly had to re-read the letter many times before the words sank in. She couldn't understand the change in her husband. His letter sounded almost reasonable. There was none of the bitter innuendos or recriminations that his previous letters had been full of. She felt it was too good to be true, but realised that he would have had a nasty shock when he opened her last letter. Bill would have been devastated to hear about Polly's death. That might have turned his mind. She was glad she was able to tell him in a note. She wouldn't have wanted to break the awful news face to face with him. She wouldn't have liked to see his reaction.

Bert came home from work when she was starting to read the letter again.

"Is that from your Bill?" Bert asked as he took off his jacket.

"Yes, he talks about having a long hard slog for the last few months, and they're having a bit of a rest before the next push. He doesn't say where, but then he wouldn't be able to, would he? He's talking about swimming in the sea and the men being allowed a bottle of beer each."

"Sounds as if he's having the time of his life over there instead of fighting a war."

"I think he makes light of it because he can't tell me what's really going on. The censors would black it all out anyway, wouldn't they?"

"It's nice to know they can grab a bit of fun while they can. Them lads will see some horrors, Agnes. He won't be the same when he comes home, you know."

"You'll know all about that, won't you, Uncle Bert."

"Aye, lass. I saw some bad things in the last war. Killing someone, well, it does sommat to you, inside like, you know? Well, you won't know, of course. I hope you never do."

Agnes shivered. She hadn't killed anyone, but she knew what it felt like to be responsible for someone's death.

"Be kind to your Bill when he gets back, Agnes."

"That's a strange thing to say, Uncle Bert. He's my husband. Of course, I'm going to be nice to him." Agnes couldn't bring herself to look at her uncle as she spoke the lies.

"Listen, Agnes. I have eyes and I have ears. I know you and Bill don't have the kind of marriage that me and Hilda enjoyed. I know your dad wouldn't have been happy with the union that your mother organised for you."

Agnes froze and looked into her uncle's face, searching his eyes, afraid to see the truth in them.

"Don't look so scared, Agnes. I'm not about to say owt about your little Harry. Me and Hilda knew there was something about the way you and Bill got together so fast. Trudie was wrong to encourage you to start seeing him so soon after your dad died. Anyone could see he was wrong for you."

As Agnes listened, she felt relief washing through her. Bert thought Harry was Bill's child, but guessed that he'd been conceived on the wrong side of the blanket. He didn't know about Andrew, thank goodness.

"There was something about that lad, Agnes. I can't put

me finger on it, but there was a reason he wanted to marry you so fast, and I don't think it were owt to do with the fact that Harry was on the way."

"Uncle Bert, you don't know what you're talking about!" Agnes tried to cover the trembling of her hands by clasping them together. "We had a whirlwind romance, that's all. I think I missed me dad so much, and Bill was around and he was nice to me. You know how it is sometimes." She couldn't believe how easily she was fabricating the past.

"Aye, I know it can happen like that, Agnes. But I don't think that's what happened with you two." Bert fixed her with a stare. "I knew me cousin's lad. He was a lazy so-and-so and always out for an easy life. That's why he took a job at the bank. He had a head for figures and it got him out of doing the heavy labouring that most lads get into around these parts."

"You can't blame Bill for having a brain and using it, Uncle Bert." Agnes's heart was beating fast. She wondered where this conversation was leading.

"I think he used his brain all right when he married you, Agnes. I doubt his heart had anything to do with it."

"Uncle Bert!" Agnes tried to sound affronted. "What are you saying?"

"I was at your wedding, Agnes, and you didn't look like the happy blushing bride I expected to see. You looked sad and there was something about your eyes that didn't quite fit with the rest of your face, lass. Oh, you put on a good act for the priest, but I could see through it."

"You asked me at the time if I knew what I was doing." Agnes felt her world shift. If Bert found out, or guessed the truth, what would he do? Her uncle was a very perceptive man. She decided to call his bluff. "I remember thinking then that you might know what me mam had done."

"What did she do, Agnes?"

"She helped me and Bill to get together. That's all." Agnes didn't dare say more. Bert didn't know enough details to put the whole sorry story together, and she didn't want to give him anything else to think about.

"Then what happened to your dad's money, lass?" Bert pushed for more. "How come Trudie had to get a job at the pub, if she had all that money from the bakery in the bank?"

"She wanted to get out of the house. She missed me dad and needed some company. There's no big mystery, Bert!"

Agnes forced herself to smile around the lies that fell from her lips.

"That doesn't explain why you carried on working with first one and then two bairns to look after. What happened to the money when Trudie died, Agnes? Why didn't it come to you?"

"Because me mam were old fashioned and believed a man should take care of the money in the family." Agnes lied easily, she didn't want Bert to dig any deeper.

"Well, I'll be having words with your husband when he gets home. He shouldn't be keeping you short like that when he has all that money salted away!" Bert changed his tone and spoke more softly. "That money should have been yours, Agnes! I can't believe Trudie would have done that to you."

"Well, she did." Agnes swallowed back her anger and her fear. She had to convince her uncle to keep quiet. If the truth came out about the real reason that Bill had all the money, then more secrets could be uncovered, and the whole mess would unravel and leave Agnes and her children alone. No one would want to have anything to do with her if they knew the whole truth. She called Bill a monster, but she was no better. She watched her own father die in her arms, and instead of getting help, she had put him in the river. What kind of a daughter does that? She knew it was an accident, but if the truth ever came out, she doubted that the authorities would see it that way.

"It's not really owt to do with me, Agnes. I'll keep me nose out. But I'll give you a piece of advice, lass, if you'll let me."

"What's that, Bert?"

"From what I've heard from our Polly and what I've seen with me own eyes, I don't think you're very happy with Bill." He paused, waiting for Agnes to comment, but she kept silent. "Well," Bert said after a few moments, "That silence tells me more than any words you might have said to defend your sham of a marriage."

Agnes flinched.

"Folks talk, Agnes. Your neighbours aren't deaf, you know! They heard the rows between him and your mam, and between the two of you."

"So you've been listening to gossip."

"I'm on your side, lass. I don't like to see you unhappy. Whatever the reason you had for marrying Bill Smithson will always be a mystery to me. I knew he wanted our Polly, but she was too blind to see a good thing when it was staring her in the face. Not that his dad would have liked him to marry our Poll, me having left the church as I did, but she were too busy with that philanderer anyway."

"Why didn't you say anything to me before, Uncle Bert? Why didn't you have all this out with our Polly?"

"Don't you think I didn't try? I told her what was staring her in the face, but she wouldn't have it. Charlie Watson was the only man for her, no matter that he already had a wife and children."

"She knew that Bill wanted her?" Agnes could hardly draw her breath to speak. "Polly knew? Even when I was getting married and she were my bridesmaid? You're telling me that she knew how Bill felt about her?"

"She thought you loved him, Agnes. Why would she spoil your happiness?"

"Because she knew that Bill didn't love me!"

"But you all ready knew that, didn't you?" Bert said quietly.

"Oh, Bert, what a mess I made of things."

"I think your mam had more than a bit to do with the mess you made, didn't she?"

"How much do you know, Bert?" Agnes decided to face the truth head on. She was sick of the lies, but she knew she couldn't tell him the whole truth. He would never understand about her dad.

"Not even half of it, I'm betting. But I know enough to appreciate that it probably wasn't your choice to marry Bill."

"There was no other choice, Uncle Bert." Agnes sighed.

"Do you want to tell me?"

Agnes decided to confide in her Uncle. Not about everything, she could never do that, but he knew enough about her charade of a marriage to deserve the truth about Bill. So she told him about Andrew, and about her dad being against him because he was a Protestant. She told him about the night her father died, sticking to the story she had concocted with Andrew, that Seth never turned up for the meeting, and then Andrew had bad news from Ireland and had to return there.

"What news was it that made him go away and never come back, Agnes?" Bert asked gently.

"I don't know what it was, Uncle Bert." Agnes couldn't think fast enough to fill in that blank in the story.

"It must have been bad. I thought you said he loved you."

"He did, Uncle Bert. I loved him too."

"But he didn't come back for you."

"No." Agnes stared at her clasped hands.

"And you were pregnant?" Bert asked.

"Yes, but Andrew didn't know that when he left. I didn't know until a month or so later."

"Do you think he would have come back for you if he'd known about Harry?"

"I don't know." Agnes shook her head.

"So your mam arranged for Bill to marry you to give the bairn a name, and offer you a way out."

"That's about it, Uncle Bert." Agnes felt ashamed and hung her head low.

"And the money from your dad's bakery?"

"That was the only way me mam could get Bill to agree to it. She offered him it as my dowry."

"I knew it!" Bert thumped the table. "I knew there was something fishy about what happened to that brass."

"You won't say anything, will you, Uncle Bert?" Agnes pleaded. "Please don't make this worse than it is."

"How can it get worse, Agnes?"

Agnes realised that it could get much worse if Bert knew the complete truth, but he seemed happy enough with the part of the story she'd told him.

"The way I see it, Agnes, you're tied to a man you don't love. So you either make the best of it and welcome him back with open arms, and you stop all this rowing that gives the street cause to gossip."

"Or?" Agnes raised her eyes to meet his.

"Or you start to live the life you want to live, not one that others made for you. Without him."

"How can I do that with three bairns and another on the way? I can't leave him. I can't afford to."

"Money isn't everything, Agnes. Me and Hilda had no more than a few coppers left over at the end of the week, but we had the happiest marriage a man could hope for. It's not what's in the purse that counts, lass. It's what's in here." Bert tapped his chest. "If you don't have that, then what's it all about?"

"You make it sound so easy, Uncle Bert."

"It won't be easy, Agnes. I won't pretend that. But if you don't love Bill, and he doesn't love you, what are you doing together? It's a waste of two lives, love."

After Bert had left to do his shift on fire watch and David went to do his home guard duties, Agnes thought about the discussion she'd had with Bert. The two six-month-old babies were tucked up in bed, and Harry was sitting at her feet playing with his painted boat. She didn't want to put Harry to bed, he was company for her, and so she let him play. She picked up the knitting needles and yarn from the bag by her chair and began to work more rows on the cardigan for little Alice.

She felt the baby moving inside her, and realised that her life would change again very soon when the baby came, but hoped things wouldn't change too much. She was enjoying the company of her Cousin David and Uncle Bert, and hoped the disruption of a new baby wouldn't drive them to look for a place of their own. Bert had already told her that he didn't want to impose for too long, but also said that he would stay as long as she wanted him to.

She had enjoyed a few long conversations with Bert since he and David moved in with her, and she had come to realise that he wasn't the ogre that her mother or Polly had made him out to be at times. She found him to be sensitive and thoughtful. He had strong opinions about the church, and a strong sense of right and wrong, which made him seem a little abrupt sometimes, but Agnes had come to recognise that he was a good man with a generous heart. She was glad she'd told him about Bill, even though he had guessed half of the story already. She only hoped he would never guess the rest of it. She knew her uncle would not condone what happened to her father. Even if he believed it had been an accident, he would never understand why Agnes had felt it necessary to tip him into the river and pretend she'd never seen him that night. It even looked bad in her own eyes when she saw it through the distance of years. How could she have behaved in such a way? Because she loved Andrew with all her heart, she answered herself, and she would have done anything to protect him. She didn't want to see him charged for something he hadn't done.

Agnes wondered where Andrew was now. He'd never tried to contact her since she said goodbye to him on the canal side. Andrew didn't even know that Harry existed.

Andrew could have written to her, he knew the address. She often wondered why he'd never tried to contact her. She would have liked to know what happened to him. She was curious to know if he still loved her, or thought of her. She couldn't contact him. She had no idea where he might be, but

Andrew would know exactly where Agnes was. He had no excuse for not writing.

So much had happened in her life in that short time. She wondered what Andrew had been doing. Had he gone to Cork as he said he would? Was he still there? Would George come across him as she hoped he might? Would he get her message? Would he still want to honour his snowdrop's promise? If she were to divorce Bill, there'd be no reason why she couldn't marry Andrew, but would she still want to? So much had changed. Would he still love her? Did she still love him?

Agnes sighed and put her knitting to one side. "Come here, Harry. It's time you went to bed." She lifted her son onto her lap.

"No want bed, Mammy." Harry leant against her.

"Well, we'll have a bit of a cuddle first, shall we?" She stroked her son's head.

"Sing bonny man, Mammy?" Harry asked, sleepily.

Agnes began to hum the tune of 'my bonny lies over the ocean,' and realised with startling clarity that her feelings for the boy's father had changed. She no longer thought of Andrew, in the same way that she had three years ago. When she was pregnant with Harry, Andrew was all she could think about. He filled her wakeful mind in the daytime, and she dreamt of him every night. She now knew that her love for Andrew had grown dim with the passing of time, and lately, another man was filling her thoughts and her dreams.

Chapter Nineteen, Friends and lovers

With Agnes's baby due any day, she had given up work at the mill. Even though she had only worked half days for the last six months, standing on her feet all afternoon was taking its toll on her health. Swollen ankles were the first sign of stress on her body, and under doctor's orders, Agnes agreed to stay at home with her children.

She loved spending time with her little ones. Harry was nearly two now and was quite the little man of the house. He looked after his baby brother and cousin like a mother hen. Having the two nine-month-old babies so close in age was like looking after twins, although they couldn't be more different. Alice was dainty and sweet natured, where Thomas was a chubby baby with a tendency to throw a tantrum or sulk if he didn't get his own way. If there were trouble, Thomas was usually behind it.

One Sunday afternoon, Agnes was hanging some laundry on the line in the yard when she heard Harry shouting and Thomas screaming. She ran back inside to see Harry holding Thomas tightly in his arms and the baby was screaming and struggling to escape.

"Let go of him, Harry!" Agnes demanded. "Tell me what's going on."

"Thom hurt Ally, Mammy."

Agnes went to pick Thomas from the floor. "What have you been up to you little tyke?"

"He 'natched dolly!" Harry told her. "You thay not 'natch."

"That's right, Harry. Good boy for remembering that you shouldn't snatch things from each other. But you have to see that Thomas is only a baby, and he doesn't remember the rules as well as you do."

"He hit Ally!" Harry threw in for good measure, standing tall and trying to look grown-up and important.

"We must not smack, Thomas." Agnes said to the younger child. "Now go and say sorry to your sister." She put the baby on the floor and watched him crawl to Alice, who stared at the commotion with wide eyes, from the rug.

"Go on, Thomas." Agnes encouraged. "Say sorry."

Thomas put his arms around the little girl and hugged her gently.

"That's a good boy. Now! Play nicely. No more arguing, do you hear me?"

Agnes turned to the pot sink and began to peel potatoes for a meal she would make for her family. She realised she had referred to Alice as Thomas's sister quite naturally. She no longer thought of the infant as Polly's child. She loved her as her own, and the two boys treated her as a sibling. She turned to see that they were all happy and playing together. Thomas and Alice were giggling as they played tug-of-war with the rag doll, and Harry lay on his stomach watching them. "Be genkle, Thom." The older boy was overseeing the play, making sure his playmates played fairly.

Harry was mature for his tender years. His talking skills were improving by the day.

A knock on the door interrupted her thoughts, and she wiped her hands on her apron as she waddled to open it.

"Sam! What are you doing here?" she asked with a beaming smile.

"It's a lovely afternoon and the lads from the factory are playing a team of the lasses in a cricket match on Sand's Lane. I thought you might like to take a walk with the bairns and watch them."

"I was just starting to make the tea."

"We can take a picnic, what do you say?"

Sam was standing on the step smiling up at Agnes, and she felt her chest tighten. He was such a thoughtful man, and she knew he cared deeply for her. She knew she shouldn't encourage the feelings. Her life was complicated enough. "I don't know, Sam."

"You're worried people will talk, aren't you?"

"Well, yes! Look at the state of me!" Agnes stroked a hand over her large stomach.

"What's wrong with you, Agnes? You're ready to have a baby, and you are blooming. You've never looked more beautiful, but how can folks seriously accuse me of carrying-on with you when you're about to have Bill's child?" Sam pointed to her stomach. "It would be funny if it weren't so preposterous."

"I can't walk far, Sam. I wouldn't make it to the end of the street without me ankles flaring up." She lifted a puffy ankle to show him. "See, they're starting to swell already."

"Well, you sit down and put those poor feet up while I peel your potatoes." Sam pushed past her and limped to the sink.

"Sam Wood! What do you think you are doing?"

"Helping a friend. That's allowed, isn't it?"

"Me help, Unkie Sam?" Harry ran to the man's side and looked up adoringly.

"I don't see why not." Sam lifted Harry and sat him on the wooden drainer. "You can help to wash them."

"All right." Agnes laughed. "You win. I'll need a pan-full mind. Bert and David will be hungry when they get in. They're helping Bert's mates at the allotments. They get a few vegetables for doing some work there. I think Bert likes the company, and David has his eye on a young lass who goes there to help her dad."

"Well, being stuck in the house with all these bairns is no fun for men-folks on a Sunday afternoon."

"Then what are you doing here?" Agnes asked, smiling.

"What you got to go with these?" Sam shook a half-peeled potato at her.

"I got some mince and a couple of onions. I was going to make a cottage pie."

"That's one of my specialities. You sit back and let an expert show you how it's done."

"You're full of surprises, Sam Wood." Agnes settled into the fireside chair to watch him.

"I've got a few more up me sleeve too if you hang around long enough you might see what they are."

Another knock on the door surprised them.

"Expecting anyone, are you?" Sam asked.

"No, but I wasn't expecting you either." Agnes grinned at him as she got to her feet. She couldn't help liking this man. She ponderously made her way to the door.

When she opened the door, her eyes flew wide and she had to grip the door frame to keep herself upright. "Andrew!"

"Hello, Agnes." The Irish lilt of his voice hadn't altered. "Will you invite me inside, or will I stand here all day while you gawp at me? I've come a long way to see you."

"You'd better come in, Andrew." Agnes stepped back to let him pass her, feeling the blood quicken in her veins. She had waited so long for this moment.

"This isn't what I expected to find, Agnes." Andrew looked pointedly at her pregnant stomach, and then to Sam and Harry at the sink. "A nice little scene of domestic bliss."

"It's not what you think, Andrew." Agnes began to explain. "Sam is a friend. He's helping me out."

"So I see." Andrew glanced around the room, taking in the

two crawling babies and his gaze then rested on Harry, sucking his thumb while still sitting on the draining board. "A right little menagerie you got here, Agnes. Twins as well, eh?" Andrew's tone was accusatory.

Agnes felt he was judging her without knowing the facts. That didn't seem like the Andrew she remembered.

"What business is it of yours?" Sam asked, clearly picking up on Andrew's unfriendly tone.

"None whatsoever, or so it would seem." Andrew stood by the door. "I made a mistake, Agnes. I shouldn't have come back."

"So why did you?" Agnes couldn't disguise the hope in her voice.

"Someone gave me a message from you. Something about honouring a snowdrop's promise, but I'm thinking that message was an old one. It might have meant something if it had reached me in time."

"In time for what?" Agnes asked, breathlessly.

"Before you tied yourself to someone else and bore him all these brats!" Andrew looked pointedly at Sam.

"Now that's enough of that kind of talk." Sam strode to stand beside Agnes. "Did you just come here to insult Agnes?"

"Quite the opposite, but it looks as if I arrived a few years too late."

"Andrew, let me explain." Agnes pleaded.

"What's to explain, Agnes? I have eyes and can see the way things are. You moved on, that's plain to see." He looked at her large stomach. "When's that one due?"

"Any day now." Agnes sighed. "I know how it looks, Andrew. I can't blame you for thinking badly of me."

"I don't think badly of you, Agnes. I could never think anything, but good, of the lass who sent me away to keep me safe." Andrew's eyes softened and he looked at her with that familiar smile on his face. "I think I stayed away too long though, didn't I?"

"I thought I might have heard from you. A letter would have been nice." Agnes thought she'd mention her disappointment in him. "Why didn't you write?"

"I didn't want to cause more trouble for you. What would your mammy think of you getting letters from the Irish Protestant?"

"My mam died, Andrew."

"Oh, my love! I'm sorry to hear that." Andrew took a step towards her. "What happened?"

"Does it matter?" Agnes felt her heart softening to his Irish charm. His words sounded sincere, but she began to wonder whether he would still want her now she was no longer the young girl he fell in love with.

"And this little lot?" Andrew indicated the children with a sweep of his hand. "Who did you marry? Not ginger head, obviously. There's not a redhead among them."

Sam lifted his chin and pulled Agnes against his side, but she put a hand on his shoulder to stop him from retaliating.

"It's all right, Sam. I'll deal with this."

"Oh, you'll deal with me, will you?" Andrew smirked. "Just how will you deal with an old lover who had to live in exile because of your daddy's bigotry?"

"Andrew! Please!" She glanced to Sam and hoped Andrew would say no more.

"He doesn't know your dirty secret, does he?" Andrew smiled knowingly. "Your boyfriend doesn't know what a cold-hearted lass you really are, I'll bet."

"Don't do this, Andrew, please." Agnes closed her eyes. She couldn't believe what she was hearing. Did Andrew really think she was cold-hearted? After everything they had meant to each other? "I loved you, Andrew. What we did, we did for love of each other."

"So! You're talking of loving me in the past tense. Am I no longer the object of your desire, my love?" Andrew shook his head. "Then it was all for nothing."

"What's he talking about, Agnes?" Sam looked concerned.

"You are safe, Andrew! You walk the streets a free man. It was not for nothing!" Agnes insisted. "You could have been hanged for what happened."

"I did nothing wrong, and any court in the land would have come to the same conclusion if you'd given me a chance to defend myself! Instead, you insisted that I ran away." Andrew's voice was getting louder.

"Please keep your voice down, man." Sam asked. "You're scaring the bairns."

"I don't want to upset your children, Agnes." Andrew continued in a quieter tone. "But I've had a lot of time to think. I know now that I'll never be able to prove a thing about that night, but by running, everyone will think I'm a guilty man. Only the guilty run. The innocent have nothing to hide. Why did I ever listen to you?"

"Is that why you never contacted me?" Agnes whispered. "You blamed me for making you go away."

"Things could have been so different, Agnes. If you'd let me stay."

"You could have been hanged!" she insisted. "Or put away for life! Who would have believed what really happened? We talked about this! It wasn't just my decision. You can't lay the blame on me. You decided to go back to Ireland." Agnes was beginning to suspect that Andrew was not the man she thought he was.

Sam was looking at each of them in turn with a puzzled frown. "What exactly have you two done?" he asked.

"It was an accident, Sam. I'll explain everything." Agnes put her hand on Sam's chest. "You deserve to know the truth."

"How touching!" Andrew sneered. "Be careful of putting your trust in this woman, Sam. She'll take your heart and drop you like a hot stone as soon as a better offer comes along."

"You can't mean that, Andrew! I loved you. I loved you for years!"

"Is that why you went with another man before my feet touched Irish Soil?"

"I didn't! I would never have done that. I loved you!"

"Tell me how old that boy is." Andrew pointed to Harry cowering on the draining board.

Agnes went to lift her son into her arms. "He's eighteen-months-old. He's big for his age." She said quickly, and looked to Sam, hoping he would trust her enough and would not betray the truth to Andrew. If Andrew guessed the boy was his, it would lead to so many problems, and her life was complicated enough.

"You could have waited for me, Agnes. If you loved me, you would have waited."

"And if you loved me, you would have written to me. How was I supposed to know whether you were alive or dead?" I had no word from you, Andrew! I couldn't live on the memory of our love, though I did just that for years."

"Not years, Agnes." Andrew looked at Harry. "A few months, maybe, judging by the age of your eldest son. I can't have been the love of your life as you told me."

"Have you been livin' like a saint then for the last few years?" Sam asked. "No girlfriends? No lovers?"

Agnes saw Andrew's face flush. "Andrew, I don't think you need to answer Sam's question."

"Who did you marry, Agnes, and where is he if it's not this so-called friend?"

"My husband is away fighting in the war." Agnes didn't want to tell Andrew any more than she had to. Some inner sense told her not to trust him as she once had. "I'm surprised *you're* not in uniform."

"Southern Ireland is neutral, or hadn't you heard?" Andrew drawled. "I don't have to concern myself with a foreign war."

"I heard hundreds of Southern Irishmen have volunteered to serve. They know when to fight for something worth saving. Not all Southern Irishmen are cowards." Sam taunted Andrew.

"Don't you dare call me a coward! I don't see you wearing uniform and you look fit enough for conscription."

Sam pulled up his trouser leg to display his false foot. He bent to knock on it with his knuckles for good measure. "Some of us have already done our bit and paid heavily for it." As he straightened, he pointed his finger at Andrew. "But I'll tell you this much! I'd do it all again if they'd let me, to keep our country safe from the clutches of that monster over in Germany."

"Brave words, ginger-nut, but you're the fool. You're the one that will have to live the rest of your life as a cripple."

"At least I can look at myself in the mirror and not feel shamed, unlike the coward that you are. How can you live with yourself?"

"I told you not to call me that, and if you say it one more time —."

"Please, stop this! Stop it now! Think of my bairns. They don't need to see grown men fighting and arguing." Agnes pulled away from Sam and went to the door. "I think it's time you left, Andrew."

"Before you go, I have something to say." Sam turned to Agnes. "Don't worry, lass, I'll not cause trouble." He took a step closer to Andrew and the two men looked each other in the eye.

"Well, what is it, ginger?"

"I don't know what you've done, or what it is that you and Agnes did, but I know Agnes, and I know she's good through and through. If you don't know that, then you don't know her at all, and you don't deserve her."

"And you do, is that it?" Andrew mocked.

"I know that a grown man wouldn't let a lass talk him into owt he didn't want to do. You wanted to run because you couldn't face the music and own up to whatever it was you did. You were a coward then and you're a coward now."

Andrew flexed his hands and balled them into fists at his side. "I told you not to call me that again."

"You won't punch me, Andrew. Your sort always takes the easy way out. Agnes never took the easy way. You think it's been easy for her to raise all these bairns with no man around to help? They're not all hers, but you didn't think to ask about that, did you?"

Andrew looked at Harry and narrowed his eyes, then looked at the two infants cowering by Agnes's feet.

"No matter. We'll be glad to see the back of you. Cowards aren't welcome here."

"Are you going to let him talk to me like that, Agnes?"

"What choice do I have, Andrew?" Agnes lifted her head. "As Sam says, he's a grown man and doesn't need a lass to tell him what to do or say."

"Time to go, Andrew." Sam pulled the door open and waited for Andrew to leave.

"Do you want me to go, Agnes?"

Agnes couldn't speak. Her emotions were in turmoil. She nodded and watched him shake his head at her. She had yearned to see this man for such a long time. He had filled her thoughts and her dreams for years, and now she realised she didn't know what to think. Had she wasted her time worshipping a love that had no foundation in reality? Had she been chasing fairytales by clinging to the hope of a happy ending with Andrew? He didn't seem the man she thought he had been, and she felt bitterly disappointed with him for the way he conducted himself just now. She looked into his face and saw anger and self-pity there. She didn't recognise the man before her as the man she had loved with all her heart. She didn't see the love she had long expected to see in his eyes.

As Andrew turned and walked out of her house, Agnes felt tightness in her chest. She had loved the memory of him for such a long time, and it was painful to watch him walk away from her. She wanted to call him back, but she didn't want to see that awful look in his eyes. The look that accused and condemned her. The meeting she had hungered for was turning out to be very different to how she had imagined it would be in her dreams.

Sam closed the door and took Agnes into his arms. She clung to her friend and tried not to cry. Andrew didn't deserve any more of her tears. She could have stayed in Sam's arms forever. She felt so safe with him. Her feelings were tangled and in knots, but even while her heart was clinging to the memory of Andrew, she felt Sam was taking his place in her affections. Agnes felt confused and disorientated by her conflicting emotions. She was almost relieved when Sam's arms loosened around her.

"Do you want to tell me what that was about?" Sam asked gently as he released her.

"It's a long story, Sam." She didn't know whether she was ready to tell him, but after what he'd just heard, she thought he deserved to know the truth.

"Sit down, Agnes. I'll make us a brew and you can tell me while I finish that cottage pie for your tea."

Agnes told him the whole sorry tale, leaving nothing out. "I loved him, Sam. I was mad with love. It's the only explanation I can give for what I did. I'll never forgive meself for what I did to me dad."

"The way I see it, Agnes..." Sam came to crouch at her side. "Your poor dad was already dead. You didn't hurt him. Andrew didn't hurt him. It was an accident. I believe you."

"That means so much to me, Sam." Agnes looked into his eyes and knew he was sincere. "I'll always wonder how things might have turned out if we'd gone for help that night, but I'll never know."

"Any amount of help would not have brought your dad back, Agnes, and I know how it feels to love someone so much that you would do anything to protect them."

She couldn't look into Sam's eyes any longer. His love for her was clear, but she couldn't accept his feelings. "I'm glad you understand, Sam."

"I'll not say anything, Agnes. Your secret is safe with me. If you don't want Andrew to know that Harry is his bairn, I won't tell him." He patted her hand and got to his feet.

"It would complicate things, Sam."

"I can see that, but maybe Andrew has a right to know?"

"He gave up any rights when he decided not to write to me. He could have, but he chose not to, didn't he?"

"Whatever his reasons, Agnes, he's back now, and I have a feeling you won't have heard the last from him."

"I hope you're wrong, Sam."

"Well, we'll see. That pie is ready to go in the oven. I'll go now if you're all right, and I'll see you later."

"Thanks, Sam." Agnes reached to touch his hand. "Thanks for everything."

Chapter Twenty, Letter form a stranger

Bill's letter came in the October, a year after Agnes had written to let him know his daughter had arrived safely. It had been delivered by one of her old neighbours as it was posted to her previous address. Bill wouldn't know she had moved. She held the envelope in her hands but didn't open it. She listened to her children playing outside. Helen was asleep in the pram, by the back door. The late October weather was unusually warm, and the children were making the most of it, dashing around shouting and kicking a ball that David had given them.

Agnes stared at the small brown envelope and wished with all her heart that Bill would understand when she next wrote to him. She had decided to take control of her own life. She didn't want to be cruel and end her marriage while he was so far away, but the war gave her no choice. She'd already written a letter asking for a divorce. It stood behind the clock on the mantelpiece, but she hadn't plucked up the courage to send it yet.

She sent the last letter after she gave birth to Helen. Little Helen was born without complications late in September, a couple of weeks overdue. From the day she was born, the household fell in love with her. Bert would often volunteer to hold her, and David offered to change her when Agnes was busy dealing with the other little ones. She knew that Bill would be happy to hear the news. He never showed affection to Harry, but he certainly loved his own son, Thomas, and had a special place in his heart for Alice because she was Polly's child.

Goodness knows how things would work out if he refused her a divorce and wanted to come back and share her life again. She knew it would be a different life to the one they had before the war came along to disrupt everything. She disliked Bill before they were married, but she quickly came to hate him, especially after his cruel treatment of her. Then after she heard him confess to killing her mother, she detested him. She knew she would never be able to live with him again. Now she had moved house, and things were on a firmer footing with her Uncle Bert, she hoped she might never have to live with her husband again, and was determined to unshackle herself from the marriage as soon as she could.

Having her Uncle Bert as an ally helped her decide. They'd shared a home for almost two years now, and she felt as close to him as if he'd been her own father. He made her see that anything was possible if you wanted it badly enough.

Agnes's bedroom was overcrowded when Helen was born, and Bert suggested that he and David find other accommodation, but Agnes insisted that she was happy with the way things were. She liked having her uncle and cousin around. She didn't mind that her sleeping arrangements were cramped. When Bert recommended a solution some months later, she was happy to hear him out. Eventually he'd found a little house on the outskirts of town. It had three bedrooms, a kitchen, a parlour, and dining room. The garden clinched it for Agnes. With four little ones, a nice outside space would be perfect.

Bert had taken her to see it while David watched the children, and Agnes fell in love with the grubby cottage.

"Oh, Bert, can we afford it?" Agnes couldn't keep the grin from her face. "I love it!"

"We can afford the rent between us; if you're sure you still want me and David round your neck."

"Uncle Bert, you know I love having you live with me. What would I do for adult conversation if you weren't around?"

"It'll need a bit of cleaning up. It's been left empty for a year or so, and we'll have to build an Anderson shelter, there's no cellar."

"I'll soon see to the cleaning if you can take care of everything else, Uncle Bert!"

"Shall I tell the owner we'll take it then?"

Agnes had thrown her arms around Bert and hugged him close. "Thank you for finding us this. It's perfect!"

Bert and David made repairs to the guttering, and did some general maintenance. Bert made sure there would be enough furniture for their needs, and they had moved in the following week. Agnes set to work making the rooms fresh and clean while the children explored the new house. Harry ran from room to room with the two toddlers following him.

"Alith come see de beds! They 'normous!" Harry yelled from the top of the stairs.

"Be careful on them steps," Agnes had warned, and went to make sure the little ones were safe. "Come on, Thomas, let me help you." She held the boy's hand and followed close behind Alice as the toddling girl mounted the stairs on hands and knees.

"See de beds that Uncle Bert made? I go sleep up top!"

Harry scrambled up the ladder that Bert had made, to reach one of the top bunks.

Agnes had watched her children climbing around the two sets of bunk beds that Bert had erected against the walls on either side of the room. He'd built them for the children telling Agnes that they wouldn't always be infants. The beds would last them a good few years. Alice and Thomas could sleep on the bottom beds for now, but when Helen became old enough to leave her cot in Agnes's room, she would be able to join her siblings in the children's room.

Agnes had hugged herself as she watched her children playing together. She felt fortunate to have all this and lucky to have her Uncle Bert on her side.

Over the months since they'd moved in to the new house, Bert didn't often talk about her situation with her husband, but when he did mention it, he made sure she understood that he was there to help her, whatever she decided to do. She hadn't told him that Andrew had called to see her before Helen was born, though she'd been able to think of little else since his visit. She couldn't understand her emotions about Andrew. She had loved the memory of him for such a long time, but since she'd seen him again, the reality of him didn't match the emotion in her heart. She didn't trust her feelings. Sam had noticed that she was distant with him, and although he didn't put it into words, Agnes knew he was hurt. She didn't want to give Sam false hope, and her uncle had noticed the way it was between her and Sam, and warned her to go carefully. "Don't lead him on, Agnes. It's not fair to the lad. At least try to sort things out with you and Bill first, eh?"

If only it were as simple as sorting things with Bill. Bert had no idea that Andrew was still complicating her emotions. If only he'd never come back to stir up her feelings for him.

The letter still lay on Agnes's lap, and she couldn't put off opening it any longer. Carefully, she tore the top off the envelope and opened it to read the long letter in tiny script written on the inside of the fragile brown paper.

"*Agnes*," it began, and she thought that he could at least have used an endearment of some sort, but a simple and abrupt, 'Agnes,' was all she got.

"*I am glad to hear that my second child arrived safely. Helen would not have been my choice, but I will accept it as I couldn't there to choose the name for my own little girl.*"

Agnes's bit her lips together. The arrogance of him, she

thought, referring to Helen repeatedly as 'his' child was infuriating.

"*I'm part of the Eighth Army now. The sergeant told us there are thousands of us here in the desert, though I only see the men in my unit. It's good to know we have the manpower to do the job,*" the next bit was blacked out by the censor. "*So I won't be home anytime soon, no doubt you'll be glad to hear that. I miss my lad, and hope you are telling him who is daddy is. I would hope baby Helen will know that I am her daddy, too.*"

Agnes thought she could see a glimmer of his softer side when he wrote of his children, but realised that Bill had no softer side as she continued to read.

"*As for Bert and David moving into our house, I hope they are paying their way. I won't support your extended family. It is bad enough that I have to support you, after all that was arranged before our marriage. I agreed to it because I know it would be more expensive to put all the bairns into a nursery so you could work. I hope you know that when Helen reaches school age, I will expect you to return to the original arrangements.*"

Agnes shook her head. He was unbelievable!

"*There will be some changes when I get back. I have a lot of time to think over here. I have decided that I don't want to spend the rest of my life with someone I dislike so much. You once asked for a divorce, and I now want the same.*"

Agnes couldn't believe what she was reading.

"*My father will not be happy, and Father Brennan will be against it, but that doesn't bother me. This war has changed me. Seeing so much death makes me realise my life is precious. I don't want to spend the rest of my life tied to someone I don't desire, don't have feelings for, and can't respect.*"

Agnes shot to her feet. "You pompous, unfeeling, bullying buffoon!"

"I hope that's not aimed at anyone I know."

Agnes spun to face the door and saw James standing there with his kit bag over his shoulder. "James! What a lovely surprise!" She ran to give the young man a hug. "Did your dad know you were coming home?"

"No, I thought I'd surprise you."

"Well, you did that, James! Come in." Agnes stood back to let her cousin enter their new home and tucked Bill's letter into her apron pocket. "What do you think of our new home?"

"It's grand, Agnes. You've made it nice, I can tell."

"How long are you home for?"

"That's the first question everyone asks!" James laughed. "Can't wait to see the back of me, eh?"

"Not at all, you daft thing. You know how pleased we are to see you. Your dad and David will be over the moon."

"They gave me a few days off. I've been thrashing the hell out of Jerry for the last few weeks and I'm exhausted."

"Oh, lad!" Agnes went to take his jacket and could see the dark circles under his eyes. "Come and sit down and I'll make you a nice cup of tea. Bert and David should be home in an hour, so you can put your feet up and have a snooze if you like."

"You wouldn't mind?"

"Tell you what, James. Go get into bed and have a proper sleep. You look like you need one."

"You're one in a million, Agnes. Are you sure you don't mind?"

"My house is your house, love. We share the rent, and your dad won't mind if you share his bed. The bedroom to the right at the top of the stairs is yours."

"Don't bother with the tea, Agnes. I'll have one when I wake if that's all right."

Agnes watched him wearily make his way upstairs. James was doing an amazing job. He was flying bombers from a base down in Lincolnshire, and by the sound of it had been working nonstop. He looked exhausted, and she felt so sorry for the young man.

"Woo dat man, Mammy?" Harry came running into the house. "Where is he?"

"That's our cousin James, Harry. He's very tired and he's gone for a sleep, so can you keep the noise down?" Agnes asked her son.

"Why, Mammy?"

Harry had reached the age of questioning everything. 'Why,' was his favourite word. Agnes ruffled his hair and told him to go and play. Harry ran outside to his siblings, shouting to tell them to keep quiet. Agnes smiled and shook her head at the boy.

She pulled the letter from her apron pocket and read it through one more time. She couldn't believe that Bill had changed his mind. She could divorce him. She would get him out of her life. It was the best news she could have hoped for. She didn't know where to start, or who she would need to see to start the proceedings, but she knew that her Uncle Bert would help her. She couldn't wait for him to get home.

She busied herself making a potato and onion pie for tea, with a scraping of cheese in the pastry to make it tastier. She fed Helen and called the children to eat theirs before Bert and David came home. The children were all ready for bed when Bert and David came through the door.

Agnes put a finger to her lips and pointed to the kit bag that stood against the wall. "James is home," she whispered. "He's asleep upstairs."

Bert and David grinned widely.

"Why the whispering?" David asked.

"He's tired out, poor thing. I don't think he's had much sleep in the last few weeks. That's why they sent him home for a rest."

"It'll be good to see him." Bert took his work boots off by the door. "What's for tea?"

Agnes got the plates from the oven and put them on the table in the dining room. "Come through here and have some peace from the little ones while you eat."

"It's nice having our tea in the dining room!" David grinned.

"Aye, my Hilda would have liked this house."

"It's a lovely house, Bert. The children love the garden. They've been out there all day."

"Well, I'll be able to pay a bit more of the rent soon." David told them. "I'm going down the mine from next week. I joined Bevin's Boys. I'm old enough, and strong enough, and I know the job, so don't try to talk me out of it, Dad."

"I wouldn't talk you out of it son. Why would you think I'd want to?"

"I thought you might want me to join the proper army and go and fight for me country."

"Staying at home and keeping the country going is just as important, lad. I wouldn't want to think you were overseas risking your life."

"It's a dangerous job, David. Are you sure this is what you want to do?" Agnes asked.

"He'll be safer here in Yorkshire, lass, and he'll not have to face the kind of thing that I had to in the last war. I wouldn't want hat for a son of mine. I'm glad you'll be staying home, lad." Bert patted his son's hand.

"Eat your tea while it's warm." Agnes told them. "I saved

some for James for when he wakes up. I'm going to put the bairns to bed."

"Come and give your Uncle Bert a cuddle afore ye go up." Bert called to the little ones.

Harry was first in the queue to climb on Bert's lap. "Night Unkie Bert." The little boy kissed his uncle's cheek.

"Night, son." Bert lifted him to the floor and scooped the two toddlers into his arms. He kissed them while they wrapped their arms about him. "Night, night, you two. Be quiet for your mammy and go straight to sleep."

"Don't wake your uncle James." David called softly as they trooped up the stairs.

When Agnes reached the top of the stairs, with Helen in her arms, James was coming out of the bedroom. "I hope we didn't wake you, James."

"No, I think it was the smell of that pie that woke me. I'm starving!"

"It's in the oven, James. If you wait two minutes, I can get it out for you when I've settled these into bed."

"I can do it, Agnes. I can see you've got your hands full. Night, night, you lot. I'll give you a game of footie tomorrow."

Agnes ushered the little ones into the beds.

As she was tucking Harry into his top bunk, he asked her, "Mammy, is dat my daddy?"

"Goodness, no, Harry. It's Bert's son, and David's brother. James is our cousin."

"Where my daddy?"

"He's away fighting the Germans, you know that."

"Him come home, Mammy?"

"I don't know, love." Agnes didn't want to get into the complicated discussion with her son who was too young to understand. "Go to sleep now."

She closed the door and stood in the semidarkness at the top of the stairs. If she got a divorce, the children might suffer. They wouldn't have a daddy around after the war. Then she realised that lots of children wouldn't have a daddy after the war. Lots of men wouldn't survive to come home to their families. Her children would be no worse off than any of them. She had no reason not to go through with what Bill had asked. She would ask Bert for his advice at the first opportunity.

Chapter Twenty-One, Realisation

Agnes was Christmas shopping while Bert looked after the children for her. The shop-fronts were uninviting; a few had Christmas goods on offer, but all the window displays were in darkness because of the blackout. Food was rationed so strictly that Agnes feared the Christmas table would be a poor affair this year. Tinned salmon and beef paste wasn't what she would have preferred to offer her family, but she was hoping to find some tobacco as a present for her uncle. She'd managed to buy some wooden blocks for the babies and a fire engine for Harry in a second-hand shop. She'd knitted some socks for David, and although the presents weren't the most imaginative she'd ever given, at least she had been able to get something for everyone.

She had invited Sam and his father for Christmas dinner. She knew that Bert couldn't openly approve anything other than friendship with Sam, while she was still married to Bill, but her uncle kept his thoughts to himself. He knew she had seen the solicitor he had found for her, and although the man had warned her that it would take a long time, she knew the divorce could go through. She had another appointment with him in January. Bill would have to pay all the costs because she had no money apart from what he sent her. He would also have to admit adultery, and would have to provide a witness willing to testify that he had, but amazingly, he had agreed by letter to do everything asked of him.

She still didn't dare to encourage Sam in case anything went wrong. She wanted to wait until she was a free woman before starting a relationship with her friend. She wasn't sure whether Sam was what she really wanted. Seeing Andrew a year ago had upset her, and although she knew it would probably never have worked out with her Irish lover, she wasn't sure Sam would be able to fill the void Andrew had left in her heart. She knew Bert worried that Sam might get hurt, and he'd told Agnes that it was obvious to him that Sam wanted more than friendship. Agnes knew that Sam was waiting for her to respond to his gentle advances, but told herself that she had nothing to reproach herself for. Agnes had flirted a little with Sam, but she told Bert he had nothing to worry about because nothing had happened. Sam always treated her with respect, and never overstepped the boundary of friendship.

By the sound of the news broadcasts, it looked as though the war might soon be over. Germany had turned away from Britain and was now locked in battle with Russia. America was in the fight since Japan had bombed one of their harbours last year. Britain had enjoyed success in battles at El Alemein, and Rommel withdrew from El Agheila a few days ago. Agnes had reason to hope peace might come soon.

"Hello, Agnes!" Enid called and hurried over the street to join her. "I haven't seen you for such a long time. How are you?"

"Oh, we're all right, Enid. How are you? How's the nursery doing?" Agnes glanced at the town hall clock.

"Booming, Agnes. We've taken on another lass, and we have more than forty children, in shifts, like. Wouldn't do to have them all at the same time. What you got?" Enid looked at the bags Agnes was carrying.

"Nothing too exciting, Enid. You know what it's like with the rationing. I was hoping to find some tobacco for a present for me Uncle Bert, but no one seems to have any left."

"Well, Christmas Eve morning is a bit late for shopping for tobacco, love. It will all have sold out. You could try that little newspaper shop on Daisy Hill. He might have some cigars for a price."

"Oh, thanks, Enid. I'll go there now."

"How's little Helen doing? I haven't seen you since she was a month or so old, she'll be a year now won't she?"

"Oh, she rules the roost! The others adore her. If she cries, there's always one of them to rock the pram for me. They fight over the privilege." Agnes laughed. "I'm sure our Alice thinks she's a living dolly."

"Have you heard from Bill? I bet he's pleased he's got a little girl."

"I had a card from him a few days ago. It didn't say much, but he's happy about Helen." Agnes didn't want to discuss the details of her martial breakup with her auntie's friend.

"Well, I'll let you get on, lass. I can see you'll have your hands full when you get home."

"Bye, Enid. Happy Christmas."

Agnes made her way to the little shop Enid had suggested, her mind filled with thoughts of Christmas and the chores waiting for her when she got home. She wasn't looking where she was going and apologised instinctively when she bumped into someone.

"No need to apologise, Agnes."

The Irish voice stopped her feet from moving. She looked back into Andrew's face and her mouth fell open. "I thought you'd gone back to Ireland," she blurted.

"I thought I'd stick around and see what happened." He pointedly looked at her flatter stomach. "You had the latest bairn then?"

Agnes felt awkward. She didn't know how to talk to the man who was now like a stranger. The Andrew, who stood before her, bore no resemblance to the Andrew she had dreamed about for so many years. He looked the same, but something had changed and Agnes couldn't work out what was different. "I had a little girl."

"So now you have two of each. Oh, no, of course, they're not all yours are they?"

Agnes heard the derision in his voice and quickly turned to walk away from him. She didn't know how she felt about this man, but she didn't like his tone. When his hand shot out to grab her arm, she was shocked. "Let go of me!" she demanded.

"Don't walk away, Agnes. I want to talk to you. Please." He added.

Agnes shrugged her arm free of his grasp. "All right, I'm listening." She faced him with more daring than she felt inside. "Though I think we said all that needed saying last year, don't you?" She felt her heart hammering in her chest. He still had the power to unnerve her.

"I judged you harshly, Agnes, and I've had a long time to think about everything. I've thought about you constantly." He touched her sleeve. "Will you at least tell me who you married?"

"That's no concern of yours." She was wary of him, and didn't want to give him a chance to get close to her. She didn't know how she would react if he took her into his arms. She didn't trust herself.

"When did you get married, Agnes? How long did you wait before you fell in love with someone else?"

"What's it to you, Andrew?" Agnes stepped away from him to put some distance between them. "You didn't think to contact me. How long did you wait before you bedded another lass? I won't say, 'fell in love with', because I don't think you know what the meaning of the word is." She was finding the strength to resist him, and his abrupt attitude was strengthening her resolve to keep him at arm's length.

"I loved you, Agnes. With all my heart and soul."

"If you did, Andrew, why did you abandon me?"

"You told me to go!" Andrew spluttered.

"And your love for me was so great that you disappeared without a trace!" Agnes felt bitter now at all the long months she spent hoping to hear from him.

"I still have feelings for you, Agnes."

"I'm not interested, Andrew." She recognised the truth of her words as she said them and laughed. "We never stood a chance, did we?"

"What do you mean?"

"You were the first man that ever showed interest in me, and I fell for your Irish charm. I thought you loved me. I wanted to spend the rest of my life with you. I believed you when you explained about the pregnant Irish girl you ran away from, but now I'm not so sure that story rings true. The more I think about it, the more I don't believe it. You knew the Catholic faith wouldn't accept a Protestant husband, so how come you would think my dad would be any different?"

"I told you the truth, Agnes. I had no idea your father would be so lacking in understanding."

"You knew, Andrew. You knew that what we had would never end in marriage. You strung me along, and flattered me to sleep with you once you were sure you could get away and not have to face any consequences. I played right into your hands didn't I?"

"You've got it wrong, Agnes." Andrew protested feebly. "You dad's accident changed everything.'

"Yes it did. But the outcome would have been the same whether he'd lived or died. I know that now. You would have left me eventually."

"I'm wasting my time here, aren't I?"

"Well, that depends on what you wanted to achieve in coming back." Agnes narrowed her eyes, "Why are you still here, Andrew? You say you've thought about me constantly, but you've been in town for a year and not tried to see me again. Why?"

"You've changed, Agnes."

"I hope I have! I wouldn't like to be the same lovesick girl you left behind. You haven't changed, Andrew. You seem changed from how I remember you, but that's because I saw you through different eyes then. You sweet-talked me and I fell for your cheap lines. I don't think we would have lasted more than a few more months under ordinary circumstances."

"Do you really think so, Agnes? If that's true, I wasted so much time journeying back here."

"We have both wasted our time. I wasted years yearning for something that was never meant to last. I'm glad you came back, Andrew. I'm glad I've seen you again today because you've opened my eyes. We never loved each other. Not really." Agnes realised that she meant every word. "Will you go back to Ireland now?"

"And leave you in peace, Agnes?" Andrew sneered at her. "You'd like that, wouldn't you? You'd like to keep your dirty little secret hidden."

"It wouldn't do you any good to expose it." Agnes said nervously. "You'd be in more trouble than me if it ever came out."

"What if I'm willing to risk that?"

"You wouldn't!" Agnes began to panic then remembered what Sam had said, and felt her courage return. "You're a coward, Andrew, so you wouldn't ever own up to what happened. I'm not afraid of you or what you threaten you might do."

"Brave words, Agnes. But can you really be sure I won't tell?"

Agnes looked into Andrew's face and realised that she never really knew him at all. He reminded her of Bill when he was in the mood to bully her. She didn't understand how she could have fallen for him, or believed she could have loved him so deeply.

"Well? Cat got your tongue?" Andrew taunted, childishly.

"You won't tell, Andrew. You've too much to lose. Go back to Ireland and leave me in peace, will you?"

"I might stick around. It could be interesting to watch you squirming, wondering what I might do."

Agnes flinched at his harsh words, but she felt anger bubbling up inside her. She decided she needed to take control. "Don't stay around too long, or the authorities might start asking questions. Tell me, why is a fit young Irishman so interested in England?" She didn't like being intimidated, and thought of a way to make Andrew feel insecure. "You might get arrested as a spy. I've heard that foreigners can't be trusted. Someone might notice you acting shifty and report you."

"Who would report me?"

Agnes stared at him and straightened her shoulders.

"You wouldn't!"

"Try me." Agnes saw him draw back but resisted the urge to smile. "If I see you again, I'll be tempted to tell someone."

"You are a hard-hearted bitch, Agnes Garrity."

"If I am, it's down to you." Agnes realised this was true. She would never have done what she did to her father if it weren't for her infatuation with Andrew. She knew now that it hadn't been love. Real love is a much deeper emotion, but she hadn't recognised that until a few moments ago. What she felt for Andrew was a shallow passion. It wouldn't have stood the test of time if circumstances hadn't given it an added dimension of fear and desperation.

"I pity your husband." Andrew turned his nose up at her. "He's away being a brave soldier and his wife is carrying-on with a cripple behind his back. How is ginger-head? Still sniffing around, is he?"

"I feel pity for you, Andrew. You'll never know what real love feels like because you are too selfish to give love unconditionally. That's what real love is. You call me hard-hearted, but your heart is made of ice. I hope you find someone who might thaw it for you, but I doubt that will happen." Agnes turned to leave him, but Andrew caught her arm.

"Don't leave it like this, Agnes. We meant something to each other once. We can't part like this. I'm sorry. I don't want to hurt you. I don't want to make life difficult for you. I don't mean any of those nasty things I said just now." Andrew pleaded with her. "I'll go back to Ireland and leave you alone, if that's what you want, but leave me with something, Agnes. Don't think badly of me for wanting you."

"You don't want me, Andrew. You want the memory of me, and that girl doesn't exist any longer." Agnes softened her tone. "I thought I loved you, Andrew, and I believe you thought you loved me too. Now I know what real love is, and what we shared doesn't even come close."

"Your husband must be a very lucky man."

"He will be." Agnes walked away with her head held high.

The wireless was playing softly in the background as she let herself into the warm kitchen. Bert was feeding Helen from a spoon, and Harry was playing with a paper angel on the floor with Alice and Thomas.

"She can fly, see?" Harry fluttered the paper wings of the angel. "She fly up chimly to daddy mismas."

"They look happy enough. Thanks for minding them, Bert."

"Mammy, look Unkie Bert made." Harry waved his paper angel at Agnes.

"She's lovely, Harry." Agnes took off her coat and began to unpack her shopping. "I'll pop upstairs with this bag."

"Is that bag of goodies for Santa?" Bert grinned up at her.

"No, it's for all my family and friends, and you're not to peek until tomorrow." Agnes ran up the stairs to hide the bag under her bed. She'd wrap them in newspaper later when the children were in bed. She sat on the bed and looked through her purchases. The toddlers would love the wooden blocks, and she knew Harry would be thrilled with his red fire truck. She was glad the newspaper shop had a small box of cigarillos that she would share between her uncle and Sam's father, Peter. She paid dearly for them, but she had saved some of her allowance from Bill each month so she could treat her family.

She took out the blue silk tie that she found in the Salvation Army shop and stroked the soft fabric. She hoped Sam would love it. She sighed as she thought about him, and recognised that the feelings she had for him could no longer be hidden. She must have loved him for months, but had only recognised the depth of that love when she was talking with Andrew earlier. She didn't know how she could keep this revelation to herself. She wanted to shout it from the rooftops, but knew that Bert would want her to keep a lid on things until her divorce could be finalised. He was an old-fashioned man, with old-fashioned ideas, and she wouldn't want to go against him for the world.

She put her treasures under the bed and went to make a start on her chores. Christmas wouldn't wait, and she had pies to bake and vegetables to chop.

"Would you like me to take over, Uncle Bert?" Agnes asked as she reached the bottom of the stairs. "You can go to the Crown Arms if you want. I can finish feeding Helen. It's Christmas Eve, after all. Don't you want to go and spend it with your friends?"

"No, that's all right. We're done here aren't we, little lass?" Bert gently shook the feeding bowl. "She's taken the lot, bless her."

"She'll soon get as big as her brothers and sisters if she carries on eating like that." Agnes smiled with pride.

"Funny how we think of them all as full brothers and sisters isn't it?" Bert commented. "After all, the only two with the same mam and dad are Thomas and Helen."

"Bert, be careful what you say in front of big ears there." Agnes nodded at Harry. "I'm sure he understands a lot more than we give him credit for."

"Sorry, lass. I didn't think. They are all in the same family, no matter how they came to be in the world."

"That's what I think too." Agnes took her baby from Bert's arms and held Helen against her shoulder to pat her back. "Though we are a strange assortment, aren't we? And we'll be even stranger to our friends and neighbours when they hear I'm getting divorced."

"You won't be the first, Agnes." Bert said, kindly.

"No, but I think I'll be the first Catholic around these parts to sever the knot officially. It'll be a proper scandal, won't it?"

"That shouldn't bother you too much, Agnes. It's more than two years since you went to church, not counting our Hilda and Polly's funeral. You're not having second thoughts are you?"

"Goodness no!" She turned to Bert. "In fact, I can't wait to get rid of Bill. I know now that it's Sam I want, and I think he's waited long enough for me."

"You won't do anything about Sam until the divorce is through, will you, Agnes?" Bert asked. "He'll wait, lass. I know he will."

"I know he will, too, Bert, but I don't know how much longer *I* can wait. I want to tell him how I feel. I have all this love sparkling inside me and if I don't tell him soon, I'll burst!"

"Well, it won't harm to tell him, as long as you behave yourselves and don't do anything about it until the time is right."

"You wouldn't mind?"

"Why would I?" Bert smiled. "You remind me of my Hilda, lass. She could never keep a secret. Got all excited as you are now and, oh, well! It does my heart good to see you so happy."

"Thanks, Bert. You're one in a million, do you know that?" Agnes went to hug him with one arm, keeping the other firmly around her little girl. "This is going to be the best Christmas ever."

"Listen, they're playing that Bing Crosby song. Turn it up a bit, Agnes."

They sat quietly listening to the words of White Christmas.

When the news broadcast came on the voice listed the names of ships lost and towns bombed. It was depressing to hear and Agnes reached to switch off the wireless.

"This war will go on for years. Haven't we had enough fighting and bombing?" Agnes wrung her hands in her lap.

"What's that?" Bert opened his eyes.

"How many years will this last, Bert? Will the children grow up knowing nothing but war?"

"It's out of our hands, lass. We can only do what the politicians ask of us. The last war went on for four long years, and we thought it was the war to end all wars, but we were wrong."

"Well, I'm not going to let it ruin everything."

"What you going to do, lass?"

"Let's give these children a night of fun and laughter. No more war talk tonight. It's Christmas Eve." She bounced baby Helen on her lap and reached to tickle Thomas at her feet. "We're going to get ready for Father Christmas, children. Who wants to help me put up your stockings?"

"Me, Mammy. Me! Me!" Little Harry jumped to his feet excitedly. "Is daddy mismas coming soon?"

Chapter Twenty-Two, Divorce

Christmas morning was chaotic. The two toddlers couldn't believe their eyes when Agnes showed them what was inside their stockings. Harry whooped with joy when he discovered his fire engine. Bert and David gave the children more gifts. Helen and Alice each unwrapped a faded handmade pink teddy bear, and Thomas had a brown one, all from Bert. "They're not new, Agnes," Bert whispered.

"I wanna teddy bear, Unkie Bert." Harry looked enviously at his siblings' gifts.

"No, lad. I got sommat else for a big boy like you." Bert gave him a newspaper-wrapped parcel.

Agnes watched her son open the package to find a patchwork brown dog with a red collar and lead. His eyes grew wide and he ran to hug Bert.

"What you going to call him, son?" Bert asked.

Harry looked puzzled.

"He has to have a name. Rover or Butch or something like that."

"Wover!" Harry said decisively. He put the dog on the floor and dragged it around by the lead. "Come, Wover!"

Agnes laughed at her son taking the toy dog for a walk around the parlour. "Where did you get that? It's like new," she asked Bert.

"Some lasses at the iron works set up a stall a few weeks ago. They'd all been making toys and socks and stuff in their spare time to sell for Christmas presents, and the boss said they could sell 'em in the canteen. I saw that and thought of Harry."

"It's perfect."

"And this is for you." Bert handed her a small parcel.

Agnes carefully opened the package to find a bright-blue scarf with red roses printed on it. "It's very bright and jolly, Uncle Bert!" Agnes wrapped it around her throat. "Perfect for spring. I love it. Thank you." She took if off and put it on the dresser.

Sam and his father arrived later that morning, bringing more gifts for the children.

"They are so spoilt this year!" Agnes said after she thanked them.

After Agnes gave out her presents and watched the delight on their faces, Sam's father, Peter, thanked her and reached into his pocket.

"This is for you, Agnes. We both put towards it, so it's a joint present." Peter handed her a small piece of cloth tied up with string.

Agnes opened it and started to laugh. The bright-blue scarf had red roses printed all over it.

Bert began to laugh too, "Great minds think alike, Peter!" He went to the dresser and waved the first scarf in the air.

"Well, now I can wear one around me neck and one on my head, a matching pair!" Agnes giggled.

"You could always take one back and exchange it for another colour." David suggested. "Where did you get them?"

"Err, the Sally Army," Peter said, sounding embarrassed.

"I won't be swapping either of them, I love them both!" Agnes assured the older men. "And I don't care where you got them, it's the thought that counts, and I'm so lucky to have all you lovely men thinking so highly of me."

"Well said, Agnes!" Bert told her. "Now where's that dinner you promised us? Me belly thinks me throat's cut!"

Agnes served the Christmas dinner of tinned salmon fish cakes with roast and mashed potatoes and vegetables. She'd made a parsley sauce to go with it, and made some jam suet pudding for desert with dried egg custard. After everyone had given their compliments on a lovely dinner, Agnes set about clearing everything away. Sam came to help her with the dishes in the kitchen, and Peter and Bert retired to the parlour with their cigarillos. David excused himself to go and meet his sweetheart and Sam and Agnes exchanged smiles as the young lad put his coat on.

"Why don't you bring her back for tea? It's only beef paste sandwiches, but she'll be welcome." Agnes suggested.

"Give over, Agnes." David blushed. "We've only been walking out a few weeks. It's nowt serious."

"I should think not, you're both too young for that." Sam said.

"Well, how old are you, Sam? Old enough to stop shilly-shallying, I think, eh?" David grinned.

"You keep your nose out!" Sam flicked the drying cloth at the young lad.

"I'll see you later, Agnes." David smirked at Sam as he left them.

"What was that smirk for?" Agnes asked Sam.

"I think young David sees more than he lets on."

"What do you mean?"

"Oh, nothing." Sam sighed.

"Nonsense!" Agnes turned to face him. "You tell me what that was all about, Sam Wood." Agnes laughed at her friend. She was eager to break the news to Sam of her new found feelings for him, but planned to tell him later, when they would have the house to themselves.

"Later, Agnes, we have the dishes to attend to."

"Spoilsport!" Agnes turned back to the sink, telling herself that she could wait. She knew David had seen the way things were with Sam and her. She wondered whether he'd been talking with his dad and knew of her plans to divorce Bill. No matter, it would be all around town soon enough, then the gossip mongers would have a field day.

The children were tucked in bed after a very excitable day. David and Bert had taken Sam's father with them down to the Crown Arms and Sam had offered to stay with Agnes to keep her company. Peter and Bert had exchanged a glance when Sam told them he preferred to stay at home, but Agnes was glad they decided to keep their thoughts to themselves. She'd been waiting all day to get Sam alone. She couldn't wait to talk to him about the future.

The wireless was playing Christmas songs, and the flickering fire cast a warm glow over the parlour. They were seated on either side of the fireplace, facing each other, relaxing at the end of a lovely day. It was the perfect setting for talk of romance.

"I'm glad I've got you to myself at last." Sam looked into her eyes. "I have something to tell you, and I'm not sure you're going to like it."

Agnes's heart sank. This isn't what she had been dreaming about all day. She'd imagined taking Sam's hand and declaring her love for him. Then she saw herself falling into his arms and allowing him to kiss her for the first time. Now he was looking at her with a sad expression, and she dreaded what he was about to say. "It seems as if you don't like what you have to say to me either. What is it, Sam?"

"I'm going away, Agnes."

"Where to?"

"I can't tell you. It's war work."

"But why? Why are you going anywhere?"

"There's nothing around here for me, Agnes. I feel useless and I feel this war is passing me by. I need to be involved, Agnes. With the war and with living my life."

"I thought you were happy here."

"I have been, Agnes."

"Then what changed?"

"I had a letter from, well, from someone who knew me in the army. They offered me a posting and it's too good to turn down."

"What will you be doing?" Agnes couldn't believe her dreams were being snatched away from her.

"I'm not sure what they want me to do, but it's to do with helping the army, so I can't talk about the details."

"You're going to be a spy!" Agnes gasped. "Oh, my!"

"It's not like that, Agnes. I'll be based here in England, down south somewhere. I can't operate overseas, in the field like, because of me foot."

"Well, that's a blessing."

"Not for me. I'd rather be over there doing something worthwhile, but if all I can do is, well, I can play my part over here, and that will do. I want to be useful, Agnes. You can see that, can't you?"

"You've been useful here, Sam. The folks at the mill will miss you."

"I don't mind about them. It would be nice to know that you'll miss me, Agnes."

"Oh, Sam!" Agnes put a hand to her mouth. She didn't know what to say to him. Should she declare her love now after he'd told her he was leaving? Would it be fair of her to mention her feelings?

"I know we're only friends, Agnes, but you must realise that I would have liked us to be much more than that. I've recognised at last, that you can't be anything more than a friend to me, so I have to move on. You have a husband, and although you've told me the circumstances of your marriage, and I know you don't love Bill, you've never given me reason to think you might someday have feelings for me."

"Sam, please!" Agnes wanted to stop him from saying more, but didn't know how.

"I know, Agnes. I know!" Sam reached across and took her

hand in his. "You have nothing to give me but friendship. I understand that. I hoped for more, but I can see I'm wasting my time. This opportunity has come out of the blue for me, but I'm taking it because it will get me away from here."

"Away from me?" Agnes could barely speak, her heart was hammering in her chest, and every atom in her body was screaming to tell him of her feelings, but her head was whispering, keep quiet. Common sense was holding her tongue. She didn't want to spoil Sam's ambition of going to help his country. She knew how useless he'd been feeling since he came home injured so soon in the war. This new position, whatever it was, would give him back his self-respect. She didn't want to stand in his way, but realised that if she told him how she really felt, he might not want to leave her.

"I wouldn't put it like that, Agnes. You can see why I have to go, can't you?"

Agnes nodded, not trusting herself to speak.

"I can't stand by and see you and know I can't have you. It's getting harder for me, Agnes. One day I'm going to make a complete fool of myself, over you, and I'll never live it down."

Agnes shook her head. It didn't feel right. This is not how her plans for tonight were supposed to go. "You're wrong, Sam!" She stood, and tugged on his hand until Sam got to his feet. She lifted her face to his and when he still didn't take the hint, she put her hands on either side of his head and pulled his lips down to hers.

Sam took a moment to respond, but within seconds, Agnes felt his arms wrap around her and she felt a warm glow spread through her whole body.

Eventually, Sam pulled away from the kiss. "Are you sure this is what you want from me, Agnes?" He looked down into her face with hopeful eyes.

"More sure than I've ever been of anything in me life, Sam."

"Then why didn't you tell me afore now?"

"Because I didn't know meself until yesterday. I mean, I knew I cared about you. Loved you, even, as a very good friend. But I couldn't tell you, I didn't think it was fair, I mean I didn't know how much I felt about you then." Agnes knew that Sam wouldn't like to know that she'd seen Andrew again, but she had to tell him. She wanted everything to be open and honest between them. Sam knew all her secrets and didn't condemn her. She knew he would understand. "Then yesterday, I bumped into Andrew again, and —."

"Is he still in town?" Sam interrupted. "What did he have to say for himself?"

"You have nothing to worry about, Sam. I sent him packing. He won't be troubling me again, I'm sure."

"So how did your Irish friend change your feelings for me?"

"You know I thought I loved Andrew very much." Agnes watched Sam nod. "I pined for him when he went away, and built him up to be some kind of hero. I hoped he would someday turn up and rescue me from the life my mother organised. When he turned up before Helen was born, I didn't recognise the man I loved, but then Andrew was never that man, do you know what I mean?"

"I think I understand, Agnes. Go on."

Sam was smiling down at her now, and it was good to feel his arms around her. "Well, I still thought of him after that day, but I was confused. I thought I knew what love was. I thought I was in love with him, but yesterday, seeing him and talking to him, well, somehow, I came to understand that what I had with Andrew was nothing more than a passing infatuation."

"So you don't love him anymore?"

"I never did, Sam. Real love is a much deeper feeling."

"Tell me more." Sam's eyes twinkled in the fire glow.

"I love you, Sam. You've been a good friend, and have always looked out for me and the children. The bairns adore you, and I'm sorry it took so long for me to realise that I feel the same way they do."

"You do?" Sam's eyes widened.

"I do!"

Sam leant to kiss her again and she felt her insides doing somersaults as she realised that he felt exactly the same way about her. This time the kiss deepened, and Agnes felt the heat of desire flushing through her, but Sam kept control and pulled away. "Sorry, Agnes. You'll have to keep me at arm's length if you want me to behave myself from now on."

Agnes sighed and laid her head on his shoulder. "If it were up to me, I'd let you misbehave anytime, but I have Uncle Bert and the bairns to think about."

"What have they got to do with any of this?" Sam's voice held a note of humour. "They can't see us?"

"Well, it seems I get pregnant at the drop of a hat, so it wouldn't be wise to tempt fate. It wouldn't look good in the divorce courts if I turned up expecting, would it?"

"You're getting divorced!" Sam looked shocked. "But you'll be shunned by everyone you know, Agnes!"

"Not everyone, Sam." She smiled up at him. "And I don't care what people say. I'm going to live my life for me, not how anyone else tells me I should."

"Will the church let you?"

"They can't stop me!" Agnes sighed. "Uncle Bert is helping me, and Bill has finally agreed to do all that he needs to do, to make sure the paperwork will be in order. Bert said I shouldn't say anything to you until the divorce came through, but I couldn't wait that long. It can take years, and after what you said tonight about going away, I was afraid I might lose you altogether."

"I'm glad you told me, Agnes. What a waste of two lives if you'd stayed quiet."

"Will you still go?" Agnes asked in a whisper.

Sam pulled her closer and held her tightly. "I have to go, Agnes, but now I can go with a happy heart, knowing you'll be waiting for me when I get back."

"When will that be?"

"I have no idea, love. You will you wait for me, won't you?"

"I will." She reached her lips to his for a chaste kiss. "Just make sure you come back to me safe and sound. I need you, Sam Wood."

Chapter Twenty-Three, Regrets

Agnes walked home with an armful of daffodils. She'd promised Bert and David that she would go with them to lay flowers on Hilda and Polly's grave that afternoon. Two years had passed since the fateful day that took them, and Agnes felt such a lot had happened. She was on her way back from her appointment with the solicitor and was feeling a strange mixture of elation, regret and concern. Her own life was moving along and changing beyond what she had ever thought possible, she was leaving behind the past that was full of unhappiness but her divorce was small news in comparison to what was happening in the world.

The country was full of American and Canadian troops, and the feeling in the towns was upbeat and optimistic. With the help of her allies, people thought that Britain would surely be getting the upper hand soon in this war. The Germans had surrendered at Stalingrad, and people everywhere were talking about Hitler's army being defeated soon.

Agnes wasn't sure whether it would be worth it to pursue her divorce under the circumstances. The world was a precarious place, with death and destruction everywhere. Who knew what might happen? Her solicitor told her that the only way to act was to expect she and Bill would survive the conflict, and if they did, and they didn't want to be together, then the sooner the proceedings were started, the better.

Bill had provided the evidence and witness testimonies needed to prove his adultery, and in return, she had agreed Bill could keep all his savings. It hurt her to know that he was still clinging to what was rightfully hers, but she kept remembering her uncle's advice about love being more important than money. She knew now what it meant to love and be loved deeply. She would willingly give up everything she owned to be Sam's wife. Her father's money meant nothing to her, and although she regretted how Bill came to own it, she wouldn't miss what she never had.

Sam had left after the New Year. He journeyed to the south coast to work on a project to help deliver oil to the troops in Europe. He couldn't discuss details with Agnes, but she knew his engineering skills would be involved. She already knew he was a good engineer, because the mill didn't want to let him go the first time he joined up, but the army had given him further training, and now they wanted him back to use his skills for his country. She waved him off at the railway station, feeling proud of him, but afraid he would be going into danger. Even though he assured her that his job would be on British shores, she couldn't help being concerned for him. Southern England was getting a beating from sporadic air attacks, and nowhere was safe, these days.

Thornbury had fewer and fewer raids in the last months. The Anderson shelter at the bottom of Agnes's garden had been more useful as a playhouse for the children than a safe haven. It had only been used as a shelter twice when the sirens went off, scaring people from their beds in the middle of the night. Each time, Agnes listened to aircraft droning overhead, dreading the sound of explosions, but they never came. The aircraft flew on to deliver their carnage elsewhere, leaving her afraid and with her mind full of terrible memories. The awful raid that had killed Polly and Hilda two years ago had not been repeated. The town had moved on, damaged buildings had been demolished and bomb sites cleared, but for Bert, David and Agnes, the memory was still fresh and painful.

They left for the graveyard with Bert carrying the flowers and holding Harry's hand, David pushed the pram with the two toddlers in it, and Agnes carried young Helen in her arms.

The graveyard was deserted. An icy wind blew from the north, but it remained dry. The children were warmly wrapped against the cold, and the small gathering stood around the wooden marker with heads bowed.

"Should we say a prayer or something?" David asked.

"Hilda wouldn't want any prayers, and Polly, well we all know what our Polly thought of church."

Agnes smiled. "I wonder what heaven is making of our Polly? She was one of a kind, wasn't she?"

"She were a bugger, that's for sure!" Bert huffed.

"I miss her." Agnes took the daffodils from Bert and placed them by the wooden cross. She glanced across to the door of the church when she saw someone coming out. Father Brennan caught her eye and started to make his way to them. "Oh, my! That's all we need!"

"Leave him to me, Agnes." Bert turned to face the priest. "We're not here for a lecture, Father."

"I know why you're here, Bert, and you have my sympathies." The priest bowed his head reverently. "However, it has come to my knowledge that Agnes here is seeking to divorce Bill, and I can't let that go without comment. I'd be failing in my duty to ignore such a grievous sin against one of my flock."

"If you knew the truth of our marriage, you'd not be so quick to defend Bill." Agnes told him.

"Agnes, you don't need to explain yourself to Father Brennan." Bert warned. "He's only doing his job."

"This isn't a job, Bert, it's a calling." The priest smoothed his hand over his white dog-collar.

"Aye, well!" Bert lifted his chin. "Whatever you call it, being a priest isn't an excuse for meddling in people's lives."

"I take an interest and try to look after my congregation." Father Brennan straightened his shoulders and faced Bert. "I always have their best interests at heart."

"Even when you're persuading young lads to go and sacrifice their lives for future generations? Where does God stand in that statement, Father?" Bert squared up to the priest.

"God doesn't start wars, Bert. Men do!"

"So why does God allow men like Hitler to get to power in the first place?" Bert asked. "Like I said; where is God when you need him?"

The priest tapped his chest. "He's in here." He reached to touch Bert's chest. "And in here, if you'll let him in."

"Can we just have some peace to remember our family?" Agnes asked. "If we wanted you to preach to us we'd come inside where it's warmer."

"You'd be welcome." Father Brennan gestured to the door of the church. "But that will change if you go through with this nonsense that you're planning, Agnes."

"It's clear to me that you've been speaking to Mary and Edwin." Agnes held her youngest daughter close to her chest to protect her from the bitter wind. "They wouldn't know that the divorce is Bill's idea because he'll have told them that it's my doing. Well, it's not! I'm not contesting it, because it's what I want too, but it was Bill that asked me for a divorce, Father, not the other way around."

"I can't believe that of Bill Smithson." The priest shook his head. "There must be extenuating circumstances." He looked at Agnes with narrowed eyes.

"He committed adultery, Father. You'll be able to read all about it in the papers when it goes to court." Bert told the priest, jumping in to defend his niece. "This lass has done nothing wrong, despite what you might have heard from the town gossips."

"I don't listen to idle chit-chat, Bert."

"Well, don't be so quick to judge her, that's all I'm saying. There are two sides to every story."

"I'm more than willing to listen to your side, Agnes." The priest said quietly.

"I'm cold, Unkie Bert." Harry tugged on his uncle's coat. "Wanna go home."

"I think that's a good idea, son." Agnes took her son's hand and began to walk away from the graveside.

"If you need to talk, Agnes, I'll be here for you." Father Brennan called to her.

Agnes continued walking; the priest would be the last person she would want to talk to. She heard David and Bert say their goodbyes to Father Brennan, but couldn't hear what the priest said, and then she heard the pram wheels on the path and knew they were following her.

When they got home, David lifted the two little ones from the pram and hurried to stoke the fire. They were all cold from standing in the graveyard and the long walk home in the bitter wind hadn't helped. Helen was crying with hunger, and Harry's knees were blue.

"Come here, little man, let me get you warm." Bert wrapped Harry in his coat and went to sit by the fireside with him in his lap.

"I'll boil the kettle. This one needs something to warm her belly, and we could all do with a cup of tea to warm us up." Agnes hurried to get the kettle.

"What will happen if you get divorced, Agnes?" David asked as he piled more coals on the glowing embers. "I mean, will you be able to go to church again? Will it be allowed?"

"I think I can still go as long as I'm not the guilty party, but it doesn't matter, because I wouldn't want to go anyway." Agnes told him as she prepared the tea and got the baby some food from the dresser cupboard.

"You wouldn't be able to get married in a church again, and if you did remarry in a civil ceremony, the church wouldn't recognise that marriage." Bert clarified for David's sake.

"Do you think you'll marry Sam?" David asked.

"That would depend if he asked me." Agnes couldn't help smiling as she broke some Rusk biscuits into a bowl. It was what she hoped for.

"I think he'll ask you." David grinned at her. "He's proper daft on you is that man!"

"I hope so, 'cause I'm proper daft on him too." Agnes reached to ruff up David's hair, but he ducked away from her hand. "What about that lass you've been walking out with? Are you proper daft on her?"

David flushed and glanced at his father. "It's nowt serious."

"You've been seeing her a few months, I'd say that was serious, wouldn't you, Bert?"

"Don't rush the lad, Agnes." Bert was smirking at his son. "He'll take his time and make sure Betty is the right one before he decides to make it official with us."

"Like you did with me mam?" David asked.

"No, lad." Bert's face took on a wistful look. "I knew from the first day I set eyes on her that she was the one for me." Bert shook his head. "Took me some time to convince her of it, though!" He smiled. "But she couldn't resist me charm for long."

"You two had something special, didn't you, Uncle Bert?" Agnes knew her aunt and uncle's relationship had been very different to her own parents.

"Aye, we did. I miss her sommat shocking!" Bert's eyes filled with tears, but he blinked quickly to stop them from falling. "Where's that tea, Agnes?"

Later that evening when the children were all in bed, Agnes had the house to herself. David was out at the home guard depot, and Bert had gone for a pint with his work pals.

The parlour was warm and she snuggled into her chair with a cup of tea in her hand, listening to the wireless playing soft music. She allowed herself to think about the past, and realised that she had changed a lot from the young girl who fell in love with an Irish charmer. She'd been so unsure of herself back then. She thought of herself as a plain Jane, too tall for any lad to consider as a serious girlfriend. She was content to live her life on the outskirts of her friends and family, and the only thing she had to look forward to in her future was a lonely existence as a spinster. When Andrew came along, he had blown her off her feet, and she had allowed herself to be thrilled by him because flattery was something she had never received before. He was intoxicating, and her love for him made her life brighter and more exciting. Her love of him made her do things she would never have considered doing. It made her reckless and foolish.

Now she knew that the feelings she had back then were

transient. She'd been in love with the idea of love, and that came nowhere close to what she now felt in her heart for Sam.

In the quiet of the house, she could face her past and she realised that, at last, she had forgiven herself for the mistakes she had made. She blamed herself for years for the death of her father, but Sam had helped her see that she was not responsible for her father's reaction on that night. She was not accountable for his temper or his aggressive actions that led to him falling to his death.

She was foolish to try to cover up the facts of the accident, and stupid to hide the truth and help Andrew get away, but it was done and it was in the past. With Sam's help, she could learn to live with her regrets. Especially as Sam knew everything and supported her in coming to terms with her guilt. Sam was a remarkable person, just like her uncle Bert. She knew she would have something special with Sam if this damned war would let them be together.

Sam had written to her from an address on the south coast. He talked about the icy weather and the bombing raids. He told her he'd watched some dogfights in the skies over Dover, where spitfires darted through clear blue skies, shooting at a German Messerschmitt. He wrote of the aircraft looking like birds of prey, circling and spitting bullets at each other. His words made her realise that Sam was in danger. The south coast was the most probable landing site for an enemy invasion, and the dogfights were proof that the war was not too far away from where Sam was stationed.

She went to the dresser and took his latest letter from the drawer to read it again. She knew every word by heart, but it felt good to see his writing.

"Dear Agnes, I miss you, and wish we could be together, but I can be patient, knowing that you will be mine eventually. When this war is over, and it will be over one day, we will live in peace with all our bairns. The ones we already have, and the ones we might have together. We'll have a dozen at least, and we'll love them all the same."

Agnes couldn't believe Sam already thought of her children as his. He hadn't actually asked her to marry him, but they had drifted into an understanding of sorts. She didn't need a fancy proposal. Just knowing that Sam loved her was enough. She knew Harry adored Sam, and her son would be over the moon if he could call his hero daddy. She wasn't so sure about the others, though. Bill would want to be involved in their lives, and although it would be complicated, they would have to find a way to make it work. Sam was her future, no matter what Bill, Bert or Father Brennan had to say about it.

Chapter Twenty-Four, Freedom 1944

Agnes and Bert were waiting for the evening news broadcast to start. Christmas had been a poor affair this year, although they had tried to make it fun for the children. Everyone had been saying all year that it would be over by Christmas, especially since the Normandy invasion in June then the liberation of Paris in August. They really thought the end was in sight, but the Germans and Italians dug their heels in and the slaughter continued. Earlier in December, thousands died on both sides in the Ardennes offensive, and hopes of an early end to the conflict faded.

On the home front, things seemed to be easing. This Christmas, churches were allowed to light the stained-glass windows. Bombing raids were a thing of the past. The country was troubled by doodlebugs, which the Germans sent over haphazardly. The pilotless flying bombs fell randomly, so blackouts wouldn't help to defend against them.

The government was generous with the rationing of sugar and sweets, so the children had a feast of sweet and fancy treats. They were now in bed, sleeping off the exertions and excesses of the exciting day.

Agnes was waiting to hear if there was news of the fighting in Italy. She knew Bill was over there. He'd sent a card to Thomas and Helen with the words 'Christmas Greetings from Italy,' printed on the front. She had read his words of endearment to his children, but they almost stuck in her throat. If only he could bring himself to treat all the children the same, but she knew he never would. She didn't look forward to him coming home. She hadn't seen him for more than four years, and she'd be happy if she never saw him again. At least they were now divorced and she could get on with her life but she knew Bill would want regular contact with his children once he came back to England.

In the eyes of the law, she was a free woman, but in the eyes of the church, she would never be. She and Sam planned to marry when the war was over. They'd waited this long, and both agreed that to marry with the war still hanging over them would not be ideal. Sam still worked on the south coast, though Agnes didn't worry about him as much as she had. The doodlebugs were the biggest threat to his safety, but he was just as likely to get struck by lightning as by one of the hit-and-miss flying bombs.

Sam had been able to tell her a little about what he was doing down there. He managed to get back to Yorkshire a few times on leave, and Agnes was always happy to welcome him back. She loved to hear his stories, cuddled into his arms by the fire. He was using his engineering skills to help deliver much-needed fuel to the troops over the channel. He worked as part of a large team of engineers to lay pipes under the water, a daring move for the divers and submariners involved, but Sam's skills were needed on the shore. He had reassured her that he was not in danger. He had reached the rank of sergeant and carried himself with pride and confidence. Gone was the youthful bravado he used when Agnes first knew him when he flirted with her in the café. They had both matured during the long years of the war.

"Shall we have a tipple, Agnes?" Bert interrupted her thoughts. "To warm our spirits this Christmas Day?" Bert already had two small glasses in his hand and a dusty bottle of cherry brandy tucked under his arm. "I've been saving this for the end of the war, but it might turn to vinegar if we wait that long."

"How long have you had that, Bert?"

"Since me and Hilda got wed. It were a wedding present from me dad and we were saving it to celebrate our Ruby Anniversary, but that won't happen now."

"Was it in the house when the bomb dropped?" Agnes couldn't believe how such a fragile bottle could have survived the impact.

"Aye, it was. Some of the wardens collected what they could from the debris, as you know. I got them few photos." He pointed to the framed photographs of Hilda and Polly on the dresser. "A few nick knacks of our Hilda's and this." He waved the dusty bottle in the air.

"Why now, Bert?"

"Because we can't get a decent drink for love nor money these days, and I remembered I had this."

"I wonder if it tastes all right?" Agnes watched her uncle open the bottle and pour the red liquid into the glasses.

"There you go, get that down you, lass." Bert handed her a glass.

"Mmm, that's got a kick to it!"

"Turn the wireless up, Agnes. That's the news coming on now."

Agnes reached up to turn the dial and heard the newsreader talking about Glen Miller.

"Captain Miller's plane went missing on the fifteenth of December, just ten days ago. He was on his way to perform a Christmas day concert for the allied troops in Paris. In his own words, he wanted to, 'bring a touch of home to our fighting lads.' After ten days with no sighting of his plane, we must presume that Captain Miller and all on board have perished."

"Oh, no! His poor family." Agnes looked at the wireless, waiting to hear more.

"Wonder what happened?" Bert took a sip of the brandy and grimaced. "This is a bit sweet, isn't it?"

"Sounds as if they don't know." Agnes had been listening to the voice from the wireless. "It must be terrible to have someone go missing like that. You'll always wonder what happened, won't you?"

"That's war, lass. You never know what's round the corner. You can't make plans in a war."

"That's why Sam and me decided to wait to get married."

"Not like our James, eh?"

"No, but I can understand why James wanted to marry his sweetheart. Young love is so intense, isn't it?"

"Are you speaking from experience, Agnes?"

Agnes smiled at Bert.

"I can't remember meself. It was so long ago when I was James's age."

"You were lucky, Bert. Your young love grew into the lasting kind. I'm not sure many people get to know the kind of love you and Hilda had."

"She was special, but you know that."

"So are you, Bert!" Agnes raised her glass. "To love!"

"I'll drink to that." Bert took a sip and grimaced again. "I'm not sure I can finish this, though."

"James's sweetheart sounds nice, doesn't she? His letters are full of her."

"From Norfolk, he says. She joined the WAAFs and ended up working in the mapping room at his airbase. Sarah they call her. Nice name that, isn't it?"

"She must be clever, eh?"

"Not so clever if she agreed to marry our James!"

"Oh, Bert! Our James is a lovely lad. He's caring and gentle, but he's brave as well. You should be proud of him."

"I am proud, Agnes, but I'm scared I'm going to lose him."

219

"He's done well to survive so far. Let's hope his luck continues."

"Let's hope this blasted war ends soon so we can all stop worrying about our loved ones. And we might be able to get a decent drink at last!" Bert took another sip of the cherry brandy and shuddered.

Agnes was helping Helen to get dressed when she heard a knock on the door.

"Can you try to put your socks on, Helen?" Agnes got up and went to open the door.

"All right, Mammy."

"She's a big girl, Mam. Helen can do it, can't you?" Harry watched over his younger sibling.

"I'm a big girl. I'm older than Helen and I can get dressed all by myself." Alice boasted.

"Well, get a move on, we have to take Harry to school soon." Agnes told them. "Thomas, did you put a handkerchief in your pocket?"

"I'll get him one, Mam." Harry dashed into the kitchen.

Agnes shook her head and smiled. Harry was still the mother hen with the little ones. She opened the door, still smiling, but was surprised to see her ex-father-in-law standing there. He looked dreadful. His face was grey and he was twisting his hands together in front of him.

"Edwin! What are you doing here?"

"I'm sorry to call so early, Agnes, but we've had some news."

"What is it, Edwin? You look terrible."

"I've been up all night. Mary said I should have come yesterday, but I was in shock. I could hardly string two words together. I'm not much better today."

"You'd better come in, Edwin." Agnes's thoughts were whirling. It had to be about Bill. What had happened?

Edwin stepped inside and took off his cap. "Mary didn't want to come. She misses the bairns, but you know what she's like."

"Yes, Edwin. I know." Agnes nodded and turned to the children. "Go and play in the dining room for a minute or two. Thomas, you can get your new train set out that David made for you." She turned back to Edwin after the children had charged from the room. "I don't like them to hear grown-up

220

conversation, especially if it's about them. Harry is of an age to understand more than he should."

"How old is he now?" Edwin asked absently, but Agnes could see he had more important things on his mind.

"He's five, Edwin. He's at school now." Agnes briefly thought that she should be leaving soon to take Harry to school, but had a feeling the school would understand if he were to take the day off.

"Mary is missing out so much by not seeing the bairns, Agnes."

"Yes, Edwin, I know she is. I told her the last time she came that if she isn't prepared to treat all my children the same, she won't be welcome. I know that Harry and Alice aren't your kin, but they are only children. They don't know there's a difference, so I won't have Mary bringing treats for the other two and leaving them out. It's not fair."

"I know, Agnes, but she won't budge on it. To her, Thomas and Helen are family, the other two aren't. I can see how it is with you, though. It might all change now, anyway." Edwin twisted his cap in his hands.

"What's happened, Edwin?" Agnes couldn't wait to hear his news. She could see it was something bad, but hoped it wouldn't be bad news for her.

"We had a telegram yesterday, Agnes."

"About Bill?"

"Aye, he were killed in action on the twenty-eighth of December."

"What! No! Oh, Edwin, I'm sorry." Agnes was genuinely sorry for the elderly man, but she felt nothing for herself. She was thinking of the lengthy and expensive divorce she had gone through, and realising that it hadn't been necessary after all.

"They sent the telegram to us as we are next of kin on his papers."

"Yes, I understand, Edwin. With the divorce I wouldn't be the first one they'd contact, would I?"

"There's more, Agnes, and you won't like it."

"What's that?" Agnes had an idea about what she wouldn't like, but let Edwin explain.

"Bill's money. He told us some time ago that if owt happened to him while the bairns were still young, it should come to us. To me and Mary. We'll get to hold it in trust for them until they're old enough."

"When you say, bairns, you mean Thomas and Helen, don't you? Harry and Alice will get nothing." Agnes tried to keep the anger from her voice. Edwin was grieving, and she didn't want to add to his pain.

"Well, they're not Bill's children, and Alice isn't even yours, so no." Edwin looked puzzled. "Why would you expect it to be any different?"

"The children are all mine, Edwin and don't you forget it. Polly gave me Alice to bring up as me own, and that's what I'm doing. As for the money!" Agnes tried to lower her tone. She didn't want the children to hear raised voices. "You know as well as I do, that money was me mam and dad's hard-earned cash and life savings. It should have come to me, but instead it found its way into your son's grubby hands and I never saw a brass farthing of it."

"Agnes, it's not my doing. It's the way things are."

"Sorry, Edwin. I'm not angry with you. That money has been a curse to me since the day I married your son and my mother handed it to him. You take responsibility for it. I'm beyond worrying about it now."

"Mary said you'd be angry about it."

"About the money?"

Edwin nodded, but couldn't bring himself to look at Agnes.

"I'm not angry, Edwin. Look, I can see this is difficult for you. I'll make us a cuppa, eh?"

"Thanks, Agnes. That would be nice."

"You just lost your son, Edwin. I'm not heartless, no matter what others say about me."

Harry charged in from the dining room, closely followed by the others. "Look at me, Mam!" Harry shouted.

Harry had a metal colander on his head, Thomas had a pan on his head, and each boy had a gun shaped wooden stick under their arms that David had made them for Christmas.

"We're soldiers, and we're goin to win the war, Mammy!" Thomas ran after Harry around the room.

"I want to be a soldier!" Alice demanded and stamped her foot. "Harry won't let me play!"

"I wanna be a sholder as well!" Helen pouted.

"Girls can't be soldiers." Harry shouted as he dashed by his sisters.

"I can be a sholder if I want!" Helen copied Alice and stamped her little foot.

"Quiet now, children. We have a visitor." Agnes got their attention. "See! Your granddaddy has come to see you."

Edwin shot Agnes a look of surprise.

"Are you my granddaddy?" Harry asked.

"I can be if you want me to be." Edwin nodded at Agnes.

"Are you a soldier?" Thomas asked Edwin.

"No, son. Not in this war." Edwin shook his head at the small boy.

"Why not? Our daddy is a soldier." Alice said, importantly.

"I'm too old to be a soldier."

"Mam says I'm too young, but when I'm older like David, I can be one then." Harry looked at his mother. "Can't I, Mam?"

"Hopefully, the world won't need soldiers when you grow up, Harry." Agnes touched her eldest son's head.

"What 'bout me? I be a sholder when I grow big?" Helen jumped up and down.

"And me!" The other two chorused.

"Oh, you lot!" Agnes laughed.

"Me have a go, Harry?" Helen made a grab for Harry's gun.

"Oh, go on, then!" The older boy gave her his helmet too. "But only for a minute!"

"You're a good lad to your sister, Harry." Edwin smiled at the boy.

"They are all good bairns, Edwin. They all deserve the same treatment from the adults in their lives." She chose her words carefully because the children were still around. "If you can get Mary to see that, there's no reason why my bairns can't enjoy having a grandma too."

"I'll try, Agnes, but don't hold your breath."

"I won't, Edwin. I'll get that tea now, shall I?"

Agnes watched the children playing as she made the tea. To an outsider they looked like any ordinary family, and she hoped she could keep up that appearance for their sakes. She would have to tell them about Bill soon. She didn't know how they would take the news. Their daddy was a man who sent letters and cards. None of them would remember him as a living breathing father. Helen had never met him and the two middle ones were only babes in arms the last time he was home. Agnes thought that Harry might have some hazy memories of Bill, but as Bill had never given him any attention, he probably wouldn't even have those.

Maybe it was the best thing that could have happened for

her family. Bill had done her a favour by getting himself killed in action. It was no more than he deserved if he really had killed her mother as she suspected. She would never be able to prove it now that he was dead, but the world, or at least her part in it, would be a much nicer place now that he was gone. The children wouldn't miss him. They would come to know Sam as their father, and all memories of Bill would be wiped from their minds. The only fly in the ointment as far as the children were concerned might be the situation with the money, but she needn't worry about that until Thomas and Helen came of age to inherit it.

Chapter Twenty-Five, Victory in Europe

Sam came home for the Easter holiday, and Agnes invited his father over for Sunday dinner with the family. David had been playing April Fool's jokes on the children all morning, and the house was filled with laughter.

"Having Easter Sunday fall on All Fools' Day has made for an entertaining morning." Agnes greeted her guests at the door and showed them in. "Make yourselves at home if you can find a space to sit."

The parlour was full of children's toys and games, discarded dressing up clothes and various kitchen-wares they had used in their games.

"I'll tidy up, Agnes." David started to pick things up from the floor.

"I'll help." A petite blonde girl offered.

"No Betty, you're a guest." David told her.

"You muck in if you like, Betty." Bert told the young girl. "If you're going to be part of this family, you'd better start how you mean you to go on."

Betty smiled shyly and went to help her boyfriend.

"She seems a nice lass." Sam whispered to Agnes as he put his arms around her.

"She's fitting in. She'll do." Agnes whispered back. "I'm so glad to see you."

"What you got for dinner, Agnes? I always enjoy your cooking." Peter asked.

"I got a couple of chickens from Frank at the allotment. Bert helped him out a few weeks ago with digging the ground over and he gave us these." Agnes pulled a tray out of the fireside range with two small steaming chickens on it.

"Oh, they look grand, Agnes!" Bert came to sniff them. "I can't remember the last time I tasted a chicken. Me mouth's watering already." Bert reached to pull a piece of meat from the leg of the nearest bird.

"Hand's off, Bert." Agnes slapped her uncle's hand gently. "There's not much to go around as it is." She laughed as he pulled his hand back and cringed.

"You're a mean woman!" Bert pulled his bottom lip out at her and everyone laughed.

"Why don't you take the children outside while I set the table and put the dinner out?" Agnes suggested.

"David, can you take charge outside?" Sam asked. "I'll give Agnes a hand here."

David and Betty ushered the children outside into the warm sunshine. Peter and Bert followed them and the parlour suddenly seemed bigger and quieter without the family filling it up.

"Peace!" Sam lifted his face to the ceiling. "At last!"

"It won't last long, we'd better make the most of it." Agnes walked into his arms and rested her head on his shoulder. "I miss you so much, Sam."

"Well, let's hope it won't be for much longer, Agnes."

"We keep saying that this war is nearly done, but still it goes on. When will it end, Sam?"

"We're almost there, Agnes. The Germans are losing on all sides now. We destroyed Dresden in February and we took Cologne last month. With Russia on our side, it will all be over soon."

"I hope you're right, Sam. When I listen to the news about what those Germans have been doing to the Jews, it fills me with fear. What if they invaded here? What would they do to us?"

"That's not going to happen, Agnes. We've got them on the run. It's only a matter of time."

"Hold me, Sam. Make me feel safe, like you always do."

"Glad to be of service, my lady." Sam wrapped his arms around her and pulled her closer.

Bert came into the kitchen and coughed loudly. "I thought you two were getting our dinner on the table!"

"We thought you were entertaining the bairns." Agnes pulled away from Sam and smiled at her uncle.

"Peter has a bit of baccy, I'm just getting a light." He reached for the box of matches on the mantelpiece.

"I got you some, too, Bert." Sam pulled out a packet of American cigarettes from his jacket pocket. "I have friends in high places. Here you are."

"Thanks, lad. You know how to cheer a bloke up. You haven't got a bottle of brandy tucked away an' all have you?"

"No such luck! Sorry."

"You two carry on, I can wait a bit for me dinner now I've got these." Bert grinned at them and went back outside.

Agnes laughed. "Trust Bert!"

"You like him a lot, don't you, Agnes." Sam looked serious.

"He's the best, of course, I do."

"I'm going to ask him to be me best man."

"Oh, that's lovely, Sam. He'll be thrilled."

"It won't be long now, Agnes. We'll be together soon, you'll see."

All through April the news was full of allied successes in Germany. The German war machine was failing at last. At the beginning of May, the announcement of Hitler's suicide shocked the world, and Agnes began to hope that the end really was in sight. A few days later German troops surrendered in Italy. When the wireless broadcast the unconditional surrender of all German troops to the allies on the seventh of May, Agnes was jubilant. The country waited with bated breath for news from Churchill that the war in Europe was over. When the wireless broadcast his speech to the nation, cheers could be heard in all the streets around.

Along with the rest of the country, she wanted to do something special, and joined the rest of the street in organising a victory party for the declared holiday on the eighth of May. The schools were closed, and places of work shut down too. Spirits were high as tables were laid in the streets with an odd assortment of food items. Anything people had in their pantry was brought out. Tins of salmon and bully beef were opened and placed on plates next to fish paste and thin slices of cheese. Mountains of bread were buttered and homemade pickles of all descriptions were brought out of storage. Agnes baked some scones, and other neighbours brought cakes and biscuits to the tables. Potatoes cooked in various ways were stacked on trays. There were baked potatoes, piles of mash with sausages stuck in them, plates of fat fried chips and thin scalloped ones. Bowls of shredded cabbages and carrots steeped in vinegar and pies of every description weighed the tables down.

A record player was set up in someone's doorway, and Glen Miller lived on as his music filled the street. Teenagers danced, and children ran around with excitement, though few of the little ones realised the importance of the day.

Agnes invited all her friends and family to the party, and the neighbours had done the same. Hundreds of people filled the long street, and all the visitors brought more food and drink with them.

"We'd better fill our bellies today, 'cause none of us has owt left in the house to eat for the rest of the week!" Enid laughed with Agnes.

"Who cares!" Agnes answered. "The war is over at last! I can't believe it."

"It's not over for some of them, lass." Bert said quietly. "They're still fighting in Japan and that's set to go on for a while. Vicious buggers them lot, you know."

"Well, let's hope it's over for them soon." Enid said. "But I'm not going to let that spoil today for us. We're having ourselves a party to remember!"

"We won the war! We won the war!" Harry chanted as he led a group of youngsters around the street. He wore his colander helmet and his brother Thomas wore a saucepan. A column of boys marched behind them, wearing an assortment of kitchen pots and pans on their heads and waving flags of red white and blue.

"Where are your sisters?" Agnes called to her sons.

"Talking to Granddaddy over there." Harry waved his flag at the end of the street. "Grandma's there too."

Agnes looked to where she could see Edwin and Mary with her two little girls and frowned.

"Trouble?" asked Enid.

"I hope not, Enid." Agnes decided to make sure Mary was behaving herself. She didn't want Alice to pick up on any bad feeling the woman might show her. "I'll be back soon."

"Go easy on them, Agnes." Bert called as she left them.

Agnes saw Mary glance up, and she put a welcoming smile on her face. "Hello Mary; Edwin. I'm glad you could make it."

"Thanks for inviting us." Edwin nudged his wife.

"Yes, Agnes, thank you." Mary smiled tightly.

"Come and find a place to sit before all the chairs get taken." Agnes led them back to the tables outside her front door. "Come on girls, I'm sure you must be hungry by now."

"Can we have cake before our sandwiches, Mammy?" Alice asked.

"Harry said we could eat whatever we wanted today." Helen said.

"Did he now?" Agnes chuckled. "Well, it is a special day, I suppose you can."

"Yippee!" Alice took a slice of cake from the nearest table and broke it in two. "Here's some for you, Helen." She shared her cake with her sister.

228

"That's nice to see." Edwin commented.

"They share everything. I taught them that from an early age. With four so young together, it's the only way to keep the peace."

"Well, that will change as they get older, I'm sure." Mary said, and her cheeks flushed pink.

"I'm not sure it will, Mary." Agnes said pointedly. "Lessons learned from the cradle usually stand the test of time."

"It's easy to share when all you have is a piece of cake. Thomas and Helen will have much more than that in a few years, and I'll be surprised if they want to share it with their so-called siblings." Mary sniffed and lifted her chin.

"If you're intent on spoiling this day, with your mean mouth and petty favouritism, you can turn around and go home." Agnes hissed at her ex-mother-in-law.

"Now then, ladies! This is a party. Let's not spoil it by bickering." Bert came to join them.

"I need to find the boys." Agnes left Bert to smooth Mary's feathers. The woman was infuriating.

When Agnes returned with her sons, the feasting began. Talk centred on the recent weeks leading up to the ending of the conflict, and spirits were high. Agnes ignored Mary and concentrated on her children, making sure they had enough of the right kind of food, steering them to the savouries, with a promise of cake if they ate at least one sandwich first.

"I already had cake," Helen boasted to her brothers.

"Me too." Alice preened.

"Well, you'll have a salmon sandwich now." Agnes said firmly.

"Aw, that's not fair!" Thomas pouted. "Why can't we have a cake first?"

"You're a boy and boys can't have cake!" Helen taunted.

"We can!" Harry joined in the banter. "But we need big strong muscles, Thomas, so we have to eat sandwiches first. We don't want to grow up like girls, do we?"

"No!" Thomas picked up two sandwiches and began to eat them with big bites.

"Slow down, Thomas." Agnes laughed at her sons. "There's plenty more, no one will take it off you."

"He's quite the diplomat isn't he?" Edwin nodded at Harry.

"He's the peacekeeper all right." Bert told his cousin.

"He must take after his granddad Seth." Mary added. "God rest his soul."

"Aye he was always the one smoothing things out when lads came to blows after a few pints in the Crown Arms." Edwin smiled.

"Aye, I can see Seth now." Bert had a faraway look in his eyes. "Shouting the odds at me after I told him I'd done with going to church."

"Shouting at you?" Agnes was surprised. "That wasn't usually my dad's way."

"There's a lot you don't know about your dad, Agnes." Bert smiled warmly at her. "He had a right temper when he was roused, you know."

"No, I err, I didn't know!" Agnes was amazed at this revelation.

"Oh, it took a lot to make him lose his temper, but when he was riled, everyone knew to get out of his way." Edwin told her.

"Why? What was he like?" Agnes couldn't believe she was having this conversation. The only time she had ever seen her father lose control was the night of the accident.

"I remember the time he found out that you'd been carrying-on with that Irish lad. Some friends of ours knew his family in Ireland you know." Mary told her.

"No I didn't know!" Agnes was shocked that all this was coming out now, after all this time.

"Well, they told your dad how he'd got a lass into trouble and scarpered over here to get out of marrying her. Your dad went wild."

"I had to hold him back, Agnes." Edwin admitted. "He was all set for searching him out and giving him what for!"

"Not me dad!" Agnes couldn't believe what she was hearing, but she could picture Seth the night of the accident. She had a clear image in her mind of her father. He was out of control. He was seething with rage and although she hadn't realised it at the time, she knew now that he had been intent on doing Andrew some serious harm.

"It's a good job your young man was called away back to Ireland. I'm sure your dad would have murdered him if he'd found him." Mary said smugly. "Peace-maker, indeed!"

"Ah, to be fair, Mary, Seth was usually the one to calm things down when they got heated." Edwin said to his wife.

"Trouble was no one could calm him when he got

overheated, eh?" Bert chuckled. "He was a right character, Agnes."

"It sounds like it." Agnes shook her head. She didn't know what to make of the revelations. If Andrew had stayed to face the music, and if the case had been allowed to go to court, would all this have come out then? Would the court have heard what her father's temper was like? She'd lived all her life thinking her father was good natured. Right until his last night she had thought her father was a fair-minded, composed and calm parson, but she was learning she was wrong about him.

"Well let's hope Harry didn't inherit his granddad Seth's temper, eh?" Edwin said.

"Well, he won't have inherited our Bill's bad moods, that's for sure." Mary started laughing then stopped herself. "I'm sorry, lass." She looked at Agnes. "I didn't mean to say that."

Agnes looked at Mary and shook her head. It wouldn't matter how hard she tried to keep the children safe from knowing their chequered ancestry, there would always be people like Mary who wouldn't be able to keep their mouths closed.

"I think we should let the children go and play while the sun is still shining." Agnes turned to her children seated beside her. "Have you all had enough to eat?"

"More cake, Mammy!" Thomas demanded, pointing to a plate of dried-fruit buns.

"All right, take one more each and away you go to play."

"Yippee!" Helen grabbed two cakes from the plate.

"I said one more, Helen." Agnes warned and wagged a finger at her youngest.

"Sorry, Mammy." Helen put one back and ran to join the others.

"They are so well behaved, Agnes." Enid remarked. "You've done a grand job to say you raised 'em without a man around."

"I suppose I'm just a bag of wind then, Enid!" Bert chuckled. "Don't forget, I've been around them since they were born."

"Well, of course, you have, Uncle Bert. And we wouldn't have managed without you, that's for sure." Agnes leant against her uncle.

"But all that will change soon, I'm guessing." Bert's eyes twinkled.

"Why's that?" Enid asked.

"The war is over, and I'm hearing wedding bells ringing in me ears." Bert grinned at Agnes.

"Wedding bells?" Mary sat up straighter. "Bill is hardly cold in his war grave and you're talking about getting married again! It's disgraceful!"

"Bill wasn't my husband, Mary. We divorced, remember?" Agnes said sternly.

"In the eyes of the church he were your husband until the day he died." Mary lifted her chin. "And that was not too long ago. You're a widow, Agnes and you should be acting like one, not planning your next wedding. Have some respect for the dead, will you." She sniffed and took out a handkerchief to dab at her eyes.

"Now, Mary." Edwin patted his wife's shoulder.

"I'm not listening to this!" Agnes pushed her chair back from the table and stood. "Your Bill was no saint, and if you knew the truth about how he treated me and me mam you'd know the real reason why I couldn't bear to be near him. I won't stand by and listen to you telling me why I should be mourning him. I'm glad to be rid of him permanently if truth be told. There! I've said it! I'm glad he's dead!" Agnes spun on her heel and hurried away from the table, leaving people gasping and gawping at her.

She knew most of the neighbours barely tolerated her. She was little more than a loose woman in their eyes. A divorcee was a rarity and she knew that some people still crossed the street to avoid her since her divorce had been in all the newspapers. Even though Bill took the blame, the shame of it still fell on her shoulders. It was also common knowledge that Harry was barely born on the right side of the blanket, and that added fuel to the gossip's inflammatory version of her character.

This last little outburst would give them something to talk about for weeks.

Chapter Twenty-Six, Surprises

Agnes was nervous as she set foot inside the church for the first time in years. She hoped Father Brennan would be charitable and honour his promise that she would always be welcome in God's house. She automatically crossed herself and bobbed to the altar before she made her way to the office at the other side of the entrance.

Her knock was answered in seconds, and she smiled at Father Brennan's look of shock when he saw her standing there.

"Hello, Father Brennan."

"Hello, Agnes. What a surprise."

"I wondered if I might have a few words. That is if you're not too busy."

"Come in, Agnes." The priest stepped back to allow Agnes into his office. "What can I do for you?"

"Will you marry me, Father?"

"I don't think that's allowed, Agnes." Father Brennan smiled at his joke.

Agnes smiled too; glad to see that the priest was trying to make things easier for her. "Oh, Father, you know what I mean."

"Sam Wood, is it?"

"Aye, it is."

"Is he of our faith, Agnes?"

"He's like me, Father. He was baptised a Catholic, but he doesn't attend church."

"Well, you would both need to attend my church if I were to agree to marry you here."

"Why?" Agnes was prepared for his request.

"Why do you want to marry in church, Agnes? Do you want a traditional ceremony? The pomp and circumstance, the pretty dress and the flowers? Or do you want God to sanctify and bless your union?"

"I'm not sure to tell you the truth, Father." Agnes admitted. "I want my vows to mean something this time, and saying them in church seems more important somehow."

"Are you telling me that your vows didn't mean anything the last time I stood before you and heard them?"

Agnes realised she had said too much and the priest was quick to pounce on her mistake.

"Father, my marriage to Bill was, it was, err..." She

couldn't finish her explanation. She didn't know how to tell the priest of her sin.

"Would you like to come to confession, Agnes?" he asked her gently. "Whatever you say to me here in the office will be public and I'll be at liberty to discuss our conversation with anyone who might be interested. However…"

"But, Father!"

He put up his hand to stop her interruption. "However, Agnes, if you have things you would like to say to me that you would prefer to remain private, then we can go to the confessional box now. It's your choice."

Agnes thought about it, and decided she would like to unload the guilt and the suffering she had kept to herself for years. Telling Sam everything had helped, but the secrets still weighed her down, and it would be so good to tell someone in authority the truth at last. She simply nodded and got to her feet.

Once settled in the small box, she listened to the priest saying the prayer, and then she began the ritual of confession as she remembered it from being taught as a little girl. "Bless me father, for I have sinned. I don't know how long it has been since my last confession, but such a lot has happened, and I'm truly sorry for everything. Some of it weren't my fault, but I should have tried to stop it, I'll never forgive myself, but I'm hoping God will help me to live with it."

"My child, why don't you start from the beginning? It's clear that you have a lot to get off your chest. Tell me the whole story. I have lots of time."

Agnes took a deep breath and started with her affair with Andrew. She explained her infatuation and the reasons she thought she'd fallen for the Irish charmer. "He told me I was the most beautiful girl in the world, Father, and I believed him. I know I'm not beautiful, but he made me feel so special."

The priest remained silent as she went on with her story, moving on to the night her father died.

"So you see, Father, it was an accident. We didn't mean for it to happen, but I thought that Andrew would be blamed for his death, and I couldn't bear to lose Andrew." Agnes wept as her story unfolded, partly from guilt, but also with relief that at last she was admitting her sins. "I was foolish, because I lost him anyway." Agnes paused to wipe her face and blow her nose.

"Then I found out I was pregnant, and me mam made me

234

marry Bill Smithson to save us from the shame of it. She paid him all me dad's money. It was the only reason he agreed to wed me. We never loved each other."

Agnes continued her tale, crying with shame as she told of Bill's treatment of her, of his taunting and his admission to killing her mother. She thought she heard a gasp from the priest at that point, so she paused.

"He actually said those words in your hearing?"

"He did."

"Go on, child."

When she'd finished, she waited for the priest to speak.

"I've never heard a confession quite like that one, and although you have committed sins, the sins of others are plain to see in your story.

"I know you have lived a good life in the last few years, despite the fact that you don't come to Mass. I know you try to be a good person. I'll give you your act of contrition, make sure you perform this sincerely, my child."

Agnes listened as the priest listed her penances, and ended with "Go in peace to love and serve the Lord."

She replied, "Thanks be to God." Then she left the box. She knelt in a pew and said her prayers of penance, feeling lighter with every prayer she recited. When she finished, some time later, she left the pew and was halfway up the aisle to leave when Father Brennan called her back.

"Agnes, wait a minute, please."

"Yes, Father?" Agnes smiled. She couldn't believe how much better she felt after unloading her deepest secrets.

"Come into the office, Agnes, I have something I think you'll find interesting."

Agnes followed the priest, wondering what he might have for her.

"Sit down, Agnes." He sat opposite her and they faced each other over a wide desk. "I'm not supposed to discuss the details of your confession outside the confessional, but something you said in there sparked a memory. While you were praying, I came to look for something and when I found it, I realised that this could be very important for you." He slid a piece of paper across the polished wood. "Read it, Agnes," he prompted.

Agnes unfolded the sheet of paper and read the few words written there. Bill's signature was written at the bottom, with two more signatures and dates beside it.

"What is this?" Agnes asked, already beginning to remember her mother's words about a will, and Bill's comments on the night he confessed to pushing Trudie down the stairs.

"I believe that is Bill's last will and testament, Agnes. He leaves you everything."

"But his mam and dad said he told them it was all to go to them for safe keeping."

"Well if he didn't write it down and have it witnessed, it can't be proved. Word of mouth wills don't stand, Agnes. This is proof of his real intentions." Father Brennan picked up the paper. "With your permission, I'll take this to a solicitor to verify it for you."

"But Bill said he'd burned that will." Agnes checked the paper again to make sure it looked like Bill's signature.

"It is a legal document, Agnes. Solicitors always keep copies of wills."

"Did Bill know about the copy?" Agnes asked.

"There would be no reason to suppose he would know about it. We used a legal writing pad with carbon paper. The solicitor wrote the simplified wills and the boys signed them. We handed the top copy to the boys to give to their families, and we moved on to the next one. I kept the copies because the solicitor was going to join the Royal Air Force. It seemed safer to keep them here in the church where the families would know where to find them."

"So there is no other written will? I mean, he didn't write another one?"

"Not as far as I know, Agnes, but I'll have to ask his mother and father to make sure, and I'll take this to another solicitor to have it fully checked and authenticated."

"You'd do that for me, Father?" Agnes couldn't believe what was happening. Her life was changing because of her decision to come here today. It was too much to take in.

"Leave it with me, Agnes." Father Brennan got to his feet. "I'll show you out."

Agnes stumbled from the chair and made her way to the door of the church in a daze. "I don't know what to say, Father."

"Come to Mass on Sunday, Agnes. For old time's sake, eh?" He smiled at her. "Please bring Sam if he's willing."

"I don't know." Agnes faltered.

"If you both come to Mass at least once a week, I can marry you here. It's your choice."

After everything that had happened in the last hour or so, she had forgotten the reason she came here in the first place. "Oh, I see. Well, I'll ask Sam."

"I hope to see you on Sunday, Agnes."

Agnes walked home on shaking legs. The weight of her secrets had been crushing her for years, and now she felt lighter, but confused. Should she start going to church again? Should she persuade Sam to go too? Was it worth it? She would have to get the children baptised, and she would have to be sincere in her promises to God. Could she do that? After all she'd been through, could she?

What about the will? Father Brennan said he would try to get a solicitor to verify it, and then the money would be hers. How much money? She had no idea what her dowry had been worth. She needed to see Sam. She would have to collect the older children from school in an hour, and then she would get Helen from Enid's house. It would be her youngest girl's fourth birthday soon. They'd planned to have a little tea party for her, and tell the children of their plans to get married. Agnes knew they'd be excited at the news.

They discussed getting married after the war in Europe ended in May, but Sam wanted to wait until his work was completed down on the south coast. The war had finally ended with the surrender of Japan at the beginning of the month, and Sam was, at last, demobbed last week.

He was back home with his dad, and would begin working at the mill next week, but he wasn't happy. Agnes knew that millwork wouldn't satisfy him after the important work he'd been involved with. She knew he'd been offered work in Cumbria by one of his army bosses. He talked of little else, but Agnes was reluctant. If he decided to take the job, it would mean moving to the Lake District, and it was so far away from everything and everyone she knew.

As she walked, she came to realise that Sam was the most important thing in her life apart from the children. She loved Bert and David, but there was nothing else to keep her here in town. Not even Bill's money was important to her. Love was what mattered. Real love. The kind she felt for Sam. She began to run, she couldn't wait to tell him her news.

"Sam!" She burst through the door into the house where Sam lived with his father. "Where is he?" she asked Peter.

"He went for a walk, Agnes." Sam's father shrugged. "Said he wanted to do some thinking."

"Where did he go?" Agnes was eager to talk to Sam.

"Sand's Lane is where he usually goes. Try there, lass."

"I will, Mr Wood." Agnes dashed away and ran over the bridge. Her headscarf had come loose so she grabbed it from her head and continued running.

She was out of breath when she finally reached the cricket field at the end of the lane, but she could see Sam's ginger hair in the distance, shining like a beacon amidst the green of the grass and the shrubs by the river.

"Sam!" she called, waving her bright-blue headscarf to get his attention. She continued to run, holding the stitch in her side. "Sam!"

The tall red-headed figure turned and began to hurry towards her. "Agnes, what's wrong?" he called as he began to run to her.

Agnes stopped running and slowed to a walk to catch her breath. She let him come to her and opened her arms to embrace him.

"What's happened, Agnes? Not one of the bairns?" Sam looked worried.

"No, silly, nothing's wrong." She hugged him tightly. "I wanted to tell you how much I love you."

"Is that all?" Sam smiled. "Well, I know that all ready."

"No, Sam! That's just it. You don't!"

"Don't I?"

"I love you, Sam Wood, and I'll go to the ends of the earth to make you happy. If you want us to move to Cumbria, we'll go with you."

"Agnes, do you mean it?"

"More than anything."

"We might have to live in a boarding house until we find something to rent. There aren't many houses around where the job is."

"I'll live in a tent if I have to." She grinned up at him. "If it means we can be together and you can be happy doing a job that you love."

"Oh, Agnes, you make me so happy."

"I'm glad, because that's how you make me feel. Every time I think of you."

"I'm so lucky to have found you, Agnes."

"We're both lucky, Sam. Don't ever forget that. I won't."

"How did it go with Father Brennan?"

Agnes decided not to tell Sam about Bill's will. It might not come to anything, and she didn't want to spoil the moment by mentioning her ex-husband. "He said that if we agreed to go to Mass at least once a week, he would agree to marry us in the church."

"I think I could manage that." Sam nodded. "But we'll have to tell him we'll be moving away. It's only fair for him to know that we won't be continuing to attend his services after the wedding. I'm not sure I'd want to go to church wherever we lived."

"I'm not sure he'll still want to marry us if that's the case. He's all for sincerity, is Father Brennan."

"Would it matter to you so much if it has to be a civil wedding, Agnes?"

"Not a bit, Sam. I thought it would, that's why I went to see the priest, but I know now that all I care about is you. I don't care how we do it. I just want to be yours and I want you to belong to me."

"Well, we don't need to get married to know that, my love."

"Are you suggesting we live in sin?" Agnes tried to look shocked but couldn't help smiling at him.

"No!" Sam pushed her away, gently. "We've been good so far, let's not spoil it. I'll make an appointment with the registry office as soon as I can. And while I'm there, I'll ask about adopting the bairns. We can't have them having a different family name to their daddy can we?"

"Oh, I love you, Sam Wood!" Agnes threw herself at him and felt his arms enfold her. "You make me feel so safe and happy."

The wedding took place in a small and dingy registry office at the top of Daisy Hill in town. Bert, David and James were there with Betty and Sarah, James's new wife. The children sat quietly through the exchanging of vows and when the registrant announced that Sam and Agnes were man and wife the four little ones cheered.

"Are you our new daddy now, Sam?" Harry asked.

"I would be honoured if you'd call me daddy, Harry." Sam lifted the young boy into his arms.

The others clung to his legs shouting, "Daddy! Daddy! Daddy!"

Harry put his little arms around Sam's neck and hugged him tightly. "I'm glad you're my daddy, Sam."

"How would you like to be called Harry Wood instead of Smithson?" Sam asked him.

"Don't know." Harry looked confused. He turned to his mother. "Do I have to be called Harry Wood, Mammy?"

"Not if you don't want to, Harry. But my last name is Wood now because I'm married to Sam and that's his name."

"So if Sam is my daddy, I can be called Harry Wood?"

"If that's what you want, son." Sam had a tear in his eye as he watched the young lad work it out.

"All right then." Harry nodded solemnly and looked down at his siblings around Sam's legs. "We're gonna be called Wood, we're gonna have Sam for a daddy!"

"Hooray!" they chorused.

"Come on, we have a party to get to." Bert ushered the wedding party out of the office and onto the street. "We can't let you go without a send off, can we?"

"The train leaves at five, Bert. We can't stay long." Sam warned him.

"You can have a drink with us before you go. The bags are all packed and waiting at the station for you."

"I can't believe we're really going!" Agnes grinned.

"Well, if you don't like it, there's always a bed for you at our place." Bert assured her.

"What, with all of you?" Agnes looked at her two cousins with their new partners. "James has moved back in and David won't be long until he and Betty make it official. You won't have room for this little lot."

"Nevertheless, Agnes. There'll always be a home here for you and the bairns. I'm going to miss you all." Bert's eyes were glossy and he blinked rapidly. "But we'll come up to visit you when you're settled."

"You'd better, Uncle Bert, because we'll miss you too." She gave him a hug and turned to take her husband's hand. "We won't always be staying in the boarding house that Sam found for us. We hope to get somewhere nice with room for you to visit us." Agnes could already picture a little cottage in the countryside. "Let's go have that drink. We should toast our future happiness. It's tradition."

"Just the one, then." Sam relented and walked behind Bert and his family, holding tightly to Agnes's hand. The children followed behind, giggling and skipping excitedly.

At the Crown Arms, a few of Sam's friends and some of the neighbours had gathered to say farewell to the family.

"Congratulations, Agnes." Enid gave Agnes a kiss on the cheek. "We'll miss you."

"Thanks, Enid. I'll miss you too." Agnes knew she would miss all her friends, and especially her Uncle Bert, but also knew she was doing the right thing in moving away. A fresh start would be good for them all.

Agnes saw Edwin and Mary seated in the corner and went to talk with them. "Thanks for coming," she began. "I know it's not easy for you to see me marry Sam and take your grandchildren away."

"Well, you got what you wanted, didn't you!" Mary spat. "Our poor Bill not dead a year and you're already dancing on his grave."

"Mary, don't!" Edwin put a hand on his wife's arm. "We talked about this. Don't spoil it."

"Spoil what? Spoil this strumpet's idea of a wedding?" Mary bristled with indignation. "They didn't even get married in the church and Father Brennan said he offered to marry them, but oh, no! Not miss high and mighty. The church is only good for what you can get out of it, isn't that right, Agnes Smithson, or Agnes Wood as you are now?"

"What do you mean, Mary?" Agnes stretched to her full height and looked down at her ex-mother-in-law.

"You'll find out soon enough when Father Brennan catches up with you."

"What's she talking about, Edwin?" Agnes asked.

"Our Bill's will, lass. It was proved to be right and proper. We had to give the money back to the solicitor. Father Brennan said he'd try to see you before you leave today to explain everything."

Agnes clamped a hand over her mouth and stopped breathing for a few seconds. "You mean it? I'll get me dad's money?"

"I think you have to open a bank account so they can transfer it over to you." Edwin explained.

"How much money are we talking about, Edwin."

"You don't know?" Mary's eyes widened. "You can't tell me you didn't know what your mother gave our Bill."

Agnes shook her head.

"What's going on over here?" Sam came to her side. "There's a party going on over here in case you hadn't noticed."

"Sam, they just told me about Bill's will."

"What about it?" Sam asked.

Father Brennan entered the pub and went straight to Agnes. "Can I have a quiet word, Agnes?"

"No need for secrecy father." Mary got to her feet. "We already told her!"

"Sit down, Mary!" Edwin pulled on his wife's sleeve.

"I'll not be staying to take part in this mockery of a wedding."

"Actually, Mary," Father Brennan looked at Agnes. "This wedding will be much more pleasing to God than the one where Agnes married your son." He turned to the older woman. "Not all marriages are made in heaven, as the saying goes."

"What do you mean by that?" Mary blustered. "Explain yourself man!"

"I don't have to explain anything, Mary. Search your heart and find the truth of what I'm saying. Come Agnes, we need to talk." Father Brennan led Agnes and Sam to the far corner of the public house where they could have some privacy.

"Thank you, Father. You've been so understanding." Agnes began. "I'm sorry we didn't take you up on your offer of getting married in the church."

"We didn't want to be hypocritical. Is that the right word, Father?" Sam asked.

"Yes, Sam. I know, and I have to respect you for that. So many would have taken the easy way and gone along with what I asked to get the big ceremony and the frills of lace and the show of a full church wedding. If you have lost your faith, I can understand why a church wedding wouldn't be what you'd want. I hope you find your faith again. Both of you. I'll pray for you."

"Thanks, Father, but —.'

"Thank you, Father." Agnes cut short Sam's reply. "Mary told me you have news about Bill's will."

"I need to know the details of your bank account, Agnes, and if you don't have one, you must open one soon and let me know so I can tell the solicitor where to deposit the money."

"We don't have an account, Father." Sam answered for her. "But we'll open one as soon as we get settled."

"You're moving to the Lake District, I hear."

"Yes, we leave in an hour or so."

"Well, send me the details when you can, Agnes. I'm sure the money will help you find your feet in a new place."

"Do you know how much money there is, Father?"

"You really don't know, Agnes, do you?" Father Brennan shook his head. "Your father was a good businessman and he had quite a bit in savings. I believe your mother sold the bakery after his death?"

Agnes nodded and blushed. The priest knew all the details of that night, but was honour bound to say nothing.

"The total sum amounts to something over four thousand pounds."

"Are you sure it's so much?" Agnes gasped. "That means I'll be rich!"

"You will be a wealthy woman, my child. I'm sure of the amount, Agnes." Father Brennan smiled at her amazement. "I think with Bill's banking background, he invested your dad's money well. The investment has grown in the last few years. Spend it wisely, Agnes. Make your father proud of you."

"I will, Father. Oh, I will!" Agnes turned to Sam to hug him. "Can you believe it? I had no idea!"

"Neither did I, my love." Sam said quietly. "What will you do with all that money?"

"You mean, what will *we* do with it, Sam."

"It's your money, Agnes. It's from your ex-husband. I can't have any part of it. It wouldn't be right."

"We are married now, Sam. What's mine is yours. Didn't you hear the vows I said to you?" She smiled up at him.

"I'll leave you to enjoy your wedding feast. I'm sure you'll have a lot to discuss on your train journey north."

Father Brennan left them and Agnes turned to say thank you to him once again, but saw him talking with Edwin and Mary and decided to leave it. Instead, she turned back to Sam.

"That money was never Bill Smithson's by right, Sam. I told you what happened. It was me dad's money, and it were always meant to come to me one day. If I hadn't been so stupid, and if my mam hadn't thought she knew best it would have all turned out differently."

"But four thousand pounds is a fortune, Agnes."

"I know!" She squealed with delight. "We could buy a house!"

"We could get you a little business to keep you busy." Sam suggested.

"We could keep the bairns in clover for years on that." Agnes hugged Sam tightly.

"We don't have to decide now." Sam looked into her eyes. "We have all the time in the world Mrs Woods."

"And the world is at peace at last."

"Mammy, Mammy, come and cut the cake!" Alice ran up to pull Agnes back to the party and Sam followed, holding tightly to her hand.

The world had turned full circle, from peace to war, to peace again, and Agnes felt her life had turned with it. She'd spent years in the cold depths of despair, feeling guilty and ashamed. She wasted years waiting for a love that was never meant to be, hanging on to the snowdrop's promise of better times to come. Now she realised that the snowdrop had kept its promise, but it wasn't in the way she'd expected. She felt she was on the threshold of a new life. She felt full of joy and happiness like she'd never known before. Her springtime was behind her, and she was moving into the summer of her life with her children and her husband.

THE END

About the Author

Pearl A. Gardner lives in West Yorkshire, England.

She has enjoyed some success with short story fiction, winning some national competitions. Her articles and stories have been published in popular magazines, both fiction and non-fiction, but she is concentrating on full length works now.

Pearl has a wide ranging and eclectic author list that includes many genres from chick lit romances to science fiction, which she writes under the author name of P.A. Gardner

The following is not a comprehensive list. If you would like to see more work by Pearl A. Gardner, simply search for her name in Amazon.

Further Reading, fiction and non-fiction novels by Pearl A. Gardner

The Scent of Bluebells – A World War Two romantic saga

In spring of 1939, eighteen year old Amy falls in love with Jimmy and life seems full of promise for the young girl from a northern mill town. War was brewing in Europe, and it would change her life forever.

Through the following five years of turmoil, Amy endures heartache and loss. Her husband returns briefly and leaves her pregnant with his child. She writes to him of the news but shortly before the baby is born, Jimmy is reported missing in action and presumed dead.

After more than a year with no further news of her missing husband, she slowly begins to enjoy freedom and independence like she'd never known before.

The war continues with no news of Jimmy and she dares to love again.

Will this love survive the war?

Will Jimmy be found?

It's Penguin Shooting Day – A true diary account of the first weeks following brain injury.

From my son-in-law, Simon's, point of view, he awakes in a bizarre place full of strangers and doesn't know why he is there. His yesterday is ten years ago, and the only memories he has between then and now seem to be no more than hazy fragments. However, his first words to his wife, Natalie, when he wakes from the coma are, 'I love you, honey.' Even though he doesn't remember who she is, he knows that he loves her.

Amazingly, his emotions are still intact even though his memories don't support them. He has no recollection of his wedding day, or of his daughter's birth but the love he feels for his wife and child are overwhelming in their intensity.

So we use Simon's emotional strength and Natalie's inspirational positivity to form the foundations of a future we can only begin to imagine.

Pushed on the Shelf – a romantic comedy.

Forty-something Trisha is reeling from the shock of being dumped by her husband, Alan, aka DISCWIFF (Dick in Sports Car With Foot Fetish.) Trisha now has to support her two children financially, as DISCWIFF has set up home with TITSNOBB (Tits no Brain Bimbo) and left her in a house that is about to be repossessed.

With no qualifications or experience, the job market looks bleak, but she is determined not to go under.

Trisha feels as if her life is being lived inside a pressure cooker that's ready to blow a gasket. Something has to give, but what?

Ella's Destiny – A romantic saga with a hint of sci-fi and a touch of time travel.

War is imminent when Ella Stevens applies to join the Eden Venture in the hope of saving her teenage children and salvaging her failing marriage. Amid riots and unrest the family travel to their designated camp where they prepare for a future beyond anything they could have imagined.

During a perilous journey through space and time, Ella realises her marriage can not be saved, but is determined to fulfil her dream of finding a better future for her children. Arriving at the fresh new world, filled with hope and endless opportunity, Ella begins to build a life without her husband. However, the settlers soon discover that Eden is not the paradise they hoped it would be.

With no escape from the hostile and dangerous environment, survival becomes a priority. Ella embraces the challenges of her life with a new-found courage and moves into a future that no one could have predicted.

Science Fiction, Published under the name of P.A. Gardner

Pearl's science fiction novels are set in the real world, with true to life characters living through extraordinary circumstances. Based on scientific facts and extensive research, her science fiction works are believable, page turning stories that raise questions about the world we live in.

They Take our Children, Book One, The Truth Revealed– Soft science fiction / family saga about alien abduction.

Courtney is an astonishingly beautiful teenager. She is also a brighter than average young woman but is otherwise as ordinary, happy and well adjusted as any other girl her age.

On her sixteenth birthday, Courtney's neurotic mother, Helen, calls her a monster in a fit of rage. The teenager runs off, causing panic in the family. Courtney's father, Gavin, has long suspected something sinister hiding in his wife's history, but nothing could have prepared him for the truth. Helen's father, George, tries to reveal what he knows about the mystery but the family find it hard to accept his far fetched version of events as realistic.

Weaving between past and present the facts about Courtney's shocking alien origin are exposed and the search for the whole truth begins.

They Take our Children, Book Two, Taking Control– Second book in the two book series about alien abduction.
Courtney's family is drawn into the murky world of ufology experts. Subterfuge and concealment become a part of their lives as they search, for the secret, to open the gateway to the second dimension where they hope to meet face to face with the aliens who abducted Courtney's cousins.

Talk of government agencies and 'above top secret' organisations make them fearful but when they discover how much information has been covered up about the alien abductions, they become even more determined to take control and find the missing children.

Discover more about Pearl A. Gardner on the web site
www.pearlagardner.co.uk

Connect with Pearl A. Gardner
Email: pearl@pearlagardner.co.uk

On Goodreads
https://www.goodreads.com/author/show/7350328.Pearl_A_Gardner

On Facebook
https://www.facebook.com/pearlagardner

On Twitter
https://twitter.com/PearlAGardner

Dear Reader
I really appreciate that you took the time to read this work of fiction. I hope you enjoyed reading it as much as I enjoyed writing it.

I would be grateful if you could leave a review of the book on Amazon, Goodreads or your favourite review site.

If you have not enjoyed this book, or found faults with the work, please feel free to contact me to let me know how I may be able improve your reading experience of this novel.

With very best wishes from the author,
Pearl A. Gardner

Pearl A. Gardner